# Reading, Writing And Necromancy

## WOMBY'S SCHOOL FOR WAYWARD WITCHES

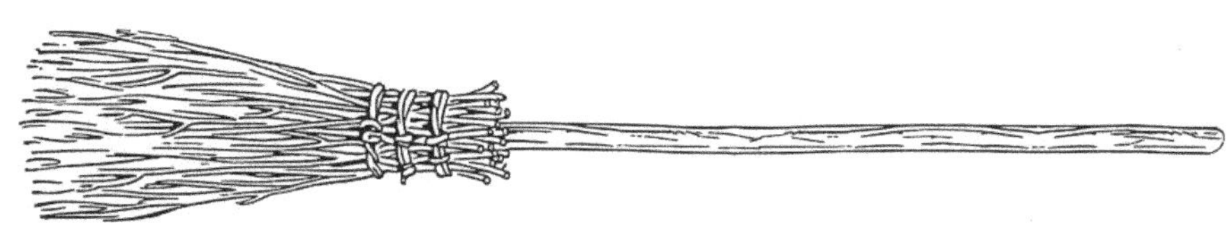

SARINA DORIE

ISBN: 1722645547
ISBN-13: 978-1722645540

## OTHER BOOKS IN THE WOMBY'S SCHOOL FOR WAYWARD WITCHES SERIES LISTED IN ORDER

Tardy Bells and Witches' Spells
Hex-Ed
Witches Gone Wicked
A Handful of Hexes
Hexes and Exes
Reading, Writing and Necromancy
Budget Cuts for the Dark Arts and Crafts
Hex and the City
Spell It Out for Me
Spiders Are a Witch's Best Friend
Hex Crimes
My Crazy Hex Girlfriend
Wedding Bells and Midnight Spells
All Hexed Up

# CONTENTS

# AUTHOR'S NOTE

If you are reading this far in the Womby's School for Wayward Witches series, I'm guessing you have read the other books as well. Whether you have stuck with the series because you love the quirky characters, you want to know if Clarissa will turn into a wicked witch like her mother, or you are waiting to see what happens with Felix Thatch and Derrick, I appreciate your enthusiasm.

If you haven't already signed up for my newsletter, I want to encourage you to do so. This helps me as an author connect to my readers, lets you know when books are being released, and gives me a way to gift you with free books and short stories.

You can find the newsletter sign-up on my website: sarinadorie.com or you can go to: https://www.subscribepage.com/q6h1q2

Happy reading!

# CHAPTER ONE
# The Morning After

Golden sunlight filtered in through a window, but I turned away, not wanting to leave the sanctuary of sleep. A draft of wintry air chilled my naked skin, and I pulled the covers up to my chin. I'd been dreaming of curses cured by magic, unrequited yearning finally satisfied, and true love.

A masculine arm slipped around my waist, reminding me I wasn't alone. Derrick pulled me closer. He smoothed my hair away from my face and kissed the back of my neck.

A wave of déjà vu washed over me. Was I dreaming? This was always the nice part of the dream. It never lasted. I wanted to savor this moment, but I couldn't. This happy dream always shifted into a nightmare. It never ended well. I blinked the cobwebs of sleep from my eyes, my apprehension growing.

"Clarissa, this is how I always imagined it would be," Derrick murmured into my hair.

That was always the kind of thing he said in dreams before the tornado stole him away from me. That storm always mirrored what had happened in real life when our magic had exploded, causing the house to collapse and taking the life of my sister, Missy.

Something was different this time. I examined the room around me. Paintings, tubes of acrylics and oils, and assorted art supplies filled the small studio. Across from the bed, a sweater and a canvas hid most of the full-length mirror I'd hidden the night before. A painting of me rested against a trunk. It was a younger version of myself with auburn hair. Blonde highlighted the locks instead of the hot pink I sported now.

This wasn't my childhood room. I wasn't dreaming. This was real. Derrick was here and with me. It was all my dreams come true—my good dreams.

I sat up, clutching the blankets to my chest. I gulped in air, not realizing I'd been holding my breath. For once, everything was right.

"What's wrong?" Derrick asked. "Are you okay?"

I took in his tousled blue hair and his five-o-clock shadow. His brow crinkled up in concern.

I threw my arms around him and hugged him. "I didn't kill you with my magic." I covered his face with kisses. No tornado had come this time. I had controlled my powers. I wasn't like my biological mother.

He laughed in the same good-natured way I remembered from our teenage years. "That's right. You cured me. Your kisses are magic, just like in fairy tales."

I was pretty sure it was more than kisses that had cured him.

It all seemed too good to be true. I stared into the azure of his eyes, feeling like I was falling into a cloudless sky. "How is it possible I cured you unintentionally? Thatch said I had to perform an elaborate spell."

"Why do you have to bring him up?" he groaned. "He's such an asshole."

"Don't say that. Felix Thatch is my friend, and he was trying to help you. He made me collect all those things—virgin tears and unicorn poo—" And a few other more disgusting items for the spell.

I hadn't used a dragon egg or unicorn horn to cure Derrick. The only ingredient that might count was my own virgin blood combined with my affinity. "But I didn't need any of those things. You aren't invisible. You remember me. And you aren't cursed."

Derrick reached across me and fumbled with something under the bed. "Is that why you let him tie you to a tree in the forest? For unicorn excrement?" He found a half-full bottle of cola.

I took it he didn't know about the unicorn semen.

I nodded. "We were gathering ingredients for a potion. It was to cure you. I had to be bait to lure a unicorn."

"That is so messed up." Derrick took a swig from the soda and offered it to me. "Have you ever considered there wasn't a spell? He might have been giving you busywork because he's trying to distract you."

"I'm pretty sure he had a spell in mind." I wasn't typically a cola drinker for breakfast, but Derrick didn't have running water in his room or much else. I took a few tentative sips.

"Think about it. If I hadn't been there to stop those chimeras, they would have eaten you," he said. "That jerk just left you there."

"He said he'd put up wards to protect me. But I wouldn't feel the fear needed to lure the chimeras, which would call the unicorns, if I didn't believe I was in actual danger."

"Clarissa, there weren't any wards." Derrick frowned. "That's why I intervened."

Derrick had always been a bit of a kidder. I wanted to believe his words were a joke, but he was so serious. It had been Derrick who had rescued me, not Thatch?

It had been Derrick I'd kissed in the darkness that night in the woods, not Thatch. Thatch had put me in actual danger—and lied about it afterward? A spark of anger flared in me. "As Josie would say, what a bag of dicks."

Derrick fell back laughing.

I could have gotten killed gathering ingredients to save Derrick. I had no doubt Thatch was collecting all those ingredients for a reason. It just happened I didn't know what that reason was. I no longer felt certain of Thatch's intentions. Some of those ingredients had been listed in the spell at the back of Alouette Loraline's journal. It was possible Thatch might have decided to try to solve the Fae Fertility Paradox with the spell I hadn't finished decoding in the book.

He'd chided me for trying to investigate something so dangerous, but it wouldn't surprise me if he intended to do the same thing.

"Uh-oh," Derrick said, kissing the crinkle in my brow. "I know that look."

"What look?"

"The one you make before you get yourself in a heap of trouble." Derrick squeezed me to him.

I wanted to stay snuggled in his arms and talk to him about my suspicions, but my bladder was full, and I was thirsty for more than carbonated corn syrup.

"Do you have a restroom nearby?" I asked.

He jabbed a thumb toward the door. "I usually use the bushes around the back. Of course, I'm also usually invisible when I use them. Otherwise, the nearest indoor restroom is down the tunnel of spiderwebs toward the great hall."

My stomach grumbled. "I should go get something to eat and drink."

"What time is it?" he asked.

I poked him in the side. "I don't know. *Someone* confiscated my cell phone."

"Sorry about that. It's part of my job. Thatch wanted me to keep an eye on you and make sure you didn't do anything that got you kicked out of the school. He was adamant about me confiscating your phone. I turned it in to

Mr. Khaba—but don't worry. I didn't say the cell was yours. He thought it was a student's." He stared off into the distance, brow furrowing.

"Now that you're my boyfriend, can't you just steal it back for me?"

"Boyfriend?" He blinked in surprise.

From his wide eyes, my confidence faltered. "I mean—well—we were dating before, when we were in high school. And now we've slept together so . . . um. . . ."

"We went on *one* date when we were in high school and kissed twice since then." His lips twitched into an amused smirk. "Do you assume you're dating everyone you sleep with?"

"Yes." Not that my magic made it easy to sleep with men. "I mean, no. I don't have a lot of experience with dating, and I don't know the right lingo. I haven't ever. . . ." I swallowed. Nervous anxiety churned inside me.

His grin widened, and he kissed my nose. "I know. I'm your first. I was just teasing you." His smile turned shy. "But I hope you'll *want* to be my girlfriend."

I squeezed his hand, relieved he felt the same way. "Yes. I want you to be my boyfriend. I've wanted that since we were in high school."

"Good." He leaned in and kissed me on the cheek. He pulled me closer, peeking under the blankets and waggling his eyebrows. "Maybe we should make up for some of that lost time we weren't together?"

I shook my head. "Don't even think about it. I need to eat and shower and powder my nose." I wiggled toward the edge of the bed.

He poked me in the side. "I have a feeling that isn't what you're going to be powdering."

I hesitated at the edge of the bed, a spike of anxiety shooting through me at the idea of exposing myself. Last night had been the first time he'd seen me naked—the only time anyone had seen me completely naked. I'd felt comfortable and confident—or at least not awkward like I was now.

"I, um, would you. . . ?" Words suddenly eluded me. I motioned for him to turn, like I was fifteen again and tongue-tied. Now I was twenty-two and tongue-tied. I worried he would think I was a prude or immature or weird.

Derrick winked at me and turned away. "Anything for you."

That was it. No complaints or teasing. He knew me that well. Derrick was the perfect gentleman I'd remembered. I collected my bra and underwear from the floor and hurriedly dressed.

Derrick remained facing the window. "While you're out, do you think you could bring me something to eat and some clothes?" He gestured to the pair of underwear on the floor and a coat hanging over the foot of his bed. "Believe it or not, these are all the clothes I've got. An invisible man with a heat-conducting spell doesn't need much else. It might look a little weird if I walk around naked now that people can see me."

I laughed so hard my bladder almost burst. "Breakfast in bed it is." I jammed one foot into a striped legging, trying not to lose my balance.

Derrick ran a hand through his blue hair. "I wonder what Mr. Khaba is going to say about this turn of events. He's not going to be able to employ me as an invisible security guard if I'm not invisible."

"I guess you'll become a visible security guard."

"Maybe. Funny thing about that. . . . I was cursed and went to Thatch for help—or maybe he came to me. My memory is a little hazy still. I don't remember being invisible before asking for Thatch's help."

"Do you know where my shirt is?" I asked.

He turned, but with his hand covering his eyes. I laughed at his goofy attempt to pretend he wasn't looking at me half undressed.

He peeked through his fingers as he scanned the room. "I got the job here because the school happened to have a vacancy for a security guard. They were specifically looking for an invisible man. And I was invisible. Thatch recommended me for the job and told Khaba I would be a perfect fit. It's a little too coincidental now that I think about it."

I spotted my pink blouse in the bed behind him. I tugged it out from under his leg and pulled it on over my head. "What are you saying? Thatch cursed you, not the Raven Queen?" I said it half jokingly, but as soon as the words came out, my mouth went dry.

"I remember the Raven Queen. Sort of." He shivered and wrapped his arms around himself. "She used pain magic to torture me. She drained me. Not completely, but enough that I was in so much pain I wished I was dead. Thatch was there in her castle. He watched her, and she invited him to. . . ." He traced his fingers across a scar on his arm. "Everything about him is foggy."

I climbed back into bed and hugged him. "It's okay. It's over now. You're safe at the school. She can't get you here."

"Maybe." He grabbed me by the shoulders, fear in his eyes. "Clarissa, you've got to be careful around Thatch. I don't remember what he did to me, but it wasn't all happy rainbows and yippity-skippity rescuing. He still works for her. And she wants you."

## CHAPTER TWO
## The Roommate from Hell

Avoiding the most frequented routes, it took me forever to navigate to the avocado-green hallway built in the seventies before ducking into an older brick hallway and up a cobwebbed stairwell to the dormitory wing with its white plaster walls. Muscles I hadn't even known I possessed ached in my hips and pelvis from the previous night's extracurricular activities. I walked slowly, my progress to the women's dorms hindered by my sore muscles.

After making a quick stop in the women's restroom, I headed to my dorm. I unlocked my room and nearly collided with Vega Bloodmire, my evil roommate. Being a Sunday, she must have decided it was Gothic-casual day. Instead of one of her flapper dresses or a business suit with a pencil skirt, she wore an all-black day dress befitting the twenties era. The ensemble was complete with her short bob haircut and a sparkly headband.

Vega looked me up and down, her blood-red lips curling into a sneer.

I stumbled away from her. "Good morning," I said.

She reached out with a long, slender arm, snatched me up by the front of my shirt, and yanked me into the room. I tripped over the Art Nouveau rug near the door. The ornate patterns of flowers formed a giant skull. I stubbed my toe on the coffin sticking out from under her bed and plopped onto her pristine bedspread. The homicidal Downton Abbey vibe to our room was her doing, not mine.

The cuckoo clock on the wall between our beds showed it was only ten after seven. I had plenty of time to get dressed and go to the great hall for breakfast.

She slammed the door and turned to me.

I scooted off her bed. "What was that for?"

"You never came to bed last night." She advanced on me. "Where were you?"

I edged around her bed toward mine. "None of your business."

"It is my business." Her dark eyes gleamed with danger.

I backed past her wardrobe, toward mine. When I neared the plant hanging from the ceiling, the Venus flytrap's jaws snapped at me.

I ducked away. "Since when do you care?" I would not allow Vega to intimidate me. Even if she was taller than me. And could do magic. And was majorly creepy.

"Since Thatch tasked me with keeping an eye on you," she said.

"You aren't my babysitter anymore."

I opened the doors to my wardrobe to pick out a dress, but the wardrobe closed itself again. I turned back to her. Vega held her wand. A cloud of faint blue light with yellow sparkles faded from it.

She lifted her chin. "Thatch expects me to know where you are from ten p.m. to six a.m. If I keep you from leaving your bed and wandering around the school during the middle of the night, Thatch promised I'll get the tower next year instead of Josie Kimura."

Ah, so that was her motivation. Not caring about my safety, of course.

"Where. Were. You?" She leaned in close, nostrils flaring. I had no doubt she could smell my fear.

I tried to think of something plausible. "I was with Josie. All night. We stayed out late at, um, the Internet café. I didn't want to get caught coming back, so I spent the night in her room."

Her eyes raked over me. "I don't believe you."

She jabbed me in the stomach with her wand. She didn't even have to use magic to make it hurt.

"Ow! Stop it, Vega. I'm back. I won't tell Thatch you weren't watching me, okay?"

She waved her wand over me. My feet lifted off the floor. I tried to push her away and run, but I couldn't move. It felt like she'd bound me with invisible rope. My back slid up against the wood of my wardrobe as she made me levitate. My face was now level with hers.

"Tell the truth, and I won't hurt you . . . much." Her voice was the low purr of a kitten.

I had no doubt she would. A wave of sweat washed over me. When all else failed, the only thing left was the truth. "Fine. I was with my boyfriend. We were in his room."

She snorted, she scrutinized me again, and then she laughed. "You? A boyfriend?" She cackled and shook her head. "You expect me to believe that? Who would want to date you?" The maniacal hysteria coming from her rivaled the Wicked Witch of the West.

She wiped the tears from her eyes and sat on my bed. "Is that the best lie you can come up with?"

"Um, yes." I continued to struggle against the invisible ropes holding me. I managed to kick one foot free.

Vega's cool gaze slid over me. "The first explanation was more believable. If you were with Josephine Kimura, what would you two losers be doing that was worse than sneaking out like children to spend time at the Internet café?" She tapped the foot of my bed with long lacquered nails that matched her crimson lipstick. "Were you doing something . . . lewd with each other?"

"No," I said quickly. I hadn't been doing anything risqué with Josie. It had been with Derrick. Technically I was telling the truth.

Her lips curled into a knowing smile. "What were you doing with Josie? Making out? Stroking each other's . . . egos?"

"No!"

She sighed in exasperation. "Let Thatch waste magic questioning you. I have better things to do today." She rose and headed toward the door.

"Aren't you going to let me go?"

"You want to learn magic. Figure it out yourself." She closed the door behind her.

My electrons must have been supercharged after all the friction I'd stored up with Derrick because I was able to make the power in my affinity swell with ease. Electricity crackled over my skin, and I broke her spell. I fell to the floor, banging my knees, free but not without taking a beating.

I walked into the great hall refreshed and showered, a spring in my step as I thought about rejoining Derrick. Students sat at tables, talking and eating breakfast. Latecomers to breakfast filtered in through the Stonehenge-like archways, painted mustard yellow and avocado green.

For once I was blind to the seventies colors vomited across the walls. All I could think about was my joy radiating out of me like the sunniest of days. I had never imagined my reunion with Derrick would be so perfect and magical. His love and acceptance of me was everything I had hoped for. My life was perfect.

The moment I spotted Felix Thatch, my confident stride faltered.

Thatch sat at the teacher's table on the dais. A public appearance from him was noteworthy considering how infrequently he ventured out of the dungeon.

His shoulder-length hair glistened blue-black in the morning light, like raven feathers. Even from a seated position, he loomed taller than Jackie Frost and Josie seated at the table. His tweed suit hugged his lean frame. The vest and cravat gave the suit an old-fashioned look.

I considered ducking down and slinking out one of the many archways.

I could wait until he left before getting breakfast. In that moment of hesitation, he spotted me. His lips curled upward. The expression took years from his face and made him uncharacteristically handsome.

He looked human. Like someone with a heart. Looks could be deceiving.

A smile from Thatch was never a good sign.

If I ran now, it would look suspicious. I lifted my chin and strode forward, pretending he had never put me in any jeopardy. I tried not to think about losing my virginity with the best friend Thatch had purposefully tried to hide from me. He had lied to me about Derrick and said I couldn't see him.

Couldn't *see* him. The invisible man. Har har.

He probably thought he was funny.

I forced myself to look away from Thatch and pretend to examine a poster advertising Josie's after-school Weaving Club. The room would have given off the air of a sacred site full of wisdom and learning if it hadn't been for the seventies-era paint slapped onto the stone. The ceiling tapered upward to a point, like the underside of a giant witch's hat. Banners with each of the team colors decorated the walls, clashing with the yellow and green walls and stained-glass windows.

I passed sleepy students at tables, eating oatmeal, fruit, or toast. A student waved to me, and I waved back. I plastered a smile on my face, trying not to allow my apprehension to show.

I glanced at Thatch again. My eyes narrowed. He had kept Derrick from me and made him forget me. Derrick seemed to think Thatch was working with the Raven Court.

After all the ways the Raven Queen had hurt Thatch over the years, I didn't believe it was possible that he would work with her. He loathed her. She'd killed one of his sisters and turned the other into a bird.

Besides that, Thatch was my friend. He wouldn't do anything bad to Derrick. He wouldn't hurt anyone. Even so, my suspicions battled with my respect for my colleague. I wished I had talked to Derrick more before I'd left him.

I had made it one third of the way through my mission. Now I just needed to grab extra breakfast and find some clothes in Derrick's size before I returned to him. I needed to not raise Thatch's suspicions.

Josie Kimura sat next to Thatch. That was odd. She didn't like Thatch.

She eyed me over her black-rimmed glasses and gave me a pleading look. Streaks of her midnight hair had been bleached and dyed the hue of lavender. They matched the purples of her patchwork dress and witch hat.

"Good morning," Thatch said with uncharacteristic cheeriness.

"Uh-huh." I was having a tough time thinking of the correct social responses.

Maybe his good mood had something to do with him getting laid. Or maybe he was smiling because he was about to bust me. I had hoped Vega might not tattle to Thatch about my disappearance, out of the motivation that it might help her get the tower next year.

"It's going to be a lovely day," he said with a joyous sigh.

Josie gave him a sidelong glance, an eyebrow raised.

It was hard to tell what was going on in Thatch's head. He poured himself a coffee and prepared it, a little smile on his lips. Was he happy he was about to crucify me for doing something I wasn't supposed to?

I sat down in the chair, wincing as the seat met my aching muscles.

"You look well, Miss Lawrence. I take it you retired early last night?" Thatch enunciated each word with his crisp British accent. "No nightmares?"

He knew. There was no way I was going to answer that. I smashed a butter knife through a biscuit, half of it splintering into crumbs as I tried to butter it. I did my best to change the subject. "Fancy seeing you here, Mr. Thatch. I've never seen you eat breakfast with staff."

He waved a hand airily. "I do venture out of my dark hole occasionally, Miss Lawrence."

Josie leaned toward me. "Jeb is away. Thatch got stuck with breakfast duty."

He leaned in conspiratorially. "I hear the headmaster is bringing in a new staff member today, our new History of Magic teacher. Hello, smaller class sizes!" He spoke like a normal human being, not a depressed, monotone teacher from another era.

Josie mouthed the words, "What is he on?"

I plunged forward, trying to cover for myself before he decided to question me about where I had been the previous night. "Hey, Josie, thanks for letting me sleep in." I gave her a look that I hoped conveyed I wanted her to play along. "It was nice having a slumber party in your room last night. I got one night of sleep without Vega's snoring." I poured myself a glass of orange juice.

"Huh?" Josie asked.

I kicked her under the table. "I don't know how you put up with Vega as a roommate last year. Thanks for letting me spend the night in your room."

"Oh yeah. No problem." She glanced at Thatch.

I was afraid she was going to give me away with her lack of guile.

I hurried on. "It's too bad we can't be roommates. That would solve one third of my daily problems having to put up with Vega."

"Yes, such a shame," Thatch said. "But that would be impossible."

"Maybe next year," Josie said, giving him a sidelong glance.

I was sure he would find some way to make Vega babysit me next year if he could.

Thatch sipped at his coffee. "Just moments ago, I was asking Miss Kimura about what she intends to do with her day. It looks like she'll be covering detention for me." He chuckled. His eyes were tired.

Josie sighed despondently. No wonder she looked so depressed.

"Tell me, Miss Lawrence, what are your plans?" Thatch's tone was cloying, his eyes sparkling with sinister interest. "Something about you seems different." He stroked his chin with a long finger.

I stiffened. He knew. He could divine things. Or maybe he was like a unicorn and sensed the lack of virginity radiating from me.

"Have you changed your hair?" he asked.

"Mmm," I said around a mouthful of biscuit. I wondered what Derrick would want for breakfast.

I loaded my plate with one of everything. If we'd had eggs and bacon I would have brought him that, but there wasn't any left. I stacked pastries and fruit.

"Someone has quite the appetite," Thatch said. "Do you usually eat a trough of breakfast?"

Oh no! I was going to give myself away. He would know I was bringing Derrick food. I removed a banana and a slice of toast from the plate and returned them to their stacks.

Josie turned to Thatch. "A trough? Really? Are you trying to imply that Clarissa is a fat pig?" She snatched up the toast and banana I'd returned and replaced them on my plate. "If that's how much she wants to eat, what's it to you?"

"I didn't say she was fat . . . yet." A wrinkle creased his brow. "That is just like you, Miss Kimura, twisting something I say into an insult. It's no wonder you don't have a boyfriend."

Josie stood up, spilling a cup of coffee. Thatch clucked his tongue in disgust. He removed his wand from an inner pocket in his jacket and waved it over the mess. The cup righted itself, and the liquid refilled.

Josie straightened her conical hat. "I'm done. Are you coming, Clarissa? You can bring your plate with you."

I stood to follow her.

Thatch grabbed the back of my sweater and yanked me back into my seat. "Not so fast. We have matters to discuss."

That sounded ominous.

# CHAPTER THREE
## Merlin's Balls

"Stay," I mouthed to Josie. I was faced away from Thatch, so I didn't think he could see me pleading with her.

Somehow, he did.

"No, she can't," he said. "Miss Kimura has detention duty today. If only she was better at budgeting her time like you and I." He waved her off.

She lingered.

He casually aimed his wand at her feet. "Go. If you don't, I'll be forced to jinx you into compliance."

She gave me an apologetic grimace before stalking off. I didn't blame her. He'd used that spell on me to get me to leave a school in the Morty Realm once. I'd had no control over my legs, and they just kept walking. At least with freedom she could choose to go instead of being forced.

I served myself a helping of oatmeal and spooned brown sugar and cinnamon into it. There was no point in pretending all this was for me if he already knew. Maybe I could ask Thatch for clothes for Derrick. They were about the same height. Thatch might even be taller.

He didn't look angry. More concerned than anything else. I could work with concerned.

Thatch steepled his fingers. "I know what's eating you."

"Do you?" Could he possibly have known how much had changed in the last twenty-four hours? Did he understand the battle raging inside me? I worried he was a liar and a villain with nefarious intentions. But what if he wasn't?

I hated thinking ill of a friend. This was the conflict eating me up inside.

"You don't have to worry. I've taken care of your little problem," he said.

"*What* problem?" For a moment I thought he meant Derrick—that he'd taken care of Derrick.

He leaned back with the satisfied air of a Venus flytrap that had just swallowed a canary. "Miss Periwinkle. I persuaded her not to tell anyone about your secret. You're welcome."

"Oh, um, thanks." I had completely forgotten about the librarian.

After Miss Periwinkle discovered my affinity and researched the Lost Red Court and the extent of my powers, she'd discovered I could increase the magic of others like my biological mother. Plus, she'd seen my powers at work.

If she had asked nicely, I would have helped restore the youth that my biological mother had stolen from her. I wanted to assume Alouette Loraline had accidentally stolen it from her, but I didn't know.

Instead of asking, Miss Periwinkle had blackmailed me. When the spell had gone wrong, I'd gone to my mentor, Thatch.

He must have been able to fix things because she'd been young and beautiful again when I'd gotten a peek at her through the magic mirror window to his room. And Felix Thatch must have been quite smitten with her from the eyeful I'd gotten of the two of them.

No wonder he looked so tired.

His smile turned smug. "Aren't you going to ask how I secured secrecy on your behalf?"

"No. And I don't want to know." I glanced at the students sitting at the tables. This really wasn't the time or place to hear about his sexual exploits.

A smirk played at his lips. "Wiseman's Oath."

"Oh, that's all?" A binding spell wasn't the lurid explanation my mind had jumped to.

"What did you think I was going to say? A blood ritual?"

"Yep, you read my mind."

He shook his head and clucked his tongue. "You always think the worst of me, don't you?"

His words couldn't have cut me more. I avoided his gaze. I did jump to conclusions—especially about him.

This conversation had taken a drastically different turn than where I thought it had been going. Thatch's good mood could be explained by getting laid, not because of sinister plot. Maybe he had a soul after all.

I wanted to ask him about Derrick. Maybe Derrick had been mistaken about him.

A student squealed at a table nearby, drawing my attention. Josie lingered there, talking to Chase Othello, one of my students with bright orchid hair. Josie smiled at me. My friend hadn't left after all? Even after Thatch had threatened her? She had to be the most loyal person I knew.

I smiled and waved her off, no longer worried. I ate my oatmeal, trying to figure out how I could possibly ask Thatch about Derrick without giving away I knew the invisible man was my best friend from high school. Thatch had been specific that Derek needed to forget about me because the Raven Queen had cursed him to kill me or kidnap me or something vaguely ominous. But it wasn't true. Derrick remembered me—and remembered something suspicious about Thatch turning him invisible. I couldn't ask about that, but I could ask about something we had already discussed.

"Do you remember that time we went to the forest to collect . . . stuff?" I asked.

Thatch scanned the sea of students. "If you're bringing this up because you want me to finish collecting the remaining ingredients for the spell, you'll have to be patient. I am preoccupied with other matters at the moment." He didn't sound angry as he said it, just matter-of-fact.

*Play along*, I told myself. "Why have you never given me the list? I could gather everything for you."

"You wouldn't know what half the items are, nor do I think you would be capable of collecting the more dangerous items like the dragon eggs."

"It's too bad I don't have smart friends who are witches and unicorns."

He snorted. "Very well. I'll give you the list."

That was too easy. I would normally have been jumping up and down in joy, but I was having a hard time remembering how I usually behaved around Thatch.

My mentor scrutinized me. "Just don't try to collect the dragon egg yourself. We don't want you to get hurt. Make that annoying unicorn who likes to hang around here do it for you. With any luck, he'll get himself burned alive, and that will be the end of your unicorn problems."

"You don't want me to get hurt," I repeated. My oatmeal was tasteless mush, even after spooning in sugar and butter. I couldn't hold it in any longer. "But you were the one who tied me to that tree as bait. I almost became chimera food that night."

"I wouldn't have let anything happen to you." He sipped at a mug of coffee. "Is that why you're so grumpy this morning? Josie convinced you I don't have your best intentions in mind?"

"You left me alone. Those chimeras attacked, and they almost killed me. You told me you warded the tree, but you lied."

"You're being overdramatic. I never left you alone. Nor did they come close to killing you." He didn't confirm or deny what Derrick had told me about the wards.

Had he known Derrick had been there? I couldn't tell. I couldn't ask.

I piled my plates on a tray, ready to leave.

"So, who is all that food really intended for?" Thatch asked.

"Brownies," I said. It was a pretty good excuse. I'd seen Vega set out food for the cleaning staff. "I have a lot of laundry I want them to take care of."

"That isn't going to work. It's school food. They make the school food. They have higher standards than their own cooking."

"How do you know? Have you ever tried leaving out school food?" I drained my orange juice.

"Why do you never listen?" Thatch asked.

Sebastian Reade sat down on the other side of Thatch, ignoring me. The foreign language teacher was a middle-aged man with silvery hair. He reached for a roll, a dreamy expression coming over his face.

"Wow, I am in love," he said to no one in particular.

Thatch turned to him.

It was the distraction I needed.

Sebastian smiled and sighed. "I heard Jeb hired a new history teacher. I had no idea she would be so beautiful. I just ran into her outside the library."

I slid my tray away and backed from the table slowly, not wanting the motion of my escape to catch Thatch's eye.

Thatch snorted. "That isn't our new history teacher. It's the librarian."

"We're getting a new librarian too?" Sebastian asked.

"No, that's Miss Periwinkle."

Sebastian laughed. "You can't be serious." He stopped laughing when he saw Thatch's stern expression. "Do you think she would go on a date with me?"

"She's out of your league." Thatch leaned forward conspiratorially. "In any case, I hear her boyfriend is a sadistic Merlin-class Celestor who removed the eyeballs from the last man who ogled her. I advise extreme caution."

# CHAPTER FOUR
## The Emperor's New Clothes

I headed straight for Derrick's room in the unused wing of the school. I had to duck under spiderwebs and climb over rubble to get there. The stone walls near his room were painted with murals of me, Cthulhu, and a few of his other favorite things.

I knocked on his door. There was no answer. It was unlocked so I went inside and set down the food. I waited for over ten minutes, but he didn't return. I didn't blame him for not waiting. I had taken almost an hour to shower and get food.

His coat was gone, so I supposed he might have gone to talk to Khaba. He'd sounded concerned about his job security.

In my haste to leave the cafeteria, I had failed in my mission to acquire Derrick clothes. He probably still needed some. I couldn't imagine what he was wearing. I left the tray of food, and I went to Khaba's office in the administration wing, but the door was locked and the room dark. The principal wasn't in either, but that was no surprise. Even if it hadn't been a Sunday, Jeb was never in.

I headed to my room next to see if there was anything I could find for him there. Fortunately, Vega was gone. All my clothes were child-sized due to my diminutive stature. I considered where I would be able to get Derrick clothes that would fit him. Derrick was taller than Pro Ro and most of the other male teachers. The only person his height was Thatch.

Since it was a Sunday, that meant Thatch would have cafeteria duty until nine. If I hurried, I could sneak into Thatch's private quarters and grab a pair of pants and a shirt for Derrick. Thatch had been livid that one time I'd looked in his desk for Post-its. I tried not to think about how he'd react if he caught me stealing his clothes.

This time, I wasn't going to get caught. Plus, we were just going to borrow the clothes. Derrick could get dressed and then go into Lachlan Falls to buy something. Then we could wash Thatch's clothes and return them. Easy peasy. Or so I tried to convince myself.

What Thatch would do if he saw those clothes on Derrick was a different problem. Then again, if Thatch saw Derrick wasn't invisible, that trumped appropriated clothes.

I powerwalked to the hallway with the tapestry of the dragon and knight in battle. The moment no students were in the hallway, I ducked into the dark passage. I felt along the wall. I wished I had my cell phone to use as a flashlight. I followed a turn in the stone corridor until I walked into a set of armor. I groped the metal man until I found his arm to give him the secret handshake and pulled his arm down. The grinding of stone and a faint glow came from around the corner.

A bluish rectangle of light shone around another tapestry. I ducked underneath and hurried toward the windows set in the walls. Each window revealed a different bedroom, the sizes and positions of the windows reflecting where mirrors were placed in the rooms. Most of the dormitories were empty, but Pro Ro still lay asleep in his. Grandmother Bluehorse sat in her housecoat drinking coffee at a table. The view into these rooms was silvery and bright, a ghostly version of the world.

I passed the rooms by until I came to Thatch's. The blanket had been removed from the mirror, and I got an unobstructed view of his unmade bed. Maroon curtains were untied from the posts and draped around the canopy bed.

I touched the surface of the mirror, the glass rippling like water. It was cold and thick, sucking at my hand like a bog. I stuck my hand through the looking glass. My fingers were silvery blue like the scene on the other side. I pushed the rest of myself through the cold surface, arriving in his private quarters.

The room was empty. The door to the bathroom was closed as was the one that led out to the short hallway to his office. I tried not to examine the clothes littered around the floor too closely. At least Miss Periwinkle wasn't in his bed any longer.

Immediately I went to Thatch's dresser. Each drawer reflected his orderly existence, everything neatly folded and organized. I found socks in the second drawer and undershirts in the third. There was no way I was going to touch his underwear in the top drawer. There wasn't a need for ascots or cravats so I skipped that one. I considered whether the loose pajamas in the bottom would be more comfortable or it would be more appropriate to give Derrick slacks and a button-up shirt.

I went for the wardrobe next and selected a pair of gray pants and a button-up shirt from the back. I considered taking the vest and jacket but decided not to. A door creaked behind me.

"What are you doing?" a woman's voice asked.

I whirled. Miss Periwinkle stood in the doorway to the bathroom, a towel wrapped around herself.

Craptacular. I was caught.

## CHAPTER FIVE
## Don't Mess with a Siren

"Sorry, I didn't know you were here?" The statement came out a question.

I hadn't suspected Gertrude Periwinkle would be there, not with Sebastian Reade saying he'd just seen her in the library. But apparently, she'd come back for more of Thatch. Maybe this was why Thatch had given Josie his detention duty—so he could spend time with her instead. Maybe that was why he was too busy to search for ingredients for that spell.

Gertrude Periwinkle's long blonde hair dripped water onto the wooden floor. She was no longer the old wrinkled prune she had been the day before, but a young woman my age. She was inhumanly beautiful, as radiant as an angel. Beads of moisture on her skin caught the vague illumination from above so that each droplet shone like a diamond.

Her perfect pink lips puckered into a frown that would have looked more in place on her old body than this new one given to her through my magic. "How did you get in? Do you have a key?"

I hugged the clothes to my chest. "Yes."

Her eyes narrowed. Maybe she knew I was lying. Miss Periwinkle was a Celestor, and they were known for their divination abilities. Not that Vega had tried very hard with me.

"What are you doing in *my* boyfriend's room?"

"Oh, um, don't mind me. I just had to get some clothes."

"For Felix? Why didn't he ask me?" She looked more hurt than angry now.

"For someone else." I backed up until I reached the door. "Sorry for the inconvenience."

"Give me your key," she said.

"Huh?" I groped for the handle behind me.

The chill in her voice could have frozen the flames of hell. "There isn't enough room for both of us in his life. Give me your key."

"I don't have a key." I opened the door, ready to make my getaway.

She lunged forward and pushed the door closed. "Yes, you do. You just told me you had a key. How else did you get in?"

I sighed in exasperation. "Okay, I lied. I used magic to get in."

She snorted. "I think we both know how inadequate your magic skills are."

There was no way I was getting away easy now. She was going to tell Thatch I'd been here stealing his clothes. I tried to think of a way out of this.

"Look," I said. "I'm not supposed to be here. But neither are you. The school rules forbid fraternizing with colleagues. Unlike you, I'm not naked."

Her face turned red. "Those rules were created for *you*. For your protection." She spat out the words like they tasted bad in her mouth.

"Exactly. All that sex magic and fertility stuff might endanger me. You probably were just using the shower in the dungeon because it's so much less moldy than your wing. I'm sure that would go over well with Jeb and Khaba, especially considering you *used to be* a siren and people at this school think sirens are the equivalent of succubae."

A vein pulsed in her forehead. She didn't look as pretty with the red splotches breaking out across her face. "Fine, have it your way." She dropped her hand from the door and stepped back. "Just know this isn't over."

I hurried out the door.

She shouted after me. "And if I ever catch you in here again, I'll yank out your entrails and use them to hang you from the highest tower of this school."

Gertrude Periwinkle and Felix Thatch were made for each other. I couldn't wait to see what impending doom fell upon me when Thatch learned I had been in his room.

# CHAPTER SIX
## Invismo Winslow

Derrick still wasn't in his room when I returned with clothes. Where was he, and why was he taking so long? Maybe he was looking for me? I found a blank page on his sketchpad.

I used one of his fancy markers to write a note:

*I came, I saw, I conquered. Actually, I just brought you food and clothes. I suspect you should keep a low profile until we talk more. I'll be back later.*

*XOXO*

*C*

I didn't know what to do now. The idea of Derrick wandering around the school *visible* made me nervous. I didn't know how Thatch would react. Maybe I should have just told him. Still, he had forbidden me from seeing Derrick. I couldn't imagine he'd be happy.

Even if Derrick had gone somewhere like Lachlan Falls for clothes, Thatch might see him walking on the school grounds to get there. If Thatch was working for the Raven Queen, I was in this mess way over my head.

I needed help.

Josie sat behind a tall stack of essays in her classroom. I took it detention duty hadn't yet begun for her. She moaned the moment I walked into her room.

She removed her black-rimmed glasses. "Please say you're my fairy godmother come to take me to the ball and you have a herd of small mice to do all these papers for me."

"Sorry, no such luck. I'm the kind of wonderful friend who's here to add to your problems."

She laughed, thinking I was joking. "I wish I had started this three days ago, but I was grading last week's essays. And before that, it was more essays. I hate teaching Morty Studies. I so much wish I was teaching the History of Fae Studies, but they wanted someone who had lived in the Morty Realm for this." She laid her head on her arms. Her patched witch hat fell onto the floor. "I need to learn not to procrastinate. Why do I do this to myself every time?"

"I *could* tell you why *I* procrastinate." I picked up her hat and placed it on my head. "But I'll tell you later."

She lifted her head, her wan smile conveying little appreciation for my sense of humor. "Funny."

I sat down at one of the desks that was probably too small for most teenagers but fit me. "I need to talk to you about last night."

"You're going to tell me why you told Thatch you spent the night in my room? I take it this had nothing to do with Vega's snoring and bad breath?"

I glanced over my shoulder. No one was in the hallway. "I have a boyfriend."

"No way!" She jumped to her feet and snatched her hat off my head.

I thought she would smile and congratulate me. Instead, she smacked me with her hat. It probably hurt the hat more than it did me.

"Have you gone crazy, girl?" She smacked me again.

I backed away. "What was that for?"

"You can't have a boyfriend. You'll lose your job. Jeb said no sex. Remember? We don't want your fertility magic to make this school all Fifty Shades of Magic and set off already horny teenagers."

"My magic isn't like that. I think. . . ." I lowered my voice. "I think maybe Thatch misled Jeb and Khaba into believing my magic would do that. I think he's been lying, but I don't understand why." I went over to the door and closed it before launching into the full story.

I told her everything: about my previous relationship with Derrick and what had happened when we'd kissed when I'd been fifteen; Thatch's explanation that I was forbidden from seeing Derrick until his curse was lifted because it was too dangerous; his explanation that I could break Derrick's curse by collecting ingredients for a spell; and I recounted the events involving the invisible man, one of the school's security staff, and how he had been following me the previous semester. I explained Thatch had given Invismo an incentive to watch me to make sure I didn't do anything stupid that would get me fired.

He had neglected to tell me Derrick was the invisible man.

Josie stared at me in shock. "Thatch is the most legit bag of dicks ever! You couldn't *see* him because of his curse? Is that supposed to be a joke?"

"Yeah, I guess. So now I don't know what to do. I discovered the invisible man was Derrick. I broke the curse without Thatch's help. I've cured him—which I think Thatch didn't want me to do because Derrick remembers him being employed by the Raven Queen. He thinks Thatch cursed him or something."

"Fucking A." She waved a hand at the stacks of papers on her desk. "Why did you have to tell me this on the day I have so much work to do?"

"I'm sorry. You always give good advice. I didn't know what to do."

"Duh. You have to tell Khaba. But don't tell him you slept with Derrick. Tell him you tried the spell and cured him."

"Will he believe me?"

"It doesn't matter if he believes you. He's like a lawyer. He's obligated to report your admission of misdeeds." She leaned forward. "That means you can't ever tell him you broke a school rule. He's Fae, and he lives for rules. Got it?"

Ten minutes later, I sat in Khaba's office with Josie. The smile slid from our dean of discipline's face as I told him an abbreviated version of events.

Khaba ran a hand over his bald head. "What do you mean Invismo Winslow isn't invisible anymore?"

"Derrick Winslow," I corrected.

Khaba paced the small expanse of his office, though I didn't see how he could stand to walk at all considering how tight his leather pants were. His hot-pink, leopard-print shirt was unbuttoned down to his navel, exposing his washboard abs. Fae magic radiated off him in a cloud. He was so beautiful it made my eyes water if I looked at him too long.

Josie stared at him dreamily.

Khaba ceased pacing. "By the way, is he hot? I always imagined he would be sexy."

"*I* think he is." I cleared my throat. "But let's get back to the important issues. . . ."

Khaba crossed his arms and leaned against a hot-pink file cabinet covered in unicorn stickers. "Like the fact that you lifting his 'curse' means I'm going to need a new security guard."

"By important, I meant Thatch's ulterior motives."

He ignored me. "Do you know how hard it is to find an invisible man who isn't a pervert? I had to fire the last one for peeking in the girls' locker room while students were undressing." He gazed into a crystal ball on the filing cabinet. "Invismo was a sweetheart."

Derrick had always been a nice guy. That time my sister had put alcohol and probably a roofie into my drink at homecoming, Derrick was the one who had cleaned up my vomit and taken care of me. He had refused my suggestions to make out, explaining how that would be taking advantage of me. Even as an adult he'd been reluctant to kiss me, afraid he was taking advantage of my affinity.

"But just because he's visible now doesn't mean he can't have a job here, right?" I asked. I'd only gotten him back the day before. I didn't want to lose him again.

Josie nudged me. "What about Thatch?"

"What are you going to do about him being employed by the Raven Queen?" I asked.

"Honey, I need evidence. Right now, it's Derrick's word against Thatch's." Khaba drummed his fingers against the pink file cabinet. "Who would Jeb believe? Who would the Witchkin Council believe? A teacher with a . . . *fairly* clean record? Or some kid whose memories have been tampered with by the Raven Queen herself?"

"What do you mean by 'fairly' clean? What did Thatch do?" I asked.

"People suspected he was involved in experiments with Alouette Loraline, and he was taken into custody. Heck, I suspected he was guilty. He was released due to lack of evidence. Jeb vouched for him, claiming he'd been a victim in the entire thing." He rolled his eyes in disgust.

Khaba didn't come right out and say my biological mother had tortured Thatch to near death, but that had to be the reason why Jeb felt sympathy for him.

"But you think Thatch still works for the Raven Queen?" I asked. "You think he has an ulterior motive to teach me dark magic to summon a demon like my mother did all those years ago."

"Yes." He looked me up and down. "How did you know that's what I suspected?"

"Um. . . ." It probably wouldn't do to say I had accidentally overheard his conversation with Jeb in the hallway of mirrors during the first semester when they'd been talking about Thatch. It had been right before Jeb had "rubbed Khaba's lamp." I suspected Jeb had done a lot more than rub the lamp tattooed on Khaba's body.

I hated having so many secrets.

Josie cleared her throat. "I don't disagree Thatch is a grade-A alpha-hole, but summon a demon? That's a little much, even for him."

Khaba removed the crystal ball from his file cabinet and sat in his pink chair. "Thatch was *friends* with Clarissa's biological mother. He was the one originally sentenced for her crimes before they knew she was involved. He didn't argue on his own behalf. Jeb thinks it's all because he was too addled and drained after what she did to him. I tend to think she would have killed him, rather than leaving him for dead and letting him take the blame, if he hadn't been in on the plan."

Another reason Thatch must have resented me, the daughter of the woman who left him to be blamed for her crimes.

Khaba set the crystal ball on his desk. "In any case, Jeb will be unconvinced by conjecture and hearsay. The first thing I'll need to do is interview Invismo and use memory charms to help him remember. There still might be remnants of curses or counter curses on him. I can see if I'm able to detect the origins of the magic and the purpose. Afterward, I'll have a better idea of what to ask Thatch." He smoothed a hand over his bald head. "Our delightful alchemy instructor didn't inform me you and Derrick knew each other when we hired you. He didn't mention you were high school sweethearts, or that Derrick had been abducted by the Raven Queen." Khaba waved a hand over the crystal ball. "Those are the kind of employment details I would expect to be informed of before hiring someone."

White light clouded the sphere. Thatch's face appeared. He was laughing, but it was hard to tell with the absence of sound if it was a good-natured chuckle or a maniacal mwah-ha-ha-ha villain laugh.

I leaned forward to gaze at Thatch. "If you start asking Thatch questions, he's going to know Derrick isn't invisible anymore. He might do something to Derrick."

Khaba shrugged. "Thatch is a Merlin-class Celestor. He's clever, sneaky and highly skilled. Even if Invis—Derrick manages to sneak around without being spotted, Thatch probably has alarms and wards set up in case of a possibility like this. He's got to suspect one of the major spells he had cast has been tampered with."

"Please don't start asking Thatch yet," I begged. "Question Derrick first. We can see if we can find evidence to prove Thatch is still working for the Raven Queen first. Or we might find he's totally innocent."

In any case, I didn't want to endanger Derrick. But Khaba was right. If Thatch was behind Derrick's invisibility, it was only a matter of time before Thatch figured out I'd broken the spell. I didn't know how long we had or what he would do when he did find out. We needed to know if Derrick was safe or if the Raven Queen would be coming for him.

Somehow I had to prove or disprove Thatch's involvement in something diabolical, for Derrick's safety and for my own.

# CHAPTER SEVEN
## Stinky Pinky

Josie, Khaba, and I exited from his office together, heading toward Derrick's room. Khaba had used his crystal ball to determine where Derrick was—and he was back in his room—so we would soon resolve this issue.

With Khaba's Fae magic, we hoped to find answers to some of the missing pieces of this puzzle. Josie linked arms with me as we descended puke-green stairs.

"Are you sure you have time for this?" I asked Josie.

"I want to meet your boy—ahem—your friend from high school." She glanced at Khaba.

His full lips curled into a smile. "I'll pretend I didn't almost hear that."

I nudged Josie. "Not that I don't want you to meet him, but aren't you supposed to be covering detention duty today?"

"This will just take a sec."

"Procrastination," I teased her.

I was so glad we were going directly to Derrick. Khaba would help me resolve this problem. It would be a relief to know Thatch's intentions.

Before we'd gotten to the main floor, I noticed the pungent smell in the air. It was musky like a wild animal, reminiscent of goat or bear. Cedar and decaying mulch were mixed in, and for the briefest moment I thought of Julian Thistledown, the green man who had tried to use my affinity against me.

We exited the hallway, and before us loomed the largest mass of fur on legs I'd ever seen. The shaggy man—I thought it was a man—was taller than Thatch. The fur was chestnut, so thick and dense it was impossible to tell what gender it was, but the creature held itself like a man.

"Howdy!" Principal Jebediah Bumblebub waved at us from behind the creature.

The creature's head came up to the top of Jeb's hat, which looked more like a Stetson with a cone attached than a witch's hat.

The furball blocked my path to Derrick.

Josie halted, her feet rooting into the floor as Jeb and the shaggy beast approached.

"Is that a. . . ." I lowered my voice. It was considered rude to ask what a Witchkin or Fae was. "Sasquatch?"

A squeak of noise escaped Josie's throat.

The pungent odor rolled off the giant animal in waves. I covered my nose and mouth with my hand, trying to block it out. My eyes watered at the smell, and I blinked back tears. As overpowering as it was, oddly, part of me liked the masculine musk underneath everything else. It was just a lot all at once.

Khaba nudged me with his elbow. "Clarissa, you're being rude."

"What?"

"Remove your hand from your face," he whispered.

There was my Morty upbringing again. No one had ever told me it was impolite to try not to gag when I found myself staring at Chewbacca.

Jeb waved to us. "Good golly, there's some of my school's finest. Y'all, won't you say howdy to our school's new History of Magic teacher." He looped his fingers through his belt. It must have been a special occasion. Jeb usually saved his large W belt buckle for school events. And he'd curled his mustache into four loops today instead of two. His long silver beard hid most of his bandana.

I had a feeling my quick excursion to see Derrick was about to get derailed.

"I am so excited to be here!" The sasquatch's voice was high for a man. Or maybe the voice was low for a woman. There was so much hair everywhere I couldn't tell what gender the Fae creature was.

"Jeb has been telling me all about your school's—our school's—programs. The moment he told me there was a yoga class, I was sold." The sasquatch's brown eyes looked to Josie. "It will be great working with you. This is my dream come true." Bigfoot fidgeted before us like an eight-foot-tall puppy.

Khaba held out his hand. "I'm Khaba. I'm dean of discipline at Womby's. I'll make sure you get a handbook with all our rules." He looked the sasquatch up and down. "You might want to check rule five, the one for pants."

The sasquatch looked to Jeb, eyes growing wide.

Jeb tugged at his beard. "Khaba, don't you be such a stickler. I told Professor Anotklosh Johnson—"

"Please, call me Pinky, sir. Anotklosh Johnson is my Fae name." Pinky's voice was nasally. I still couldn't tell if Pinky was male or female. I kept trying to figure out if I saw breasts under the fur or any sizable mounds anywhere else, but I didn't want to ogle and be rude.

Jeb tugged on his beard. "Ahem, err, Pinky. I told Professor Pinky—what was I saying?"

"You made the rules. I enforce them," Khaba said. "Professor Pinky is going to need to wear pants while working in the building."

"Sasquatches do not wear pants." Pinky's brown eyes settled on Khaba. "Clothing is a Fae construct used to oppress sasquatch people."

While the fashion police were having their argument, Josie clutched at my arm. Her eyes watered, and she stared at the floor. Miss Periwinkle hurried down the stairs and rushed past us, arms full of books. She looked young enough to be a student. I wondered if Jeb even knew she was the librarian. She was wearing her black Victorian dress with the high collar and cameo made of a skull, but her witch hat was absent.

She tossed her vivacious long hair over her shoulder, flashing the kind of smile one might see on a Cheshire cat. A chill settled over my spine. I didn't know what that sinister cunning in her eyes meant, but I had a bad feeling about it.

"Okey-dokey. Well," Jeb motioned to me. "This is Miss Lawrence. She teaches fine arts and crafts."

Pinky nodded. Before Jeb could introduce Josie, Pinky said, "Hi, Jo, nice to see you again."

"Hi."

"You two know each other? That's mighty convenient," Jeb grinned.

Pinky smiled, revealing straight white teeth my late father would have been proud of considering he had been an orthodontist. "We used to teach at Zeme's Academy for Plant and Animal Magic. How long ago was that? Three years ago?"

"So that's an Amni Plandai school?" I asked.

"Mmm," Josie said. Her face was pale. Maybe it was the smell.

"I always wondered about where you'd went," Pinky said. "You left so suddenly in the middle of the year. There were all these rumors that you had gotten ill. I'm so glad we'll be teaching together again."

I kept listening to Pinky, trying to figure out some hint whether the sasquatch was male or female.

"Mmm," Josie said.

"I'll leave y'all to show Pinky around the school. I've got some business to attend to in the office," Jeb said.

"Sorry," Khaba said apologetically. "Now isn't the best time for a tour. Perhaps I could assist Pinky later. I have some dire school business to attend to." He hooked his arm through mine, tugging me in the opposite direction.

"I've got to get back to my office. Mrs. Keahi's been pesterin' me to answer all the letters that have been stacking up. She insists I take a looky at the bills." Jeb turned to Josie. "Miss Kimura, can you take Mr. uh, Miss, uh, Professor Pinky on a tour?"

Jeb didn't know what Pinky's gender was either. I tried not to laugh. Even with all that fur covering Pinky's face, the confused expression was clear.

Josie yanked her arm from mine and backed away. "I have to finish grading . . . stuff. Plus, I have detention duty to oversee. Sorry. Bye."

Pinky waved. "See you later, Jo. I'll drop in on your classroom. I'd love to catch up on old times."

"Miss Lawrence? Please say at least one of my staff members is free." Jeb fidgeted with one of the curls of his mustache.

"I have business with Miss Lawrence," Khaba said.

"Mr. Thatch is free," I said. Okay, so I did take a sliver of delight in unloading the stinky sasquatch off on Thatch. I grabbed Mr. Khaba, tingles of energy prickling my fingers. "I need to help Mr. Khaba with a security issue."

Khaba nodded solemnly. "A dire security issue."

Jeb harrumphed.

Khaba and I started away. Jeb shook his head, not pleased. He spoke to Pinky, heading toward his office. I wanted to get to Derrick's room so Khaba would be able to work his djinn magic. The guidance counselor shouted from the stairs behind us. I ignored Puck.

"Is Pinky male or female?" I whispered to Khaba, who usually knew the answer to everything with his superior Fae magic.

"Male?" he asked. The question in his voice gave me pause.

"I guess we could ask Josie," I said. Until then, calling Pinky *it* didn't seem like the most respectful pronoun. *Xe*, I decided. I would ask Josie about *xir* later.

"Oi! Miss Lawrence!" Puck called. "I've been looking everywhere for you."

Not another interruption. I didn't have time for this. I needed to talk to Derrick.

Puck, a short man with wild blond hair, panted as he ran up to us. "I've been manually transferring all the teachers' grades and comments onto the midterm report cards we need to send home to parents next week. I noticed yours are missing."

My annoyance turned to alarm. "What do you mean? I put them in your box weeks ago."

"You did, but they're all blank."

This was a teacher's worst nightmare.

"They shouldn't be. I remember doing them."

Jeb sidled up to me. "Miss Lawrence, bless your heart! Did you use disappearing ink? One of the students gave one of the old art teachers a pen with disappearing ink once. What a calamity that was!"

"No! I used pencil. I put them in Mr. Puck's box. My grades were done." Panic rose up in me.

Jeb tsked and headed toward his office with Pinky.

"Do you have any backups? You're going to have to redo them." Puck waved me after him.

It had taken days to fill in the grades from my book and write a comment in every single box by hand. I'd done a little each day that week. I was not a procrastinator. I was a good teacher. Why couldn't Puck have told me this three weeks ago when I'd turned in grades? What kind of school sent out report cards a month after the end of the semester?

Maybe this was how the world worked without computers.

I looked to Khaba in desperation. "Can you fix this with magic?"

"Why don't you see if you and Puck can figure this out? I'm going to take care of . . . other business." He gave me a meaningful look.

In the counseling office, Puck showed me the blank report cards. This was worse than not saving a document on a computer.

Gertrude Periwinkle passed by the open door of the office, a satisfied smile on her face. A sinking suspicion weighed me down.

Son of a witch! She had done this. That sneaky librarian had gotten her revenge.

# CHAPTER EIGHT
## The Wrath of the Librarian

I had underestimated the librarian's penchant for revenge.

Puck didn't trust me to work on report cards without screwing them up. He made me bring my grade book to the office and fill them out in the counseling center. I sat at the intake desk where I imagined a secretary would sit if the school could afford one.

I worked for hours, but I found it difficult to concentrate on grades when all I wanted to do was find Derrick. What if he was in danger from the Raven Queen? Thatch had said that without a permanent cure, Derrick was like a bomb that could go off at any moment. It was hard to believe Thatch would keep him around if he actually posed a threat to my safety.

Unless he didn't pose a threat and never had. For all I knew, it was all a fabricated story, like so many of the other ones Thatch had told me to persuade me to do something. I hadn't forgotten how he'd tried to con me into believing he was my father to make me cry so he could collect virgin's tears.

I forced myself to focus on grades. When I rose to get lunch, I found Puck blocking my path. "Not so fast. You aren't allowed to leave until all that is done." His hair looked more wiry and wild than ever.

"I just want to grab a sandwich and have a quick restroom break." I stepped to the left.

He shifted in front of me. "Not allowed."

"What do you mean that isn't allowed? How can going to the bathroom not be allowed?"

"You can use the faculty latrine." He nodded to the hallway past the reception desk and offices.

I trudged down the hall past the mailboxes. Puck's office reminded me of a Zen garden with bonsai trees planted around rocks and a pit of pea gravel raked into artful patterns. Sunlight shone from an immense skylight.

I wasn't sure how he got work done in there without a desk. It certainly involved magic.

The next room I passed was the room of school records past. It was filled with file cabinets and went on into infinity. It was a lot like Mary Poppins' purse, how it went on forever, but the outside of the room didn't look any bigger. I imagined that took even more magic.

I passed the conference room, the staff room with the steam-powered magic copier, and a few closed doors. At the end of the hallway was the latrine. Not a restroom, but some grody wooden room with flies buzzing around it. Why didn't we use magic to make that shithole nicer?

Josie stopped by to pick up mail at two. When she heard Puck was holding me hostage and hadn't given me a lunch break, she brought me an apple. By five o'clock, my handwriting in the comments boxes was close to illegible, but I had finished.

Silas Lupi came in to check his mail just as I was finishing up with the last report card. He whispered something to Puck about picking up Miss Periwinkle's mail for her.

When I was done with my torture session, I stepped out into the bright corridor, my eyes hurting. I still wanted to go see Derrick, but now it was dinnertime, and I was ravenous. No doubt, Derrick would be as well.

I headed toward the cafeteria. I could get a tray of dinner for Derrick and myself and head back to his room. I planned to ask him if Khaba had been successful in drawing out memories.

As I stepped through one of the Stonehenge archways into the busy cafeteria, students waved at me. Imani Washington came running up to me, her pigtails flopping with the bounce of her every step. She was petite and freckled like me, but her skin was dark and her eyes as brown as the earth.

"Miss Lawrence, I've been looking everywhere for you!" she said.

Why did people have to keep saying that to me today? Already it sounded like I was going to get sucked into another problem.

Greenie, her best friend, a girl with viridian skin and leaves growing from her hair, joined Imani. "You need to see. He's been cursed. He's been acting strange for hours."

They tugged me in the opposite direction of the food.

"Who has been cursed?" I asked.

"Mr. Thatch," Imani whispered. "Something is wrong with him. Seriously."

"What's wrong with him?" I asked in alarm. "Have his eyes turned all black?" His eyes had done that once before when he'd been in the throes of pain magic. It had made him look like those in the employment of the Raven Court—which he probably was.

"No. It's weirder than that," Greenie said.

I couldn't imagine anything worse. I jogged through the hallway with them. Even more interestingly, they led me toward the front courtyard.

"Wait?" I asked. "He isn't in the dungeon?" Thatch hardly ever left his moldy lair.

"No. He's outside acting strange."

Okay, so this was already suspicious. "Does he have his bird with him?"

"No."

Just as we stepped out into the frigid March air, Vega stepped into my path. "No running in the school." She looked to Imani. "Five points from the Celestor team." She looked to Greenie. "Five points from Amni Plandai." She looked to me. "Five points from. . . . Oh, it's you. Can't you just learn some magic to make yourself taller than the students?"

Imani grabbed my arm and dragged me down the steps. The air was cold, and I wrapped my arms around myself. We passed a frozen fountain. Our feet crunched over icy earth. The stark branches of trees lined the path.

We found Thatch sitting on a bench smiling. The way he stared off into the distance, his usually somber face transformed with a cheerful smile, didn't look natural. I understood why Imani and Greenie had thought he was cursed, but surely Thatch wasn't one to succumb to enchantments so easily.

Two students walking by on the path snuck furtive glances at him. He held a daisy and twirled it between his fingers. I don't even know where he had found a flower considering how bleak the grounds looked right now.

"Go back and get some dinner," I told Imani and Greenie. "Nothing is wrong with Mr. Thatch."

More likely this was what love did to Thatch. Though, I hadn't ever imagined Thatch would let himself get this stereotypically sappy.

"There is something wrong, Miss Lawrence," Imani said. "You know he doesn't smile. Please, check on him. Please."

I couldn't very well tell students Thatch wasn't his normal self because he had gotten laid—which probably hadn't happened for a hundred years. Maybe that had broken his resting-bitch face curse.

Tears filled Greenie's eyes. "He's been hexed, hasn't he? Can you see if there's dark magic at work?"

I waved the girls off. "Get some dinner before it gets *Lord of the Flies* in the cafeteria." Even if dinner was flavorless and bland, it was still food, and there never seemed to be enough of it.

I hugged my sweater around myself and made my way over to Thatch.

"Beautiful day, isn't it?" He scooted down the bench to make room. He patted the wood.

The two girls huddled together, glancing over their shoulders as they headed back to the school. The building looked like an octopus with multiple personality disorder, each wing stretching out from the center built in a different style and during a different era. Wood was layered over ancient stone and sections of brick. The towers at the end of wings didn't match in size or shape.

Reluctantly I sat down. "So, um, you came outside? I didn't know you did that. Everything okay?"

"You're so droll! It's not like I'm a vampire and I'm allergic to sunlight."

"Right." The girls stood at the top of the steps. It looked like Vega was scolding them for something.

I turned back to Thatch, finding myself tongue-tied.

I had found my long-lost love and cured Derrick with magic—or sex. Why was it such a surprise Thatch might have benefited from a little sex magic too? Sneaking peeks at his contented face, I wanted to congratulate him and talk about our mutual happiness. I wanted to trust him and tell him all about Derrick.

I knew Thatch was a good person deep down. He was like Severus Snape from the Harry Potter series, the guy who pretended to be bad, but would turn out to be the hero in the end. Or perhaps I only wanted him to be a hero.

"There's a . . . curious matter I ought to mention." He tore his gaze away from the flower to look at me. "I was speaking with Miss Periwinkle earlier. . . ."

Panic jump-started my heart. She'd told him about me stealing his clothes. I was in such trouble. I stood. "Sorry, gotta go."

He grabbed the back of my sweater and tugged me onto the bench. He spoke slowly, enunciating each word with his British accent. "Why does Gertrude think you have a key to my room?"

"No idea."

"You don't have a key, do you?"

"No."

The sun sank behind the boxy structures of the school, casting us in gloomy shadows.

Thatch smelled the flower. "I confiscated your lockpick kit, and you don't have another. Correct?"

I nodded, waiting for the question to come. *What were you doing in my room?* He twirled the flower between his fingers. I slid away from him and rose. He didn't stop me this time as I walked away.

*That* was strange. He didn't act suspicious or question me further as he usually would have. I glanced over my shoulder at him. He did seem a little too happy. I ascended the steps.

"Ugh," a deep female voice said from the shadows of the doorway. Vega Bloodmire, my evil roommate, crossed her arms. "Where's the nearest rubbish bin? I'm going to vomit."

I glanced behind me. Thatch plucked the petals of the daisy, smiling.

"That is the most cliché thing in the world," she said. "I can't believe I ever dated that man."

Eew. Now *I* wanted to barf.

I quickly piled my plate with food and snuck away to the spiderweb hallway that led to the section of the school in ruins, tripping over a bit of rubble along the way to Derrick's room. A roll fell onto the floor. His room was locked, and I knocked.

He peeked out. "It's about time! Where were you? You said you'd be back." He opened the door wider and let me in.

"Ugh. Thatch's new girlfriend erased the report cards I filled out and made my life miserable today."

"Thatch doesn't have a girlfriend. Wait! Do you mean Vega Bloodmire?" He wore the white T-shirt I'd brought him earlier. The fabric hugged his muscular chest. He hadn't dressed in the rest of the clothes, though, just a pair of boxer shorts he'd found under his bed. I hoped they were clean.

We ate dinner, a bland curry that Derrick improved by adding the magic ingredient: salt. He lit candles around the room to brighten the gloom. The romantic lighting cast the rugged angles of his face into sharp sections of golden light. He was even more handsome than I remembered from high school. And just as quirky with his sky-blue hair.

As I told him everything that had gone wrong that day, he fell back onto the bed laughing. "Miss Periwinkle and Thatch. That is hilarious! Was he really plucking daisy petals? She's so old!"

"Not anymore. I fixed the glamour spell that made her look that way. That's how I got to be trapped in her office the other day when you came and blew the door down." I set my empty plate aside before any of the curry sauce got on his bed.

"And the first thing he does to *help* her is hook up with her?" Derrick laughed harder. "How could she think you're going to steal Thatch from her?"

"Shh!" I said, covering his mouth to muffle his unguarded roar. "Someone might hear you."

"No one comes back to this wing." He mussed my hair, pink locks flopping into my eyes.

I smoothed my hair into place again. "My students meet in that room you painted with the murals."

"Yeah, but they think I'm the school ghost and it's haunted back here."

He walked across the room to the dresser he'd painted in a kaleidoscope of patterns, setting our tray on top. His boxer shorts hugged his muscular backside.

"How come you aren't wearing the clothes I brought you?" I asked. Not that I minded his choice of attire, but he had asked for clothes. "After all that work to steal clothes that would fit, the least you could do is wear them."

He opened a drawer and withdrew a handkerchief. "Sorry to break the news to you, but I'm too fat for Thatch's clothes."

I eyed the shirt stretched tight across his muscular chest. "You aren't fat."

"I know."

At least if the clothes didn't fit him, I could return them to Thatch's wardrobe, preferably without him or Miss Periwinkle noticing.

He plopped down next to me and dabbed at my cheek with his handkerchief.

"Did I get food on my face?"

"Yep." He leaned in close to kiss my cheek. Or I thought he was going to kiss me. Instead, he poked his tongue out and licked me. "Right here too."

"Gross!" I scrubbed my cheek with the cloth. "Why did I decide I liked you?"

"You don't *like* me, you *love* me." He winked. "You want me to be your *boyfriend*." He scooped me up and kissed my cheek for real this time. His lips trailed across my jaw and down my neck, nibbling and tickling with his teeth. "I think you got food down here too."

"I doubt it." I giggled.

He buried his face in my cleavage. "You definitely dropped something down here."

His hands were warm on my back, one of his thumbs dipped beneath the edge of my blouse, stroking a sliver of skin. Arousal blossomed inside me. I wanted to lose myself in the pleasure of his touch like I had before. My affinity fluttered to life inside me. Now wasn't the time for magic. I visualized it decreasing and staying contained.

Focusing on my affinity squashed my rampant hormones. My mind sharpened and remembered what was important. "Did Khaba ever find you today and talk to you about doing memory magic?"

"No."

I kissed along his jaw. "We should find him and get him to help you remember so we can figure out if Thatch still works for the Raven Queen."

"Ugh, why do you have to bring him up? Can't we just have a romantic evening and not think of the dungeon master?" He squeezed me closer.

I drew away enough to stare into his sky-blue eyes. "How can I think about being romantic when Thatch might find out about you being visible at any moment and do something nefarious?"

He planted a peck on my lips. "I'm sure he's too busy with Miss Periwinkle to be interested in me right now."

"Let's go see Khaba. He's expecting you." I slid off his lap and stood.

He tugged me closer again. "Mr. Khaba isn't going anywhere. He can wait."

I started to protest. He kissed me again. At first his lips were soft and hesitant, but as they pressed against mine, he kissed me more deeply, more passionately. The taste of his lips, salty and sweet, and everything I wanted, drowned out all other ideas in my head. He held me close, the familiarity and tangibility of his body too alluring to ignore. I wrapped my arms around him and threaded my fingers through his hair. His erection pressed hard and insistent against my leg. I wanted to be wrapped in the warmth of his embrace. Every part of me not in contact with him felt naked and cold.

He broke away, his breath tickling my hair against my cheek. "We can go see Mr. Khaba if you want."

"Never mind." I kissed him again.

"I might as well get rid of some of these clothes. They're too small anyways." He pulled his shirt off. I smoothed my hand over the contours of his muscled chest. As a teenager, I had never imagined he would look like an underwear model underneath his clothes.

Desire spiked inside me. My affinity mirrored the rise in my arousal. I calmed it again. Now wasn't the time for magic.

He lay back on the bed, pulling me down with him. We fumbled with my clothes. I didn't feel any less bumbling than I had the night before. We laughed as my arm got caught in my sleeve and one of the hooks from my bra snagged my ponytail.

Derrick chuckled as he unhooked it. "Life never has a dull moment with you around."

My words came out mumbled against his mouth. "I think you mean there's no end to the goofy things I end up doing to myself."

"Yep."

We both laughed again. I couldn't believe how lucky I was. Finally, I had Derrick, just as I'd always wanted.

His lips trailed down my body, stopping to pluck at my breasts and nibble at my belly. He kissed me between my legs, and I arched up to meet him. He stroked me until I cried in pleasure.

"I want you," I said.

I was slippery and ready for him. Or I thought I was. His finger dipped inside me. That penetration was where the pleasant sensation ended. My muscles ached where he dragged against me. I felt ragged and raw inside.

I told myself it was a tolerable level of torment considering the reward that would be coming. He shifted so that he faced me. His smile was so sweet and reassuring, it made all apprehensions melt away.

The moment his erection slipped between my legs and pressed against me, pain jolted through me. The red magic in my core transformed to lightning and sharp spasms stabbed in my belly. The energy shot through me, fighting to be released from my body and into the origin of my pain. It took all my will to contain that magic and make sure I didn't shoot lightning out of my vagina and into him.

"No! Stop!" I said, squirming back.

"What is it? What's wrong?" His eyes brimmed with concern.

He withdrew so quickly, I feared I had shocked him.

"Did I burn you?" I asked.

"Burn me? No, why would you think that?" He repositioned himself beside me.

"I—my magic—it hurt when you touched me. I almost lost control of my affinity and shot lightning at you. I'm sorry."

The magic tumbled around inside me, slowly subsiding as I calmed. I shivered, and Derrick covered me with the blankets. His arm was warm and secure around me.

He smoothed hairs from my face and kissed my forehead. "Are you all right now?"

"Maybe. The last time that happened . . ." I swallowed. "It was with Julian. I was trying to protect myself, and I killed him. I gave myself electrical burns."

"Shocking."

I didn't laugh. I could see why Derrick and Khaba got along.

He touched the tip of my nose with his finger. "Some men complain they can't find a woman hot enough for them. I have one that's so hot, I don't know what to do with her."

I rolled my eyes.

"Do you think it's because of last night?" he asked. "You still hurt too much from losing your virginity? Maybe your affinity is protecting your body right now?"

I shrugged. "I don't know. It's plausible."

He hugged me to his chest and cuddled close against me. "That means I need to be careful and only give you good feelings so you'll shoot out rainbows instead of lightning."

"Easier said than done."

He laughed. "Challenge accepted."

"Derrick," I groaned. "Does everything have to be a joke to you?"

"Not everything. You aren't a joke to me." He dipped his head down, brushing his lips against the corner of my mouth.

He teased me with an almost-kiss. I turned to meet his mouth, but he pulled back just enough that my lips missed his. His smile was mischievous. He kissed me, softly and tenderly. His lips grazed across my cheek and down my neck, dizzying me with desire.

"How do you do that?" I asked.

"Magic." He grinned. "Can we just lay here naked for a while?" He kissed me again.

"Okay."

He pressed his mouth to mine. "Naked and making out?" He cupped my breast.

My answer came out mumbled against his lips. "Okay."

"And you'll let me touch you if I'm careful?" His hand left my breast and stroked between my legs.

I moaned by way of response. I was slippery and wet where he caressed me. My affinity burned red-hot inside me, but it didn't threaten to jolt out of my body like before. I visualized it subsiding.

He kissed me deeply, and my breath caught in my throat. I melted into hungry abandon, clutching at him and claiming his lips all for my own. He was mine. This moment was mine. I wouldn't allow my affinity to ruin it. I sank deeper in the swell of pleasure as he continued to touch me.

Delicious waves rose up inside me and crested. I cried out in ecstasy. All the while, I kept my affinity in check. It roiled like serpents and pressed against my diaphragm, the magic unspent and wanting to break free. This might have been the first time in my life that it hadn't exploded out of me.

He stared into my eyes. "Was that better?"

"Yes."

"Good." He kissed my nose. "I love you."

"I love you."

"You're probably just saying that because I gave you an orgasm." He winked.

"Probably." I laughed, and he did too.

We lay in each other's arms, huddled under the blankets and basking in the paradise of each other's warmth for several minutes. As the oxytocin subsided, my worries returned.

"We really should go see Khaba now," I said.

"I would do anything for you," Derrick sat up and reached for the T-shirt he'd earlier dropped on the floor. "Even squeeze myself into Professor Jerkface's clothes for propriety—for you."

I could only hope Khaba would help us discover the truth about what had happened to Derrick.

# CHAPTER NINE
## The Usual Suspects

Khaba wasn't in his office, which wasn't really a surprise considering he usually patrolled the school, alert for students up to mischief. Derrick and I snuck to the corridor where the knight-and-dragon tapestry hid the hall of mirrors. No one was around. We ducked under the tapestry.

From up ahead came a light and whispers.

"Uh-oh," I said.

I recognized the feminine laugh of one of those students. Maybe I should have at least waited until after the students' curfew to go out.

"Define 'uh-oh,'" Derrick whispered.

We rounded the corner. A group of students sat on the ground in the middle of the hallway. The bluish glow of cell phone screens lit six faces and the dank stones around them. They sat around eating potato chips and candy. Beyoncé blared out from one of the phones. It looked like a party.

Among the group were Hailey Achilles and Maddy Jennings, two of my students. Hailey was athletic, with pointed elf ears poking from her long dark hair. Even when her Elementia magic was at rest, a faint orange light glowed in her eyes. Maddy was a beautiful blonde siren. The girls' smiles slid off their faces as they saw me.

Why did I have to be a teacher? Couldn't I just have a covert mission with my boyfriend without running into students? Sheesh.

"Shit! Teachers!" one of the boys said. Two young men ran the opposite direction.

"Freeze," I said.

Naturally, they kept running. I remembered how well chasing students had gone the last time I'd tried to apprehend them in one of the school's secret hallways. Another boy held up his wand. A red-headed boy that might have been Ben O'Sullivan hid his phone. It was hard to see now that they'd put away their cell phones and the only light came from wands, but the squashed goblin features of one of the boys looked like Balthasar Llewelyn.

When trouble was at hand, Hailey, Ben, and Balthasar always seemed to be near.

Balthasar muttered under his breath, his wand glowing brighter.

"Don't!" Hailey said, tackling Balthasar to the ground. "I don't want to get suspended from another game!"

"Get off me!" He raised his fist and punched her in the shoulder.

Maddy remained seated, watching them with wide eyes.

"No fighting," I said.

Hailey raised her wand. It glowed with hot red sparks.

"No!" I said.

Before I could do anything, wind whistled down the passage, pushing so hard my feet skidded against the floor. I fought against the current. Students fell into each other. The pushing of the wind shifted to a sucking sensation. The wands whipped out of their hands and scattered to the floor. The cell phones flew into the air and clattered onto the stones next to me. Balthasar lay flat on his face. The students who had run off yelled from up ahead. They tumbled back, somersaulting through the air as if carried on the breeze. They collided into Balthasar. Another phone tumbled forth and fell at my feet.

"Whoa! She can do magic," someone said. It sounded like Ben.

"That wasn't Miss Lawrence's magic," someone else said. He was right. It was Derrick's. I glanced behind me. I couldn't see him in the shadows.

Balthasar crawled forward, stretching his fingers out for his phone.

I kicked it behind me. "Why are electronics not permitted on campus?"

No one answered. Someone's labored breathing came from behind me. Presumably Derrick.

"Why are students not allowed to use cell phones?" I asked in my sternest teacher tone.

Maddy hung her head in shame. "It depletes our powers and makes us too weak to learn."

"We need to be strong to protect ourselves from Fae," Hailey said.

"And why does the principal expect students to stay away from the secret passages in the school?"

"Because he doesn't want us to get hurt," one of the boys said. "Plus, he doesn't want us to steal the answer keys to the spring exams . . . again."

"I will be confiscating your phones and wands and turning them in to Mr. Khaba," I said.

"Ugh! No fucking way!" Balthasar said.

I was about to correct his language, but it turned out I didn't need to.

Hailey kicked him. "Shut up, before you get us in more trouble."

"I want all of you to go to your rooms." Everyone started forward. I put up a hand. "Except you two, Maddy and Hailey. Stay for a moment."

Hailey and Maddy exchanged glum looks. The young men glanced over their shoulders at Maddy with longing as they departed. Possibly this was because Maddy was a tall blonde, looking more mature and voluptuous than any freshman needed to look, thanks to her siren ancestry. The boys' feet crunched over empty wrappers and potato chips as they departed.

I looked to Hailey. "I am very disappointed in you. I thought you were going to follow school rules and try harder not to get in trouble."

"We weren't the ones using the phones," Hailey said. "And we weren't going to go any farther into the secret passages."

"What were you doing down here?" I leaned against the wall.

"We just wanted to celebrate." Hailey kicked at a plastic wrapper on the floor. "Balthasar broke into the counseling office and took pictures of our report cards. I passed first semester with Ds in Morty Studies, Latin, and Beginning Alchemy and a C in your class. Ben and Balthasar both got D minuses in alchemy because they've been studying."

I patted her on the shoulder. "There's nothing wrong with being proud of your achievements. You just need to do it somewhere more appropriate. And without electronics." Preferably after report cards came out. Though I couldn't completely blame them for that; they'd been waiting an entire month for their grades.

"What are *you* doing down here?" Maddy asked.

"Catching delinquent students." I wagged a finger at Maddy. "You are supposed to be staying away from boys. You haven't learned how to control your siren magic."

She stared out into the darkness past me. "It's okay. Miss Periwinkle helped me tone it down with glamour. Today when I was in the library with her, and she was training me to be her assistant, hardly any boys talked to me or drooled all over themselves as I checked out their books."

I doubted that. Then again, now that I wasn't Maddy's mentor, I wouldn't be drawing out her powers. Gertrude Periwinkle might be able to teach her how to channel her powers.

"In any case, I would feel better if I knew you were safe in the girls' dorm," I said.

"We're really sorry. It won't happen again," Hailey said, edging closer to the direction her friends had gone. "Can we go now?"

I pointed to the litter. "After you clean up your mess."

They groaned in unison. Derrick snickered somewhere in the darkness behind me.

"Can I have my wand back so I can see at least?" Hailey asked.

I kicked a stick of wood at my feet toward her. She snatched up a different wand and used a flashlight spell. The two girls crouched and picked up the garbage.

"I think Study Club really helped," Hailey said as she pushed potato chips into a pile. "I might even pass some classes this semester too." She smiled, excitement in her voice. Most students would rather be passing *all* classes. Considering Hailey's record, this was still an improvement.

"Me too," Maddy said. "Except for Miss Bloodmire's class. Wards are difficult."

"They are," I agreed. I pocketed two phones and three wands.

"This is the first time I've ever passed more than the coach's classes." Hailey jumped up and down in excitement.

I smiled along with her. Maddy stared into the shadows past me. I turned, catching a black silhouette shifting in the darkness.

Male pheromones never escaped Maddy's notice.

"Who's that?" she asked.

"No one," I said quickly. "Who was what?"

"Who?" Hailey looked around.

"I see." Maddy smiled. "Miss Lawrence was down here because she has a secret *boyfriend*."

"No."

She walked confidently into the gloom. She didn't need a wand. Her skin glowed with pearlescence, and she reminded me of moonlight as she stepped into the shadows. She turned back to me, hands placed on her hips. "You had someone with you when you first found us. He had blue hair, and he wasn't a student."

Curse Derrick and his blue hair! The last thing I needed was for Maddy and Hailey to tell Thatch they'd seen me hanging out with a tall man with blue hair. We were going to have to get him a hat.

I lowered my voice to a whisper. "I'll buy you each a candy bar if you promise not to tell anyone you saw him."

Hailey rolled her eyes. "It's going to take more than that to buy my silence. I know teachers aren't supposed to bring boyfriends to their rooms."

"I'm not in my room." A smile stretched tight across my lips.

"No. You're just alone with him in a secret passage."

Maddy nudged Hailey. "Shush." She looked to me. "We aren't going to tell on you, Miss Lawrence. You don't need to buy us candy." She whispered to Hailey. "Miss Lawrence let us stay with her at Christmas. Do you really think she's going to do that again if you blackmail her with candy?"

"I wasn't blackmailing. She offered!" Hailey turned to me. "Just so you know, I wasn't going to narc on you." Hailey shoved her wand up the sleeve of her sweater. It looked like the black cardigan my mom had bought her at Christmas. "I'm keeping my wand."

The two girls left with armfuls of garbage. I took out one of the cell phones and used the flashlight feature. They'd missed a box of Red Hots. I didn't even know how they got Morty junk food in this realm. There had to be a black market for this stuff.

I dropped the scattered candies into the box and straightened. I turned and collided with Derrick. He caught me and held me against his chest. I leaned my head against him, listening to the steady rhythm of his heartbeat.

"Tell the truth." Derrick whispered into my ear. "You're going to keep those phones, aren't you?"

"Are you going to tell Khaba if I keep one of them?" Whichever one had better music, a flashlight app, and other desirable features.

"It depends. Do you intend to bribe me with candy like you do with your students?" He squeezed me tighter.

"No. I have other bribery in mind for you."

He tickled my ribs. "I like the sound of that."

I squirmed out of his arms before I burst out laughing and drew anyone's attention from outside the hallway.

Derrick laced his fingers through mine. He walked alongside me, his eyes growing thoughtful. "Maddy Jennings. She's the one you have to watch out for."

"Why do you say that?"

"With Hailey, you know where she stands and what she wants. She's bribable. Sirens aren't as easy to figure out. They want attention, and they don't want attention. They want a man and at the same time, they resent him and want to kill him."

"That's a stereotype. Maddy isn't like that." Neither was Miss Periwinkle. She'd renounced her siren ways to derive her magic from the stars and celestial bodies like Celestors.

We whispered as we traversed the secret passage to the suit of armor, around the corner and under the next tapestry. In the hallway of mirrors we saw that Khaba wasn't in any of the rooms. Thatch's mirror was covered with a blanket again. I tried not to think about what was going on beyond that curtain.

Josie was sprawled across her bed in her purple Eeyore pajamas, reading a book. She wore her long hair in two ponytails, looking far younger than someone in her twenties.

I stuck my head through the surface of the mirror. "Hey, Jo! Can we come in?"

She shrieked and dropped the book she was reading.

"Sorry! Didn't mean to scare you." A disembodied head probably looked freaky coming out of a mirror.

The time I'd walked through her mirror to get her help with Julian, she'd been asleep and hadn't seen me exit the mirror. Afterward she'd come with me to the hallway of mirrors, but she hadn't seen herself emerge from the mirror.

"Clarissa?" Josie asked. She shoved the book under her covers and approached the mirror on the wall. "What's going on?"

I pushed against the taffy-like surface of the mirror. The glass was cold and slithered against my skin as I forced my way through. It resisted me at first, then sucked at me like it wanted to pull me in.

"I wanted to talk to you," I said.

Josie had a desk and wardrobe like my room, but that was where the resemblance ended. Rather than a homicidal Downton Abby vibe, it was cozy and cheerful with a plump easy chair in the corner made of bright yellow fabric. Two chairs were pushed in at table decorated with a lace cloth. The walls were adorned with weavings, and doilies covered every surface that could be covered. Her bed was bigger than mine and covered in a multicolored quilt.

I had been in her room a couple times before, but I had never seen the bags filled with balls of yarn or the knitting needles out until now.

Derrick came through next. As his head and shoulder emerged, he looked like he was made of silvery glass. The shape of his face and arms reflected the colors of the room, shifting as he moved in a dizzying kaleidoscope until he parted from the surface and looked like himself again.

He shivered and shook himself. "That felt like icicles melting under my skin."

Josie looked him up and down. "Wow. You're Clarissa's boyfriend? Invismo?"

"You can call me Derrick." He smiled at me shyly and blushed. "But, yeah. I'm the long-lost boyfriend."

Josie shook his hand and introduced herself. He already knew who she was—he knew who everyone at the school was—but he didn't interrupt. Graciously he smiled and nodded.

Josie invited us to sit down.

Derrick leaned against the bedpost. "Thanks. I'll stand." He tugged at the slacks self-consciously. He hadn't been lying when he'd said they were too small for him. The way they hugged his butt was adorable. He hadn't buttoned the shirt all the way up since it was so tight across his shoulder blades.

I sat down next to Josie on the bed. "Do you know where Khaba is? We need him to help Derrick remember his past."

"Oh boy, I've got the perfect spell for finding him. I've been waiting for an excuse to use it!" She dug through a ball of yarn next to the bed, finding a bundle of herbs in the bottom. She approached the mirror on the wall and threw a pinch into the air, then waved her wand at the glass. A ray of green light, followed by the aroma of mint and lavender, wafted from her wand.

She closed her eyes and said, "Mirror, mirror on the wall, show me the hottest hottie of them all."

Our reflections clouded over. Khaba appeared in the mirror. He wore the same pink leopard-print shirt as earlier. The image was clearer than a video call on Skype.

"Cool," I said. This was like a fairy tale.

Behind him was a cobblestone interior. From the fiddling and dancing going on in the background, it looked like he was in Lachlan Falls at the pub. He sat at a table with a model-worthy red-haired man in a kilt.

Khaba leaned forward, touching the man's arm flirtatiously. "Does anyone care about who wears the pants in a relationship anymore?" His eyes raked over the other man's tartan kilt.

Josie snorted out a laugh. "Isn't he hilarious?"

I gave Josie a sidelong glance. She would say that, the girl with no gaydar. We were so lucky this is where we had caught Khaba, not somewhere more private.

I shifted on the bed. Her hardback book poked me in the thigh.

Khaba's date downed his ale. Both of them stood.

"Um, Josie, how do we get ahold of him?" I asked. I didn't want a peepshow of what came next.

She strode forward and banged on the mirror. "Hey! Khaba! Can you hear me?"

I folded my legs underneath me, accidentally kicking her book out from under the covers. The title sounded like something Japanese: *The Fine Art of Shibari and Kinbaku.* I didn't know what that meant. It wasn't a term that had ever come up in the limited amount of anime I had watched. Knowing Josie, it probably had something to do with weaving or textiles. I shoved the book back under her blankets.

Khaba blinked. His eyes shifted across the mirror. "Josie? I told you not to use this spell unless it's an emergency." The man in the kilt gave him a puzzled look.

"It is an emergency," Josie tugged me closer to the mirror. "Sort of. Clarissa found you-know-who, and they want you to come here to do you-know-what."

"That isn't an emergency." Khaba glanced at his date. "I have a true emergency right now off campus, and it involves me and my kilty pleasures."

"First of all, I know you're not shopping for kilts. I can see you at the Devil's Pint." Josie clucked her tongue.

I cringed at her cluelessness. Derrick snickered. I shushed him. I didn't want to hurt Josie's feelings.

"Second of all, alcohol is not an emergency," Josie said. "We need you here for a school-related matter."

"The nature of my emergency has nothing to do with alcohol and everything to do with a ride on a kilt-a-whirl." He eyed the man who was impatiently waiting near him.

Josie crossed her arms. "You have a duty to serve this school as our dean."

"Slave to the lamp or slave to the school, it makes no difference. I still don't have a social life," Khaba said with a sigh. "I'll be back at Womby's . . . soon."

The mirror fogged up before clearing and returning to normal.

"How about some tea?" Josie asked.

Half an hour later, a cloud of smoke materialized in the corner of her room. Khaba's silhouette appeared through the haze.

"It's what I've always wished for! Khaba in my room!" Josie jumped up from the table and ran to the bed, seductively striking a pose.

Khaba grew more solid through the cloud, though the smoke only increased in the room. He no longer wore hot pink. His pants were white, but just as snug. I'd never seen him in a magenta sweater vest with nothing underneath, but he managed to make it work. He strode toward Derrick. He didn't appear to notice Josie trying to catch his eye from where she lay across her bed.

"Invismo! Nice to *see* you!" He looked Derrick up and down. "My, aren't you . . . yummy?"

"Heh, thanks. That's what the ladies tell me." Derrick shook Khaba's hand. "Please, call me Derrick. There's not much use in a cool nickname now that I'm not invisible."

Khaba slapped Derrick on the back. "So, let's get down to business. I understand you have a favor to ask me." He waggled his eyebrows. "You do realize anything you want me to perform with djinn magic requires you rub my lamp first."

"Right," Derrick said. "Hasn't your lamp been rubbed enough for the evening?"

Khaba grinned. The smoke grew denser, obscuring Josie's furnishings and the textiles on the walls. Warm swirls tickled around my ankles. Josie coughed and waved the smoke away from her face.

I could barely see myself in the haze, let alone anyone else.

"Um," I said, waving a hand at the smoke with growing concern. "Is something on fire?"

"No, it's my magic," Khaba said. "Men aren't allowed in the women's dormitories. I thought it best to grant Derrick's first wish in the privacy of my office."

The smoke slowly dissipated. Derrick no longer leaned against a bedpost. He lounged against a file cabinet. He stepped back in surprise. I sat in a chair before Khaba's desk.

Josie lay sprawled across his desk. "Ow," she said, wiggling away from a tray of papers and sliding off.

Khaba opened a drawer in the file cabinet. "All electronics go in this drawer." He arched an eyebrow at me.

How did he know? It was so unfair!

"Those aren't mine." At least, they weren't anymore. I emptied my pockets into the shadowy abyss. The phones didn't make any noise as they dropped down. "We confiscated those from students earlier." I peered into the void, trying to see the bottom.

"Careful." Khaba placed a hand on my shoulder. "A student once fell in that drawer trying to retrieve his iPod. He never came out."

I straightened.

He nodded to my other sweater pocket. "Tell me those are wands in your pocket. Because if not, there are some things I don't know about you—including how happy you are to see me."

He opened another drawer. This one didn't look like a bottomless pit. There were wands, half-eaten bags of candy, a knife, a dildo, one box of cigarettes, and two bongs. I suspected those were all the nonelectronic items he'd confiscated from students.

I set two of the wands inside. I kept the third one. "Do you want to know who the students were?"

He glanced in. "No need to. I know those wands: Ben O'Sullivan and—hmm, that's odd. Sherice Stevens?"

"Sherice wasn't with them," Derrick said. "Dwayne Evans and Balthasar Llewellyn were. One of them probably stole it from her."

Khaba appraised Derrick with respect in his eyes. "I see you aren't a complete waste, even without your invisibility."

I had inwardly grumbled about finding students, but now I wondered if it had been a blessing in disguise. If Khaba saw Derrick as valuable, he might not need to fire him. "That's right. Derrick used his magic to collect the wands and cell phones. We caught students in one of the secret passages. He makes a great security guard."

Khaba grimaced.

I went on. "Think of how great he'd be with an invisibility cloak, or hoodie or whatever it is my students were wearing last semester when we thought they were trying to steal answer keys. He could still be a valuable asset to the school. You should have seen him tonight . . . busting students." I faltered, seeing the way Khaba was giving me that look. His dean-of-discipline look.

"Let's just drop this topic before I ask what *you* were doing in a secret passage, Miss Lawrence," Khaba said.

Oh. Me and my big mouth.

"It's all right. I was keeping her out of trouble." Derrick playfully nudged me with his shoulder. "Like I always do."

"Enough chit-chat." Khaba removed his vest and turned so that we could see where the tattooed lamp on his flesh had migrated. He sat in his cushy chair behind his desk. "The sooner you rub my lamp, the sooner I can grant your wish."

What a relief the lamp was between his shoulders rather than somewhere risqué.

Derrick massaged Khaba's shoulders without complaint. Khaba raised his eyebrows at me. "You get back here too. You and Inv—Derrick have the same wish."

"I can help," Josie said.

"I only have enough time for *this* wish. Your wishes would take far too long."

She giggled. "My wishes would take all night."

"My point exactly." He smirked. "Plus, it helps if you know your wish and keep it in mind as you rub the lamp. I doubt you would be able to think of anything other than my hot body."

"I could! Come on, I want to help. You never let me rub your lamp."

Khaba kicked his feet up on the desk. "You can rub my feet if you want."

I stood next to Derrick, massaging Khaba's right shoulder. I wondered how this magic was any different than my affinity. The magic of the Lost Red Court worked through the human body, usually with touch, but not always through sexuality like a siren's or a green man's. Thatch had said Red affinities used electrical impulses, which is why we weren't weakened by electronics. If I was touching someone, I could increase another Witchkin's magic, like I had with Miss Periwinkle and Maddy. Like I had with Derrick in the past. Theoretically that meant I should be able to increase Khaba's abilities to detect whether Derrick's memories had been tampered with and what might be the truth.

Physical contact alone wouldn't activate my powers. The touch had to be pleasant for me. I didn't know if I could use my magic without drawing attention to myself. I didn't want to endanger myself like I had with Julian by revealing what I was to a Fae—even if Khaba was my friend.

I glanced at Derrick. He looked up from kneading Khaba's muscles. "Should we switch sides? You know, to make things even?"

"Good idea," I said.

As he scooted around me I took that opportunity to lean against him. I pressed my lower back against his crotch. He arched himself away from me. His tight pants became a whole lot tighter. He shook his head at me, looking like he was trying hard not to laugh.

Two seconds of grinding was not enough to make magic happen.

As we massaged Khaba, I leaned closer to Derrick. I crossed my arm over his. He bumped me with his hip.

"Are you concentrating on your wish?" Khaba asked.

"Yes," Derrick said.

I refocused my attention on wanting him to help Derrick remember.

Khaba nudged Josie with one of his bare feet.

She blinked her eyes open. "Yes," she said.

"Think about their wish. Not yours."

I stared into Derrick's eyes. He smiled. A flutter of energy uncoiled inside me. Red light twitched in my core. Khaba took in a sharp breath.

I shifted my hip so that it touched Derrick and repositioned my foot so that his feet sandwiched it. The contact of his body against mine sent little thrills through me. A mischievous smile curled his lips upward. He dipped his head lower, his mouth inching toward mine.

I glanced at Josie. Her eyes were closed.

I placed my hand over Derrick's. His lips brushed against mine. Pleasure swelled in my chest, flashing through my nerves and tingling out of my hands.

"Son of a succubus!" Khaba bucked in his chair like an electric jolt had gone through him. He kicked Josie, knocking her out of her seat. His chair pushed back with enough force to roll over my feet.

He fell onto the floor ungracefully. "What did you just do?"

I stumbled away from Derrick, into the wall. Derrick tripped into the filing cabinet. Khaba's cheeks were flushed, and he was breathless when he lifted himself from the floor. Josie replaced her glasses on her face.

"Um, sorry," I said. "Did I do something . . . bad?" I hoped I hadn't drained him. Or burned him. He was my friend. I was afraid I had done something horrible to him.

Khaba fanned himself. "I haven't felt magic like that since . . . huh." He looked me up and down. "Your magic is like your mother's."

Alouette Loraline had been powerful. Did that mean I was powerful? As much as I wanted to be a respected witch, every time I did something that reminded people of my biological mother, I suspected it drove me closer to the dark side.

I bit my lip. "I'm sorry. Did I hurt you?"

He smirked. "Hardly."

"Where's the lamp now?" Josie asked.

Khaba glanced over his shoulder and waggled his eyebrows at us. "Looks like it migrated south for the rest of the evening. No worries. I've been rubbed enough for the day to satisfy the requirements of my magic."

Khaba gestured for Derrick to take a seat. "Let's get this party started."

Derrick sat down, the back of his pants splitting with a loud tear. So much for returning those pants to Thatch without him noticing.

"How about for your first wish I fetch you a pair of pants?" Khaba asked. "That doesn't even require any magic."

Khaba's memory magic was in between the dream magic I'd discovered I could do and Thatch's torture chair to draw out fears. After Derrick had stated his wish out loud, he sat in a chair across from Khaba, eyes closed, hands on the armrests. The hot-pink pants Khaba had brought him looked like capris on Derrick's long legs, but at least he could sit comfortably enough to meditate.

"Sink into the memory," Khaba said. "Imagine yourself there again."

Derrick's brow crinkled. Khaba leaned toward the crystal ball on his desk. It flashed yellow and white.

Josie and I had somehow managed to squeeze both our butts onto the other chair in Khaba's office. We both were petite, but not small enough for this to be comfortable. I leaned forward to see, accidentally jostling Josie. Khaba lifted the ball and squinted. He set it down again.

The ball on Khaba's desk started off the size of an apple, but as Khaba waved his hand over it, the orb grew to the size of a beach ball. White light flashed within and it clouded over. The sphere expanded further. I leaned back now.

The image within was warped, but I could see Derrick chained to the walls of a dungeon. It didn't look that different from the school dungeon where Thatch chained students as part of their detentions.

I was so fixated on Derrick's image, I didn't realize the crystal ball had expanded again. The barrier of glass passed through me, containing all of us. I was inside the sphere and inside the memory. Derrick was no longer seated beside me. He was a participant in his memory.

Khaba walked around to where Josie and I sat off to the side. "We are here as observers. Don't touch anything. Don't say anything. As long as you remain still, you won't interfere with his memories."

We watched Derrick struggle against manacles holding him against the grimy stone. He was dirty and shirtless, cuts and burns etched into his skin.

His blue hair was shorter than it was now, closely cropped to his skull, reminding me of a military haircut.

Footsteps echoed down a set of stairs. Will-o'-the-wisps floated along the ceiling, bumping into each other and careening into walls.

Derrick yanked at the manacles, the metal jangling. His eyes went wide with terror. He pulled on the metal so hard it cut into his wrists and tore at his skin. Fear radiated from him like a perfume, settling onto my skin. My heart raced alongside his.

Something bad was coming. I wanted to tell Derrick it was okay. I wanted him to understand this was the past, and it wasn't real anymore.

The Raven Queen glided down the stairs and over the floor. Light caught on the sheen of black feathers that made up her dress and hair. Her black crown reminded me of an oil slick, a dark rainbow made of jagged points. Her eyes were all black like a bird's. She tilted her head at Derrick, studying him with disinterest.

Lurking in the shadows behind her stood Felix Thatch.

# CHAPTER TEN
## The Raven Queen's Servant

"Mr. Thatch! Help me, please!" Derrick's voice came out a rough rasp. He sounded thirsty.

"You know my prisoner?" the Raven Queen asked. Her voice was deep and sultry, the purr of a tiger before it strikes. A hint of a French accent laced her words.

"He was one of my students." Thatch glanced over at Derrick. "Briefly."

Thatch stood beside the Raven Queen, his gaze raking over trickles of water dripping down the walls and then Derrick with the same disinterest. His expression was like her own, cool and cunning. From his gleaming midnight hair to his pale complexion and lean build, he looked like he could be one of the Fae of the Raven Court. The thought sent icicles down my spine.

"It has come to my attention this Witchkin knows Clarissa Lawrence, daughter of Alouette Loraline. Perhaps I should remove his entrails and leave him somewhere for her to find with a little note that says, 'This is what you get for refusing my offer.'"

Thatch said nothing.

"Please, Mr. Thatch." Tears ran down Derrick's grimy cheeks. "Please don't let her kill me."

The Raven Queen lifted Derrick's chin to look into his eyes. "Kill you? I didn't say anything about killing you." She leaned her head back in a throaty chuckle. "Removing your entrails is painful, but it won't kill you. It's the blood loss that kills you. That takes hours. Or the infections. That could take days."

Derrick looked to Thatch in desperation.

"He isn't going to save you, *mon cher*." She raked a talon-tipped finger against his jaw. Droplets of crimson formed under his chin. "Look into my eyes."

Derrick turned away.

"Think of her. Remember a fond memory," she said with uncharacteristic tenderness.

"No. I won't let you do this to me."

"Think of what her skin feels like against yours. Remember how soft her hair was against your face. How she smelled."

Derrick squeezed his eyes closed and tried to twist away. She sandwiched his face between her palms, keeping his head still. Her lips parted, and she inhaled. As she did so, his breath was sucked out of him. In the gap between their faces, tiny particles glowed as they left him. He shook uncontrollably. He gasped and choked.

I'd seen this before. I knew what someone looked like when they were being drained. She stepped back, licking her lips in pleasure. Derrick sagged limply in the manacles. His eyes were dark and bruised.

She leaned in again.

"I beg your pardon," Thatch said, each word slowly enunciated. "Have you considered how leaving this one for dead will fail to serve your true agenda?"

The Raven Queen idly ran a finger down Derrick's chest. She drew a little *x* over his heart. "I don't know what you mean."

"Derrick Winslow is acquainted with Clarissa Lawrence. He gained her trust and would easily be able to do so again. Rather than use him as a message, you could instead use him as a messenger."

She drew away from Derrick. "You have my attention."

"Let him go. Allow him to go to her on his own."

I wanted to believe this was Thatch's way of plotting to protect Derrick, but if it was, why hadn't he told me about any of this? He'd kept Derrick a secret from me, hadn't revealed the nature of his curse, and told me the Raven Queen would use him to get to me. He'd never told me he had rescued Derrick. I watched in silence as Khaba had advised, a million questions in my mind as I did so.

"What good will it do me to release him?" the Raven Queen asked.

"If you plant the right seeds in his head, he will bring her to you. He will convince her of your true intentions to . . . help her." Thatch placed his hand on his heart as though he spoke with complete sincerity, though his tone held a nuance of mockery. "Rather than drive Miss Lawrence further away by showing what you intend to do with her friends and family, show her the wonders of your magic. Show her your mercy. Convince Derrick why she needs you. He, in turn, will convince her. Having her trust already, he will do a far better job of it than I will be able to do."

"Hmm," she said. She ran her hands over Derrick's shorn hair.

"You have given him the stick. Now give him the carrot." Thatch waved his hand at Derrick. "You are the Queen of Pain *and* Pleasure."

She gave Thatch a disapproving smile, as though he were a naughty child she couldn't help finding amusing. "You've grown far too soft at that school. I think you like this one."

"I'm impartial to all things, save my queen." Thatch bowed. "And what I may do to serve your agenda."

"I will give him pleasure. I shall gift him with so much indulgence and gratification it will hurt." She laughed. "But first, I want to see you use your magic. Entertain me. You know what I like."

Thatch bowed his head. "As you wish, my queen."

He withdrew his wand.

Anxiety rose in me. I didn't know if it was my own or Derrick's I was feeling. I didn't want Thatch to be a bad person. Surely he must have been pretending he would hurt Derrick so that he could help him escape.

He stepped forward, walking back and forth in front of Derrick, looking him up and down. A smile twitched his lips. Slowly he lifted his wand and raised it to Derrick's arm. He slashed it into his flesh like a knife, opening a wound deep enough that it exposed the muscle. Derrick cried out.

My stomach flip-flopped at the sight of it.

Derrick's eyes went wide. He tried to pull away, but the moment he straightened his legs, his knees went weak again. I didn't want Derrick to have to relive this horrible moment. I would have done anything to save him from this torment.

I reached out, wanting to reassure him, but I couldn't see my hand. I was invisible in his memory, a ghost of the future. I fumbled for his hand, giving it a squeeze to let him know I was there for him, even if neither of us could see me.

I felt the pain rushing up his arm. I gasped at the suddenness of sensation in my own arm. Lightning flared into my veins from where the wand jabbed me—him.

My brain was confused. I felt light-headed and foggy. Or was that the room that was foggy? I felt as though I was falling into a jumble of images and sensations. Feathers brushed against my skin, the caress unexpectedly pleasant. Lips nibbled my neck, but I didn't know whom they belonged to. Nor did I care. I sank deeper into contentment. Black magic glittered before my eyes, dazzling me, lulling me into a trance. In my ears a thousand pleasant songs played at once, overwhelming my senses. There were words in that song, a suggestion I could almost hear. They tasted like blood and promises.

I was no longer myself. I was Derrick, surrounded by another world of dark magic and temptation.

The Raven Queen's mouth tasted cold like winter. She was as sweet as honey and more bitter than black coffee, sour like lemons, and saltier than a lake of tears. Every sense came crashing down on me at once. Talon-tipped fingers raked across my flesh.

I wanted more.

The chaos of pleasure and pain melted away. There was nothing left. I was filled with an empty aching hunger that consumed me.

Thatch's arms lifted me—no—Derrick from the floor, heaving him into a standing position. "Get up, Derrick. I need you to help me."

My perspective wavered, first anchored inside Derrick and then shifting so that I observed the scene from the outside.

Derrick leaned against him. "Where are you taking me?" Derrick's words came out slurred.

"Somewhere safe. To the school."

"I'm not going to do what she asked," Derrick said. "I won't ever hurt Clarissa. I won't take her here."

"I know you won't."

Thatch walked slowly, allowing Derrick to limp along.

The taste of winter returned to my mouth. The song of tears washed over my skin. Colors flashed before my eyes, and I tasted music. Everything crashed together. The world didn't make sense. Pleasure built inside me, but laced in the thrill of revelry came dark waves of pain. The searing stab of electricity rushed through my veins again.

I screamed.

"It's okay, honey," Josie said. "Derrick is fine. It was just a memory."

I blinked my eyes open. I sat on her lap in the chair in front of Khaba's desk, my arms hugged around her. I was shaking and crying.

Khaba held the crystal ball in his hand, frowning at me. "That was unexpected."

Derrick blinked, and his brow was furrowed as he took in the sight of Khaba's pink office. He left his chair and crouched on the floor next to me. "Clarissa, are you all right?"

"What happened?" That was all I could manage. My throat was a dry desert.

I looked from one face to the next and wiped my eyes. They all looked so calm. I didn't know how anyone could be calm after that. Cold sweat made my shirt cling to my back, and I shivered.

Derrick lifted me to my feet and hugged me to his side. "What did you see?"

"Feathers and music made of tears and blood and promises." I tried to find words to make sense of it. "Someone was kissing me. I liked it and I didn't like it. I think I was you."

Derrick's brow furrowed. "I don't remember that."

Khaba rubbed his chin. "Clarissa saw more than I saw, apparently. More than you did." He returned the crystal ball to the holder on his desk. "You have more memories locked away in there. What we saw is incomplete and . . . patched together."

Derrick rubbed my back.

"Let's have you come back tomorrow for another stab at this." Khaba gave me a sidelong glance. "Without Miss Lawrence."

I pushed a handful of sweaty pink hair out of my face. "Why?"

"I don't want you absorbing my magic or Derrick's memories to try to make things easier on him."

"I wasn't—"

Khaba put up a hand. "Not on purpose, no. But memory magic is tricky, especially when you're close to someone. It isn't uncommon to take someone's pain because the witness struggles knowing they'll relive it. That was your fear, wasn't it?"

I shook my head. But I knew he was right. That had been my concern as the memory had started to go downhill.

"I can tell the memories aren't accurate, but it would be easier for me to decipher what is and what isn't real without you screaming." Khaba arched an eyebrow at me.

"Oh," I said.

Me and my big mouth. Literally.

"But we saw enough to know Derrick is safe, and Thatch is trying to help him?" I asked.

"No," they all said at once.

"You can't be serious, Clarissa," Josie said.

"Thatch tortured me." Derrick stared into my eyes, the vivid blue of his own so bright it reminded me of a cloudless sky. "Didn't you see that in the memory?"

"To prove to the Raven Queen he still serves her—which he doesn't. He took you here to the school to keep you safe. And you haven't tried to lure me to the Raven Queen." That had been Thatch's fear, the reason he had said he didn't want me to see Derrick, but I'd cured him. We weren't in danger of that anymore.

"You heard Mr. Khaba. That memory wasn't real." Derrick's brow crinkled up in concern and he shook his head. He took my hands in his. "When are you going to stop seeing the best in people—even when there's nothing there to see? This is just like Missy. You would never believe she was a wicked witch who intended to hurt you until it was too late and she tried to kill you. You're doing it again, this time with Thatch."

I wasn't biased. It was true I wanted to see good in Thatch, but that didn't mean he wasn't trying to help. I was nowhere closer to figuring out if Thatch's intentions with Derrick were malicious.

The yellow glow of sconces lit the dark hallway. Derrick held my hand as we walked with Josie away from Khaba's office. His feet and the top half of his head were invisible because Khaba had given him an invisibility hat and shoes. It was seriously creepy seeing the top half of his head gone, but at least it covered his blue hair.

"Maybe you should consider. . . ." Josie pointed her glowing wand at Derrick's hand holding mine.

"What?" I asked.

"Being a little less obvious. You aren't supposed to have a boyfriend. Your magic isn't supposed to be able to handle men, right? Think of how much trouble you'll be in if Jeb catches you." She lowered her voice to a whisper. "I'm surprised Khaba didn't say anything. Your chemistry is like a nuclear reactor. You're going to attract attention."

I waved her off. "You're being a worrywart."

"It's hard to resist you, after being apart all this time, but I don't want you to get in trouble." Derrick withdrew his hand from mine, his smile sheepish as he gazed into my eyes. "After Vega falls asleep, you can sneak out, and we'll hold hands as much as you want."

I intended to do more than hold hands with him.

The hall was empty now that the students had gone to bed, which was kind of a shame considering how I would have liked to confiscate some troublemaker's phone and keep it for myself as a weapon. We headed past the great hall and up a flight of stairs toward the dorms. Because of the randomness of architecture, we had to pass the men's dorms to get to the next set of stairs that led up to the tower were Josie's room was located.

I froze when I heard a woman's laugh coming from farther down the hallway of men's rooms. The woman's voice was high and sweet with the timber of a lullaby.

"That sounds like Miss Periwinkle," I said.

Whatever she was doing up here instead of her private quarters through the library, I did not want to find out.

Derrick grabbed my hand and tugged me backward. "That means Thatch will be with her."

All three of us ran in the opposite direction, back down the stairs to the main corridor that led around the great hall. As we did so, a putrid stench of rotting garbage and wild animal wafted toward us. We rounded a corner, nearly colliding into Pinky, the stinky Sasquatch.

"Oh, hi, guys!" Pinky said with eight feet of enthusiasm.

"Ugh," Josie said.

I fought the urge to cover my nose and mouth.

"It's nice to see you again, Jo," Pinky said, voice as high and nasally as ever. "I got lost trying to find the restroom. Miss Bloodmire told me the only functioning toilet is in the counseling office. That's going to be a drag if I ever wake up in the middle of the night and try to find it. . . ."

Josie shook her head. Derrick and I gave each other sidelong glances. I was sure Vega's picture was in the dictionary next to the word "bitch."

"What?" Pinky asked.

"Vega was playing a trick on you," I said.

Josie pointed down the hall. "There are restrooms on the teacher side of the dormitories and ones on the student side, in case the others are all full."

I wondered which one Pinky used, the male or female restroom. Maybe sasquatches didn't have genders, they were all "xe."

"Oh," Pinky laughed and slapped a knee in good humor. "Well, it wouldn't be a new job without a little hazing. Jo, do you remember Mr. Booker from Zeme's? Did he punk you on the first day too? He tried to sic a herd of unicorns on me. Fortunately, unicorns and sasquatches are like this." Pinky crossed xir fingers. Xe looked to Derrick as if realizing he was there for the first time. "Oh, hi, I don't believe we've met. I'm Pinky. I'll be teaching history."

I glanced over my shoulder. I didn't see anyone coming or hear Miss Periwinkle, but lingering outside the main corridor was risky considering how many people traversed this way to get to other wings.

Derrick reached out and shook Pinky's hand. "Some people know me as Invismo. I work in security." Derrick pulled more of the hat over his face, making himself look like the headless horseman.

Pinky chuckled.

"Maybe we should get going," I said. "It's almost time for teacher curfew."

"Are they really strict about that at this school?" Pinky asked.

"It isn't smart to wander the halls after dark. Too many accidents happen," Derrick said.

I couldn't tell if he was being serious or joking. Sure, a few accidents had happened, but I was pretty sure that had been Julian's work—and certain students. I had left my room after lights-out when I'd gone into Lachlan Falls to go dancing. Of course, Khaba had been chaperoning, and I had a feeling no monster out there would want to mess with his Fae magic.

"Right," Pinky said. "Can I follow you up to the dorms? It's going to take me a while to get used to the layout here."

Derrick gave my arm a squeeze. "I'll see you . . . later?" His brows lifted hopefully.

I nodded. After Vega went to bed. That was what we had talked about anyway.

Derrick skipped down the hallway. He glanced back over his shoulder and smiled at me.

Pinky looked from Derrick to me. "Are you two . . . um . . . Jeb told me dating among colleagues isn't allowed."

"That's right," Josie said quickly. "No dating. They're just friends."

Pinky looked to her, head tilting to the side. "That's too bad."

We walked in the direction of Josie's room. I wondered if Pinky's room was that way too.

A moment later Derrick came running back to us. "Thatch," he panted and kept running.

I looked around, my heart thump-thumping. There was no telling what he'd do if he saw Derrick not invisible. Then again, maybe he wouldn't care. Maybe he would laugh. He'd been in a good mood earlier.

Somehow I expected his reaction would be less than pleasant.

Pinky looked from me to Josie. "Mr. Thatch? Isn't he one of the teachers here?"

"Yes, once you meet him, you'll know why anyone would run from him," Josie said.

Derrick disappeared down the hallway and up the stairs to the men's dormitory. We followed at a slower pace.

I whispered to Pinky. "If you don't mind, could you not mention you saw Derrick tonight?"

"Derrick?" Pinky asked.

"She means Invismo," Josie explained.

Pinky took the stairs two at a time, pausing between each step for Josie and me. "Why?"

"Um. . . ." I said trying to think of something plausible.

"Uh. . . ." Josie said.

"He's supposed to be invisible. You aren't supposed to see him," I said. That was half the truth anyway.

"Got it." Pinky made a zipping motion across xir mouth, locking it with an imaginary key and throwing the key away. "No problem. I'm great at keeping secrets. Right, Jo? Just like at Zeme's."

"I wouldn't know. I don't have any secrets," Josie said quickly.

I elbowed her in the ribs. She ignored me. My best friend had a secret. That was interesting.

Derrick came running down the stairs. "Periwinkle and Bloodmire are coming. I need to hide."

He looked around frantically. Voices came from the hallway below. Male voices. My heart pounded frantically. We were about to get caught. What would Thatch do?

Thatch rounded the corner. There he stood.

# CHAPTER ELEVEN
## Sasquatch Ex-Machina

Thatch spoke with Pro Ro. Both men halted on the steps. Pro Ro grimaced, looking at me. I wasn't his favorite person considering the way I'd torn his turban off months earlier when I had succumbed to thinking my biological mother was under his turban. I had read too much Harry Potter for my own good.

Pro Ro—Professor Darshan Rohiniraman—wore a navy-blue turban and the kind of full beard that would make a lumberjack jealous.

Thatch's smile faded. Ice settled in the pit of my stomach. I turned to look at Derrick, but he was gone. Pinky shifted on the steps, looking like xe was about to stumble forward. Xe righted xirself, edging toward the wall. A section of the pink pants Khaba had loaned Derrick was visible to the right of Pinky's leg.

Derrick was hiding behind the furry mountain! I scooted closer to Pinky to hide the bright pants. My eyes watered at the proximity to sasquatch musk.

"My, my, what do we have here?" Thatch asked with a sinister gleam in his eyes. "Teachers out after curfew. You should be ashamed of yourselves, setting a bad example for the students."

I swallowed.

His nostrils flared, and he sniffed at the air. As he eyed Pinky, his lips twitched downward. Pro Ro covered his nose and mouth, his eyes watering. Thatch leaned in and said something to the other teacher, and Pro Ro immediately removed his hand from his face, his gaze raking over Pinky.

"What are you going to do?" Josie placed her hands on her hips. "Report us to Khaba? It's not like you're in bed yourself."

Pro Ro gave an uncomfortable laugh. "No one is going to report anyone. We're all teachers. At least, I think we're all teachers." He looked to

Pinky.

Pinky introduced xirself. Pro Ro followed suit. I tried to look casual as I stood there, helping hide Derrick. Sweat trickled down my back. It was difficult to focus on Pinky's friendly banter. Flashes of Derrick's memories kept playing before my eyes. I felt the caress of feathers and the lance of pain as Thatch stabbed his wand into Derrick's arm.

Thatch's eyes narrowed as he studied me. "Something is different about you, Miss Lawrence."

I shook my head.

Vega's deep voice drawled out from above. "If you ask me, she's gotten shorter." Vega stood at the top of the stairs, hands on her hips. She wore a black-sequined dress with fringe. From the sparkly headband and long string of pearls, it didn't look like she was headed for our dorm room to go to bed.

Gertrude Periwinkle stood at her side. Her attire was subtler, her dress long and collar higher. Her dress was just as Gothic, but an earlier era, perhaps Edwardian. Her lacy gloves reminded me of spiderwebs, and the flowers and skulls on her witch hat were simultaneously elegant and creepy. Her pale skin and fair hair glowed in the dim light, her siren beauty drawing all eyes.

The two ladies looked like they were going out on a school night.

Thatch touched a hand to his heart. "My, aren't you ladies a vision of loveliness."

Josie made a face like she was going to retch.

Pro Ro stared at Miss Periwinkle, his jaw dropping. "I don't believe we've been introduced."

"Hi, I'm Pinky," said the sasquatch with a wave. Pinky fidgeted in place, looking very much like xe wanted to walk up the stairs and greet her, but xe remained on the steps.

From xir breathlessness, I had a feeling Pinky was male. Then again, maybe *she* was a lesbian. I wasn't attracted to women, but I had a hard time tearing my gaze from Miss Periwinkle's beauty.

Gertrude Periwinkle glided down the steps, smiling shyly at Pro Ro and Pinky. Her coquettish affectation flickered to annoyance when she saw me on the other side of Pinky. Her gaze flickered to Thatch and back to me. He wasn't standing that close, but I supposed he was closer to me than anyone else. From the daggers in her eyes, it looked like she still thought I wanted to steal her boyfriend. Craptacular.

I started to shift away, and then remembered I couldn't move because of Derrick's hot-pink pants. Pro Ro raced up the steps to meet Miss Periwinkle, distracting Thatch and causing him to ascend after the other teacher.

"I'm Darshan Rohiniraman, but my students and most of the staff call me Pro Ro." He reached for her hand, but she didn't take it.

"I know," she said. "You teach divination and soothsaying."

"And yoga," Pinky said cheerfully.

Rumor had it Pro Ro didn't know anything about yoga, but that hadn't stopped Jeb from giving him the class this semester.

Thatch slid in between them, cutting Pro Ro out of view. "Are you going out?" His brow furrowed, his expression pensive.

"Yes." Miss Periwinkle's smile grew strained. That was interesting. She hadn't told him—her supposed boyfriend. I felt bad for my nemesis.

Vega descended the steps, her heels hammering against them like nails on a coffin. "What is that nasty smell? Either the students set off another stink-bomb spell or someone needs to shower."

Pro Ro's eyes went wide. He glanced at Pinky. Josie stared at the floor.

Thatch's eyes were glued on Miss Periwinkle. "I didn't realize you and Vega had plans."

Vega covered her mouth and nose with a handkerchief. "Please don't say this stench is going to taint this dress. It's already hard enough getting the smell of gin and cigarette smoke out of my clothes." Vega went on to complain loudly.

I was more focused on Thatch and making sure he didn't see Derrick. He offered Miss Periwinkle his arm, and the two of them continued down the steps. He said something too low for the rest of us to hear.

Vega nudged me and then Josie with her wand. "What are you two lesbos doing?"

I ignored her.

The high sweet lullaby of Miss Periwinkle's voice caught my attention from the steps below. "A girls' night out. I hope you don't mind. It's been ages since I've gone dancing."

"I would have taken you," Thatch said.

"Yes, but you hate dancing. Besides, I don't even know if I can dance anymore. Wouldn't that be embarrassing for you to see?" She laughed. The sound was like wind chimes and water bubbling in a brook.

The way Thatch leaned toward her was filled with such longing, I doubted he cared if she made a fool of herself dancing. He obviously was smitten with her. He didn't act like a soulless servant of the Raven Queen. He had a heart and cared about people.

Pro Ro and Pinky continued staring after Miss Periwinkle.

"Ugh, is no one listening to what I just said?" Vega asked. "What is wrong with you fucktards?" She stomped after them.

I breathed a sigh of relief.

Pro Ro sighed dejectedly. "Well, I guess I should be going to bed. It's not like I have anything better to do. Too bad I don't know how to dance." He started up the steps, turning to glance over his shoulder at Pinky. "Are you coming?"

"In a minute," Pinky said.

We stood on the stairs until Pro Ro left.

"Is everyone gone?" Derrick whispered.

"Hopefully," Josie said.

"Good thinking," I said. "I would never have thought of using Pinky as a human shield."

Derrick stepped out from behind Pinky. "Thanks, I owe you one."

Pinky crossed xir arms. "Okay, I gotta say, this goes way above and beyond avoiding someone. I might be the new teacher, but I'm not dumb. What is going on here?"

"Nothing," I said.

Josie bit her lip.

Derrick stared up into Pinky's brown eyes. Considering Derrick's height, it was incredible he needed to stare up into anyone's eyes. "I'm Clarissa's boyfriend. If Thatch finds out we're together, he'll probably fire her—or me."

It wasn't an implausible lie. He was more convincing than I was too.

"But that woman we just saw—wasn't she Mr. Thatch's girlfriend?" Pinky asked.

"You saw how he was about catching us out after teacher curfew," Josie said. "He is such a hypocrite."

Pinky nodded. "Man, this is going to be a rough year, isn't it? It's hard enough coming in halfway through the year—after the semester has already started—and trying to figure out the culture of the school with the kids, but there's all these tricky social dynamics with the staff I'm going to have to navigate. Sheesh."

Xe didn't know the half of it.

After parting with Josie and Pinky, Derrick and I went back to his room.

"How long until Vega gets back?" he asked.

I sat down on his bed. "It's hard to say. I probably shouldn't stay more than a few hours. It's a school night."

"Then we had better put this time to good use." He waggled his eyebrows suggestively. He patted the chair and the hook on the door until he found what he was looking for. He went through the motions of putting on a coat, though I couldn't see one. The air shimmered, and he was invisible.

"What are you doing?" I asked.

"Giving you a fashion show. I want you to tell me how I look."

I shook my head, laughing. He was so random. "Nice, I guess."

He pulled down his ski cap and strutted across the room. He was mostly invisible except for the tan of his neck and the neon pants.

He tripped into a trunk. "It might help if I cut two eyeholes in this thing too. I can't see where I'm going."

"Isn't it, you know, invisible?"

"Not the inside."

"All you need is an invisibility scarf and a pair of invisible pants and you can show Khaba you can still be an invisible man."

He rolled the fabric of the hat upward, revealing the solemnness of his expression. "I don't know if I should stay and keep working at Womby's."

"What do you mean? You can probably find a pair of invisible pants in Lachlan Falls. We can keep you secret until we figure out Thatch's motivations."

He sat on the bed beside me. "I already have him figured out. I don't think I should be here. He can use me against you."

"No, he can't. He won't." I scooted forward so I could see his expression. "Even if there was a spell on you, I broke it. If he commands you to do something outrageous, you'll have the free will to refuse. But I don't think there is any spell on you like that." I didn't think Thatch would do that. If anything, Thatch wanted Derrick close so he would be safe from getting snatched again.

Derrick removed his coat and tossed it aside. "What if there still is a spell, only I can't remember it? Something more than the invisibility and my memories being erased that the Raven Queen did to me? All it will take is a magic word or a command to turn me evil."

I crossed my arms. "You're being an Eeyore."

"You're being naive."

My face flushed with heat. I turned away from him. He was wrong.

"Consider for just a minute. . . ." he started.

"No."

"Clarissa, stop defending him."

"Stop attacking him."

"I'm not. This is the Raven Queen I'm talking about. She wants you because your affinity is useful for her. She knows where you are. She knows about our relationship, thanks to Thatch. She knows she can get to you by using me." His voice rose. "If she decided I'm not valuable to her as a spy or a puppet, she'll just go back to her original plan and pull out my entrails and leave me for you to find."

The cold draftiness of the room seeped under my sweater and chilled me. I remembered those shards of confusing memories. I didn't know what they meant, just that it was bad.

"Look, I don't want to fight," Derrick said. "I just don't want you to get hurt. I'm afraid we aren't safe here. You aren't safe." He gathered me up in his arms and kissed the top of my head.

My anger melted away as he hugged me. Whether it was my affinity, or my need to be comforted, I didn't care. I turned to face him and sank into the sanctuary of his embrace.

"What do you suggest?" I asked. "That we run away?"

"Can you think of a better solution?"

# CHAPTER TWELVE
## One Shade of Gray

My dreams were haunted by the taste of pleasure and pain. The Raven Queen smiled at me, whispering a lullaby as she drank in my soul.

I woke up with Derrick spooned behind me. His arm was draped over my ribs, making it difficult to breathe. The weight of his words came back to my mind. I shifted his arm lower so I could move. He stirred in his sleep.

I hadn't meant to fall asleep in Derrick's bed. We had whispered plans and possibilities to each other late into the night. As much as I had originally wanted a romantic, passionate night with him, our discussion about all the ways we might die was too strong a killjoy.

I sat up. "What time do you think it is?"

"Hmm?" Stars shone through the skylight above.

"I should get back." I didn't need Vega catching me out of my bed two nights in a row. Talk about living dangerously.

Derrick yawned. "Stay here and keep me warm." He snuggled closer.

"I really need to go."

He withdrew his arm. "Okay."

I didn't move. It was too comfortable. He poked me in the side. I squirmed toward the edge of the bed. He sat up and scooted out from behind me.

"You don't have to get up," I said. I groped through the darkness for my sweater.

"There's no way I'm letting you stumble around the school in the dark by yourself."

"I don't *stumble.*" The moment I said it I stubbed my toe on the trunk.

"That's right. You meant to do that."

A breath of wind warmed brushed past me. The candles around the room glowed blue before fading into a more natural orange. I found my sweater draped over the chair and covering my wrinkled blouse underneath. I straightened my striped stockings and slipped my feet into my Mary Jane shoes.

Derrick pulled his pink pants over his underwear and groped around for his invisible jacket. I suppose that was the problem with invisible clothes. You had to remember where you left them.

"Those pants are going to give you away if Thatch sees you."

"No, they won't. Everyone will see hot-pink pants and assume they're Khaba's."

"Maybe you should dye them black or gray so you'll blend in with the shadows."

"Or I could use magic to change their color."

"Really?" Giddy delight filled my heart at the idea of seeing him perform magic. It wasn't like I hadn't seen spells before—or even his—but sometimes I couldn't get over the fact that I now lived in place where miracles and fantastical things could come true.

"Stand back. This is going to be an experimental spell." Derrick waved me behind him.

I moved. Derrick had never done anything dangerous with his magic—if one didn't count the tornado—and that was partly me drawing out more power in him than he knew he had. Even so, the idea of experimental magic didn't sound reassuring.

Derrick removed the pants—which I didn't mind at all. He laid Khaba's pink pants next to Thatch's gray slacks on the bed. He looked under his pillow and felt along the mattress.

"What are you doing?" I asked.

He pressed his palms together. "The problem with an invisible wand is you have to be able to remember where you left it."

I wondered what else Derrick had lost.

He closed his eyes and gestured with his hands. The motions were somewhere in between voguing and sign language. Blue light glowed between his fingers. The air of the room turned warm and then cold. A breeze turned the pages of his open sketchpad on the table. The candles flickered and spluttered out.

Derrick spoke, but most of his words were drowned out by the whistle of wind breathing in from under the door. "Gray and gloom enhance the pink in this pair of pants."

The glow of magic illuminated the two pairs of pants as they twisted together in a dervish. Wind blew more fiercely, snuffing the candles. I staggered back. The blankets flapped back against the wall. I couldn't tell what color the pants were anymore. The cyclone of fabric slowed. The glow faded, along with all the light in the room.

Derrick picked up the pants. Candles sparked back to life. In one hand he held a pair of torn hot-pink pants. In the other he held Khaba's wider, but shorter-legged pants. They were now gray. I stared in horror as I realized what he'd done.

"Perfect. Now the pants are charcoal instead of hot pink." Derrick turned to me. His smile faded.

I suspected the anxious expression in his eyes was due to the horror in mine.

"You turned Thatch's pants pink." I said. "Now how am I going to get them back to him without him noticing?"

"Seriously? They have a giant rip in the back." He dropped Thatch's pants on the floor and dressed in the gray pants. "Were you going to just slip them into his closet and think he wasn't going to notice? He would do some kind of homing-beacon spell that would point to you as the thief. Or me as the person who tore his pants. Just let him think the brownies didn't return the pants after washing them."

"I don't want to be a thief. I planned on returning his pants," I said.

He kept staring at me like he wanted to say something. He laced his invisible shoes, sneaking looks at me.

"What?"

"Um, nothing. I'm sorry." He bit his lip, eyeing me. "I don't want to make you mad."

I went over and hugged him. "I'm not mad." I kissed his cheek.

"You're right about the color pink," he said. "It really is . . . conspicuous. Gray is a much better color for being incognito." He looked at me and then looked away again. "Have you ever thought about . . . ahem . . . gray as a hair color?"

My eyes went wide. I had a feeling where this was going. "You're kidding me."

"Heh."

I ran to the mirror and slid the painting over. My beautiful pink hair was dull and gray.

"Derrick!"

"I'm sure we can change it back. Maybe Josie or Khaba can help."

I shook my head in exasperation. "It's a good thing I love you."

We headed to my room, Derrick using his wand to light the way. He kept the light dim, with just enough to see by. With his invisibility clothes and dark pants, he was impossible to see now. I didn't like the idea of having gray hair at my young age, but it probably was more practical for clandestine adventures in the middle of the night.

"There are so many times I've been out after dark that Vega has never said anything. I can't believe she had a fit about it last night," I whispered.

"The difference is that you come back. Last night you didn't." Derrick's voice came from beside me, but I couldn't see his face with the invisibility clothes. "You had her worried. She's not a bad roommate. She's looking out for you."

"Only because Thatch makes her."

He grunted. I didn't say I thought Thatch was the one looking out for me. That would have just started us arguing again.

I thought I caught a whiff of cigarette smoke. I eyed the shadows. It wouldn't have surprised me if one of the students was smoking in a secret passage somewhere. Or if one of them had lit the school on fire again. I hoped it wasn't the latter.

He walked up the creaky stairs to the women's dorm. The light of Derrick's wand illuminated a portrait on the wall of an old man in a witch hat. Out of the corner of my eye I thought I saw the silhouette of a bird shift across the painting, but when I looked, I only saw our shadows.

Derrick kissed me on the forehead outside my door. I stood on tiptoe, wanting more than a chaste kiss.

The light of his wand faded. Fabric rustled.

He gave me a quick peck on the lips. "I'll see you tomorrow. Or maybe that's today. I don't know what time it is. It's probably after midnight." His warmth withdrew as he stepped back.

I unlocked the door. An oil lamp burned in the room. I didn't remember leaving a lamp on. Perhaps Vega had. Her bed was neatly made. She wasn't back yet. I turned back to Derrick, a smile on my face.

A light flared in the darkness of the hallway. Vega leaned against the wall, the tip of her wand glowing brilliantly white. She still wore her black flapper dress.

She advanced, bringing with her the odor of sweat and cigarette smoke. "What the hell are you doing?"

"Me?" I asked.

"Who else would I be talking to?" She grabbed the front of my sweater, yanked me back out into the hall, and slammed me against the wall. "You're going to tell me where you were tonight, and if you try to lie to me, I'll make you regret it." She shoved the wand under my chin menacingly.

# CHAPTER THIRTEEN
## Romantic Rivals

I stared at Vega in terror.

She shook me. "Where were you?"

"With Josie?"

"Bitch, please!"

Her breath smelled of alcohol and tobacco smoke. Up close I could see her lipstick was smeared. I turned my face away and tried to breathe clean air.

"Ahem," Derrick said, probably a little too quietly to get the attention of Miss Drama Queen.

"Fine, you want to do this the hard way." Vega released me, but I remained pinned against the wall. She flourished her wand in the air, about to hex me. "I'm not above torturing this out of you."

"Actually." Derrick coughed from the darkness behind Vega. "She was telling the truth. Miss Lawrence was in Josie Kimura's room earlier."

Vega whirled. She squinted into the darkness, waving her wand to the left and right. "Who's there?"

Vega's lips moved, and pinpricks of white drifted out of her wand, floating in the air and radiating larger. They glowed like stars. The fragrance of night air intensified, cool and crisp and tasting of moonlight and the cosmos.

"I can't see you. Where are you?" Vega said.

"You aren't supposed to see me. I'm invisible. I work for security."

"I don't believe you." She waved a hand in the air. A grid of lines appeared a foot out around Derrick, flashing blue and purple. In front of him glowed the school crest. Underneath was beautiful ornamental writing that looked like it could have been Arabic.

"That's Khaba's stamp of protection." Derrick sounded cheerful and calm. "He only does that for classified staff."

Go, Derrick! He didn't sound intimidated or scared at all. He was handling Vega with far more ease than I did. It looked like being escorted by a security guard might have provided a good alibi for me.

My relief was short-lived.

Her eyes narrowed. "You're that perverted invisible man who peeks on us while we're showering, aren't you?" Her wand glowed red.

"I will have you know I never spy on women in the shower. That was the former invisible man. And I don't go into any of the staff quarters, locker rooms, or student dorms." Derrick peeled back enough of his ski cap that his grin was visible. "They call me Invismo. You've never met me, but I've seen you around."

Vega crossed her arms. She eyed his pants, the only other part of him visible. "I see you now." She pointed her wand at him. "What are you doing outside my room?"

I squirmed against the wall, trying to free myself.

"I was walking Miss Lawrence back to her room. As I said, she was with Miss Kimura earlier," Derrick said. "And then I escorted Miss Lawrence to Mr. Khaba's office."

A smile twitched the corners of Vega's lips. "Oh, was someone in trouble?"

"Lots of trouble." Derrick laughed.

Vega laughed along with him. She stepped toward Derrick, her gaze resting on his full lips. "You look familiar. Have I seen you before somewhere?"

"Probably. But I doubt you would notice me."

The evil look in her eyes was replaced by something else I wasn't used to seeing in Vega. Curiosity? Interest? "I have a feeling I wouldn't forget you."

He laughed, sounding nervous. I had a bad feeling she might try to test him like she had once done to me.

She lifted her chin. "Do I scare you?"

"Well, yeah." He cleared his throat. "I mean, maybe 'scared' isn't the right word."

Her nostrils flared. Surely she could smell the fear on him like a wolf about to close in on the prey. She was about to go in for some below-the-belt magical punch. I wiggled against my invisible bonds. I had to save Derrick from her evil clutches.

"Maybe 'intimidated' is more accurate." Derrick flashed a sheepish smile. "I've always been kind of a dunce around beautiful women. I say stupid things." He grimaced. "And the fact that you're beautiful and an incredible teacher, and you're one of the most skilled Celestors at

Womby's—"

"Stop." She backed away, blushing. "Flattery will get you . . . everywhere."

"Uh-oh." Derrick laughed. "I better be careful."

OMG. My boyfriend was flirting with my wicked roomie. My face grew hot. I was not jealous. He was just doing this to save himself from getting cursed.

"How tall are you?" She smoothed the curve of her bob away from her cheek. "We don't have many male teachers at this school past six foot. It makes dating difficult for a woman such as myself."

Barf!

"There's Mr. Thatch," I said. "And Pinky the Sasquatch."

"Thatch is a fucktard. And I wouldn't screw that mangy furball if my life depended on it."

Derrick cleared his throat. "Miss Bloodmire, according to the school rules—"

"Call me Vega."

"Dating is not allowed between coworkers. As one of Mr. Khaba's employees, one of the school's disciplinarians, I wouldn't want to break any rules and be a poor role model for others."

"You can discipline me any time." She winked at him.

"And speaking of naughty girls, let's get Clarissa—err—Miss Lawrence to bed before she causes any more trouble tonight."

Her smile faded as she followed the turn of his chin toward me. "Ugh, are you still here?"

"I wouldn't be if you would release me from your spell," I said.

"Right." She waved a hand in the air. The invisible coils holding me in place faded.

I walked into the room, hesitating when I realized Vega wasn't following me inside.

Derrick shifted the fabric back over his face, obscuring his features. A sliver of neck remained.

"Do you like coffins?" Vega asked.

Derrick's voice came out muffled against the knit fabric. "Good night, ladies."

I gathered up my pajamas from a drawer.

Vega closed the door, a contented smile on her face. "I call dibs on the invisible man."

"What?" I stood.

She opened her wardrobe, snatched up a nightie from where she'd left it folded on top of her rows of shoes and swished past me to the dressing screen in the corner.

"You heard me," she said. "He's mine."

The white paper of the screen was decorated with Japanese-style cherry trees ending in blossoms of red. From far away, the screen always looked beautiful. You couldn't tell until up close the red was the blood of impaled birds and insects.

I fought the mixture of rising emotions in me. I should have been relieved Vega hadn't tortured me into telling her I had been with Derrick. I wanted to count my blessings that she hadn't done anything to Derrick—that he had disarmed her with his charm. Even so, jealousy spiked through me when I thought about him flirting with her.

She draped her black dress over the side of the screen.

"No," I said, surprising myself with my vehemence. "You can't have him."

Vega could take up the shelves and crowd her homicidal furniture onto my side of the room if she wanted, but she was not going to get my boyfriend.

Vega snickered. "Don't try to fight me for him. We both know I'd win. Besides, he's out of your league."

I undressed on the outside of the screen. There was never any telling how long she would hog it.

"No, he isn't," I said. "He's perfectly my league."

"He probably doesn't think so. In any case, he has that innocent boy next door charm that would be delightful to corrupt. I doubt he has any idea how hot he is."

"How do you know he's hot? Most of him was invisible."

"I saw what counts."

What was that? His mouth and his pants? "I'm sure D—Invismo can make up his own mind about who he wants."

"Let's be logical. What would he want with someone like you? You don't even look like you've hit puberty. Except for your hair. Nice look, by the way. Did you hear gray is the new black? It adds years to your face."

Sometimes I didn't know who was worse, Vega Bloodmire or the Raven Queen. The Raven Court was out there, somewhere far away, trying to make my life miserable. Vega was right here in my room torturing me daily.

The following morning, I had difficulty forcing myself out of bed—no surprise. Now that I had a boyfriend to spend time with, I had stayed up too late and was now paying for it. I rolled over and closed my eyes, dozing off again until Vega slammed our door on the way to the bathroom.

Rubbing my eyes, I forced myself up.

I did a double take in the mirror as I brushed my hair. I'd seen women with gray and silver hair, but this wasn't either. It was the same charcoal as Thatch's pants, an almost black. If only I'd brought more hair dye with me from my mom's house. I didn't want to wait for her to send me some in the mail, and I doubted they sold hot pink at Brooms, Magic Carpets, and More or at Potions Emporium in Lachlan Falls.

In the cafeteria, students' heads turned as I passed. Jeb sat at the staff table. I was glad to see Thatch wasn't present, but then he rarely showed up for breakfast or lunch unless we were short-staffed. I would swear he got out of all the unpleasant duties.

Jeb stood when he saw me, his jaw dropping. He clutched at his chest, and I thought he might have a heart attack.

"It's her!" Jasper Jang, the theater and music teacher stumbled out of his seat.

I looked around, confused. "Who?"

No one answered.

"Good morning, Jeb," I said. "Is everything . . . all right?"

"Miss . . . Lawrence?" His face was pale. "Is that you?"

"Yeah." I looked down self-consciously. "It's the hair, isn't it? I look like I'm twice my age." I hated it when Vega was right. I hoped that was the only thing she was right about. Doubt niggled at my mind; Derrick might be out of my league. He might get tired of me.

I pushed that thought away. He had loved me all these years. He wasn't going to suddenly stop. If Thatch and Gertrude Periwinkle could still love each other after so many years and have a happy ending, why couldn't I?

Then again, maybe I shouldn't have been comparing my happy ending with Derrick to the evil lovebirds.

Jeb yanked on his mustache so hard he looked like he might pull off the lip attached to it. "It ain't that, it's just. . . ."

Jasper laughed nervously, sounding like a hyena on crack. "What did you do to yourself?"

I tried to consider the best explanation. "It was a magical hair-dyeing accident." That was close enough to the truth.

"You look like . . . your mother," Jeb said.

"Oh." That was what this was about? My biological mother had black hair and creamy skin. I suppose my freckles at least saved me from looking completely like her.

Students kept staring and pointing. Jackie Frost and Puck walked into the cafeteria from under one of the arches closer to us. Puck's eyes went wide with fear.

For the briefest of moments, a thrill of excitement ignited guilty pleasure in me. People were afraid of me. I'd never had that effect on anyone before.

I felt powerful, like the kind of teacher no one messed with. Staff wouldn't dare make snide comments to me or talk about me like I wasn't there at meetings if they feared me.

I was the daughter of the wickedest witch of all time.

I bet Puck regretted making me redo report cards now. If Gertrude Periwinkle saw me like this, she'd think twice about blackmailing me or playing malicious tricks on me. I smiled.

It was Imani, her brow furrowed as she stared at me that reminded me I didn't want to be feared. I didn't want people to think I would fall into the footsteps of a woman who had killed others and worked for the Raven Court.

The last person I wanted to look like was Alouette Loraline. I offered Jeb an apologetic smile. "Sorry, about that. I didn't mean to give anyone a fright. I don't suppose you'd be up for restoring my hair to the way it was?"

Jeb sat down. His faced relaxed into a relieved smile. "It would be my pleasure, darlin'." He didn't even get out his wand. He waved his hand in front of me. Sparkles shimmered and flashed before my eyes. The air tasted sweet and salty, cool and starry.

Jasper Jang's eyebrows rose.

"Is it as bright as it was before?" I asked.

"It's brighter," Jasper Jang said.

"Cool." That was good enough for me. "Thank you!"

Jeb excused himself as I gathered breakfast. Students continued to point.

Imani ran up to me while I was eating. "I love your new hair, Miss Lawrence. It's perfect for second semester." She ran off before I could respond.

Uh-oh. Now what color was my hair?

I should have focused on work because it was a Monday. Ignoring my better judgment, I slipped off during my prep period, hoping to visit Derrick. When I peeked into his room, I found a note sprawled across his sketchpad:

*Went to Lachlan Falls for a new pair of pants. You'll see me later. Actually, you won't* see *me! LOL*

I hoped that meant he would find me at lunch or after school. In his mirror I found my hair had been turned auburn, not pink. It had been years since I'd seen my natural red hair. It made me look like Pippi Longstocking. The sight resurrected every carrot and ginger joke I had endured in my childhood.

This was not how I wanted people to see me. Maybe Josie could help me. Unfortunately, she was busy teaching.

I considered asking Vega for help with my hair, but I didn't want to end up bald. As I prepped lessons in my room, I kept thinking about my hair. Derrick had never seen me as a redhead. What if he thought I looked like a dork?

Maybe I could solve my hair problem myself. I still had time. I went to the library. The card catalogue was not my friend—nor was Miss Periwinkle. She was unlikely to help me. Fortunately, I found Maddy, Imani, Greenie, and Hailey doing research for a school project.

"Can anyone help me with the card catalogue? I need to find a spell for hair dye."

Hailey's eyes went wide as she took in my new—old—color. Apparently she hadn't been at breakfast.

"Why? That is a great color. Is that natural?" Greenie asked.

Hailey rolled her eyes. "You don't ask women that question. It's rude. It's like asking if you're naturally ugly."

"Shut up!" Greenie said.

"No, you shut up."

Maddy stood. "I can help you with the card catalogue. Miss P showed me, and I've been helping students find books." She glanced at a table where Silas Lupi, one of the teachers, sat. "Although some people insist on only letting Miss P show them." She rolled her eyes.

Maddy helped me find a book on minor glamours and showed me where it was on the shelf. "Do you want me to check it out to you?" she asked.

I hesitated. I had never been able to check out books before without Miss Periwinkle intercepting me and telling me every book I wanted was off-limits for one reason or another. I glanced at Silas Lupi and lowered my voice. "Sure. There's something else I'd like you to help me get."

"Love potions?" she asked with a smile. "Those books are always checked out."

"No. I need to find out about . . . the Raven Queen."

Her eyes went wide.

"Is that a restricted subject?" I asked. "Since she's the enemy of pretty much all Witchkin, I thought it might be a good idea to read up—"

"You don't have to explain yourself to me. I saw her mark on you—back when the King of the Pacific wanted to see who you belonged to—when you and Mr. Thatch saved me."

"I don't belong to her," I said a little louder than I intended.

"No, I get it. You want to be prepared for when you have to face her. Miss P suggested I do the same thing about the King of the Pacific. She even loaned me a restricted book on Fae so I could read the chapter about merpeople and sirens."

"It sounds like your apprenticeship in the library is going well," I said.

"Yeah, I love it here. It's my second-favorite place—after your room of course. Did you see Mr. Puck just changed my schedule? I'm in your seventh-period class again!"

"I'm in your class too," Hailey said from across the room. "Puck paired me with Maddy as her buddy."

Maybe I hadn't been as quiet as I thought. Great. Silas Lupi continued reading his book. He didn't glare at me for wanting to know about the Raven Queen.

Imani poked Hailey with a book. "Shush. This is the library."

The door to Miss Periwinkle's office creaked open. Her hair was damp under her witch hat like she'd just finished showering. That was possible considering the hall to her room was through her office. She didn't live in the dormitories like the rest of the teachers, and she had her own bathroom. Though I thought she preferred Thatch's.

Silas Lupi stood and rushed over. "Miss Periwinkle, how lovely to see you! What a coincidence seeing you here!"

Right. Like she was going to buy that line. She was a librarian. This was the library.

"I have an important bibliographic question for you," he said.

She smiled coyly. "Do you? Is it related to the question you asked me yesterday?"

He chuckled.

I was almost positive he taught a class this period. Had he left his students to come down here and flirt? That was pretty irresponsible. I would never do that. I would only use my prep period for flirting with Derrick.

Miss Periwinkle's office door opened again. Thatch strode out. His shoulder-length hair was also damp. Had he just gotten out of the shower too? They'd probably been showering together. Ick.

Thatch's smile brightened when he saw me. "Miss Lawrence, what are you doing here? You aren't going to try to sneak off with any of our restricted books, I trust." He spoke jovially as if he might be teasing me.

Miss Periwinkle glared at me.

I held up my hands before his girlfriend shot lasers out of her eyes at me. "For the record, I've never stolen any books from this library or any other ones." Sure, I had fines when I kept the books too long, but I always returned the books.

Silas Lupi cleared his throat. "As I was saying, I'm looking for this rare book that I was hoping you might help me locate. . . ."

Thatch circled around the counter. "You look different, Miss Lawrence. You changed your hair, didn't you?"

Greenie and Imani whispered something I couldn't hear.

"He didn't ask if it was natural," Hailey said from across the room.

I flashed a great big fake smile. I hated my hair.

Thatch nodded to Hailey. "I don't have to ask if that's Miss Lawrence's natural color. I've seen her with this color before."

"When?" Miss Periwinkle asked, her voice shrill.

I scooted farther back.

"About that book—" Silas said.

I wondered where Silas Lupi's wife was. Did she know he was spending his day in the library drooling over the librarian? Or did she think he was in his classroom?

Maddy looked from Miss Periwinkle to Thatch. I was pretty sure she got what was going on between Mr. Oblivious and Miss Possessive Girlfriend.

Thatch shrugged. "Years ago. I've known Clarissa forever."

"Clarissa," Gertrude Periwinkle repeated.

"Miss Lawrence," he corrected.

Miss Periwinkle's smile remained in place, but the barbs in her voice prickled the air like porcupine quills. "You didn't tell me you two knew each other before she was hired on. I thought we didn't have any secrets, Felix."

"About those books," I said to Maddy. "Maybe later when the library isn't as busy."

After making a beeline out of the library, I went back to my classroom to finish my lessons. At lunch I went to Josie's classroom to talk to her about my hair. The moment I stepped in and saw who was there, I backed on out. Pro Ro sat in one of the student chairs, his belly hanging over the desk attached to it. I had never thought of him as being rotund, but his cheeks were round, and his beard hid the shape of his face. His loose kaftan shirt camouflaged his physique.

"Please, Miss Kimura. I'll pay you." Desperation leaked into his voice.

I ducked back from the door. I didn't want to interrupt this conversation. Eavesdrop, maybe, but not interrupt.

"As enticing as it is to have even less free time . . . no," Josie said.

"I'll do anything." He lowered his voice. "I happen to be very good at love potions. Real love potions, not those paltry charms students are always trying to replicate."

The silence stretched on. I wondered if she was thinking about it.

"I know you have feelings for Mr. Khaba," he added. "I have a spell that would work on a Fae."

I considered noisily stumbling into her room to announce my presence so he wouldn't go any further. Josie and Khaba were both my friends. I didn't want her to succumb to temptation. I didn't want Khaba's free will to be taken away. I knew what that was like with the vulnerabilities of my affinity. No one deserved for such a thing to happen to them.

I stepped into the doorway. Seeing the rage on Josie's face convinced me to step out again.

"Do you think I'm such a dunce at magic that I couldn't make my own love potion if I wanted?" she asked, her voice rising. "Or do you think I'm such a hag that I can't get a man to find me attractive without magic? Not to mention potions and spells that brainwash someone are illegal. And immoral."

"No! I'm—no—I didn't mean to imply—I apologize. I shouldn't have suggested it. Excuse me." The desk creaked. "Please forgive me. I'm just desperate. I don't know what to do."

"You had all last semester to figure out how to get your shit together. If you're this desperate, go ask Vega or Thatch to brew you a competency potion."

"Yes, of course. Excuse me. I shouldn't have troubled you with this." His voice grew louder. It sounded like he was headed toward the door.

I didn't want to stay standing outside like someone eavesdropping—which I was. I tried to casually stroll into the doorway as though I had been heading that way.

Pro Ro bowled into me, knocking me back. It was a lot harder to ignore the size of his belly when it plowed me over.

"Pardon me," he said. He did a double take. "Ugh. You."

He kept on walking.

I waved, trying to think of something to say. "Nice bumping into you."

Josie scowled at her desk. Her eyes went wide, seeing me. She did a double take too. "Love the hair."

"Don't remind me." I nodded to the doorway Pro Ro had just exited from. "What was that about?"

She removed her glasses and wiped them against her turquoise-and-orchid lace dress. "He's trying to get out of teaching yoga."

"Oh? He still hasn't convinced Jeb to give him a different elective?"

"Jeb is fruit loops." She leaned back in her chair. "Last year he thought the electives I teach should be karate and Chinese. Apparently because he thought I was Chinese American, not Japanese American. And all Asians are ninjas good at martial arts."

"So how did you get out of it?"

"I didn't. The first day of class I told students I was going to teach Japanese instead of Chinese and a third of them transferred out. Puck was angry as hell, but whatev. For karate I got Puck to change the course listing to Bushido instead."

"Wait, so that's samurai stuff?"

"Yeah, the way of the warrior. I taught a bunch of Japanese culture stuff: Zen meditation, shodo calligraphy; ikebana flower arranging; haiku poetry writing; and some Japanese spells. We did a unit on martial arts, but it was small. I had to seriously study up and called in a guest presenter. The kids actually liked it, and I'm teaching it again this semester."

"Maybe Pro Ro could do the same."

She snorted. "That's sort of what he's been doing this semester, teaching theoretical yoga. The kids are tired of book learning. They want meditation and exercise. I heard Balthasar Llewelyn threatened to turn him into a pretzel if he didn't teach something impressive soon."

I sat on the edge of her desk, avoiding the messy piles of paper. Her desk was a lot like mine. "I know you're busy with lessons, but I wondered if you could help me."

She leaned forward with interest. "Is this a boy problem?"

"Yes—no. Hopefully not." I waved a hand at my hair. "I want to get rid of *this*."

"Why? Is that your natural color? You do realize Morties pay a lot of money for that shade of auburn."

"I don't care. I want it gone. It was an accident." I went over to the door and closed it. I filled her in on the exploits of my previous evening.

She laughed when I came to the part about Derrick turning Thatch's pants hot pink. "You should sneak them back into his closet. It will be hilarious."

"No," I said firmly. "We need to change his pants back." I continued with the rest of the story.

She shrugged when I was done. "Okay, I'll fix Thatch's pants. And I'll change your hair back if you really want. It's not a complicated spell, but just so you know, it doesn't last as long as hair dye."

"That's fine." What a relief it was possible. "When can we get started? Do you think we can do it before Derrick gets back? I don't want him to see me like this."

She laughed. "What? You think he'll dump you because you're a ginger?"

"No, of course not." It was a silly fear. He wouldn't do that. But maybe he would just prefer not to date a ginger.

"Let's wait until after dinner," Josie said. "There are a few items I have to collect. We can do the spell in my room."

Derrick still wasn't back after school, nor could I find him before dinner. A worm of worry wiggled into my brain that something might have happened to him. I pushed it away. There were only a dozen apparel shops in Lachlan Falls. What if none sold invisibility clothes? Derrick would probably have to travel somewhere farther away.

Josie and I ate dinner together and then we went to her dorm room. I brought along Thatch's pants too. Her cauldron was boiling on her desk. A soupy mixture that looked like lime jelly percolated within. The room smelled like mint, lavender, and freshly cut grass.

She retrieved a spell book from a shelf and added a few mushrooms and a vial of something that sparkled like glitter to the mixture. The pleasant smell turned putrid, almost as bad as a sasquatch. The spell she chanted didn't take very long. I didn't understand the words because she used a Japanese spell. I hoped this was going to work better than the spell she'd used to try to fix my mouth after Vega had sealed my lips together.

Josie touched her wand to the cauldron and placed the pants inside. The green liquid turned hot pink. She wrung out the pants and set them aside. They were still pink.

Maybe the spell needed a minute to activate.

She motioned to the cauldron. "Now your turn. Dunk your head in."

"It won't hurt? The water was just boiling."

"You'll be fine. That was a magical boil, not a physical boil induced by heat."

Had it been Vega saying this, I wouldn't have believed her. But this was Josie, my best friend. I held my breath and dunked my head in. The water was warm, but not hot. I pulled my head out. She handed me a towel.

I ran over to the mirror. My hair was a bright, beautiful pink again. Yay!

Thatch's slacks were also still pink. Boo!

"What about Thatch's pants?" I asked.

"I'm not fixing anything for that bag of dicks."

"Please! It's not for him. It's for me. So he doesn't kill me. Do you want him to kill me?"

She groaned. "Only for you. And you know what—because I don't want him to kill you, I'll sew the pants for you too."

"Oh Josie, you're the best!"

"I know." Her eyes twinkled maliciously. "But just so you know, I'm going to embroider the words, 'Property of an asshole' on the backside."

"Don't you dare! You're a teacher. We're supposed to be good role models."

"Whatever. Do you remember that time he switched everyone's prophecy chocolate?"

I checked Derrick's room again. He wasn't in, and the page in his drawing pad remained turned to the note he'd given me. I flipped through the pad for a blank sheet. Inside were drawings, some in pencil, others in ink. Fantasy creatures filled most of the pages, the same subject matter I remembered from high school. Many pages contained caricatures of the teachers. I found a scowling Thatch pointing to a student chained in the dungeon, a malevolent Vega cackling over a cauldron, and a bumbling Jeb lassoing himself with a rope. Derrick's style was cute and whimsical. I remembered how much I had wanted to draw like him in high school. I wasn't even sure what my style was. It felt like forever since I'd drawn for the enjoyment of it.

I flipped another page, finding one of myself. I sat at a messy desk, my arms covered in striped sleeves that made me look witchy. An apple sat in one corner. I read a book called *Witchcraft for Dummies*. Above my head floated art supplies. A paintbrush splashed color onto a canvas. A frog hopped out of a top hat. Herbs mixed into a cauldron.

I wondered what he was trying to say about me. Reading a book with that title implied I was a dunce of a witch—which I knew. Yet, all the magical things happening behind me implied I could do magic. Did that mean he thought I was a better witch than I did?

I studied the confident lines of his pen, his attention to detail, and the way he made me look like a cute cartoon. I turned a page and found more studies of my face. My eyes were always a little too large and innocent, making me look more like a child than an adult. My freckled nose was more upturned than in real life. I filled pages of his book.

How had it been possible that he wouldn't have remembered me? He drew me like someone he had always known he loved. Why had I worried about my hair being red earlier? I felt ridiculous.

I found a clean sheet and wrote:

*XOXO You know where to find me.*

I returned to my dorm room, expecting he would show up at any moment. But he didn't. The hours ticked by, and I reluctantly got ready for bed. He still didn't come. Vega came in, crowding the little room with her presence. I lay awake long after she went to sleep, but I didn't hear any creaks outside the room or within. When Vega's cuckoo clock chimed eleven, I thought I heard a creak outside my door. I snuck out into the hall, prepared to say I had to use the restroom if Vega questioned me.

"Derrick?" I whispered.

No reply.

Derrick hadn't returned.

# CHAPTER FOURTEEN
## Staff Infection

On Tuesday morning, Vega's cuckoo clock let out a murderous scream at six in the morning. Since my bed was closest to the window, it was my job to open the shutters to let in the light. Vega was on the side of the room near the door that led out to the hallway to the bathroom. I stayed out of her path. She could keep first dibs on the showers.

I had dibs on Derrick. I smiled at that.

I hadn't seen him since Sunday night. I wanted to go to the other side of the school to find him, but I had too much to do. After getting ready and snagging a blueberry bagel from the cafeteria, I swung by the administration offices to check my mail and pick up my newest schedule. I would swear five new students had been added to every class each week, and only three students had left. The constant student schedule changes interfered with teaching the curriculum.

I had more duties this semester too: lunch duty almost every day, plus hall monitor duty after school three days a week and a Saturday detention once a month. The newest teachers like Pro Ro and me had the most, only second to the five duties that had been piled onto Pinky. The department heads like Thatch, Bluehorse, Frost, and Kutchi had the least amount of duties.

Pro Ro came into the office, frowning when he saw me.

"Good morning," I said.

He said nothing.

"That's a good color on you," I tried.

Gold was a good color on him. He had dressed in his usual loose kaftan, but gold patterns decorated the dark blue sleeves. Pro Ro lifted his nose and continued to the mailboxes.

A note in my box reminded me we had a staff meeting at three thirty after school. New class lists had been placed in my box with some names updated in bold for some reason. Puck had slipped in a note that said he hadn't been able to prepare prophecy chocolate a couple weeks ago at the start of the semester, but it would be ready on Friday. I wasn't sure I wanted another chocolate that would divine how salty and bitter the school year would be. If I didn't think it would hurt Puck's feelings, I probably would have thrown the chocolate away.

I had homeroom first period this semester. I was pleased I had several returning students. Homeroom was basically a study hall, but I used the first twenty minutes of class to teach study skills.

"This is stupid. This is supposed to be naptime," one of the boys with a widow's peak and webbed fingers complained.

I had no idea what he was. I'd learned not to ask about students' heritage early on. "What teacher at this school lets you take naps in class?"

"All of them."

I sincerely doubted that.

Ben O'Sullivan lifted his chin, trying to act tough. "Hailey said she passed classes last semester cuz you taught her how to cheat on tests."

I laughed. I had sort of spun study skills like it was naughty. It was the only way to get them to pay attention. I lowered my voice. "She wasn't supposed to tell anyone. If I teach you how to pass your classes, do you promise to keep it a secret?"

Students looked at each other with wide eyes. My returning students snickered and nudged each other, already in on my unorthodox methods. None of the other teachers had taught the students how to take notes or how to study for a test at this school. I showed the students a few simple techniques for finding key vocabulary words in a textbook and then broke students into small groups, pairing new students with returning students to try it on homework assignments.

Already this was going more smoothly than last semester. A few stragglers came in halfway through the lesson, and I explained what we were doing. After first period homeroom, I taught a beginning level art class. The day was broken into four ninety-minute-block periods with a lunch break halfway through. It was an A day, so I only had one, three, five, and seven.

I expected it to be an easy day since I had all the curriculum prepared from last semester. What I hadn't counted on was having at least five returning students in each class who had been added over the weekend. Seventh period was the most crowded class with forty-two students. We didn't have enough chairs. Imani and Greenie sat on the floor in the middle of the horseshoe arrangement of desks.

I had been lucky Imani was willing to sit on the floor since this kept her farther from Maddy and anyone else whose magic might endanger others.

"I already took a drawing pretest last year with the old art teacher," a girl with goat horns said in a high-pitched teenage whine that threatened to shatter eardrums.

"Unfortunately, I don't have the old art teacher's results. This will help us to see our improvement later in the term," I explained. I was going to have to think of new activities for returning students like Imani, but I had no ideas yet.

"Why can't I just draw? You saw what I could do last semester," Jon Jefferies said.

"Suck it up," Hailey shouted from the other side of the room. "If I have to listen to you morons bitch about getting an easy A, I'm going to puke."

"Language," I said, shaking my head at her.

She smiled sheepishly.

I didn't need Puck's prophecy chocolate to tell me how much I would enjoy my job this semester. I had built relationships with the students, and they knew me. They peer-pressured the new students into behaving. It only made it that much harder knowing I might leave like Derrick had suggested we do.

I was so busy during the morning, I didn't even think about Derrick until lunch. I had cafeteria duty, which forced me to sit and eat, as opposed to grabbing food and working in my room. It would have been nice to have a chance to see him, but I expected we would have time after school.

Unfortunately, after school I had to lock up the supply closet and the classroom, which took me a few minutes because students were so excited they wanted to talk to me about projects and Art Club. There was a line for the teacher bathroom in my hallway, and there was no way I wanted to use the one in the administration wing. I went back up to the dormitories and used that one. I had ten minutes to spare before the staff meeting, but that wasn't going to be enough time to run to Derrick's room on the other side of the school and then hike back to the conference room.

I opted to arrive early, something I'd never done before. Jasper Jang, the bald music and drama teacher, sat on one end of the conference room speaking with Coach Kutchi. Our physical education teacher had short silver hair. I had joined her equestrian class this year, which mostly consisted of unicorns and pegasi. I looked forward to learning how to ride a broom next year. I waved at her when I entered the room. She looked away.

Since Jasper Jang and Amadea Kutchi were elective teachers, it would have made sense to sit next to them, but I didn't want to be the third wheel in their conversation.

When I moved to take the seat next to Sebastian Reade, he put out a hand over the chair. "Sorry, this seat is taken."

I doubted that. More likely he just didn't like me.

I held my head high and walked to the other side of the table where no one sat. This wasn't like high school, I tried to tell myself. I wasn't the most unpopular teacher because I was a grade-A dork. It was because my biological mother had cursed and killed people. It would take time before staff saw I wasn't evil like her.

I had brought my sketchbook to the meeting with me and made quick gesture drawings of Jasper and the coach. I smiled at Vega and Jackie Frost when they came in together, and Jackie nodded to me at least. They sat together farther down the table, and when Pro Ro entered, he selected a seat near Vega.

The aroma of rotting garbage and goaty musk wafted toward me. I looked up, knowing what that meant.

Pinky entered the room wearing a khaki kilt. I suspected it was a Utilikilt, which were pretty popular in the Pacific Northwest. I didn't think Khaba would object to that. Pinky seated xirself next to Vega and introduced xirself to Jackie Frost.

Vega wrinkled up her nose and sneered. She lifted a black beaded purse from her lap. It resembled something my grandmother had once owned. She removed a vintage perfume bottle with a pump out from her bag and sprayed it in Pinky's direction.

Pinky choked and coughed. "Excuse me. I'm allergic to chemicals and Morty—"

"Yeah? Well, I'm allergic to sasquatch fur and dander, and I have to put up with your presence. Do us both a favor and sit over there." She waggled her fingers in my direction. Great.

Pinky grimaced—or I suspected that was the expression I saw under all the fur. Pinky rose and sat down next to me.

"Hi," xe said.

"Hi," I said. I tried to smile. Tears filled my eyes from the strength of xir stench.

"Is everything all right?" xe asked.

I nodded. I didn't know if it was worse to breathe through my nose or mouth. If I breathed through my mouth, that meant I couldn't smell. But that also meant I was sucking molecules of rancid air into my mouth.

"What are you drawing?" Pinky asked.

I showed xir my sketches.

Xe leaned closer. I held my breath. I wanted to like Pinky, and I felt bad the other teachers didn't want to be around xir. Staff didn't treat me much differently.

The moment Josie walked in, Pinky stood and waved. "Hi, Jo! We have a seat for you over here."

Josie's smile grew strained. She looked from the empty seat next to Pinky to the one next to Vega to the one next to Pro Ro. She flashed an apologetic smile. "Excuse me, I'll be over there in a sec. I just need to. . . ." She pointed at Pro Ro and sat next to him.

"How did the first day of teaching real yoga go?" Josie asked Pro Ro. "Did you survive?"

"I showed them a couple simple poses and then Duran Pollock told me I wasn't doing Downward Dog correctly. I couldn't even remember which one that was. The students laughed at me."

Josie nodded sympathetically. "Those haters."

"I realize I don't get out of the woods much, but I thought Pro Ro was a yogi," Pinky whispered. "He's wearing a turban."

"Don't believe all the stereotypes you read about people in turbans," I said, thinking about my previous blunder when I'd tried to rip it off his head.

Pinky nodded. "You should have heard some of the rude comments that came out of the students' mouths today. It was a horrible second day. Yesterday was worse."

"I can only imagine," I said. I had gotten my dose at the beginning of the year. I knew how harsh the kids could be.

Thatch took the last remaining seat next to Pinky. I closed my sketchbook, not wanting him to sneer at my art like he had in the past. Thatch glanced over at the sasquatch, nostrils flaring. I felt bad for Pinky. Xe was clueless that xe was the smelly teacher. Someone had to tell xir.

But I didn't want that person to be me.

Khaba, Puck, and Jeb strolled in together at three thirty exactly.

"Howdy, folks. Hope everyone had a productive day full of readin', writin', and alchemy," Jeb said.

Grandmother Bluehorse shuffled into the room late, leaning on her staff. All the seats were taken. It was standing room only in the back next to Evita Lupi and Silas Lupi, the married couple.

Grandmother Bluehorse's eyes roved over the seated teachers. No one offered her a seat.

She tolerated my presence when I helped in her sophomore level herbalism class, but I wanted to do something nice for her that would make her know I wasn't like Alouette Loraline. I stood at the same time Thatch did.

"You can take my—" I started.

Thatch spoke over me, his louder voice drowning out my own. "Won't you honor me by allowing me to give you my seat?"

Darn it. So much for trying to do a good deed. Grandmother Bluehorse sat down. She sniffed the air and glanced at Pinky. That explained Thatch's motivation for being nice.

I missed what the principal had been saying. Pinky stood. Jeb motioned Pinky to the front of the room.

Jeb straightened his miniature-dragon-skull bolo tie. "For those of you who hain't met Anotklosh Johnson yet, this is our newest staff member. The professor will be teachin' History of Fae Studies. Anotklosh worked for several years at Zeme's Academy for Plant and Animal Magic. We are fortunate he—she—uh—Anotklosh became available when they experienced budgetary problems, and we were able to snatch this one up. Their loss is our gain, eh?"

Pinky gave Jeb a sidelong glance, surely wondering about the gender mix-up. How could Jeb not know what Pinky was? Didn't he have an employment form or something with Pinky's personal information?

Staff clapped with tepid enthusiasm.

"Yay," I said, clapping as hard as I could to try to inspire other teachers to welcome Pinky a little more enthusiastically. It sometimes worked with students. It didn't work on the room of adults.

"Ahem," Pinky said. "Anotklosh Johnson is my legal name, my Fae name. I prefer to be called Pinky. The kids usually call me *Mr.* Pinky."

"Oh, uh, that's right. *Mr.* Pinky." Jeb looked relieved.

I met Khaba's gaze across the room. He hid his smile under his hand. Well, there was one mystery solved.

Sebastian Reade raised his hand. "Is it true Zeme's is closing down?"

Jeb tugged at his silver beard. "I don't rightly know."

Pinky shifted from foot to foot uncomfortably. "They're downsizing so they can last the rest of the year. They haven't figured out what they're going to do about next year's enrollment. Admission is at an all-time low."

I wondered where our school was with enrollment. It seemed like we never had a shortage of charity cases: orphans or poor families who couldn't afford the other private magical schools. But the families who could afford to pay—the students with behavior problems who had been through every other school—they weren't enough to cover the costs of everyone else.

"Can I sit down?" Pinky asked.

I didn't realize how clean the air had been with him gone until he returned to the seat next to me.

"Now, this meetin' ain't just to introduce our newest staff member. We got some schedulin' issues I'd like Mr. Puck to talk to you about."

Puck sprung into place at the front of the conference table. "Good afternoon, everyone."

Teachers greeted him with the enthusiasm of zombies.

"First, I want to apologize for the lack of prophecy chocolate earlier this semester. I am swamped with scheduling this year since we let the other counselor go."

Ah, more budget cuts.

"I wonder what the second and third thing is that he's going to apologize for," Vega muttered.

Puck directed our attention to the blackboard marked with teacher schedules at the front of the room. "Some of you have been asking why so many students are in your classes this semester and why we've been shifting them around so late after our usual cutoff date for schedule changes. Largely that's due to not knowing we would have a History of Fae Studies teacher until last Friday. The names in bold on your class lists are students who are likely to be transferred out of your classes and into Mr. Pinky's."

"Thank god you have good news for a change," Jasper Jang said.

"Pardon? What's that?" Jeb asked, cupping his hand around his ear.

Grandmother Bluehorse raised her hand. "Many of those students showing up in bold on my list attended my class today. When are these students going to be switched into Mr. Pinky's?"

Jeb looked to Puck.

The little man raked a hand through his shock of hair. "I'm still working on calling in students with schedule changes. If you still have any names in bold or question marks on the list on Thursday, send those students to my office to see if they have a schedule change. I'm hoping I'll have this figured out by the end of the week, next week at the latest."

"So . . . in addition to these schedule changes, and kids on the wait list who can't get in yet, I'm going to have to wait another week to have this sorted out?" Coach Kutchi asked.

Puck said through clenched teeth, "I'm doing the best I can."

Vega muttered. "I never had to deal with this shit at Lady of the Lake School for Girls."

"You could always go back," Josie said.

The cross talk between teachers rose. Jeb looked as though he'd fallen asleep in his chair. Khaba cleared his throat, stepping forward. He redirected the meeting like a pro. "Are there any other questions regarding schedules? If not, let's move on to the next topic." He nudged Jeb.

"What? Meeting over?" Jeb stood and blinked.

"Next on the agenda is the budget," Khaba said. "Is there anything you would like to say about that, Principal Bumblebub?"

"The budget? Ah, yes, lemme see. The budget." Jeb pushed himself up. He gazed out at the teachers in the room. "It might be a little early to say, but in any case, we got ourselves a bit of a budgetin' pickle. I don't want no hard feelin's or nothin', but in the sake of bein' completely transparent, I reckon it's best to be a straight shooter. We've run into some financial issues. First it was the repairs to the greenhouse that had to be made due to a unicorn break-in."

Grandmother Bluehorse glared at me. I stared down into my lap.

"Prices of organic non-Fae food went up this year, we had additional nonpaying students added last quarter, and all and sundry of other unexpected costs." Jeb tugged on his mustache, straightening one of the curled ends. "We knew at the start of the year the budget would be tight. Even with not paying a history teacher last quarter, we're still behind in our finances. We might have been fine if we hadn't filled the History of Fae Studies position, but we need that class to provide the students with the material they need for the Fae-mandated standardized tests they'll take in the spring. If students don't meet benchmarks, we'll lose Fae funding."

Teachers turned to each other in horror. This was as bad as public schools. Only the students in public schools didn't get snatched by evil Fae who would drain them of magic and their life forces. They didn't rig the tests so students were forced to study for subjects that wouldn't help them survive in the real world. On the other hand, who actually used trigonometry formulas in daily life either?

Jasper Jang threw up his hands in disgust. "I knew it. We can't get through one staff meeting without learning someone has gotten fired or died."

"Are we going to be like Zeme's and have to close down?" Jackie Frost asked.

"Think of the children," Grandmother Bluehorse said.

Jeb's voice thundered over the teachers. He didn't even need to use magic to silence us. "Just so! That's what we're gonna need to do. Think of the students. We're fine this quarter, but third quarter we might need to cut a position. That means class size will go up halfway through this semester. It's either that or we need to cut the staff pay."

"We should cut art," Silas Lupi said. "That's what most schools do." His wife, Evita Lupi, nodded in agreement.

I glared at them. Unfortunately, it was true art was usually the first subject to be cut, at least it was in Oregon where I had previously taught.

"It's too difficult to have kids transitioning halfway through a quarter after they've missed half the lesson. You should just cut a position now and we'll deal with the increased class size from the start," Jasper Jang said.

"I agree." Vega flashed a sinister smile at me. "Cut art now."

Wouldn't that be convenient for her? Not only would she have a room to herself, but she wouldn't have to babysit me for Thatch.

Josie looked at me across the table. I wished she had sat next to me and I had someone sympathetic at my side who didn't want me to lose my job.

On the other hand, Derrick and I had been discussing how dangerous it was to teach at the school with Thatch breathing down our necks and the Raven Queen waiting for me to mess up so she could get her talons on me. If I left Womby's due to budgetary reasons, I could leave without breaking my contract.

I raised my hand. "Would it help if I resigned?"

"Yes," Coach Kutchi and Vega Bloodmire said together.

Thatch barked out a loud laugh behind me.

"What?" Josie asked.

"This is all my fault," Pinky said. "I didn't mean to disrupt a community like this."

Jeb twirled one curl of his mustache, studying me. "I don't rightly know. Do you mean that?"

Thatch guffawed louder. "Miss Lawrence is joking."

"No, I'm not," I said, turning to him.

"Aren't you the comedian? I'm sure you used to be the class clown when you were in school." Thatch's eyes narrowed in warning.

Great. He probably suspected I was up to something now.

"Um, well, I ain't rightly sure what we're gonna do about our budgetin' concerns, but I reckon it's too soon to lay off any teachers yet. I'm headin' out tomorrow to wrangle up some donors. We can reevaluate the situation closer to the end of the quarter." Jeb offered me a hopeful smile.

"Any other business before we adjourn?" Khaba asked.

The room grew as silent as a graveyard. I took it everyone wanted out of there.

As the teachers filed out, Josie made her way toward me. "What were you thinking?" She punched me in the arm.

"Ow!" I rubbed the charley horse and scooted back. "What was that for?"

"Why would you offer yourself up like a sacrificial lamb?" she demanded.

Thatch's British monotone slithered through the murmur of departing teachers. "Because Miss Lawrence *is* a sacrificial lamb."

Josie wagged a finger at me. "You're too legit to quit."

I wanted to explain my logic to her, but I couldn't with Thatch looming over me like a grim reaper.

"Boy, I really feel awful about this," Pinky said again. "At other schools they always get rid of the newest faculty members first and shift classes around so the senior teachers fill in the core classes."

"Yeah, well, this is only my first year. I don't have tenure," I said.

"No one has tenure," Josie said.

"That isn't quite true," Thatch said. *He* probably had tenure. "Miss Lawrence, if you don't mind, we have matters of your education to discuss.

It might be prudent to think about your future before you decide you no longer need to stay and learn the most fundamental skills to survive in this world."

"I can't talk now," I said. "I have plans with Josie." I raised my eyebrows, hoping Josie would get the hint and cover for me.

Josie nodded emphatically. "Yeah, we have some students to discuss who we want to make sure pass—"

"Just as I thought, you have nothing better to do." He shoved me to the door. "To the dungeon if you please."

I didn't want to talk to him. I wanted to see Derrick. Even so, I left the conference room in the admin tower, went down the stairs to the great hall, and trudged toward the dungeon. Thatch walked ahead, his brisk legs leaving me behind. I didn't jog to keep up with him as I usually would have.

He waited outside the stairwell down to the dungeon. He crossed his arms and leaned against the banister, affecting a lazy, indifferent pose. I tried not to stare at the painting of my biological mother that hung on the wall. She was striking with her midnight hair contrasting against her pale skin. Her gown was old-fashioned and Victorian, not that much different from the clothes Miss Periwinkle wore. The emerald green of a snake coiled around her arm, the head reared up and about to strike the raven swooping down from the edge of the painting. More black silhouettes of birds in flight circled the background.

Those birds had been absent the last time I'd gazed at the painting. When I glanced at the painting out of the corner of my eye, the birds shifted, and I thought I saw a shadow swoop across Alouette Loraline's face.

Thatch studied me as I approached. "You have your mother's eyes."

I tried not to think about Harry Potter.

"Um. Thanks." The dark eyes in the painting looked nothing like my green eyes. Alouette Loraline's expression was mocking, sneaky.

"It wasn't a compliment," Thatch said. "You have a sneaky look about you."

I followed him down the stairs into his moldy hellhole. We passed through his classroom, into the detention room, which was basically a dungeon with shackles and cells, through a smaller room with torture equipment, and traveled down the short hallway to his office. The semester must have been going well for Thatch if he hadn't shackled anyone to the walls to make them die of boredom today.

Thatch closed the door to his office behind us. He seated himself on the other side of his desk in his cushy ergonomic chair. I took the uncomfortable metal torture chair, trying to avoid the bolts sticking out that would snag on my skirt and striped leggings.

Priscilla ruffled her feathers in the cage in the corner, watching me with a beady eye.

Thatch folded his hands in front of him at his desk. His lips drew away from his mouth in an attempt at a smile. The expression didn't reach his eyes. He waited.

I hated it when he did this. Awkward silences were one of my weaknesses.

"Look, I know why you want to talk to me," I started.

"You aren't allowed to quit."

"It's my choice."

His lips stretched even tighter across his face. He said nothing.

"You heard what they said in there," I said. "Half the teachers wanted me gone. It would solve Jeb's problems."

"As usual, you're being overdramatic. Two teachers expressed favor of your position being cut. That isn't the same as 'half the teachers.' You've never been one to allow morons to bully you before. Why now?" He waited.

When I didn't answer, he went on. "Have you thought this through? Where will you go? You've always insisted you wanted to learn magic. Do you think you can go back to living in the Morty Realm? We both know you'll accidentally slip up and get snatched by Fae. That leaves living in the Unseen Realm, where you will have even less protection against Fae. Neither option will help you against the Raven Court. You won't stand a chance. What exactly is your plan?"

I couldn't tell him about running away with Derrick. "I don't know."

"Why would you want to quit a job we both know you love?"

"How do you know I love it here? At the start of last semester, you told me how hard it was going to be working here. And you were right. It isn't like teaching in the Morty Realm. You said everyone would hate me, students would attack me because I don't have magic, I would mess up, and you would drain me."

He leaned back in his seat. "I was being . . . harsh. I'm not going to drain you. Yes, students and teachers have attacked you, but you've done surprisingly well. If you stay, you will continue to do so."

I tried another tactic. "If they intend to fire me, now would be an appropriate time to leave."

"Jeb is not going to fire you. This school needs you. The students need you. Think about Imani and Hailey and Maddy. You've done so much good for them, and you'll continue to do so." He steepled his fingers underneath his chin. "Pray, tell me why you've changed your mind about teaching here." His voice softened, and there was actual concern in his eyes. "What happened?"

I stared at the ground, tears filling my eyes. It would have been so much easier if he had yelled at me, but he had to act nice.

I did love Womby's. I had always wanted to teach at a magic school. I felt like I belonged here. Even Grandmother Bluehorse didn't hate me now. I'd gained the students' respect and admiration last semester when I'd performed Morty magic—a.k.a. the Heimlich maneuver.

"I know what this is about." His tone was gentle.

I swallowed and risked looking up at him. His eyes were pitying. Did he know that I'd uncursed Derrick and he remembered me? He didn't seem angry, but then I never could tell how he would react to anything. Sometimes he was friendly and kind. Other times he blew up over me accidentally catching a poster on fire in my classroom.

"It's about my behavior of late," he said.

"What?" My worry turned to confusion.

"I've been distracted. Unprofessional." He left his chair and came around to sit on the edge of his desk nearer to me. "I realize I've been spiteful and unfriendly to you at times. In my attempt to make up for my previous lack of professional boundaries with you, I have worked to ensure you wouldn't become too . . . attached. I apologize if I . . . hurt your feelings. When I told you I wasn't interested in you last week, it wasn't my intention to be cruel." He swallowed. "I know what it's like to pine for someone who has no interest in you, to work with them side by side for years, and for it to eat away at you."

I shook my head. "No, that's not—no!" That was the last thing I wanted him to think. Yes, we had kissed, and I was fairly certain the attraction had been mutual in the moment, but much of that had been magic. Our affinities had that effect on people and each other. We both knew that.

Had that kiss only been a few days ago? I'd already moved on. But I supposed he didn't know that. Had I not been so focused on Derrick, I might have been hurt by the way Thatch had pushed me away.

He frowned. "I should have handled things differently." He laced his fingers together on his knee, staring down at his hands. "Can we put that behind us and work together as colleagues and equals? Do you think we can be . . . friends?"

"Friends," I repeated. "I've tried to . . . I've wanted to. . . ." It felt impossible now with all the things Derrick had told me. I wanted to believe Felix Thatch was my friend and he cared about me. I didn't want to believe he was still the servant of the Raven Queen and he was only keeping me safe so she could use me later.

At the same time, I trusted Derrick's judgment. He had never lied to me and in the years I had known him, he'd always had my best intentions at heart. I wished I'd been able to talk to him. The conflicting emotions in me swelled so high I felt like they might burst through the dam I had carefully constructed to keep all that locked away.

Had Felix Thatch been anyone else, he might have hugged me or taken my hand. But I knew better than to even try. Touch was always going to be out of the question. Instead, he poked me under my chin with his wand to make me meet his eyes.

He offered me a hopeful smile. "Shall we be friends?"

I pushed the wand away. "If you were my friend, you would tell me the truth." I needed to know about Derrick and the secrets Thatch had been keeping from me.

He chewed on his lip as if thinking it over. "Perhaps."

"No. Not perhaps. You would. A real friend wouldn't lie."

He nodded solemnly. "What is it you wish to know?"

"Promise me you won't lie." I stared into the storm clouds of his eyes, trying to decipher if I saw sincerity there, but I didn't know when he was telling the truth and when he wasn't. I still didn't know if he'd told me the truth about his childhood and he'd been raised by the Raven Queen and suffered from her cruelty—or if that had just been a story to try to make me sympathetic of him.

"As usual, my Celestor abilities of divination make your question clear in my mind. Let's just get this confession over with." He sighed. "I'm in love with Gertrude Periwinkle."

# CHAPTER FIFTEEN
## Join the Dark Side—We Have Cookies!

Felix Thatch must have been the worst Celestor ever—which would make sense because he wasn't actually a Celestor. Since sleeping with Miss Periwinkle he'd become a brainless moron who couldn't see past his nose. She had to be sucking his Celestor divination powers away with her siren magic. Or maybe that's what love did to people. All I knew was I wasn't like that with Derrick.

"That isn't a secret," I said.

His brows furrowed together. "Isn't it?"

"No. Everyone knows."

"As usual, you exaggerate. Surely not *everyone*."

"You don't have a subtle bone in your body. It's obvious who you hate." Most of the year that had been me. "It's obvious who you love. I'm happy for you. Really."

He looked completely surprised. For once I was the smart one out of the two of us. I laughed.

"And you aren't . . . hurt?" he asked.

"You deserve each other. The two of you make a cute couple." Besides the fact that they were both a little bit wicked, he had pined for Miss Periwinkle before my biological mother had aged her. He had continued to be interested in her and friends with her even while she'd looked like an old woman. It was romantic and sweet.

His squinted at me. "I don't understand. What do you want to know about, then?"

"Derrick."

He pinched the bridge of his nose. "Not this again."

"You never gave me that spell."

"Is that all?" He waved me off dismissively. "I was busy. I forgot. I'll put it in your box."

I knew what he was busy doing. Or *who* he was busy doing.

"I need to know about him. Why are you trying to keep us apart?"

"Is this the reason you want to leave? You're jealous I have someone I'm in love with, and you have no one?"

"No!" Why did everything have to revolve around him and Miss Periwinkle? Then again, if I hadn't realized Derrick was right under my nose and I could be with him, maybe I would be resentful about him and Miss Periwinkle. "Look, I just want the truth. You say we're friends and I'm a colleague, but you won't tell me about his curse."

He nodded solemnly. "Indeed, I have been keeping secrets from you about Derrick. I've feared if I told you the entirety of the truth you might do something rash and accidentally destroy the counter curses I put in place to protect you both."

Finally, it sounded as though he intended to tell me everything. I leaned forward. This is what I needed to hear to clear up everything.

"You're an adult. I should treat you like one." He tidied an already tidy stack of papers.

The way he didn't meet my eye might have been embarrassment. Or guilt. I nodded in encouragement.

He cleared his throat. "I need to get over my distrust of other Witchkin and learn to reciprocate—"

Someone knocked on the door.

Thatch stood, his head tilted to his side, a hopeful smile on his face. "Come in."

Miss Periwinkle strode through the door, wand in hand. A tray of tea levitated in front of her.

"Are those biscuits?" Thatch asked. "For me? That's unexpected."

Oh no! Not cookies. His weakness. I suspected he'd do just about anything for his doggie biscuit.

"It's just a little something I picked up in town." Her eyes narrowed at the sight of me.

The tray clipped me on the shoulder as it floated by.

"I do hope I'm not interrupting." The tray dropped noisily onto his desk.

"Not at all. Miss Lawrence and I were simply having a conference about her future at the school." He shooed me off like he would have one of the students. "Miss Lawrence, we can discuss these matters later."

I crossed my arms. "No, we need to talk about this now."

Miss Periwinkle batted her eyelashes. "If you need to speak with Miss Lawrence, and now is an inconvenient time, I quite understand. I can go back to the library." She turned toward the door. "Sebastian Reade and

Darshan Rohiniraman were asking me for assistance earlier with some research they're doing. I'll simply come back after—"

That manipulative witch!

He snagged her around her elbow. "There's no need to rush off. We can have tea now." He steered her toward his chair. "Please, take my seat." He waved me off again. "Miss Lawrence is leaving." His voice was stern and unyielding. He didn't take out his wand, but I knew that would be his next step.

Miss Periwinkle hid her smirk behind a cup of tea.

"How about we finish this conversation after dinner," I said.

Thatch nodded, but his eyes were glued on Miss Periwinkle. Some friend he was. Why did it not surprise me the dungeon was locked up after dinner?

I wanted to see Derrick, but he wasn't in his room. I worried where he could be. Khaba could help me.

I peeked in the administration wing, hoping to catch Khaba. His door was closed. His voice thundered from the other side. "Don't tell me it's 'no big deal.' If you know one of your friends has decided to run off and apprentice with an avian delivery service, the school needs to know. You can't just not report it and think we won't notice someone is absent from classes." I'd never heard Khaba raise his voice to anyone. He was always so friendly and calm.

The girl within the office said something too quiet for me to hear through the closed door.

Khaba's voice couldn't have carried louder if the walls had been made of rice paper. "No, you don't know it was her choice. That Fae may have coerced her or enchanted her. Students don't have the defenses or skills to be able to tell the difference. You need an adult to look over employment agreements to make sure you aren't selling your souls. You're too young and too naive to realize that *nice* lady with black wings and an employment offer that seemed too good to be true was too good to be true."

The description sounded like the woman could have been someone from the Raven Court.

Khaba shouted. "Friends don't let friends sign contracts in blood, especially not with Fae."

I'd never heard Khaba go this long without using a pun.

"You're Fae," she said louder, in a cheeky tone that could only belong to a teenager.

"I am indentured to this school—not an emissary of the Raven Court. My loyalties lie with all you snot-nosed brats who insist on running straight into the hands of your enemies."

The girl began to cry. I felt bad for her. She'd let her friend get lured in by some kind of scheme. I had always thought the Fae weren't supposed to be able to snatch kids or drain their souls in this realm without reason. It was in the Morty Realm that Witchkin had to be careful not to use magic or break any rules. But it sounded like the Raven Court was always pushing those boundaries to their benefit.

I walked downstairs to the counseling department where the teacher mailboxes were. Thatch still hadn't placed the spell in there. No surprise. A spider scuttled into the shadows of my box. As I ascended the stairs to Khaba's office, Juliet Stevens ran out in tears. First semester she had been in my seventh-period advanced art class. I wondered which of her friends had been lured away.

I waved at Khaba from the door. Today he wore a magenta zebra-striped shirt halfway unbuttoned.

He leaned his head into a hand, looking more depressed than I'd ever seen him. "Another one bites the dust. It's the second student we've lost in one week. A record."

"What do you mean by 'lost?' Like dropped out? Or snatched?"

He opened a drawer and removed a large glass jar full of sweets from within, plopping it on his desk with a thud. "Don't you ever wonder where students go who disappear from your class list?"

"I always thought they were being transferred to a different class or a different school."

He popped the lid off the jar and selected a neon-green candy. "Womby's is the end of the line. Students don't go here unless they have to. If they drop out of magic school early, it isn't good. Either they've been seduced by black magic or they've done something to get themselves snatched." He held out the jar to me.

I shook my head. I didn't want the mood-enhancing properties of his magical Prozac right now.

Khaba scowled. "Lachlan Falls is usually a safe place for students because we're on the border of the Unseen Realm and not directly in the Faerie Realm. Usually townsfolk keep an eye on students and look out for them." The instant Khaba placed the candy in his mouth, the tension left his frame. He relaxed into his chair. "Unfortunately, the Raven Court has been offering students 'employment opportunities.' If this keeps up, we're going to have to ban Lachlan Falls, except for escorted outings."

"Oh no!" The Raven Court had been swooping in on my students? How much of that was directed toward me? I had heard the Raven Queen say in Derrick's memory how she intended to use Derrick to get to me. What if she was now using my students to do the same? I didn't want to endanger their lives by staying at the school.

Khaba pushed the candy into one cheek, talking around it. "Can you imagine what a mess that is going to be to monitor? And how am I going to get teachers to agree to spend their evenings and weekends babysitting students on field trips to that damned Internet café?" He leaned back in his chair, a smile on his face, despite the gravity of his words as the candy worked its magic on him.

He might have felt better, but I didn't. What if the Raven Court had snatched Derrick? I glanced over my shoulder and moved to close the door. "I'm concerned about Derrick. Have you seen him? Has he checked in with you today? Or yesterday?"

"No. When's the last time you saw him?" His cheerful expression was too buoyant for the occasion.

"Sunday night."

"Oh. That isn't good. He usually stops in and drops off confiscated items or fills out reports on student infractions a few times a day, even on weekends. I thought it was odd he hadn't turned in any reports, but I also suspected he was distracted." He arched an eyebrow at me, his smirk sly, as if to imply I was the distraction. "And then he never came back to see if we could delve further into his memories, but I thought that might be explained by him not being ready to face those memories."

"Do you think something's happened to him? Maybe the Raven Queen snatched him. What should we do?"

He pointed to his back. "Get over here." He unbuttoned his shirt. "I need you to wish to find Derrick."

Today the lamp had migrated below his shoulder blades. I rubbed the knots in his muscle.

"Are you imagining your wish?" he asked.

I focused. "Yes."

"Ask out loud."

"I wish Derrick was here."

He chuckled, the good-mood candy making him sound more devious than friendly. "That's a nice idea, but let's start with *where* he is. I have limits to my powers. My magic doesn't extend far beyond the school and the grounds. I can't retrieve Derrick from off campus, and I can't transport myself beyond our boundaries—which is why I have to walk to Lachlan Falls just like everyone else. Once in a while I can transport myself if it's school business, but that takes more magic and far more rubbing."

I'd never known how his magic worked. This made sense why the art supplies he'd scrounged up for me with my wish last semester had been kind of crappy.

"So you can't ever leave here?" I asked.

"No, not with magic. Your mother saw to it that I was truly bound to the school. Not a slave to the lamp, and not stuck in the small confines of a lamp, but limited in my abilities. I can only grant wishes related to school business, not for my own personal gain." He snapped his fingers and pointed to his back. "You aren't rubbing. And you aren't thinking about your wish."

My hands were getting tired, but I dug into his muscles harder. I focused on what I wanted. "I wish I knew where Derrick was."

I considered thinking about kissing Derrick and seeing if I could enhance Khaba's powers but decided that might not be the best after the way he'd reacted to that spark of electricity on Sunday night.

"That's enough," Khaba said.

I stepped aside.

Khaba lifted his crystal ball. It started off the size of his palm but slowly decreased in size, resembling a marble. He waved a hand over his desk. The wood and paper trays wavered, sections of the desk changing to gray, other places turning green. As the desk transformed, it became clearer that we were looking down at the school from a bird's-eye view. Leave it to Khaba to create a magical version of Google Earth.

He set the marble-sized crystal in the crumbling section of the school where Derrick's room was located. "Show me where Derrick is," Khaba said.

The ball spun in a circle, wiggling one direction and then another as if trying to make up its mind. It rolled away from the debris, along the path to Lachlan Falls. Khaba pinched his fingers together. The map's details shrank in size, the school smaller and the map showing the forest. It rolled along the path. Khaba made the image smaller so that the village and the farms fit onto his desk.

The marble rolled into the village, closer to the edge of his desk. It hesitated at the perimeter of farmland before springing away from the desk and toward the wall. Khaba shot out a hand to catch the crystal before it smashed into the file cabinet.

The map faded.

"He's not on school grounds. I'd be able to see it if he was," Khaba said. The crystal swelled to the size it had been previously.

"Oh," I said in disappointment.

"We can try again later."

I nodded. I wanted to hope we'd have better results later, but I couldn't. I wanted to do something to help Derrick, but I didn't know what I could do.

"He might not have been kidnapped by the Raven Court. He might be looking for those invisible pants." He leaned toward me, the smile from his sweets gone. "Don't go looking for him."

"I didn't say I was going to."

He rubbed his bald head. "You didn't have to. It was in your eyes." He opened his file cabinet to the middle drawer of confiscated items and pulled out a bottle of alcohol. "I need more than sweets. Want a drink?"

"What do you have?" I wasn't big on alcohol. If it was something fruity I might not mind.

He flashed a smile and turned the label so I could see it was Bombay Sapphire. "I dream of gin."

That sounded like the punny Khaba I knew and loved.

Thatch probably could find Derrick, but his door was locked. The mirror was covered so I couldn't see him from the mirror hallway to determine if he was alone. Plus, I wasn't sure I trusted him with the truth. There was no way I trusted Vega. Pro Ro was supposed to be one of the best at divination. He was our soothsaying teacher. If I got his help, it didn't mean I had to tell him all the details.

I went up to his room and knocked on his door. I feared asking for his assistance was a lost cause, but I had to try.

The moment Pro Ro opened the door, his smile turned to a grimace. "Women aren't supposed to be in the men's dormitories."

I did my best not to let his grumpy expression get me down. "I'm not in your dorm. I'm in the hallway."

"What do you want?" he asked.

The strained smile on my face made my cheeks ache. "I wondered if I could ask you a small favor with—"

"I'm done doing favors for you."

I spoke quickly before he could slam the door in my face. "I'm sorry about trying to forcibly remove your turban and accusing you of cursing me. I didn't realize you were trying to protect me."

He crossed his arms and glowered at me.

"I need some help divining. I know you're really good and—"

"Haven't I already done enough for you? I covered your morning duties last semester so Thatch could give you lessons in the morning. You never even thanked me."

"I'm sorry. I didn't know. No one told me you did that. Thank you."

He closed the door in my face.

I wrote a note to Thatch to remind him to give me a copy of the spell and placed it in his mailbox. Since I didn't know what else to do, I practiced my magical exercises and went to bed. I tossed and turned so much Vega shouted at me.

On Wednesday morning I was tired and nowhere closer to finding out where Derrick had gone. The dungeon was locked up before school.

I checked my box again, and there was the spell. Thatch had given it to me! On one hand, I didn't actually need it to break Derrick's curse. But I could ask someone if it was legit and try to figure out Thatch's intentions with Derrick.

# CHAPTER SIXTEEN
## Bargaining with the Devil

During lunch duty I showed the spell to Josie. "What do you think this spell does?" There was no label at the top with the words: "Invisibility Cure" or "Un-hexing Someone After the Raven Queen Has Her Way with Him."

A student threw a sandwich at another teenager. I ran off to remind students food was for eating, not throwing. Someone slipped on the sandwich, and I had to walk that student down to the nurse's office. If the student who had slipped and hurt his arm hadn't been Ben O'Sullivan, I might have felt bad about taking him to Nurse Hilda with her healing elixirs full of bat poop.

When I made it back to the cafeteria, Josie handed me the paper. "I guess the spell looks okay. It's pretty complex, not the sort of spell I'd want to try. I'm more concerned about those ingredients. They're powerful, but near impossible to acquire. Did Thatch actually expect you to collect a dragon egg?"

"No, he wanted Bart the unicorn to get it for me."

She lowered her voice. "And the unicorn semen as a substitute for a unicorn horn? Where were you supposed to get that?"

"Um. . . ." I'd never told her I had collected that one. "Yes. Don't ask."

"OMG. I just barfed in my mouth. Okay, so maybe some of these are actually feasible." She tapped the parchment with her finger. "You know who I think would be a good resource to ask about this?"

"Please don't say Pro Ro."

"Vega."

Vega Bloodmire didn't do any favors without asking for something in return. What I could offer her, I couldn't guess. I was afraid I might have to give up something vital like my blood or all the space in my wardrobe.

Derrick was worth it.

My room was empty when I went up after school, save for the nightingales singing in their cage. They sang a beautiful song that filled the room with music. I considered letting the birds out to escape, but I figured that would piss Vega off, and I was trying to get on her good side.

It was hard to focus on meditation exercises for my affinity, or to do any of the practice I was supposed to be doing as my magical homework. All I could think about was Derrick. I got out my sketchbook and tried to draw his face from memory. Twice in my life that I remembered, magic had come out as I'd been drawing. Once I had been touching Derrick while I drew. The other time I had been thinking about him. I hadn't known what I'd been doing either time. I still didn't, but I wondered if I could combine my art skills with my magic skills and divine something useful about Derrick.

I started with the general proportions of a face, sketching the horizontal lines that showed the placement of the eyes, brows, nose, and mouth before I added a line of symmetry. While I did this, I focused on my question from earlier: *Where is Derrick?*

I visualized pouring energy into the affinity dwelling in my core. I imagined that energy pushing up into my chest and down my arms into my hands. It was a lot to think about, which may have been why my first drawing of Derrick didn't look anything like him. The second one resembled him, but his expression was pained. I pressed too hard with the pencil, digging the graphite into the paper so that even when I erased and redrew his features, Derrick's eyes looked bruised and haunted from the previous lines showing through. I couldn't tell if I was divining or just a bad artist.

Vega stormed into the room during my third drawing. I closed the sketchbook, not wanting her to see. She marched over to the dressing screen and ducked behind it, throwing her flapper-chic business attire over the top edge.

"Ugh, if I have to put up with that bag of fleas asking me one more question, I'm going to curse him," she said from behind the screen.

"Pinky?" I asked.

"Who else?"

Her wardrobe doors popped open. A black silk pajama top and pants flew across the room and dropped behind the screen.

"That furbag is always asking insipid questions. 'Where is the copy machine? How do I write up detentions? What's the procedure for students who don't show up to class?' Ugh. New teachers. Don't you hate them?"

"Heh." I was still a new teacher. "I imagine it's hard starting at a school midyear."

"Wah, wah, call the wambulance." Vega emerged from behind the screen and dropped her clothes on the floor in front of the full-length mirror. "I know what will make me feel better."

I also knew what usually put her in a better mood. "How about some candy?" I asked, trying to be a good influence.

"Not even close." She strode over to the birdcage, her smile sinister.

"Can't you feed your plant grasshoppers or mice? Do you have to do this?"

She ignored me. She snatched up one of the birds. The song became discordant and chaotic in the bird's fright. I looked away, knowing what she was about to do next. The birdsong cut out. I peeked at the plus-sized Venus flytrap on her wardrobe. One of the jaws was closed, a large lump struggling within.

All things being considered, I was lucky she hadn't fed me to her plant.

"So, um, I was wondering if you could help me with my homework," I asked.

"No. Get one of your friends to help you."

"It's homework from Thatch. He said only highly skilled Celestors would be able to understand the spell."

"Flattery isn't going to work." She lifted her nose in the air. "I'm not a narcissistic siren."

Flattery had worked in the past.

"Just look at the spell. It won't take long."

She continued watching her plant devour the bird.

"I'll pay you," I said.

She snorted. "To do your homework?"

"No, you wouldn't be doing my homework for me. You would be helping me. Like a tutor. I want to know if this is a legitimate spell or if Thatch is punking me. I don't know if—"

She gathered up her bathroom bag and walked out as I was talking. Apparently, I was that insignificant. On the plus side, she hadn't said no that time. Maybe she was thinking about it.

When she came back, I held the spell out to show her. "Will you look? I'll do something in exchange if you want. I can help clean your classroom or make posters for something you're teaching or—"

She made a face. "There's nothing you could possibly offer me that would interest me. If you ask me again, I'll hex you."

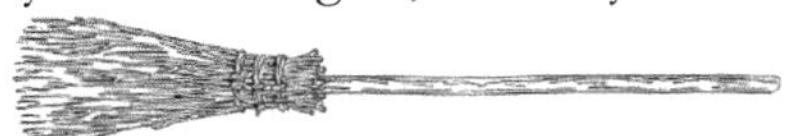

I was confident if I knew what Vega wanted, I would be able to spark her interest enough that she would hear me out. The problem was, I didn't think I had anything worth bribing Vega. I couldn't grade papers for her because I didn't know the subject matter. She wouldn't let me sub for her because she thought I was incompetent. And in reality, I was a beginner at magic, so she was right.

She hadn't seemed excited by the idea of me paying her.

I went to bed anxious. It was no wonder I had bad dreams. I kept seeing the Raven Queen in the dungeon torturing Derrick.

Before breakfast and then again after school on Thursday, I looked in Derrick's room since it wasn't locked. Everything was the same, including his note. I used the hall of mirrors to see—I wasn't even sure what I might see that would be useful. I just knew I couldn't sit by and do nothing.

I swung by Thatch's room three times. It was locked before school, an oddity for the morning person I knew Thatch to be. He sent me away when I stopped in during my prep period because he was teaching. After school the dungeon was locked again. Considering students were usually chained up in detention, this was usual behavior for Thatch.

I found Khaba patrolling the halls after dinner. I hoped he had heard something about Derrick.

He waved, but his expression was grim.

I jogged up to him. "Any news?"

"Sorry, hon. Not yet."

I lowered my voice to a whisper. "Can we go into town and see if there are any clues about where Derrick went?"

"Tomorrow I have to go into Lachlan Falls on errands. If you come with me, we'll make a few extra stops and see if anyone saw anything."

"While we're in town, could I stop at—"

"No Happy Hal's Tavern and Internet Café. You are not to leave my sight." His words came out harsh and sharp.

"Okay," I said.

He patted my arm. "Too many students have been snatched. Trouble is brewing in the Faerie Realm. I can feel it."

I would have liked to call my fairy godmother and ask her advice via the café's computer, but I would have to write her a letter instead. I went to the staff mailboxes to see if Thatch had written me a note to tell me when our next lesson would be. There was nothing in my box. I left him a note.

A scuff of noise from farther down the hall attracted my attention. I walked past the conference room to the next office. Puck sat in his Zen garden, papers flying in a cyclone around him. I ducked back out, not wanting to break his concentration.

As I passed the conference room, I stopped. The schedules were still posted, as were the duties. Being a new teacher, I had done breakfast duty for two months before I'd been switched to lunch duty three times a week. Students behaved better during breakfast. They were quiet and too sleepy to think of doing much. The downside was getting up earlier to be there for an hour and then rushing to class.

Vega had breakfast duty in the cafeteria twice a week for the next month, lunch duty once a week, and dinner duty three times a week. She'd gotten off easy, but a duty was still a duty. No one liked duties.

Maybe I did have something I could use to entice Vega.

I sat at the desk, writing my mom a letter since I didn't have Internet. The last nightingale sang a lonely song, expressing my own grief and fear with its sweet notes. I didn't look forward to adding breakfast to my schedule, but there were worse things. Like never seeing Derrick again.

I stood and stretched. Out the window, the school cast jagged shadows onto the gloomy trees toward Lachlan Falls. A lone figure strode across the school grounds past the topiary animals and toward the trees. In the dying light, it was difficult to see any details of the figure other than it was a woman in all black with a witch's hat. Her blonde hair and long cloak wafted behind her. It might have been Miss Periwinkle. Possibly Evita Lupi, because she also was blonde, but she didn't typically wear all black. Miss Keahi, Grandmother Bluehorse and Josie all wore witch hats, but none of them had fair hair.

The woman hesitated at the edge of the forest, glancing over her shoulder in a way I recognized from countless students about to do something sneaky. She crept into the forest. Was Gertrude Periwinkle meeting her not-so-secret lover for a tryst in the woods? Or was she doing something more diabolical? A few seconds later, a bird rose from the trees into the air and flew off and away. It might have been a raven, or Priscilla, or another bird. I couldn't tell.

Vega strode in. She was earlier than usual. "Get out of my way. I need the desk." She elbowed me to the side, searching through the drawers.

"What do you think Miss Periwinkle would be doing in the woods right as it's growing dark?"

"Probably having sex with one of her boyfriends. Not that I care."

"She only has one boyfriend."

"Gertrude might be a Celestor, but she's young and beautiful again, and there's no shortage of siren magic in her." She found a box of paper clips in one of the drawers and retrieved it. "Do you know how annoying it was to take her dancing with me? She stole the attention of all the good dancers—and the good-looking dancers. I don't know which of them she went home with."

It was hard to tell if this was true considering this information came from Vega's twisted perspective on reality. Anything that didn't revolve around her was inconsequential, and she was unlikely to have those facts right.

"She has a boyfriend," I said.

"I think you mean she has *several* boyfriends."

"No way! Her and Thatch are dating."

Vega snorted. "No, they aren't."

"Remember that day we saw him in the courtyard this week? He was acting all gushy, and you said it was gross. Who did you think he was in love with?"

"I just thought someone had bewitched him with a temporary spell. What do I care?" She started toward the door.

"Do you like dinner duty?"

"No." She kept walking.

"If I cover your duty this week, will you do a favor for me? It won't take long—only five minutes."

Her footsteps faltered. "I'm listening."

I held out the spell.

Vega huffed in disgust. "Is this your homework?"

"I just want you to tell me what it does."

She unfolded it and examined the list. "He expects you to do this kind of magic for your homework. Ha!"

"No. I was supposed to collect the ingredients. I want to know if the spell is real or busywork."

"Thatch is playing a joke on you. There's no way you could collect these ingredients. Those bleeding-heart liberals outlawed dragon eggs after some fucktard Witchkins hunted them to near extinction. Unicorn horns are also—oh, never mind. That's a valid substitute." She skimmed the list. "Virgin's blood or tears. Well, you shouldn't have any trouble with that considering how ugly you are. I can't imagine a man ever touching you."

I held my tongue. Now was not the time to boast that Derrick found me attractive.

She turned the paper over. "Where are the instructions?"

"He didn't give them to me."

"That's probably for the best. Whatever this potion does, it isn't meant for an unskilled Amni Plandai." She looked me up and down.

"Do you mean me?" I asked.

"Duh. Aren't you an Amni Plandai without any training?"

I looked her straight in the eye, trying not to flinch as I lied. "I don't know. My affinity hasn't been tested. Or sorted."

She studied me thoughtfully. She didn't bring up the time electricity had crackled under my skin, and I'd almost shot lightning out at her, but maybe she underestimated what I was capable of.

"Everyone always implies you have some kind of fertility affinity—nymph or siren from the way Jeb went on about not allowing dating because sexual energies might release your powers." Her gaze lingered on my small chest. "I suppose you'd be a little more to look at if you were descended from a fertility goddess. Gertrude, now she's obvious. In any case, you aren't a siren. Certainly not a Celestor."

I tried to redirect her attention back to the list. "So you can't tell what the spell is for?"

"Something big. It will require top-notch skill and the ability to harness an incredible amount of energy. I'm sure I could do it—whatever it is. It might take twenty Josie Kimuras to do a spell like this. Probably fifty fleabag sasquatches. A hundred of you."

She strode to her bookshelf, leafing through a dusty tome. She rifled through the pages. "Of course, a coven of Amni Plandai would probably use a spell like this for something paltry like saving a rainforest or healing an aging dragon's liver." She skimmed the book. "Unicorn horn is for healing—obviously. The dragon egg contains powerful properties against venom, plagues, and hexes. The virgin's blood is typically restorative. It could be a fountain of youth spell." She smoothed a hand over the flawless skin of her cheek. "Did Gertrude use this spell recently? I wouldn't mind clearing up a few wrinkles myself."

"Miss Periwinkle didn't have this list or any fancy ingredients. I think she might have used an anti-glamour spell."

She held out her hand. "Let me see it again."

I handed it over. Vega waved her wand over the paper and incanted in another language. The words of the spell floated up from the page, shifting and rearranging themselves in a complicated dance. The air tasted like cinnamon and starlight.

She waved a hand over her books on the shelves. The volumes glowed. Words drifted out of the pages in different fonts and colors. Words in the other texts that matched my ingredient list glowed in vivid purple. Vega pushed one set of words aside and waved another away. Spells with bat dung, *Tanacetum parthenium*—feverfew, unicorn horn, and dragon's egg spiraled into the air. Not all the spells contained matching words. She flicked them away.

I understood what she was doing. It was a keyword search. She was trying to find a match for the potion. This was way better than an index or a card catalog.

"Wow," I said, breathlessly watching the grace and beauty of Vega's magic.

Her spell was amazingly beautiful. It reminded me of Miss Periwinkle's reading chair with all the words scrolling by.

"It's a simple summoning charm to find a selection of text," she said.

The words from the books faded away like forgotten dreams upon waking.

"It appears I don't have this potion in any of my books."

"Oh," I said. Another dead end. I thought of Thatch's spell to examine other books remotely. "Can you look in the library? Or in Thatch's books?"

She sat on her bed. "I suppose I could go to the library and see if the spells in one of those books might match." She raised an eyebrow in challenge. "But it will cost you more than this week's duties."

"How much?"

"I figure about five minutes of my time doing this is worth about one hour of your time doing a duty. We'll see how long it takes us. I'll help you with this spell tomorrow after school." She stood, opened her hand, and the paper clips from the desk leapt onto her palm. "Until then, I have papers to grade."

Wow. I had convinced Vega to help me. As far as selling my soul to the devil went, this could have been worse. I didn't know if anything would come of this, but I felt better I was trying to help Derrick in the only way I knew how.

Vega paused at the door. "By the way, you can start covering my dinner duty tomorrow. You're welcome."

Khaba was next on my list to visit again. I stopped by at seven in the evening, but he wasn't in his office. I went to Josie's room and asked her if she knew where he was. She sat on her bed, knitting.

"I think Jeb scheduled a meeting with Khaba."

"Was it about students going missing?" Or Derrick?

"He didn't say. I just hope it wasn't about Jeb losing answer keys again." She retrieved Thatch's pants from her table in the corner. The seam had been repaired, either by magic or by Josie's flawless sewing skills.

"Thank you! They look exactly the same as when I borrowed them."

"No problem." She shrugged. "It's up to you to get this back to his room. That's the true test."

I had an idea that didn't involve getting caught by Miss Periwinkle this time. I hoped to slip them into my laundry bushel with a note that said these were Thatch's pants, and I had gotten them by mistake. If I was lucky, the brownies would return them to his closet for me.

I showed up at Khaba's office after Art Club on Friday. I was supposed to meet with Vega to go to the library and research that spell, but I'd left her a note to let her know I had business with Khaba first. I hoped he would be ready to go to Lachlan Falls.

"Any word?" I asked.

"No." He stood up from his desk. "And we're going now, before someone sends me another student in need of disciplinary action."

"To Lachlan Falls?" I was so hopeful and excited my words came out as a shout. I lowered my voice. "To look for Derrick?"

He nodded. "I don't want us out after dark. The Raven Court isn't supposed to do any snatching in the Unseen Realm, not unless someone violates a law. But their powers are strongest at night. I don't want them to lure us into a trap."

I nodded, following him out like a puppy. Sooner was fine. He closed the door to his office behind us. The lock clicked into place, even without using a key. He snapped his fingers. A sign on the door appeared that said, "Out on an errand."

We walked out of the school and along the path to the back, toward the forest. Up ahead of us a figure stood at the edge of the forest next to the path that led to Lachlan Falls. From the flowing robes and gray hair, I suspected it was Sebastian Reade. He kept turning back over his shoulder and glancing around.

"Look at this guy," Khaba said. "He thinks he's being sneaky." He shook his head. "He would draw less attention to himself if he didn't act so guilty."

My breath came out in white clouds as it met the frigid air. "What do you think he's done?"

"Internet café. Either he's coming or going. " Khaba grimaced in disgust. "If he wants to diminish his powers by going in there, fine. But if he can't act inconspicuous, the least he could do is put on an invisibility suit so he doesn't draw the students' attention."

I wondered if Josie and I acted guilty when we went to Happy Hal's. By the time we made it to the woods, the foreign language teacher had ducked into the trees out of sight. The air smelled of wet earth and decaying plants. Daylight peeked through the boughs of trees, but the shadows swallowed us as we traveled under thick patches of leaves.

Khaba prodded me. "Walk faster. I want us to arrive in fifteen minutes. We'll poke around for half an hour so we can walk back before sunset."

"Do you think we'll encounter any emissaries of the Raven Court in the forest?"

"Our grounds are warded. It's unlikely, but not impossible."

At four thirty in the afternoon, the sky was already darkening, with gloomy clouds covering the sun. I wished I had brought more than a sweater to wear, but Khaba's powerwalking kept me warm.

"Do you have a plan?" Khaba asked.

"I just figured I would ask the proprietors of shops if they had seen a boy with blue hair."

Khaba smiled and rolled his eyes.

"What?"

"Derrick isn't a boy. He's a man."

I laughed. "I forget he isn't in high school anymore. I know that's stupid. He's older than I am." I thought of Derrick's twinkling cerulean eyes and easy smile. "I thought I would never see him again. Just when we're reunited, he disappears again. He's only been gone five days, and I miss him more than before."

"Don't worry. We'll find him." Khaba patted me on the shoulder. "Now that I have a reliable security guard who doesn't sleep on the job, eat all my sweets, or keep the students' cell phones, I am not allowing him to escape. Derrick is all mine. Mwah-ha-ha-ha!" He winked at me. His humor lightened the mood.

"Not all yours," I said. "You're going to have to learn to share him with me."

"Not Vega? Doesn't she have dibs on him?"

I stared at him in shock. "How did you know?"

Something rustled in the bushes, and I stiffened, on guard that it might be the Raven Queen herself. A squirrel wiggled out of the foliage.

"She informed me." He stroked his chin. "Wouldn't it be amusing if we went back to the school and found him in Vega's coffin."

"No, it wouldn't." I didn't want to think about him in *any* coffin. I wanted to imagine him alive and healthy.

We soon reached the end of the forest path. The route to the town through the meadow was clear. We stopped at Ye Green Grocery first. Khaba stocked up on candy as I asked Clarence Greenpine, the proprietor, if he had seen a man with blue hair earlier in the week.

The old man removed his Lennon-style sunglasses and squinted at me. "As a matter of fact, a young man fitting that description did stop by and bought some chocolates. He came in asking if I knew where he could find invisibility pants. I suggested he go over to *Tartan, Stripes, and More* the next street over to see if they had any invisible fabrics."

"That's great!" I said.

"Can I interest you in some granola? It will cleanse your aura." Clarence escorted me over to the granola bins. His magic was subtle, the maple flavor of the charm he used to persuade me camouflaged by the nutty smells in the bulk aisle. All his granola was majestic and tempting, even without his Jedi mind tricks. I could have resisted buying granola, I told myself. But I didn't want to. I purchased one bag for myself and one of the special "Hempseed and More" granolas for the brownies as the obligatory thank-you gift for doing laundry.

Khaba took longer perusing the candy aisle than my mother at a garden sale. He only bought a few pounds of candies, unlike the first time I'd shopped with him. He carried the bag under his arm. "Where to next, honey?"

I told him. We tried Tartan, Stripes, and More. It was a shop that specialized in men's attire. I asked the pixieish blonde girl behind the counter if she had seen a young man with blue hair, possibly asking about invisibility pants.

"How could I forget that hottie!" she said.

For once, Derrick's blue hair was coming in handy. People remembered him. This was going better than I'd expected.

Khaba perused the racks of clothes. He started flirting with a red-haired man in a kilt. By now I'd gathered Khaba had a thing for men with elf ears and red hair in addition to kilty pleasures.

"Do you carry invisibility pants?" I asked the clerk.

"Invisibility kilts." She excitedly showed me a rack that appeared to be filled with empty hangers. She smoothed her hand over something, as if there was actual fabric there. "Feel the weave on this one."

"That's okay. I just wanted you to tell me if he had purchased a kilt or if he said he needed pants and where he might have gone from here."

"He bought a kilt, but he said he wanted to get pants too. We special-ordered them for him. The pants will be in next week."

"Where did he go from here?"

"I don't know. Do you want to see our line of invisibility socks?"

"Sorry, we can't *see* them," Khaba said, a little smirk on his face. He snagged me by the elbow and pulled me over to the corner. "The handsome young man I was just talking to told me someone he was talking to saw Derrick go into Happy Hal's."

The young man lingered near a rack of tartan kilts, pretending he wasn't listening, but he kept sneaking glances at us.

I lowered my voice. "He just *happened* to know someone who saw Derrick?" It sounded sketchy, the kind of trap the Raven Court would set up.

Khaba ignored the comment. "I'm taking you to the Internet café to do some more investigating."

"Okay."

"It isn't ideal," Khaba said. "Electricity weakens my powers. You'll be going in without me."

His new friend continued to walk with us to the Internet café. Khaba escorted me to the front door. He peeked inside, though he wouldn't enter. "I'll give you fifteen minutes to ask questions. Do not use electricity and weaken your powers. Understand?"

I sighed dejectedly.

Khaba's friend smiled at him and leaned closer to whisper something in his ear.

Khaba winked at the man. His expression became stern again when he looked at me. "Twenty minutes. That's it. Don't make me wait. It's important we get back before dark."

"I got it."

"I'll just be . . . um . . . ." He smiled at his new friend again.

I grabbed Khaba's sleeve. "Are you sure this is a good idea? That guy might lure you off and. . . ." I thought of Khaba's earlier warnings about the Raven Court.

"And have his way with me. I know." He laughed.

Khaba would have been a better chaperone if he wasn't always finding some hottie to rub his lamp.

The upstairs section of Happy Hal's contained a few adult patrons I recognized from earlier expeditions into Lachlan Falls, but many of the people sitting around tables were my students. Teenagers turned away and averted gazes. A table of boys slunk down, trying to hide behind their meals. As if I cared that they frequented the café.

I strode over to the counter.

Hal sat on a barstool, his vibrant orange hair poking out from underneath his chef's hat. "What'll it be, lass?" Before I could even answer, he waved me closer. "You want to use the private room so students don't see you?"

"No, I just have a few questions for you. Has a young man about twenty-five years old with blue hair been in here in the last week?"

He shrugged. "I see lots of lads with various shades of hair come in here, but I don't remember who I've seen, if you catch my meaning." He raised an eyebrow.

"He's a friend of mine. He went missing. I'm not trying to bust him for using the Internet. I just want to know if you saw him in the last five days."

He shook his head.

I didn't know if that meant he didn't know or he wouldn't say. "If you don't mind, I'm just going to ask around."

The way his bushy red eyebrows drew together I could tell he did mind. Before he could answer, I left the counter and maneuvered around the room. I started with the three adults. Two ate dinner together, a couple with butterfly wings attached to their backs. Neither of them had seen Derrick.

The shaggy buffalo-like creature eating a shepherd's pie in the corner grunted and shook his head when I questioned him. I moved on to the students. After five minutes, I ventured downstairs and questioned the students down there. The room was packed.

Electricity tingled under my skin as I stood among the rows of computers. The air felt charged, like lightning about to strike during a storm. I breathed in the sparks of magic. Being around electricity made me stronger. I didn't know how Hal got electricity, much less an Internet connection, but somehow he had. Maybe a Red had helped him.

Even after questioning the downstairs patrons, I was only ten minutes into my allotted time. I considered Khaba with all his rules. He was okay with people breaking the rules so long as it wasn't obvious. So long as he didn't know. It was torture leaving the computer lab, but I forced myself to do so.

I peered out the door. Khaba was nowhere in sight. I still had ten minutes. On a whim, I decided I would use the private room and call my fairy godmother to see if she had seen Derrick or had suggestions for me.

I returned to Hal and whispered, "Can I purchase ten minutes of Internet? In the private room?"

He smirked. "I was waiting to see how long before you asked."

I paid, and he showed me to the private room. I could only get to it through the kitchen. I still had to go down a flight of stairs. There were two booths. Both were empty. I had expected to see Sebastian Reade, but he might have already left. I logged on to Skype and called my fairy godmother.

"Hello, sweetie! How are you?" my adoptive mom asked.

"Fine, but just so you know, I only have eight minutes before the computer turns off."

"Are you in an Internet café in the Unseen Realm? Those are such seedy places. You never know what kind of unsavory characters you might find. You be careful, young lady." Her voice crackled with static. It was going to be one of those Skype sessions.

"Mom, do you remember Derrick?"

The silence was filled with buzzing that sounded like a demon language.

Finally, she asked, "Your friend from high school? The one with the green hair?"

"Blue hair. Yes. He came to the Unseen Realm. He was a student at Womby's and then an employee. I met him again recently."

"Oh . . . that's nice."

"What?"

"Nothing. Go on."

"You always thought he was a bad influence because he wanted to teach me magic. I know about magic now. He's not a bad influence."

"That's true." Doubt flavored her words.

"I met him this week, but now he's disappeared. I'm worried something bad may have happened to him, like the Raven Court snatched him."

"Oh dear!"

"To make a long story short, Derrick thinks Mr. Thatch cursed him with some kind of memory-altering spell that made him forget the Raven Queen."

"What? Mr. Thatch?" Mom clucked her tongue. "He wouldn't do that."

I plowed on. "I wonder what kind of spell it would take to do that. I have some potion ingredients and thought maybe you could tell me if you think they could brainwash someone." I listed off some of the ingredients.

"That's high-level magic. Potions were never my specialty. I'm good with herbs. When I use them in my cooking, it infuses the food with their medicinal properties and enhances what is already there using my affinity. I've never been one to use rare ingredients or nonherbal items."

Another dead end.

"I want you to go back to what you just said about Mr. Thatch," Mom said. "Why would he want to brainwash Derrick? He's always had the best intentions, even if he doesn't always know how to show them."

"He might still be employed by the Raven Queen and be under her influence. He's been lying to me about something, but I don't know what. I'm afraid he's going to hand me over to the Raven Court."

"How can you say that? After all he's done for you. Don't you dare accuse him of that! If he knew, that would hurt his feelings," Mom said.

Mom, the peacekeeper. She was more concerned about hurting people's feelings than someone breaking a bone.

"Mom, stop." I already regretted calling her about this. "I can't trust *anyone*. Fae and Witchkin, they all have their ulterior motives for things. Everything is about making bargains, and everything comes with a price in this world. No one does anything nice without a reason."

"That's why I came to the Morty Realm. Not everything is life or death here." She spoke quietly, yearning in her voice. "You can always come back here. If things get too dangerous over there, you could come home and lead a normal life without magic."

Wouldn't she like that!

"Thanks for the offer, Mom. But I don't think I can ever go back to a life without magic. It's in my blood. I need this world."

She sighed. "I knew you would say that."

We said our goodbyes. A little countdown clock in the corner of my computer screen told me I only three more minutes. Just for the heck of it, I typed the first four ingredients from the potion into a Google search. The top results were links to fantasy pictures on Pinterest and books on Amazon. I clicked on a few websites. On page three of Google, I found a blog for spells and potions. I doubted this was going to go anywhere, but I clicked on it.

The page was slow to load, but a photograph of an old spell written in another language appeared. The translation was typed out below. The ingredients were the same. Consumed with desire to know more, I scrolled down the page to see what the blogger said.

*This potion was found in a book that had been buried with a medieval monk. When they renovated the cathedral, they found the body sealed off under one of the floors with a book. Most of the manuscript was too far deteriorated to restore, but this photograph shows one of the intact pages. As far as I can tell, it looks like a spell for—*

My computer went dark.

"No!" I yelled. I had to get back on the Internet and find that page. I ran upstairs. Hal wasn't behind the bar. Nor was he in the kitchen. Students gave me sidelong glances.

"Where's Hal gone off to?" I asked a girl I'd had last semester.

She shrugged. "Even leprechauns need restroom breaks."

The bell on the door rang as a one of my students came in from outside. His eyes rested on me. "Yo, Miss L! Khaba's outside. He told me if I saw you in here I was to relay the message to get your butt out there."

I dashed outside. Khaba leaned against the building. His shirt was buttoned all the way up—a rarity for him.

"Khaba, I need a few more minutes. I have a good lead on something."

He pushed himself off the wall. "Someone knows where Derrick is?"

I hesitated. He wasn't supposed to know about my Internet usage. "Not exactly. About something else. There's this spell—"

"No," he said firmly. "We've already spent too long here. Sunset is in twenty-five minutes. I want you on school property before that."

"Can we come back tomorrow? This is important," I said.

"We'll see." He hooked an arm through mine and guided me along the narrow road toward the meadow. "What did you find?"

I did my best to tell him about the spell without incriminating myself. Long shadows of the buildings hid his expression in the gloom of the coming twilight. We had just stepped into the meadow when he froze.

I was already shivering, but the hairs on the back of my neck stood up. Something rustled from out in the tall grass. Khaba turned, slowly scanning the shifting plants. He pulled me closer.

Two dozen women in midnight gowns made of feathers rose from the field. Their wings flapped as they lifted into the air and circled around us. Their eyes were black like something someone would see in a horror movie.

"Hello, Clarissa," one of them said.

The raven woman's voice filled the space between us like a lullaby. The music tasted like honey and brushed against my skin as smooth as silk.

My breath caught in my throat as I tried to speak. "Hi."

"Don't respond," Khaba said. "Keep walking."

He pulled me forward.

"May we speak with you, Clarissa? We have an offer from the Raven Queen we would like to share with you." A tall and slender woman gracefully landed in front of us. Her hair was like the Raven Queen's, long and flowing into her all-feather gown. Though this woman didn't wear a crown.

"My name is Odette." Her lips curled upward. "Perhaps you've heard of me . . . from my brother."

# CHAPTER SEVENTEEN
## Sweet Temptations

I didn't know how that was possible. Odette was Thatch's younger sister—the one that the Raven Queen had supposedly killed. He'd told me the queen had torn her heart out and sent it to Alouette Loraline to show her displeasure that my mother hadn't solved the Fae Fertility Paradox.

My gaze flickered to the pink line starting at the woman's collarbone and disappearing under the collar of her black dress. Numerous scars crisscrossed her arms, reminding me of the crosshatching Thatch used in his ink drawings. This was the sister whose affinity worked best with blood magic.

"Come on, Clarissa," Khaba said, tugging me with him as he circled around the woman.

"You're supposed to be dead." I said. "Does Thatch—Felix Thatch—know you're alive?"

She laughed. "Did he tell you otherwise? He can be so . . . deceptive at times." Her voice was like a lullaby.

"You are obstructing our path," Khaba said. "I would like you to get out of our way. If you refuse, I will forcibly remove you."

Odette laughed, the sound like wind chimes. "I come in peace."

Khaba abruptly stopped. "I'll give you a piece of something if you don't leave."

She placed a hand on her chest, her eyes going wide in surprise. "I have no quarrel with you, sir. You are Fae, one of us. Are you not?" She glided back several steps, giving us more space. "Nor do we have any quarrel with . . . your charge." She spoke formally, with the same British cadence as Thatch.

Cautiously, Khaba stepped forward. He gestured for her to get out of the path. "Move along."

She flapped her wings and fluttered back another few feet, but she didn't move out of our path. She turned her smile on me. "The Raven Queen simply invites you to court. She has a proposal for you. If you would like your friend to go with you, he may do so as your guest."

"Oh?" Her words intrigued me. Then again, it might have been the way the air around her face shimmered with magic. "What kind of proposal?"

"Don't speak. It only encourages them. And don't listen," Khaba said. He started forward again.

"Clarissa has free will. She can answer if she chooses." The woman's lips curled into a sweet smile. Despite all the shades of black magic that hugged her frame, her beauty and voice sounded angelic. "She may come with us if she chooses."

It took all my will not to answer her. I wanted to melt into the lull of her voice. Khaba squeezed my arm as I stepped forward. The pain grounded me in the moment. He kept me close to his side.

They weren't attacking. So far, that was good. But with every step forward, the raven women in the rear kept pace. I didn't know why they were allowing us to get closer to the school. This smelled of a trap.

Khaba's voice was low. "I need you to do a favor for me." He shifted my hand onto his lower back before changing his hold on me around my shoulders.

Was he asking me to rub his lamp? What was the wish? I stared up at him, trying to ask without asking out loud.

I dug the back of his shirt from his pants and placed my fingers on his back. I rubbed, trying to think of how sexy he was to draw out my powers. It wasn't easy to think of my affinity and arousing thoughts when surrounded by freaky flying monkeys who wanted to snatch me.

Odette's eyes raked him over. "I sense great power in you, longing to break free. How long have you been enslaved against your will? The Raven Queen wouldn't keep such a powerful demon bound to the service of the school."

Demon? Khaba wasn't a demon. He was a djinn.

"If you join us, our queen wouldn't bind you to a lamp or ring or school," Odette said. "You would be free. You could use your powers as you like."

He snorted. "A djinn is never free. Even when he is his own master, he's a slave to his powers."

I wondered what that meant. There was a lot I didn't know about Khaba.

She continued walking backward, her pace even with our own. "It's better to be one's own master—even if it means giving some things up—than to be a slave to someone else."

"I am less a slave now than you are," he said.

I tried to remember what I had done with Derrick to give Khaba a jolt of magic. I had been touching Derrick. I didn't think the sensation had been arousing so much, but it had felt nice. Thatch had told me I needed to feel pleasure to draw out my power.

I closed my eyes and tried to block out their voices. I focused on the heat of his skin warming my fingers, the contours of the muscles of his back, and the way he held me close to his side. His embrace was safe and secure, a brotherly benevolence. I leaned my head against his shoulder.

My affinity was awake now. Not hot and overflowing like it had been with Derrick, but slowly swelling with energy. I imagined it filling my core and radiating into my hand.

Khaba gasped. "I bet you wish you were somewhere safe right now."

I wasn't sure if he directed that statement to me or the raven emissary. I kept rubbing his back, uncertain I was even in the right spot.

I said, "I wish Khaba and I were safe at the school."

The ground under my feet shifted, and a wave of vertigo washed over me. I thought I would fall over, but Khaba held on to me. The air grew warm. I blinked my eyes open. A cloud of smoke swirled around me. As it dissipated, I realized I was in my room.

"What the fuck?" Vega asked. She stood in front of the mirror. The door to my wardrobe was open. She held up one of my pink T-shirts in front of her, caught inspecting herself in the mirror.

I didn't know who was more surprised, me or Vega. She was always complaining about how much she hated the color pink and made fun of my fashion choices. I might have yelled at her, but I was more concerned about my encounter with the Raven Court. My knees turned to jelly, and I grabbed onto the chair at the desk to keep from falling over.

"Are you all right?" Khaba sat me on the bed. His brow was crinkled up in concern. "Did I drain you?"

"No, I'm fine."

He eyed me skeptically.

"Really," I said.

"What was all that smoke and mirrors about?" Vega asked. She at least had the decency to shove my shirt back into the wardrobe.

"Clarissa, if you aren't too weak, I need you to tell Jeb what happened and send him to join me in Lachlan Falls." He looked to Vega. "You, come with me. We need to retrieve all students from town. Immediately."

Mrs. Keahi was her usual crotchety old self, refusing to allow me to see Jeb. The moment I relayed Khaba's message, though, her eyes went wide.

She ran into Jeb's office. Before I could follow her in, she shoved me out and slammed the door in my face.

I went to Josie's classroom to tell her what had happened.

"Holy crap, that's bad," Josie said. "I bet Jeb has left too. I wonder who's covering dinner duty."

Craptacular. That would be me! I had to get down there before the cafeteria broke into chaos. Or before Vega caught me shirking the duty I had promised to cover for her. I could only imagine how she'd react to that.

The highest-level Celestors worked for hours to retrieve students. Later that night I heard all teachers and students came back safe.

Derrick was still missing.

I made my rounds in the morning: Khaba's office, Derrick's room, and the dungeon. I couldn't find any of them. In my mailbox a note announced that due to safety concerns, the school was under lockdown until further notice. Students were permitted anywhere on school grounds and in the woods within our boundaries, but not beyond unless they were supervised by a staff member. This would be announced by Khaba during morning breakfast and at lunch. An emergency staff meeting would be held after lunch. It might have been a Saturday, but no one was going anywhere fun with our lockdown.

Along with the note from administration, I found the note I had previously placed in Thatch's box requesting an appointment. Or more accurately, what remained of the note. It was shredded into long strips. That wasn't Thatch's usual M.O. He was more of the sort to write a scathing letter back telling me the many reasons I was unworthy of his teaching. Or to corner me in a dark hallway and tell me why I was such an ungrateful student.

More likely, this was the work of Miss Periwinkle.

Students asked me about the lockdown in Study Club in the morning, but I didn't have any answers, other than the sighting of the Raven Court. Josie and I went to the staff meeting early to get good seats. An all-staff meeting meant it would be crowded. Even arriving ten minutes early, nearly all the staff were present, even Ludomil Sokoloff, the custodian, and Mrs. Ali Keahi, the secretary. Since all adults were present, I could only hope the student hall monitors were doing a decent job overseeing the school grounds.

Josie and I grabbed the last two seats in the front next to Jeb's empty chair.

Some of the teachers were talking about the lockdown. Some were discussing their problem students of the day or the chaos of student schedule changes so late in the semester.

Khaba stood at the front of the room waiting for teachers to assemble. He wore a rainbow cheetah shirt and white leather pants so tight they left little to the imagination. Josie couldn't take her eyes off him.

Miss Periwinkle walked in with Sebastian Reade as he was in the middle of some story about how he'd heroically rescued students from werebears at his last school. She smiled politely, but she didn't look impressed.

Pro Ro stood, interrupting the foreign language teacher's story. "Please, take my seat."

"Oh, no, I couldn't," she said. She scanned the room. If she was looking for her boyfriend to rescue her, Thatch hadn't arrived yet.

"Please, I insist. I would rather stand anyway. It will be a chance to do yoga stretches in the back. I don't know if you know this, but I teach yoga." He spoke casually as if he weren't trying to impress her.

Josie nudged me. Yeah, I caught it too.

Miss Periwinkle took his seat. "I didn't know you liked yoga. You must be very limber."

The aroma of rotting garbage and musky animal wafted into the room with Pinky's entrance.

"How's yoga going for you?" Evita Lupi shouted across the table to be heard over the murmur of teachers. "I hear the students didn't have to tell you the difference between Downward Dog and Cobra today."

His cheeks turned pink. "Ahem. I've been practicing."

Pinky came in, standing behind Vega's chair in the back. She turned around and gave him a dirty look. He didn't notice.

Pinky joined in the conversation. "Did I hear you say you're just learning yoga? Hatha or vinyasa? Personally, I like Bikram myself, but I've done some yin and have been doing kundalini for about ten years."

"Wow. That's a stretch," Khaba said.

Josie tittered.

Vega stood. "For once would that fleabag bathe? He makes this room smell like a thousand unwashed armpits."

I shushed her. "That isn't very nice."

Pinky must have heard her because his eyes went wide, and he shifted away from her. Poor guy! It was hard enough being the new teacher, but having to put up with Vega's insults was the worst.

Jeb shuffled in five minutes later, whispered something to Khaba, and Khaba began.

Oddly, Thatch was absent. Could he be with . . . Derrick? All I knew was that for once he wasn't with Miss Periwinkle. If I did see him, I considered whether I would speak with him about the run-in with Odette. The woman might have been lying. Or *he* might have been lying. Though, why, I couldn't imagine, other than the fact that he was a pathological liar.

Khaba cleared his throat. "I'll keep this short and to the point. I trust you read the letter and heard the announcements earlier. Several students have been lured away by Fae. Unlike the usual occurrences, we have three—potentially four—in the last week." His eyes met mine.

My throat tightened. He meant Derrick. I didn't want it to be true.

"Witness reports suggest the Raven Court is behind this. I can confirm their most recent activity in town."

Teachers gasped and whispered among themselves. I wasn't surprised.

"But that's against the law!" Evita Lupi said.

I noticed the way her husband ogled Miss Periwinkle. It didn't even look like Pro Ro and Silas Lupi had heard Khaba. Seriously, the librarian needed to rein in the siren powers.

"Has the Witchkin Council been notified?" Grandmother Bluehorse asked.

"We have contacted the proper authorities," Khaba said. "They are unable to do anything at present because the students weren't technically snatched. Students went of their own free will."

Pinky raised his hand. "More likely they were coerced or hypnotized. They do realize that, don't they?"

"We can't prove it." Khaba's expression was grim. "We know what the Raven Court is like. They're too powerful to fight physically or politically. That's why we need to come up with a plan to keep the students safe. Kids are going to get bored on school grounds, which is going to cause behavior problems." Khaba looked to Puck.

Puck stepped forward. "Some of you may be familiar with PBIS, right? Positive Behavior Intervention and Supports. Part of this involves good classroom management. We need to give students something fun and rewarding to take their minds off recent events. Sure, we can provide short chaperoned trips to town with small groups after school, but that isn't going to be sufficient to keep the rest of the kids occupied." Puck nodded to Khaba.

Khaba waved his hand over the chalkboard. The schedules shifted to a list of activities ranging from sports to chess to basket weaving.

Puck went on. "Some of you already serve as faculty advisor for some of the school clubs. We would like to encourage the rest of you to start an after-school or weekend club. You don't have to be there to supervise the entire time, but be involved enough to help give students ideas to keep them occupied."

"More busywork," Vega said.

Puck held up a clipboard with a sheet of paper. "I'm sending around a sign-up sheet for field trips for teachers with abilities strong enough to protect students if they should encounter a hostile Fae."

"The problem isn't *hostile* Fae," Grandmother Bluehorse said. "It's having the ability to thwart a spell meant to enthrall."

Khaba nodded. "I only encourage those who feel they can fight Fae influences to sign up." He looked directly at me and gave the smallest shake of his head.

I would not be one of those teachers.

I raised my hand. "Can I go with—"

"No," he said firmly.

If I couldn't go to Lachlan Falls at all, how was I going to be able to help Derrick? I needed to find another way to search for him. Or a way to find out more about that spell.

The clipboard came around the table. Vega passed it off to someone else. Grandmother Bluehorse handed it back to her.

"Not another duty," Vega muttered.

I didn't know what she was complaining about. She had fewer duties than ever!

# CHAPTER EIGHTEEN
## Books and Babes—Check Them Out

After the meeting, Josie and I sat at the table, waiting for the other teachers to file out. Pro Ro flirted with Miss Periwinkle. Pinky lingered a few feet away from Josie. He looked like he wanted to say something, but he didn't approach us.

A spider scuttled across the table over to Josie. She held out her hand to it and allowed it to crawl across her skin. Ick. I would never be *that* kind of witch.

When the bottleneck to the door had died down, Josie and I made our way out.

Vega stood in the hallway, arms crossed. She looked me up and down. "Well?"

"Well, what?" I asked.

"I said we were doing research after school yesterday—which you blew off."

That wasn't fair! Yesterday I had told her I had to see Khaba, which had led to hours of chaos. She'd been in Lachlan Falls chaperoning students back to school.

I started, "I didn't blow—"

"Shut your piehole. Are you coming to the library or not? I've already been waiting here five minutes for you. That's one entire duty."

Ugh! The price of Vega's assistance.

"Can Josie help with—"

Josie backed away as she eyed Vega with revulsion. "No thanks."

Vega strode to the library, her high heels clattering against the floor. I had to run to keep up with her.

Miss Periwinkle sat behind the library counter, listening to Pro Ro as he leaned against it. Vega and Miss Periwinkle nodded to each other when we walked in. Maddy stocked shelves along one of the walls. She smiled, and I waved to her.

There were a lot of students in the library, most of them young men, but no one was staring at Maddy for once. Boys kept sneaking clandestine glances at Gertrude Periwinkle. A young man at the card catalogue walked over to the counter to ask a question, but Pro Ro waved him away.

Vega incanted a spell, starlight circling around her. I couldn't recall if she had done this when she'd tried to locate the ingredients by keyword search in our room. I thought the magic might draw Miss Periwinkle's attention, or even one of the students', but no one gave us a second look. And why would they? Spellcasting was normal here. Vega was a teacher. There was no reason she wasn't allowed to perform magic.

Imani and Greenie sat in one corner reading books away from the groups of boys staring longingly at Miss Periwinkle. When I looked back at Vega, she held a star in her hand. Or what looked like a star. She blew on it, and it scattered into a million sparkling specks that flew in opposite directions.

"This is different from the other spell," I said.

"Naturally," she said in her superior way. "I don't want to stand here for hours. This will take less energy and reaches farther." The sparkles shot across the expanse of the room, drifting through books and weaving up and down shelves.

"What are those stars doing?" I asked.

"Tasting. If one of them finds a match, it will tag the book and show you where it is."

A student cleared his throat behind Vega. His hair was black but glittered with starlight. From the stack of books in his arms and haughty expression, I suspected he might be a Celestor. "Miss Bloodmire, I need assistance checking out these books."

"Why are you asking me? Do I look like a librarian to you?" She grimaced.

He glanced at Miss Periwinkle, his expression transforming to longing and then annoyance. "Professor Rohiniraman keeps sending me away. He's hogging Miss Periwinkle all to himself."

Vega rolled her eyes. "I'll deal with him." She looked at me. "Go peruse without me. I trust you won't get into any trouble." She sauntered over to the circulation desk.

I strolled the perimeter of the library, studying the drifting lights. Maddy returned a book to a shelf, smiling as I approached.

"How's it going?" I asked, trying not to look guilty.

"Great!" Maddy smiled, her face radiant. "I can't believe how much easier my life is now that I'm apprenticing with Miss Periwinkle. Not that

I'm saying it wasn't great before when you were mentoring me, but you didn't know how to do glamour spells or how to tone down my magic. My affinity is way more manageable now. Boys hardly ever look at me anymore."

Of course they didn't. Every set of eyes attached to a male body in the library were too busy ogling Miss Periwinkle.

"I'm glad to hear it," I said.

I continued examining the lights dancing around the shelves.

Maddy gave a little cough. "I, um. . . ." She stepped closer, glancing back at her new mentor. "I found one of those books you were looking for, one about the Raven Court." She glanced at the librarian. "But I don't know how I'll get it to you. It isn't a book I can remove from the library."

Pro Ro was gone. Vega and Miss Periwinkle spoke in hushed tones, but I suspected from their rigid body language and red faces, they weren't exchanging pleasantries.

"No worries," I said. "I don't want you to get in trouble. If you find something else I can check out, let me know."

"Okay," she said cheerfully.

I examined the lights, trying to see if any of them looked different. Some of them slipped through the floor or floated through the ceiling. There were less stars now. I wasn't sure if that was good or bad.

I knew this spell was important in figuring out what Thatch was up to with Derrick and why he had been keeping him secret from me, but I was afraid we were going to come to another dead end. The spell had probably come from Alouette Loraline's diary, and unless she had stored an extra copy in a public place like a library—it was unlikely I would find what I needed. A student squeaked from around a row of books, over by the fiction section. I passed teen literature, all old books like *Little House on the Prairie*, *Treasure Island*, and *The Secret Garden*. The newest book on the shelves was *The Outsiders*. I could see my department wasn't the only one with budget cuts. Not that most students here had time for recreational reading.

A student rounded the corner, waving stardust away from his face. He sneezed. It drifted out his ear. The speck collided into another speck and converged. More dots joined together. It reminded me of atoms forming molecules. I didn't know what was happening. Either it was something good and they had found what we were looking for, or something bad and they were reacting to being inhaled by a student.

More and more of the lights joined together, forming a larger star. They gathered before me. I peeked around the corner at Vega, wondering if I should call her. She still stood at the desk, pointing accusingly at the librarian.

When I turned back to the light, it was the size of a tennis ball, the same as when it had started. Slowly it drifted away. I followed it around the tall bookshelves in the fiction section. I accompanied it around another wall of books and stopped when I came to a door set in the wall. It hovered in front of the door.

A thrill of excitement coursed through me. This was it. The book had to be in this room.

I tried the handle. It was locked. My hopes sank like a lead balloon. Probably this room was off-limits. The light sank to the level of the keyhole and pushed through. I placed my hand on the door again, hoping the light might work some magic that would help me. The latch clicked.

It was unlocked.

That was handy. I considered getting Vega again, but decided I didn't want to risk drawing Miss Periwinkle's attention, especially if this was a secret room of library books. I slipped through the door, keeping it ajar. The light glowed bright enough to illuminate the stairs descending to somewhere below. I hoped this wasn't leading me into the dungeon. It would make sense if it was. Thatch was the one who had the copy of Alouette Loraline's diary. Maybe I could steal it back.

My shoes made no sound over the stone floor, muffled by a hundred years of dust. The air chilled as I descended. At the bottom of the stairs, the hallway was still and stagnant.

My heart thrummed in my chest. This was it. I was about to find the answer to some—all?—of my questions.

I followed Vega's star and past rooms of books. The air smelled like vanilla cookies, which had to be impossible since no one in a forgotten tomb of books would be eating Nilla Wafers. From the stone walls, it looked like we were in the ancient section of the school, the part that had once been a monastery. I thought about the blog post I'd read mentioning the spell. Hopefully there wouldn't be any dead bodies.

The light entered a room. The air smelled fruity, like apples and autumn. A witch leaned over a book, her long wavy hair and hat obscuring her face. She held a quill in her wrinkled hand, pen poised over a line of text. It appeared she was copying a book. A golden goblet had been overturned on the table. The long-gone fluid that it once held had left a dark stain over the table.

"Hello?" I whispered.

The star hovered over the book before the witch.

I edged closer. "Excuse me."

The woman didn't stir. My heart beat harder.

I circled around the table. The woman was dead.

Of course.

From the way her shriveled skin hugged her bones like dried leather, she looked like she'd been mummified. Even in death, her features held a certain beauty, her bone structure not so different from Gertrude Periwinkle's high cheekbones, though her hair was silver, not blonde.

I wondered who she was and how long ago she'd died. The book she copied from was in another language. Maybe Old High German. I couldn't tell since I hadn't learned much Old High German. The potion she translated was incomplete. The ingredients were listed, but there was no title, and how to use it wasn't yet included. Her list did include one line mine didn't.

*The Witchkin performing this spell will need the power of a Red for this spell to—*

That was all she'd written? If this was related to the Fae Fertility Paradox, I already knew that. Why couldn't fate just give me the answers for once? I'd faced the Raven Court, Thatch's supposed sister who wasn't dead, and worst of all, Vega. Now I was faced with another dead end.

Dead end. Heh. I glanced at the corpse again.

The star pulsated, as if trying to draw my attention to the book. I could read the one translated, but not the one in Old High German. Then again, that was probably the one I wanted since the spell was complete.

Carefully, I started to slide the book out from under the head and arm of the corpse. The moment I did so, the star sank into the book. The light went out. When the seeker of the keyword match touched the book he or she sought, that must have been the signal that the magic was no longer needed.

I froze, waiting for the dead body to come to life and strangle me. She didn't.

I continued sliding the book out from under her. Something brushed my arm and I screamed. It was the witch hat. I laughed in nervousness, my heart still racing. I closed the book and fumbled for the second book. The translated volume was incomplete, but I could take both and see what else was written.

Vega had once admitted she couldn't read Old German, but I might be able to find someone who could. Darla could, but I hated to involve a student.

I removed the second book from the table. The books smelled like vanilla. Something rustled in the dark. It was just her hat or something I had bumped, I told myself. There were no such things as ghosts, zombies, or other dead things. Only witches, fairies, and bigfoot were real.

An exhalation that wasn't mine made me jump back in surprise. I dropped both books. I wished I had my phone. Or that wand I'd appropriated from a student. I couldn't even remember where I'd put it. I tried to use the Elementia spell I'd learned in Jackie Frost's class, but my hands were clammy with sweat. I was afraid to speak the Latin words out loud for fear of using them wrong and causing a dead body to come after me.

Blindly, I groped for the books on the floor. I found one book, encountered one of the seated Witchkin's shoes, and scooted on my knees as I felt for the other book. My fingers encountered another foot instead.

The breath came again. Along with it came the fragrance of berries and fruit. The foot shifted under my hand. I yanked my hand back and stumbled to my feet, tripping on the book I'd been searching for on the floor. I let out an undignified squeal.

Finally I decided it was time to shed some light on this. I used the Latin incantation and focused on the Elementia spell. The magic flashlight revealed a still and silent cadaver. Keeping my eyes on the dead Witchkin, I stooped to pick up the fallen books.

The corpse had moved both times I had touched her. My Red affinity was touch magic. Was I able to raise the dead with touch? This had to be why it was forbidden. But it didn't make sense. I wasn't aroused. Thatch had said he thought my affinity was tied to pleasant feelings. If *I* was doing this, he had to be wrong. There was something more to the magic. Either he didn't know, or he did, but he wasn't telling.

No surprise there.

I hugged the books to my chest. My heart slammed against my ribcage. I wanted to go back upstairs into the sanctuary of the library where my worst problem might be Miss Periwinkle accusing me of stealing her boyfriend and Vega telling me I owed her more duties. But as terrified as I was, I was also curious. I didn't fully understand my own powers.

I needed to.

I allowed my breath to calm and my heart to slow enough that I could form words. "Can you hear me? Are you . . . alive?"

No answer came. I crept closer.

Necromancy was forbidden. Technically, so was my affinity. But let's say I could communicate with the dead by touching their dead bodies. That would mean I could find some answers. This Witchkin scribe might be able to tell me about the text she was copying.

With one hand, I clutched the heavy tomes to my chest. I held the other out blindly until I came to the edge of the table. I positioned myself closer.

"Can you speak? Who are you?" My voice quavered.

She still didn't answer, but I wasn't touching her yet either. I scooted as close as I dared, reaching out with my hand to touch where I suspected her shoulder was. I repeated my question.

Bones shifted under the thin dress and beneath the tougher hide of her skin. I wanted to shrink away. This was seriously creepy.

A wheezing breath came out again, a gasp, and then a choking cough.

"He poisoned me." Her voice was thick with an accent I couldn't place. Her words escaped in a breathy hiss that made it difficult to understand her.

"Who poisoned you?" I asked.

Something popped under her skin beneath my fingers. It sounded like a brittle bone had broken.

"He poisoned me," she repeated, this time sounding more indignant.

She hadn't answered my question. Weren't necromancers supposed to be able to command the dead? Maybe I needed to sound more authoritative, like a dog trainer.

I pushed down my fear. I spoke louder, though I sounded just as frightened. "Who poisoned you and why?"

"He poisoned me, the bastard."

This wasn't going anywhere. I started to draw back, but she continued, "He knew I was a Red. I shouldn't have trusted him with my secrets." She coughed. The air smelled like apples and dust. "I should have checked for poison."

I fought the urge to sneeze.

"Tell me about the text you were writing," I said.

"The translation. Where is my book?" The chair creaked, or perhaps it was her body. She twisted, and more bones popped. "Did he steal my manuscript too?" Her hand clamped over mine.

I stepped back, trying to pull away, but her grip was firm. "No. He didn't get your books. I don't think he cared about those."

"Where are my books? Who has my books?" Something clunked onto the table. The corpse continued to talk, but her words came out in raspy hisses of air. I couldn't understand most of what she said. I suspected she'd lost her jaw.

Something crunched.

She said, "You have it!"

# CHAPTER NINETEEN
## Who Has My Golden Book?

I screamed. This was like that one time my dad had told *The Golden Arm* story around the campfire when I'd been a kid, and he had grabbed me. Only this was a real dead person. It wasn't a story.

"It's a library. I'm not stealing," I screamed. "I'm just going to borrow the books."

I pulled harder. I tried to use my other hand to detach her fingers without dropping the books. One of her fingers crumbled. I shrieked and tore the remaining hand away. I stumbled back, hoping she was dead again now that I wasn't touching her.

I prayed she was at peace now.

I fumbled my way out of the room, across the hallway, and up the stairs. Repeatedly I stubbed my toes and pitched onto my knees on the steep incline of stairs. The door creaked open and light fell on the stairs. A figure stood at the top, silhouetted in light.

"Please don't be Miss Periwinkle about to catch me and close me in this darkness forever," I silently begged.

Before I'd even gotten halfway up I realized it couldn't be Miss Periwinkle. This figure was smaller and didn't wear a witch hat.

"Miss Lawrence?" she whispered.

It sounded like Imani.

I fell out of the secret passage, gasping for breath. I crawled the rest of the way out and closed the door behind me.

"Are you all right?" Imani helped me up. "You look like you've seen a ghost. What happened?"

"The library is a dangerous place," I said. "I would not recommend going through that door." If Imani's powers were anything like mine, she might resurrect the poisoned scribe like I had.

"I wanted to talk to you about Mr. Thatch," Imani said.

"Yeah?"

"He isn't acting like himself. During classes, I could tell something weird was going on."

That was an understatement.

"Was Mr. Thatch in class yesterday?" I asked.

"Yeah. I guess."

"What do you mean, 'you guess'? Either he's there or he isn't."

"He was there, but he kept leaving. He said he had students in the detention room, but I know he didn't. He seemed distracted."

What was he up to?

"Would you check on him? Do you know how to check for curses and hexes?"

"Um, no." Duh. I was the least magical teacher in the school.

Her shoulders sagged. Her eyes filled with tears. I genuinely felt bad she was this concerned.

"I'll see what I can do. Okay?"

She nodded.

I was going to have to go poke around in the dungeon when he was in class. I didn't know how to do that without drawing his attention since I couldn't get to the dungeon without passing through his classroom. I might be able to use the mirror hallway to walk into his room and then go through his private quarters and office. One of these days he was going to catch me if I wasn't careful.

I no longer saw Miss Periwinkle behind the counter. Vega stood beside one of the tables, chiding a group of students about something.

My legs felt like jelly as I approached Vega. A student looked up, his eyes wide. He elbowed a friend, who stared at me.

"Do you speak any Old High German?" I asked Vega, hoping she really did.

She tugged the books from my arms and perused them. "This isn't Old High German. It's Middle High German. That's more of a Thatch specialty."

Of course it was. The students continued to stare.

Vega eyed me with a frown. "Why is a mummified hand attached to your sweater?"

"What? Where?" I spun, afraid the scribe had risen from her tomb and followed me. Something smacked into my side, and I squealed.

Vega sighed in exasperation. She detached the shriveled hand from the bottom of my sweater and held it up. "Finders keepers."

"Yeah, sure, take it," I said. I didn't want it. Had I not been so frazzled, I would have bargained with her for it.

"It looks like you found what you were looking for." Her smile turned sinister. "By the way, you were gone for a total of twenty-one minutes. I'd say that's equal to another week of covering my duties. Lucky you."

I went to Josie in her room to see if she had any suggestions for who could help me translate.

"I bet any of the Celestor teachers are good at translating," she said.

"Not Vega."

"But Thatch, definitely."

Ugh. Not him again.

There was Darla, the student who had previously told me she would help me study foreign languages. I had promised myself I wouldn't involve students in the Fae Fertility Paradox, but this wasn't about that. There was more to this spell that I didn't understand, some kind of Red magic. No matter what, I had to be careful whom I shared it with.

Wouldn't you know it, as I carried the books toward my room, who should I see outside the great hall? After all the times I had attempted to meet with Thatch to discuss Derrick, this had to be the moment I found him?

From his resting bitch face, I knew the conversation wasn't going to be a pleasant one. He marched toward me, students leaping out of his path. His face was red, and a vein bulged in his temples. It had to be about Derrick. He knew I knew. Either that or it was about the books. I couldn't allow him to get them.

As my self-defense teacher had said in college, the best defense was avoidance.

I turned and ran.

# CHAPTER TWENTY
## Josie's Revenge

I didn't know where I was running to. Thatch could use magic. My powers were limited to minor charms—and now the forbidden art of necromancy. A lot of good any of those would do me. I had to stash the books somewhere safe before Thatch found me. I wasn't far from my classroom. I locked the door and dropped the books on my desk. I shoved a stack of papers over the books and started toward the closet to make sure it was locked.

Too late. The door creaked open and out marched Thatch.

"I wondered what you had done this time." His wand was drawn. "The moment you skipped our meeting, I suspected you were up to something."

I scuttled back. "I didn't skip a meeting."

He snorted. "Then you ignored my second and third request for a meeting. I knew you had to be guilty of *something*. Now I know."

He lifted a pair of charcoal gray slacks that I had neglected to notice were draped over his arm. My eyes widened. This wasn't about the books. He knew I had stolen his pants and had been in his room.

He unfolded the pants. Pink thread had been sewn into the seat of the pants. That hadn't been there when Josie had given them back to me, but I had a suspicion the letters she'd embroidered were her doing, not the brownies'.

The seat of his pants now said, "That's *Mr.* Asshole to you." I took it Josie was a fan of eighties movies.

I tried not to laugh, but I couldn't help it. I was relieved. He was just mad about his stupid pants.

"Not funny, Miss Lawrence." He threw down the slacks on the floor.

"I'm sorry."

"You don't know the meaning of sorry."

"I didn't do it, if that's what you think."

"Do you deny these trousers were in your possession?"

I hesitated, trying to think of a valid excuse. "Look, I did have your pants, but I didn't do that. I put them in with my laundry for the brownies to return to you."

"And who do you propose did this, then? The brownies? Did profanities appear on any of your clothes during the middle of Saturday detention today?"

Why hadn't Josie listened? Hadn't she realized I would be the one to get blamed? I didn't want him to think I had played the prank on him.

I picked up the pants and studied the lettering. Josie was a skilled seamstress. I turned them and examined the pants from the inside. "I could probably pull out the thread if I borrowed a seam ripper from someone."

The brand label that had been sewn to the inside waistband was printed with the not-so-subtle message: "Made with love by Josie."

Ah, so she wanted him to know the addition had been from her. I held it up. He tore the pants from my hands, his face growing more mottled by the second. What had gone through Josie's head?

"Do you want me to try to fix the pants for you?" I asked.

"No." He wadded them up. "If this isn't the reason you've been avoiding me, then I expect an explanation. Don't try to lie to me." He strode over to my desk and sat down in my chair. "I left one note on your desk and two in your mailbox, which you refused to so much as acknowledge."

He leaned an elbow on my desk, his arm touching one of the books. The spines were exposed, and he could easily see them. As long as his attention stayed on me, and not my desk, I would be fine.

I scooted closer, shifting to the right to draw his gaze away from what was in front of him.

Thatch drummed his fingers over the papers. "I'm waiting, Miss Lawrence."

"I didn't miss any meetings, and I didn't get any notes. Every time I go down to the dungeon, it's locked up and you aren't around."

"You exaggerate. I've only kept it locked in the morning."

"And after school."

"Yesterday, yes. I was checking the Fae traps."

I stared at him, confused.

"Locations similar to the place we found Maddy. I have an inventory of where I find Witchkin students. My alarms go off when a child falls into one of them, just as it does when magic happens out in the Morty Realm." He tossed back his perfect waves of hair. "I had three false alarms last night and one today that kept me from the staff meeting."

"Oh." That sounded less villainous than it could have. "Yeah, well, I left you a message in your box yesterday, and someone returned it to my box in shreds."

His brow furrowed. "I didn't do that."

"Then who did? Could it be your new girlfriend?"

"Gertrude wouldn't do such a thing. What could possibly motivate her?"

"Jealousy."

His lips twitched, and he stared off into the distance, getting that dreamy look on his face. "Gertrude? Jealous of *me*?" His grin broadened. "That's . . . adorable."

His gaze drifted down to the stacks of art projects on my desk that I'd just taken down from the display wall.

"Um, anyway. . . ." I coughed loudly, trying to draw his attention. I tried to casually stack the papers and transfer them onto the books. The old tomes still weren't very well hidden, but I didn't want to keep fidgeting with papers on my desk and draw more attention to that area. "I wanted to speak with you about that spell. Are you going to tell me what it does?"

"After you collect the ingredients." He watched my hands.

I shuffled a pile of articles for my class the following day, hoping to draw his gaze away from the books. "Why won't you tell me now?"

"Because I enjoy infuriating you. Why are you fidgeting so much?"

"No reason." I lifted my sketchbook from the corner of my desk. "There was something you were going to confess to me the other day. Something about Derrick."

"No. I have nothing to confess."

"Stop trying to be purposefully infuriating. I want to know where he is. I'm afraid the Raven Queen has him." I bit my lip, afraid I'd said too much.

His brow furrowed. "Why would you think that?"

"Why wouldn't I?"

"Are you referring to the recent snatchings? The Raven Court is technically luring them, not snatching them." He placed an elbow on the desk again, idly stroking his chin with a long finger. "Derrick is somewhere safe. He wouldn't have any reason to go someplace the Raven Court would frequent."

"How do you know? When is the last time you've seen him?" I rephrased that. I wasn't going to let him wiggle out of telling me the truth on a technicality. "Spoken with him?"

"I've seen to it he's somewhere safe. I've been watching over him to ensure he doesn't get hurt, and that you do not either. It's possible that we've come to a time when you're ready to see him again without risk of bringing injury to him or yourself. Can I trust you not to do anything rash?

Do you think you can control yourself and not touch him?"

"Maybe. Why?" I leaned against my desk.

"It will be an experiment." He offered me a smile.

Or maybe he didn't want me to undo his invisibility.

"Have you talked to Derrick this week?" I asked.

"I've been rather busy. I will go to him tonight and set up an appointment for the two of you to meet." He stood. "Will this satisfy your wish to see him?"

I nodded, but I was doubtful. "When?"

"Tomorrow morning before breakfast, if you like. But, again, I ask that you show some restraint. Do not touch him. Will you do as I ask?"

I hugged my sketchbook to my chest. I already had touched Derrick. A battle raged inside me: to tell or not to tell? It depended on whether I trusted Thatch or not. This was the same man who had told me his sister was dead, but she'd been alive and well. Did he already know, or was that a lie?

Thatch stood. "Clarissa? Can you trust me on this?"

I wanted to trust him. I so badly wanted for Derrick to be safe and for Thatch to be looking out for him. Maybe Derrick was gone, not because Fae had snatched him, but because Thatch had sent him on an errand.

"You lied to me about Odette," I blurted out.

His brow crinkled in confusion. "How so?"

"I met her in Lachlan Falls. She was with the Raven Court. You said your sister was dead."

Thatch crossed his arms, his expression hardening into a mask. "The Raven Queen removed her heart and sent it to Alouette Loraline as a gift. I performed the spell to confirm it truly was my sister's heart. You are obviously mistaken."

I hadn't been mistaken. The woman had looked like Thatch. He had to be lying.

His gaze flickered past me, and he smiled. I turned.

Miss Periwinkle rushed through the doorway, out of breath. "There you are, love. I've been looking everywhere for you."

He strode over to her, so much joy radiating over his face he resembled a different man—someone happy. "I was having a conference with Miss Lawrence."

Her eyes narrowed as she glared daggers at me. "I don't see why it's necessary to spend so much time with her."

"My dearest Gertrude, you do realize I'm Miss Lawrence's tutor in magic, do you not? I'm going to have to meet with her on occasion. I'm afraid I've been neglecting her education of late."

He strolled out with her.

It seemed I would have to wait to find out to find out more about Derrick. Tomorrow was so close and so far away at the same time. I hoped Thatch would be able to clear everything up and Derrick wasn't missing at all.

Even so, I doubted it.

I spent another night tossing and turning. I rose early. Thatch hadn't named a time or place and there wasn't a note in my box, but all our previous planned appointments had been in his office. I couldn't talk to him there, though, because the dungeon was locked. I sat at the bottom of the steps to the dungeon, waiting. Maybe I was early.

I missed breakfast sitting there, hoping he would show up. I didn't know if it was Miss Periwinkle thwarting him or he had lied about setting up a meeting with Derrick. I checked again and again throughout the day, but the dungeon remained locked. He didn't reply to the notes I placed in his box or the ones I slipped under the dungeon door.

I worried Thatch's evasiveness was tied to Derrick's disappearance.

On Monday, I returned to the dungeon and again found it locked.

The only time I caught a glimpse of Thatch was when I returned to his classroom during my prep. Unfortunately, he sent me away because he was teaching. After school he was gone. During dinner and afterward he wasn't around. I even went to the library, hoping I might find him there. Instead I found Pro Ro and Sebastian Reade competing for Miss Periwinkle's attentions.

Worry consumed me. He'd promised to bring me Derrick. I had to confront him. I would demand to see Derrick.

I just had to find Thatch first.

On Monday night, I stood before the mirror portal, staring into Thatch's room. I hadn't been able to sleep. The blanket that had been over the mirror earlier was heaped onto the floor and no longer barred the view of Thatch sprawled across the bed. I knew it was risky, barging in on Thatch like this, but the blanket on the floor probably meant Miss Periwinkle wasn't around. It was practically an invitation to step in.

I inhaled and pushed my way through. It was darker in the room than it had looked through the mirror. A hint of ambient light came from somewhere above, but it was never clear how Thatch lit the windowless room. During the day it was bright enough one would think the entire ceiling had a skylight.

Thatch didn't stir as I approached. I hesitated, wondering how badly this could go if I startled him. He might shoot lightning out his eyes if he thought I was an intruder. I remained a respectful distance from his bed. A safe distance.

"Thatch," I whispered. "I need to talk to you."

He remained as still as a corpse.

I cleared my throat. I tried at a normal volume. "Thatch, wake up."

No response. I held up my hand and uttered a freshman-level spell used for illumination. A glowing orb hovered above my hand, filling the room with dim light. Most of my students could produce a stronger spell, but I was still learning.

I tried calling Thatch again. He shifted in his sleep. That was good. At least he wasn't dead. The blankets fell away from him. Intricate white lines covered his naked chest and arms, the patterns faint against his pale skin. He was lean, but muscular in an unassuming way. He looked peaceful, like a banished angel in repose, the subject of a Neoclassical painting. Even in sleep, his hair was immaculate, the black locks splayed across the pillow like wings.

It was the thought of midnight wings that resurrected the creepy shivers of the Raven Queen. I was here to help Derrick.

"Felix Thatch!" I crossed an invisible line separating us and shook his shoulder.

His lips curved into a smile, and he moaned. He shifted, taking my hand in his and rolling away so that I was yanked onto the bed.

"Oof," I said as I fell across him.

He blinked open his eyes. His smile faded. "Merlin's balls! What are you doing in here?" He shoved me off him.

I sat on the edge of his bed. "It's an emergency. I need to talk to you."

"Everything is an emergency with you." He sat up. More of the blankets fell away, revealing toned muscle. I hoped he was wearing pants under the covers.

"I need you to tell me where Derrick is."

"That isn't an emergency." He groaned in exasperation. "Get out."

"I'm not leaving until you tell me what's happened to Derrick. You've done something with him, haven't you?"

He rolled his eyes. "Leave."

"No."

"I want you to think for just a moment on your conduct. You break into my room. You accuse me of doing something to your friend, and you demand I tell you where he is. Why would I be persuaded to talk to you at all?"

"I can't stand it any longer. I need to know where he is. You found out and punished him and—" I was so upset I could hardly form coherent sentences. "I would do anything to make sure he doesn't get hurt. Please. I'll go to the Raven Queen if that's what you want."

He shoved me off the bed. "Stop blubbering. Go sit in my office. I'll join you in a moment. Just let me get dressed."

"You promise you'll tell me? You won't let Miss Periwinkle interrupt? She always barges in, and you let her distract you."

"What is it with the two of you? Is there some reason you aren't able to get along?"

He swung his legs over the side of the bed. From the way he carefully kept his middle covered with blankets I suspected he was naked under there. Oh boy. That was awkward.

The lock in the door rattled. He grabbed my arm and pushed me toward the bathroom, simultaneously trying to keep himself wrapped in blankets. He dropped his hand from my arm, a ball of sparkling yellow-and-green light forming. Whatever the spell was, it was too late. Miss Periwinkle was already in the doorway.

Thatch looked at me. "I hate you."

## CHAPTER TWENTY-ONE
## The Yoga Master

Miss Periwinkle's face shifted from delight to overdramatic horror. She may have tricked Thatch, but she didn't fool me. She had an uncanny ability for butting in any time I spoke with him. Surely she'd set some kind of spell to detect my presence in proximity to him.

Her face scrunched up, and she clutched at her chest like she was having a heart attack. "You said there was nothing going on between you! You said there are no secrets you've been keeping from me, but you've been lying. Obviously, she has a key."

I scooted farther away from her.

Thatch's face flushed red. "There isn't. She doesn't. This isn't—ugh." Thatch tried to stand and keep the blankets wrapped around himself at the same time, but they were tucked in, and he couldn't. "She broke into my room with magic."

Her gaze raked over his naked chest and his obvious lack of pants. Fury sparked in her eyes as she glared at me.

I inched back.

"This is not what it looks like. Let me explain," he said.

That had to be the most overused line of cheating boyfriends ever. Already I could see Thatch was going to fail.

"Explain all you want, but it isn't going to change anything." Gertrude turned to the door, sobbing. It sounded like crocodile tears to me.

Thatch yanked the covers out of the bed, fabric tearing, and wrapped them around himself as he approached her. He gave me a dirty look. "Miss Lawrence, leave."

I gestured toward the door that she was blocking. That was the only way I could get out. I didn't know how to go back through the mirror.

He placed his arm around her shaking shoulders and guided her away from the door. I made a quick escape into the hallway to his office and out the door that led to the hallway to his classroom.

I considered waiting for him like he'd originally asked but decided that between his foul mood and encountering Miss Periwinkle again, I was more likely to get hexed than find the answers I needed.

I was going to have to find another way to find out where Derrick was. I needed a master of divination. Unfortunately, convincing Pro Ro wasn't going to be easy.

Pro Ro wasn't like Vega whom I could buy with favors. I had nothing he wanted anyway. Unless. . . . He had been complaining about teaching yoga because he didn't know anything about it. I had taken yoga in Eugene. I wasn't an expert, but I probably knew more than he did.

Monday after school, I set up my students in Art Club and left Imani in charge. I found Pro Ro in his classroom at his desk, examining a star chart.

"Hi," I said from his doorway.

He didn't look up. "Go away."

"Sure thing. I was just wondering how the yoga class was going and if you needed any help. But if you want me to leave. . . ." I stepped back from the door slowly, waiting to see if he took the bait.

He stood. "Wait! Miss Lawrence, do you know yoga?"

"I've taken classes for years. We could practice together. I could see if I can teach you some new moves."

His face flushed red. "Ahem. Well, I suppose. When are you free? Are you free now?"

"I'm not dressed for yoga. How about I change, and we meet back here? Do you have a yoga mat?"

His brow furrowed. "What's that?"

Had he been teaching yoga without yoga mats? That was brutal.

"What about a towel? Are you using towels as cushions?"

"No. Should I?"

"It might help."

I went to my room and changed. I grabbed two clean towels from the bathroom. When I returned, Pro Ro wore the same loose, flowing clothes, but all the tables and chairs in his room had been pushed back.

I rolled out the towels and showed him how to use it to cushion his knees.

"Oh! That's so much better," he said.

Already I could see I was making progress.

"Why don't you show me what you can do so I can see what you're teaching the students, and I'll give you some feedback. Then I'll teach you some new moves."

"Easy moves?" he asked.

"Easy and gentle yoga." Mostly because that was all I knew.

He demonstrated Cat-Cow, Downward Dog, Upward Dog, and Child's Pose. I corrected his supine twist.

"After that, we meditate. I think most of the students fall asleep. Some sneak out." He cleared his throat. "I pretend not to notice."

I demonstrated a sequence of sun salutations, which he mastered beautifully. "So let's step up your game plan and give them some new moves. We can teach you a routine that you can do as a sequence so that one move flows into the next, and then you can repeat it multiple times."

Pro Ro grinned. "This is exactly what I need. It will take up more time!"

"Great. . . ." Here was the tricky part coming up—how to ask for what I wanted without sounding like a manipulative witch who was only teaching him yoga because I wanted something from him. Which I sort of was. My lack of social skills didn't help with this endeavor.

"So, um, so you think . . . if this is helpful to you . . . um. . . ."

He stared at me unblinking. He wasn't going to make this easy.

"Would you help me divine something when I get done showing you yoga?"

His smile turned smug. "Ah, so that's your price?"

I tried not to let the snootiness of his tone get to me. I wasn't doing this for myself. I was doing it for Derrick.

"I need to find a friend," I said. "Someone I'm afraid was snatched by the Raven Court."

He shrugged. "Fine. After you teach me yoga."

I demonstrated an easy routine. Twenty minutes into it, Pro Ro was hot and sweaty. I went slow and repeated each move until he got it. The stench of garbage and musky animal wafted into the room. I tried not to gag.

"Oh boy!" Pinky said from the doorway. "Are you guys doing yoga? You should have told me! I have a yoga mat."

Pro Ro choked and held a sleeve over his face.

We should have closed the door to Pro Ro's room, but I hadn't wanted anyone to think we were doing something inappropriate.

"How about next time?" I asked. "We're almost done for today." It was a white lie. Besides the fact that I didn't think I would be able to exercise and hold my breath at the same time if Pinky joined us, I had a feeling Pinky knew his yoga. He'd said he'd been practicing for over ten years. He would see my *years* of yoga were an amateur's three years. If I was going to get Pro Ro to help me, I would need to show him I was an expert in the field with a valuable skill he lacked.

"Oh," Pinky said, shoulders sagging. "Yeah, maybe next time." He trudged away.

His sasquatch stench lingered.

Pro Ro opened the window. Frigid air blew into the classroom, fluttering the papers on his desk.

"It isn't a good idea to stretch and do yoga while you're cold," I said. "It contracts your muscles, and it makes it harder to stretch."

"The alternative is worse," he said.

Icy raindrops gusted in, and I scooted myself farther from the window. I shivered. Five minutes into the next set, Pro Ro was in the middle of a sequence of Warrior moves when he plopped onto his towel, swearing.

"What is it?" I asked.

"My back. I'm having a muscle spasm."

I rushed to close the window, suspecting the chilly air to be the cause. "What can I do to help?"

"You said you were going to teach me easy yoga. Gentle yoga." He groaned and lied still. "That wasn't gentle."

"Why didn't you say it was too hard?"

He grunted again.

"Do you want me to get you something for the pain?" I asked. "An ibuprofen or some kind of potion?"

"I don't want any of your potions, and don't even suggest Nurse Hilda. She's a menace."

"I could get Grandmother Bluehorse. She has herbal remedies."

He rolled over and panted. "Just get out. I'll make my own tonic."

"Does that mean you aren't going to. . . ?"

"No."

Craptacular. That plan had failed.

# CHAPTER TWENTY-TWO
## A Very Bad Chocolate Prophecy

Josie burst into my classroom as I sat with students quizzing each other with notecards in Tuesday's Study Club. "It's ready! Puck's chocolate prophecy! Come to the conference room with me."

I'd never seen her so excited about anything. I leapt to my feet. "I'll be back in a few," I told the students working on Latin.

Imani gave me a thumbs-up.

Josie linked arms with me, her cheerful enthusiasm drowning out a fraction of the gloom I'd acquired since Derrick's disappearance. We traveled up the stairs to the admin wing, pausing in the doorway of the conference room. I didn't know if I wanted to taste my future. What if it was salty again? I would worry about Derrick even more.

Under each teacher's name was taped an envelope, presumably with their chocolate prophecy.

Thatch held a piece of chocolate in his hand. Josie's name was written across the envelope. Two envelopes at his feet looked as though they had been stomped on from the way they were crumpled. One was Vega's.

Why did he have to be such a jerk? Just when I thought he might not be a complete asshole, he had switched everyone's prophecy chocolate. This was the second time.

Maybe it was the pants. He knew about the pants, and this was his revenge on the both of us.

Josie drew her wand. "What are you doing with my prophecy chocolate?"

He looked at the square of chocolate in his hand. "I was checking it for poison."

"You were not!" Josie stomped over to him, reaching for her chocolate.

He held it higher than she could reach. Considering he had at least a foot on her, it wasn't difficult. She spoke in Japanese, her wand glowing green.

I stood there, not knowing what to do.

Thatch waved a hand in front of her wand, extinguishing her spell before she completed it. She punched him in the arm. He smiled and did the unthinkable. He shoved the chocolate into his mouth.

Josie shrieked. "No! Not again. It's my chocolate!" She grappled with him for her envelope, but he pushed her away and shoved another piece into his mouth.

"Guys, stop it!" I said. It was embarrassing watching two grown-ups fight like immature teenagers.

Josie jabbed her wand into his side.

"Harder. You know what I like," Thatch said, his mouth full of chocolate.

I grabbed Josie's arm before she could give him a serious blow. Anything she did would only make his affinity stronger.

Thatch's polished black shoes crunched over broken chocolate on the floor as he backed away. His face was red. He doubled over and choked.

"Josie! What did you do? You have to unhex him. You'll lose your job." I had another thought. "Plus killing someone is wrong."

"I didn't hex him. I was trying a summoning spell." Her eyes went wide.

He fell to his knees, one hand grabbing at his throat.

"Well, use some magic and unchoke him," I said.

She closed her eyes, waved her wand at him, and sang something in Japanese. Nothing changed.

She tried another spell. Still no effect.

I elbowed her out of the way. I knew Thatch hated being touched—unless it was getting punched apparently—but this was an emergency. I reached my arms around him and tried the Heimlich maneuver. He was on his knees, so I could reach him at least.

Thatch coughed up a gob of what might have been caramel, and it went flying onto the front of Josie's lavender dress. Lucky her. Thatch continued to cough. He crouched on the ground.

Josie looked from him to her dress, disgust painting her face. "I hate you even more."

Blood dripped out of Thatch's mouth.

"The chocolate was poisoned," Thatch said between coughs. "Get Pro Ro or Gertr—" A gush of blood erupted from his mouth.

# CHAPTER TWENTY-THREE
## A Taste of His Own Medicine

I shoved Josie toward the door. We needed a powerful Celestor, and who were the most powerful Celestors after Thatch? Pro Ro and Gertrude Periwinkle, apparently. But Pro Ro wasn't going to help—not after the yoga fiasco.

"You," I pointed to Josie. "Get Periwinkle. I'll get Vega."

I didn't want to leave Thatch dying on the floor, but we needed to get help fast.

As we ran out of the conference room, I passed Puck's office where he sat meditating in his Zen garden. "Puck. Emergency in the conference room."

Some of the papers swirling around him fluttered to the ground. He gave me a dirty look.

"Blood. Poison. Thatch," I said and ran out.

I ran toward Vega's classroom, one of the places I usually avoided. Students tried to stop me in the hall, but I ran past them. I burst into Vega's classroom a moment later.

She leaned over a student incanting a spell from a book. "Your pronunciation is horrible. If you don't get a handle on your Latin, you'll never master the simplest of—"

I panted. "Thatch. Poison. Conference room."

"What is this? A game of clue? I'm busy tutoring one of my juvenile delinquents." She waved a hand at the young lady.

The student crossed her arms. "I'm not a juvenile delinquent."

"This isn't a joke," I said. "He asked for you to come and cure him." Actually, not her specifically, but I was certain he would have asked for her if he hadn't choked on his own blood.

She sighed in exasperation, walking toward me. "Fine. I'm coming. But he'd better be dying."

"He is," I said.

She picked up her pace, her heels clicking against the floor in a hurried beat. I thought it might have been out of concern until she spoke. "You know, it isn't considered necrophilia if you start when they're still alive."

"What?" I asked.

"Nothing."

We found him curled up on the floor in a puddle of blood. His white cravat and shirt were splattered with more blood than a vampire horror movie. His eyes were closed. Puck was nowhere in sight.

"Too late," Vega said.

I avoided the puddle and crouched beside him. I palpated his neck and found a pulse.

I sighed in relief. "I brought Vega."

His eyes opened and fixed on Vega. I expected to see hope or relief, but instead I saw venom there. Huh. That was unexpected.

Vega waved her wand over him. Sparkles of light danced before my eyes and blinded me. The room smelled like toffee and starlight.

Thatch groaned and vomited blood.

"Fucktacular," she said. "It was someone who actually knew what they were doing."

She tried another spell. This spell didn't work either.

Miss Periwinkle rushed through the door a moment later, closely followed by Josie.

"Felix!" Gertrude Periwinkle screamed. She looked to me. "What have you done?"

She shoved me out of the way, and I landed on my butt, mostly avoiding the puddle of crimson. She dropped to her knees beside him, scooping him onto her lap—or as much of him as she could fit on her lap, mostly his head and shoulders.

Exhaustion weighed down his eyelids.

She placed a hand on his chest. Her voice erupted into a siren song, high and ethereal, filled with calm. The notes sparkled out of her mouth, flickering into brilliant flashes before dying away. It was so beautiful it hurt my eyes. I tasted fresh spring water and starlight. I couldn't tell if this was Elementia siren magic or Celestor power.

She dipped her face closer to his, the sparkles of song washing over him. He coughed again, but he didn't vomit this time. Her long blonde hair dragged in the puddle, tinting the edges with scarlet. Josie and Vega whispered something in the corner. Josie's hiss rose above the spell.

Thatch inhaled deeply and opened his eyes. My head felt light, and I realized I had been holding my breath, afraid he wouldn't survive.

He sat up, flinching and clutching his stomach as he did so.

"Don't move. You need to rest." Miss Periwinkle's hands remained on his shoulders.

Khaba and Puck burst into the room. Khaba's eyes went wide at the sight of the blood. "Fan-fucking-tabulous. What happened here?"

Vega edged toward the door. "It looks like he'll live. I have better things to do." Her usual sneer was replaced with wide-eyed trepidation.

That was unusual.

Thatch glared at her, his voice hoarse. "You evil bitch."

Vega shook her head. "I did *not* poison your chocolate."

"What?" Puck asked in indignation. "Someone tampered with *my* chocolates?"

I looked to Josie. She looped an arm through mine. Did Thatch think Vega had poisoned him? She certainly was acting guilty. Khaba's feet crunched over envelopes on the floor and broken bits of candy. He avoided the vermillion puddle.

Vega repeated herself. "I didn't poison your chocolate."

Thatch tried to rise but was too weak and fell back into Miss Periwinkle's arms. His eyes held Vega. "No, you poisoned Miss Kimura's."

She snorted. "I wouldn't waste good poison on her."

"Don't lie to me. After I detected the poison, I used an imprint charm to find the last person who touched the chocolate." His eyes burned with fire. "It was you."

Whoa! So he had eaten Josie's chocolate, knowing it had been poisoned? He'd saved her by eating it himself. He was a hero in his jerk of a way.

Thatch raised his wand, aiming at Vega. I scurried back, not wanting to get between the two of them.

"Hold on a minute," Khaba said, stepping forward, hands held up in a placating gesture.

Gertrude Periwinkle placed a hand on Thatch's, lowering his hand to his side.

"Felix," she said. "Vega wouldn't poison someone. Please, be reasonable."

He shifted as though he intended to stand.

Miss Periwinkle pulled him back down. "Stop upsetting yourself before you injure yourself worse," she said.

Khaba pointed to Josie and me. "You two. Out."

I remained rooted to the ground. Vega started toward the door. Khaba snapped his fingers at her and pointed to a chair. "Sit."

Reluctantly she did so.

Khaba nodded to Miss Periwinkle. "Please return to the library."

"But—" Tears filled her eyes as she looked down at her boyfriend.

Thatch sat up and leaned against the wall.

Khaba offered Gertrude Periwinkle a hand and helped her to her feet. "I trust he's no longer in danger." The kind smile he gave her turned to disgust as he eyed his stained fingers after touching her. His hand was hardly bloody compared to her own.

Reluctantly Miss Periwinkle exited, glancing over her shoulder at Thatch as Khaba and Puck helped him into a chair. Her apprehensive expression hardened into fury as she gazed at me. Probably she wondered what I was doing in the same room with him again.

Vega crossed her arms, her expression as petulant as a child's. "I didn't poison anyone's stupid chocolate. I just. . . ." She sighed in exasperation. "I switched them around. I thought it would be amusing. Last year when I did it, everyone assumed it was Thatch. He never denied it, so I thought—"

"It was you!" Josie shrieked. "You're the one who keeps eating my chocolate." She lunged forward. I grabbed her to hold her back.

Thatch closed his eyes and remained leaning against the wall. "Merlin's fucking balls."

"Out." Khaba snapped his fingers at us.

My feet tripped over each other as I walked out of the room against my will. Josie stumbled into me, and we fell out of the conference room and onto the floor of the hallway.

"No one is leaving until we get this figured out," Khaba said.

The door closed between us.

Josie climbed to her feet. "That could have been me." Her hands were noticeably shaking.

"I know." I pushed myself up and wiped my bloody hand on the black of my skirt. "I guess you should thank Thatch for eating your chocolate for you."

"Ha!"

Thatch had once knocked over my beer at the pub because someone had hexed it. A normal person would have just told me not to drink the overpriced swill because it had a potion dropped into it. But not Thatch. That would have shown he was a decent human being. Instead, he'd knocked it over, which had made me angry with him—until he'd revealed months later his true motivation.

Thatch never said what he meant. He never allowed himself to appear decent or caring. It was hard to believe he'd eaten Josie's chocolate because it was poisoned and he didn't want her to eat it, but it appeared to be the case. The irony of the way he tried to appear bad by being good didn't escape my attention.

Josie stared at a smear of blood on her hands.

It still felt so surreal. All I could see was the gush of blood coming out of him. "I didn't know Miss Periwinkle was a more powerful Celestor than Vega. He's fortunate she knew the counter spell."

"I don't know if she is or isn't. She might just know different magic from Vega. Her counter curse wasn't any more complicated than Vega's. But it was more specific. They're lucky it worked."

Lucky. Maybe. Or maybe luck didn't have anything to do with it.

Later Khaba came to tell me that with Thatch's imprint charm, they could see which chocolates Vega had touched. With Puck and Vega's assistance, Khaba had isolated whose chocolates had been switched. The chocolate Thatch had eaten hadn't originally been Josie's.

It had been mine.

He wasn't able to identify the originator of the curse now that Gertrude Periwinkle had destroyed it. How convenient for her. She had a cure and a way of covering her tracks.

I had a feeling who wanted me dead and why.

# CHAPTER TWENTY-FOUR
## Jinx

Multiple times Gertrude Periwinkle had interrupted my conversations with Thatch. She'd accused me of having a key to his room and implied I was trying to steal him from her. She must have been the one to poison my chocolate to keep me away from him. Only her plan had backfired, and she'd poisoned lover boy instead.

Periwinkle was busy fussing over Thatch most of Tuesday so I waited until the following day to go to the library. I was determined to confront Miss Periwinkle. Maddy sat behind the counter of the library after school, reading a book.

This was good. There were students around. Witnesses who could call for help if she tried to kill me.

"Where's Miss Periwinkle?" I asked.

Maddy nodded toward the office behind her. "In her office. She's . . . in a meeting."

Right. Is that what her and Thatch called it?

"They've been in there a long time." Maddy stared at the counter. "We could probably knock if we need her."

"No, that's all right." I lowered my voice to a whisper. "How about those books you were telling me about?"

Maddy glanced back at the office and sighed. "She has the best ones locked up. I can't officially check them out. I decided the safest—"

The door to the office creaked open. Pro Ro exited from within. His face was flushed and his hair damp. The dreamy expression painted all over his face abruptly died when he saw me. His eyes widened, and his frame went rigid. Miss Periwinkle wasn't behind him, but the door to her private quarters was ajar.

"Ahem," Pro Ro said. "Good afternoon." He quickly pushed past me.

No freaking way. Pro Ro and Miss Periwinkle? She wouldn't have invited him back to her room. She and Thatch were an item. Had they broken up? Did Thatch know about this? Maybe they had an open relationship.

Maybe it wasn't my business.

I stared after Pro Ro for a long moment. Maddy grimaced, pretending to study one of the books at the counter.

"Does Miss Periwinkle have meetings with Pro Ro often?" I asked.

"No, that's the first time with him." Her gaze flickered past my shoulder.

Silas Lupi strolled up to the counter.

"But not the first time with someone else?" I asked.

"I didn't see anything," Maddy whispered. She dipped her head back toward her book.

"Hello, Miss Jennings," Silas said with a jovial smile to Maddy. He didn't even look at me. "Have you seen Miss Periwinkle?"

"She was in her office a minute ago." Maddy bit her lip.

He arched his neck to see around us into the office. She obviously wasn't inside. He strolled back to one of the tables, glancing our way.

I lowered my voice. "Does Miss Periwinkle have meetings with Mr. Lupi as well?"

Maddy shrugged. "I don't know. I don't keep track of her schedule. It's none of my beeswax."

I'd never known Maddy to be *not* interested in every adult's personal life, especially when it wasn't her business. Maybe she was covering for Miss Periwinkle because she'd grown attached to the librarian who mentored her. Miss Periwinkle had seen to it that Maddy's siren's magic didn't draw in every boy in the school like it had previously. It could have been out of loyalty Maddy protected her mentor. On the other hand, I had experienced firsthand how convincing Miss Periwinkle could be with blackmail.

"Is everything okay? Has she threatened you?" I whispered. I didn't want Maddy to be in danger.

"Gertrude!" Silas Lupi said.

Gertrude? That was pretty informal for the Unseen Realm. Miss Periwinkle emerged from the door to her private room and into her office. She looked surprised to see Silas.

He sauntered over to the counter. "Are you available to show me that book we were discussing yesterday?"

Ugh. Gross. Not just Pro Ro, but Silas Lupi too? He was married.

Miss Periwinkle remained in her office, her fingers smoothing across a stack of books with worn covers. "I thought you were coming to discuss that book tomorrow afternoon."

"I just couldn't wait. I needed to see you—your book." His brow crinkled, and desperation painted his face. He leaned forward, half his body draped across the counter as he strained to get closer.

She smiled coyly. "I'm sorry. I haven't located the book you requested. Perhaps this evening."

"Are you sure we can't just . . . ahem." He swallowed and looked from me to Maddy. "Perhaps you could show me a different title. Just something small. It wouldn't take long."

Miss Periwinkle giggled. I had a feeling she enjoyed this attention.

"Pardon me," I said with my best imitation of a smile. "I'm first in line to see Miss Periwinkle."

I circled around the counter and barged into the librarian's office. "I'm sure it will only take a sec for her to show me the book I've been waiting to discuss with her."

I gave Maddy a meaningful look, hoping she was bright enough to catch the meaning of my words. "If we take too long, you should knock." I closed us inside her office.

Gertrude Periwinkle's indulgent smile for Silas Lupi faded. "What do you want?"

"I hope you're happy. Your spell almost cost Felix Thatch his life."

"I don't know what you're talking about." She lifted a book and flipped through the pages, feigning disinterest.

She was a dunce at looking innocent.

"If Mr. Thatch hadn't thought to ask for your assistance in curing him, he would be dead. Coincidence? Or is it you knew how to cure the poison because you were the one who poisoned the chocolate?" I crossed my arms. "But maybe you don't care. It seems you have enough lovers to occupy yourself with."

"My love life is none of your concern!" She snapped the book closed. "You don't know what it's like to be young and beautiful for the first time in over twenty years after being cursed."

"You're right, I don't know," I said. "It's hard for me to imagine why someone so incredibly beautiful would be so jealous and possessive of a man she isn't even monogamous with."

She slapped me across the face, hard enough I tasted blood. I stumbled away from her. The corner of her desk jabbed into my hip, making me flinch.

Miss Periwinkle poked a finger into my chest, just below the collarbone. "Listen to me, you little whore. You're going to keep your hands off my Felix. I don't care who else you fuck, but he's mine."

"I don't want Felix Thatch. We're just friends." I pushed her hand away. "I have my own boyfriend."

She looked me up and down and snorted. "You wish."

What was it with these snotty Celestors thinking I was incapable of landing a boyfriend? And yet, she must have thought I was competent enough or pretty enough to attract a man's attention if she feared I had stolen hers.

She backed up a step, enabling me to slide away toward the door. Most of my courage had left me by this point, but I made one last attempt to ensure my future safety.

"I wonder what Felix Thatch will say once he realizes you were the one who almost killed him. Maybe you should keep your spells and jealousy to yourself." I threw open the door.

Miss Periwinkle's voice was so quiet I almost didn't hear it. "If you try to sully my name, you'll regret it."

Maddy sat with her head bowed so close to her book, I doubted she could even read the words.

Silas Lupi cleared his throat, his eyes on the floor. "Maybe I should come back another time."

From his reaction, I suspected we had been louder than I'd realized. That had to have been an awkward conversation to overhear.

I made a beeline for Khaba's office. The door was open while he chatted with two students about attendance. He waved and shooed off the students when he saw me.

They eagerly ran off, probably relieved to get out of a chastising.

"What can I help you with?" he asked.

"I came here to tell you the name of the person who tried to poison me."

He gestured for me to enter. I did so, the door closing automatically behind me.

"I just came from. . . ." I drew in a deep breath, nervousness making my chest tighten. "Yank swig bad hunch." That didn't make sense. I tried again. "Athlete strife nonbelief incertitude for cane."

Khaba's eyebrows rose. "What?"

"What I mean to say is . . . dubiety duels spite covets thy neighbor's wife. No, that wasn't right! I mean, green-eyed gargle girls poisoned the misanthrope for duplicity. Agh!" My mouth wouldn't say the words. I tried again, but gibberish came out instead of the truth.

Miss Periwinkle had cursed me. She had ensured I wouldn't sully her name.

Khaba leaned his chin onto his hand looking exasperated. "Honey, what did you do to yourself now?"

"I didn't do this to myself. Ghouls in New York kicked squiggle boinks." I inhaled a deep breath and tried to say the librarian's name.

"Swizzle sticks." I tried to say the first letter of her name. My lips formed an *r* sound. I tried to make my mouth make a *p* instead. I couldn't do it. Maybe if I tried to say any word that started with a *p*. "Pig," I said. "Pacific. Penitentiary. Performance. Pirrrrrr—pirrrr. . . ." I could almost say her name, but the closer I got, the more the tightness in my chest radiated up my neck. My face flushed with heat. It grew harder to breathe. "Pirr—pira—Piranesi."

Khaba put up a hand. "Let me guess. You know who tried to poison you, but this person cast a tongue-twister jinx on you?"

I nodded. He laughed.

"This isn't funny," I said.

He cleared his throat. "No, of course not. Excuse me." He burst out laughing. "Sorry. I just thought of a good pun. Do you want to hear it?"

I shook my head. "No."

"I dream of djinn-x. Djinnx. Get it?"

I liked puns, but that one was lame. He kept laughing.

"Is it a student or staff member?" he asked.

"Quidditch," I said.

"Right." He drummed his fingers along his desk. "Was it Thatch?"

I hesitated. It wasn't Thatch, but Miss Periwinkle was doing it because of her relationship with Thatch. I shook my head. At least I could do that.

"Can't you unjinx me so I can tell you?" I asked.

"Sure, but that takes a lot of magic. You can make a wish if you want. I should warn you, though, my lamp has migrated . . . farther south from where it was last." The little smirk on his face told me *how* far south. "And not that I'm choosy about where a good rubdown comes from, but you aren't exactly my type."

"Oh." I could see why he hadn't offered to unjinx me now. I was fortunate his lamp hadn't been in such an inconvenient place when we'd encountered the Raven Court.

Khaba waved a hand over his desk. The surface rippled and transformed to a map of the first story of the school. It reminded me of the Google Earth bird's-eye view of the school he'd shown me previously, only this one lacked a roof. He nodded to the representation. "Place your hand over the map and show me where you were jinxed."

I studied the map, trying to figure out where Miss Periwinkle's office was located. I pointed.

"The library? In Miss Periwinkle's office?" he asked.

I nodded.

"Is she the one who jinxed you?"

I nodded.

His eyebrows drew together. "And tried to poison you?"

I emphatically nodded again.

He rose. "We're going to confront her."

"I already tried."

He nudged me with an elbow. "Tried and failed if your jinx is any indication of your lack of success. This time, you're going to have a powerful djinn with you, and I'm immune to siren magic and paltry Witchkin spells."

Khaba confidently strode toward the library. I had to run to keep up with him. This was great! I wished I'd gone to him first. He was going to find out all that she'd done, and she would get fired.

In the library, Maddy returned books to shelves along one of the aisles. She waved to me, her smile faltering when she took in the determined expression on Khaba's face. Miss Periwinkle stood behind the counter, checking out books. Three students stood in line, all young men with dreamy expressions on their faces. One of them held a flower behind his back. I sincerely hoped she wasn't sleeping with the students. I caught the tail end of what Miss Periwinkle said to one of the students.

"That is very sweet of you to ask, but you would do better to focus your attention on someone your age," she said.

I didn't know if she was saying that because of Khaba heading her way or she truly had no interest in seducing students.

"Ahem," Khaba said.

Miss Periwinkle flashed her sweetest smile at him. "Mr. Khaba, how may I help you?" Her voice purred like a sultry cat.

"Don't try that siren crap on me. Unjinx Miss Lawrence immediately."

"Me?" she asked innocently.

The students whispered to each other.

"What kind of jinx?" a tall boy asked.

"That's what happens when you don't return your library books on time," Ben O'Sullivan said, coming up to the counter with a stack of library books.

Khaba eyed the students. "Don't you have somewhere better to be?"

"I have books to check out," a young man with a goatee and spacers in his ears said. From the eclectic stack of books that included a Nancy Drew mystery and *Little House on the Prairie*, I wondered if he'd been too distracted checking out the librarian that he had no clue what books he intended to check out.

Miss Periwinkle batted her eyelashes at the students. "I'm so pleased you have such a passion for reading. I'm sure Maddy can assist you with your books." She waved Khaba around the counter. "Perhaps we should speak in private, away from the students, Mr. Khaba."

Only weeks before these young men would have loved for an

opportunity to flirt with Maddy, but today they rolled their eyes and groaned as she came over.

"I don't want that dog to touch my books," one of the boys muttered.

"Hey!" I said, "That isn't very nice. We don't talk that way about people."

"Whatever," he said.

Maddy just rolled her eyes.

Khaba and Miss Periwinkle headed into her office. I hurried around the counter to join them. Miss Periwinkle grinned at me as she closed the door in my face. I tried the doorknob, but it was locked. I knocked, but Khaba didn't open the door for me.

Did she think she could use magic on Khaba? He was Fae. His magic was more powerful than anything she could throw at him. Probably he was going to yell at her and tell her what a wicked witch she was—without me as a witness.

"Do you want me to help you check out those books?" Maddy called to the students at the counter. She rolled the cart of books closer.

"No, thanks. I'll wait," the tallest student said.

"You can wait if you want, but she'll probably be in there for a while." She shrugged and returned to work.

I didn't hear any yelling. I waited at the counter with the students. Ten minutes passed.

I walked over to Maddy. "Earlier we were talking about that book. . . ."

"Yeah, didn't you get it?" She lowered her voice to a whisper. "Hailey snuck it out for you."

"No, I did not get it. When did she borrow this book from the library?"

"A couple days ago."

"Of course." Just what I wanted, the book to be in possession of one of my students.

I soooo didn't have time for this.

Khaba emerged from the office, a satisfied smile on his face. "That takes care of that."

I rushed over to the counter, along with the teenage boys.

"Well?" I asked.

Khaba pointed a finger at me, his laugh jovial and light. "You need to start returning your library books on time."

"What?"

"You need to follow the school policies, young lady." He wagged a finger at me in mock sternness. "I will not allow staff to disregard library rules and return books late. You're fortunate Miss Periwinkle let you off easy this time. Next time she might be forced to take more drastic measures. As the school's disciplinarian, I'll be bound to see you comply."

I shook my head at him, unable to believe my ears.

The teenage boys snickered beside me. I shot them a dirty look. I was not a library delinquent. I returned my books on time. Mostly.

Miss Periwinkle stepped out of her office, her smile amused. I hated her more than ever.

How had she done it? Khaba didn't even like women.

I had failed in soliciting Khaba's assistance. I could only imagine that she had bewitched him with her siren's voice. For all I knew, she had convinced him to allow her to rub his lamp and make a wish.

I couldn't speak about what had happened because of the jinx, and I could see no male staff member would be able to resist her charms. The thing Miss Periwinkle had been the most adamant about was that I not sully her name to Thatch. I wondered if there was another way to alert him of what she was doing. Every time I met with Thatch, she interfered. He had been bewitched as well, I was certain, but if Miss Periwinkle didn't want him to think ill of her, surely her enchantment wasn't infallible. If Thatch could understand she had poisoned me, he might snap out of it.

I tried writing a letter.

*Dear Mr. Thatch,*

*I am writing you this letter because I need to speak with you about something important. I cannot talk about it in person because if I do, Miss Periwinkle will interrupt. We have already discussed how jealous she becomes every time I speak with you alone.*

So far, so good. My grammar and word choice made sense. The tongue-twister jinx might only apply to my tongue. That would make sense. Khaba had been able to ask me questions that I could nod or shake my head to answer. I continued writing.

*I need you to understand something about Miss Periwinkle. She strange gauche for phony thesaurus in the library with fishy.*

That hadn't worked as I'd hoped. I crossed off the line and tried again.

*Artificial inelegance ponders curious doubt. Pig piranha resents zealous me. Watch rival grasping djinn and tonic. Persuade hijinks skeptics of seduction.*

Sweat dripped down my forehead and my hand cramped as I attempted to defy the spell. I tried a different tactic.

*Do you have a counter spell for a tongue-twister jinx? Something that will help with handwritten messages as well? If so, would you please place it in my mailbox or send it to my classroom with a student? I need to be able to tell you about the green-eyed zealous vigilance of attentive broom closets.*

*Your friend and attentive student,*

*Miss Clarissa Lawrence*

I looked all over until I found Imani and Greenie studying in the girls' dormitory. I handed the folded note to Imani. "I need you to take this to Mr. Thatch pronto. If Miss Periwinkle intercepts you, hide it, and don't let her get it."

The two girls set their books aside.

Greenie giggled. "Is it a love note?"

"No, it isn't. And don't read it. The note is private, and it contains information about grades and. . . ." I desperately tried to think of something that would make it less interesting to students and failed. "Just mind your own beeswax and take it to him. Ask him if he will reply and send you with the response to me. I'll be in my classroom."

The girls ran off. I suspected they would read the note. Considering I didn't even know if he would understand the note, it was possible it wouldn't make much sense to them either.

Fifteen minutes later, Imani ran into my room, pigtails bouncing. She waved an envelope in her hand. "He replied. What does it say?"

Greenie ran in after her, out of breath. "He wouldn't tell us. Will you tell us?"

"He yelled at us for reading your note," Imani admitted. "But I hardly read any of it."

Greenie's cheeks flushed dark green, and she cast a sheepish smile my way. "We only glanced at it really quickly and then folded it back up before giving it to him."

On the front of the envelope was my name written in cursive with a fancy calligraphy pen. I tore the paper open. I was thrown off by the brevity of his note.

*I am determined to be an impartial and uninvolved party to whatever you and Gertrude are feuding about now. If she's jinxed you with a tongue-twister spell (which, I will point out any moron with half an education could undo) you can find the book for undoing it in the library and perform the spell on your own. I will not involve myself in your problems.*

I sank into my chair, tears filling my eyes. "I can't go to the library and check out the book." I crumpled up the note in my hands and dropped my head onto my arms. "She'll hide it from me."

"Who's Gertrude?" Greenie whispered.

"That's Miss Periwinkle," Imani said.

"Oh. She's changed since she became beautiful, hasn't she?" Greenie patted my shoulder. "Why did she jinx you, Miss Lawrence?"

I didn't want to share my personal problems with students. It wasn't professional. Then again, jinxing teachers or seducing coworkers with siren magic didn't seem professional either.

"Do you want us to go to the library and see if we can find the book with the counter jinx?" Imani asked.

I lifted my head. "Would you?"

"Of course. You're my favorite teacher."

They returned a few minutes later with news. I should have known: the five books on counter jinxes were currently checked out.

The attempted poisoning, Derrick's disappearance, and presence of the Raven Court couldn't all be separate incidents. I didn't believe they were coincidences. Miss Periwinkle was behind the chocolate poisoning. I'd seen her sneaking off into the woods, which was also suspicious.

Could it be the librarian's jealousy and hatred of me inspired her to work for the Raven Court? I was certain it had been a raven that flew up into the sky after she'd entered the forest. Maybe she could transform into a bird woman like the emissaries of the Raven Court did.

I needed to spy on her and see if I could catch her in the act. If I could prove without a doubt how evil she was, Jeb or Khaba would be forced to believe me. Maybe if I took photos on a cell phone, I could use that as proof. Josie had advised me not to use the camera feature on my phone in the past, though. Plus, I would need a phone.

I called in the favors. I asked Imani to bring Maddy to my classroom.

She came just before curfew, probably when she was released from working in the library. Her bubbly personality was gone. She stared at the floor.

I tried to reassure her with a smile. "Maddy, do you ever see Miss Periwinkle leave the library in the evening after dinner?"

"She sometimes has me lock up when Mr. Thatch comes in and they walk out together." Maddy bit her lip. She glanced around. "Have you noticed how Mr. Thatch has been kind of . . . not himself lately? Do you think maybe she cast a spell on him?"

"Probably." Who hadn't she cast a spell on? "It's none of my business, and I have way bigger things to think about at the moment." I tried to get her back on task. "What about when they don't walk out together? Does she ever go out alone?"

"Sometimes."

The librarian might have been leaving to meet one of her lovers, or even Thatch down in the dungeon. Or she might have been planning a secret rendezvous with the Raven Court.

I would get to the bottom of her mysterious disappearances and prove she was a wicked witch. Derrick might be depending on it.

## CHAPTER TWENTY-FIVE
## The Invisibility Snuggie

I returned to Khaba's office. "Do you have any more invisibility clothes?" I asked him.

He crossed his arms. "Please tell me you're not going to try to do anything dangerous or stupid."

"Me? Do anything stupid? Or dangerous?" I waved him off, trying to act casual. "That would be ridiculous." Maybe it was ridiculous to want invisibility clothes to try to secretly spy on Miss Periwinkle.

"I'm not going to ask why you need invisibility clothes in case you say something that incriminates yourself, but I will say, I'm not just saying this as your dean of discipline, I'm saying this as your friend: you need to be careful. I don't want you sneaking off to Lachlan Falls. I don't want you falling into the hands of Fae."

"You're Fae," I said with an attempt at a teasing smile.

"Ha ha. As if I don't hear that one every day." He walked over to his file cabinet and sifted through the contents. "I confiscated this jacket from Hailey Achilles last semester. If I give it to you, promise me you aren't going to sneak off school grounds." He held up his hand as though he were holding something, but I couldn't see it.

"I promise," I said.

I hoped I could keep that promise.

The piece of invisibility clothing wasn't a jacket, it was a Snuggie. I remembered Hailey using it when I'd chased her months ago, thinking she had intended to steal the answer keys. I tried it on in my room. It didn't close in the back and it was so long it dragged on the ground.

It would have come in handy for Derrick to use, except that it was such a small size. It was loose on me, but it must have been tight on Hailey. The sleeves swallowed my arms with so much extra fabric that it hid my hands. I turned it around and tried pinning the back closed with safety pins. No matter what I did, little lines of metal showed, even when I pinned it from the inside. That would give me away if I tried to use it during the day. Plus, my head was still visible.

Vega walked in on me. I hurriedly ducked into the fabric, trying to pull it over my head.

"That isn't going to work. I already saw you," Vega said. "Though, just so you know, that's an improvement for your figure."

"Um, thanks." I never knew what to expect from Vega. She might tell Thatch she thought I was up to something, or she might try to blackmail me.

Vega spritzed herself with stinky perfume and retrieved a shawl from her wardrobe. "If you really want to improve your looks, you'd put a bag over your head too."

"If I temporarily wanted to make my face invisible, how would I do it?" I asked.

"Invisibility spells are too difficult for you, so don't even bother. The best you can do is an invisibility hat or mask, but they're expensive. With your first-year teacher salary, I'm surprised you could afford one of . . . whatever it is you've got on."

"Where can I get an invisibility hat? Do you have one?"

She bumped me aside with her bony hip and applied lipstick in the mirror. "Stop pestering me right now. I have places to go and people to see."

"Khaba said we aren't supposed to leave campus."

"Who says I'm leaving campus? I have friends here I'm going to visit with."

Periwinkle and Thatch? That seemed unlikely. "Where are you going?"

"Enough questions." She whipped out her wand. "Unless you want me to make sure you're not seen *and* not heard, I suggest you shut your trap."

I pretended I was zipping my lip.

If I couldn't purchase a hat or mask, and I couldn't make my face invisible with magic, maybe I could trim off the extra fabric and sew a hood with the remnants. Of course, if I used thread, it would show like the pins. I needed invisible thread.

Fortunately, I knew just the witch with sewing skills and supplies to assist me.

Before dinner, I found Josie teaching a group of students to knit in her classroom. A sign on the chalkboard read: Knitting Club. I recognized some of the students.

Chase Othello, a student with purple hair and a lip ring, waved at me. "Hi, Miss Lawrence. Look what I'm making!" She held up a dark blue blob she was very proud of.

I pulled Josie to the back corner of the classroom and whispered what I needed. She snickered when I told her my sewing plan.

"First of all, do you know how difficult it is to sew something you can't see?"

"I already thought of that." I held up a bottle of talcum powder. "Problem solved."

She tugged on the rim of her orchid-and-mauve patchwork witch hat absentmindedly, as if thinking it over. "What do you even need a hood on this invisibility Snuggie for?"

"I'm not at liberty to say."

"Hey!" Josie raised her voice and waved at the students. "Do not eat that yarn! It will get tangled up in your intestines and cause problems. Plus, I only have so much."

Ben O'Sullivan pulled a dark blue line of yarn from his mouth. He kept pulling and pulling. He looked like he would gag. It was like a very bad magic trick.

Josie made a face. "I don't have any invisible thread. I'm going to have to dye some so it becomes transparent."

"I have a feeling if you created gray thread that turned hot pink after Thatch wore it, you can create transparent thread."

She giggled. "Yeah, that was good."

"He was really mad at me until he figured out it was you."

"I wish I'd been there to see his expression." Her giggle rose into a Vega-like cackle. Students stared at us and whispered. We snuck out into the hall to finish our conversation.

"You know, I feel a little bad about it now. I thought Thatch ate my chocolate to get back at me, but I'm not so sure anymore," she said. "I think he thought Vega hexed it, but maybe he didn't realize how severe a curse it actually was."

"Don't tell me you like Felix Thatch now." I nudged her, teasingly.

"No. He's too sneaky. I know he's hiding something. Don't you get that feeling? Like he knows something is going on, but he's covering for someone?"

I nodded. "I believe he is. Someone he cares about. Someone he *loves*." I tried to give her hints before the tongue twister took over.

She chewed her lip. "That's why you want help making this thing, isn't it? You're going to spy on Gertrude Periwinkle. She's freakier than Thatch. I wouldn't mess with her."

I lowered my voice to a whisper. "She's already tried to ghost aghast jinx school."

Darn it!

I tried again but my words came out just as jumbled.

"She hexed your tongue?" Josie asked.

I nodded.

"Have you tried talking to Khaba? You don't need to do this alone."

"Yes, I do." I carefully selected my words. "*Someone* bewitched him just like she does with everyone else. *Someone* used siren magic and makes men do what she wants. I have to find evidence of what she's doing and show someone who can resist her powers. Another woman, maybe."

"Oh! Like Mrs. Keahi!" Josie said.

Maybe. Jeb was most likely out of the question. If there was a school board, I didn't think they'd stand for it. Not that I knew if Witchkin schools worked the same way public schools did.

"Will you help me?" I asked.

She threw her arms around my neck and hugged me. "I thought you'd never ask! But you have to promise me you'll let me spy with you."

After my dinner duty was finished, Josie made me assist her in her room with the sewing. It took hours to magically "dye" thread transparent.

"Transparent thread is easier to create than invisible thread," Josie said.

"I don't see what the difference is."

"Har har," she said dryly. "Sounds like you've been hanging out with Khaba too much."

"No, really," I said.

"Transparent means the color underneath will show through, but the thread won't have any color of its own. Invisible will hide what's underneath. It takes less skill and less magic to dye thread transparent." Josie explained the process matter-of-factly, as though this was normal to her.

It was hard to talk about invisibility clothes and not think about Derrick. If we had repurposed this Snuggie earlier, we could have made him a pair of pants. He wouldn't have needed to leave the school in the first place.

After we powdered the Snuggie, Josie assisted me in cutting off the extra pieces of fabric, hemming the edges, and sewing a hood with the clear thread.

"What are we going to do for you?" I asked. "We don't have an invisibility cloak for you. How are you going to sneak around with me?"

"It's fortunate we're about the same size."

We might have been the same height, but we weren't the same size.

Josie was curvy and voluptuous, an Amni Plandai fertility goddess or some equivalent.

Josie grinned. "I'm going to teach you a replication spell for making a second Snuggie. It makes an exact copy."

"Cool! That sounds like a replicator from Star Trek." Already my mind saw the endless possibilities of where I could go with this in an art classroom. I could multiply my art supplies.

Josie held up a finger in warning. "There's a catch. Anything that happens to the original, happens to the copy—and vice versa. If the original gets a tear, the copy is torn in the same place. If the copy catches on fire, the original burns too."

So much for my plan to create hundreds of sheets of paper and supplies.

By that point, it was already nine thirty p.m. I should have been in my own room for curfew. Vega would be pissed if I made too much noise coming in when she was sleeping. I held on to my invisibility Snuggie so we could finish our project on Thursday. Already I felt better about my goal to catch Miss Periwinkle and prove her guilt.

I would catch her and force the truth out of her. I would help Derrick in any way I could, and this was the only lead I had at the moment.

On Thursday, I covered my own breakfast duty and Vega's dinner duty. I could hardly wait until dinner was over so I could work on my project with Josie in the privacy of her room. Near the end of my shift Hailey came panting into the cafeteria, her face red from running.

"There's no need to run. There's still plenty of food left," I said.

"It isn't that. I just came from the library. Maddy wanted me to give you this." She pressed a note into my hand.

I unfolded it.

*Miss P just left. When I asked if she would be in the dungeon if I needed her, she said no. She said she was going for a walk. If you hurry, you might find her outside.*

I still had ten minutes left before my duty was over. The other teachers had already gone, and most of the students had left for school clubs or gone to their common rooms to study. If I left Vega's shift and she found out, I didn't know what she'd do. If I didn't try to follow Periwinkle now, I didn't know if I would have another chance.

"Would you go to Miss Kimura's room and ask her to come down here? Tell her I had to leave to take care of something," I told Hailey.

Hailey rolled her eyes.

I ran to my room, retrieved my invisibility Snuggie and put it on. It would probably have been less conspicuous if I hadn't run down the hallway, my feet slapping noisily against the stairs, but I needed to find

Periwinkle before she disappeared. I traveled along the back wing, through the ruined section of school, and climbed over the crumbling wall. From the mound of rubble, I was able to see a lone figure in a witch hat across the school grounds about to enter the forest. I ran out the back of the school, passing topiary animals who turned their heads in puzzlement as I passed. My breath made cold clouds in the air, and my feet crunched over gravel and pressed footprints in the grass. Only at the edge of the trees did I pause.

The forest was ominously dark for this time of day, and I had no light. Nor could I carry one if I wasn't going to draw attention to myself. Up ahead, something glowed, flickering in and out of view. Miss Periwinkle was silhouetted by the light of her wand.

I continued, less noisily than before, but I was still trying to hurry. A twig snapped under my foot. Periwinkle froze. Her light dimmed, but it was still enough to see where she stood. I remained still, not daring to breathe until she continued. If she was willing to poison me and try to kill people, she would have no qualms about doing so here and leaving my body to be devoured by chimeras.

The gloom of the forest pressed in on me. A wolf howled in the distance. I shivered from more than the bite of cold.

I wished I had my phone. I only had an appropriated wand, and that wasn't any help without a good spell. I slipped my hand out of my sleeve and under the invisibility robe to grope around for my pocket to find the wand. Multitasking was not one of my stronger tasks apparently. I tripped on the hem of the robe, catching myself before I plunged headfirst into the foliage. Several twigs snapped this time. My heart pounded in my ears.

Miss Periwinkle turned around. Her eyes narrowed. I ducked down. I knew she couldn't see me, but she might be able to sense me. She kept walking along the winding path. Originally, I had thought this was the path to Lachlan Falls, but we must have taken another trail at some point, because we would have reached the meadow by now. I hoped we were still on school grounds. In the distance, water burbled over rocks.

The lullaby of a stream grew louder.

Eventually Periwinkle stopped before a rocky embankment. She sat down and removed her hat. My nose was numb with cold, and I fought the urge to sniffle. The cold must not have bothered her, though. She removed her clothes and went skinny dipping in the water. Of all the things I had imagined she might do, it hadn't been that.

I shifted from foot to foot uneasily, waiting for her to call emissaries from the Raven Court or drink a baby's blood or do something horrible. There was no reason for her to sneak off to go swimming. She could easily have invited Thatch—or any one of her lovers to go with her for this. Sure,

Khaba had said leaving school grounds wasn't permitted, but I didn't think we were even outside the school boundaries, though I couldn't be sure.

I thought about the sirens I had met earlier in the semester who had wanted to lure Maddy into joining them. Periwinkle had been the one to stop them and the one to insist there was another way for Maddy. She had insisted Maddy resist the call of siren magic and the lure of draining someone.

What if she hadn't been able to resist that call of siren powers herself? As she had said, I couldn't possibly understand how difficult it was for her now that she was young and beautiful. Perhaps my affinity had released her suppressed siren magic when she had coerced me into helping her regain her youth and beauty. It would make sense how she managed to seduce all the men in the school—though I didn't understand how she could bewitch the ones who weren't straight.

Periwinkle sat on the rocks and sang, combing out her hair and looking angelic in the gloomy light. She glowed with inhuman beauty. I leaned against a tree and sighed. She was so perfect. I would have given anything to look like her. I wasn't even sure why I had thought she would kill me.

The wind rustled the leaves in the trees. The perfume of earth and water, starlight and dusty books washed over me. My tongue tasted honey and nectar in the air.

"I know you're out there," she said. "Why don't you come out and show yourself?" Her voice rushed over me like that of a tide, drawing me closer.

My feet walked forward. I didn't want us to fight her magic. Something niggled at the back of my mind. There was some reason I was supposed to be afraid of her, but I couldn't remember why.

"You caught me, lass," a male voice said from behind me.

I flinched to the side, Periwinkle's spell broken by the gruff words, caustic on the ears after the siren lullaby. That wasn't Thatch's British monotone. Nor was it anyone else I knew.

Had I discovered Periwinkle's secret?

# CHAPTER TWENTY-SIX
## A Kilty Pleasure

The man's accent might have been Scottish, but I wasn't sure. I couldn't make out more than a silhouette on the path.

"Come closer, love," Miss Periwinkle said with a coquettish smile.

The honey in her voice compelled me to obey, but I fought against it.

He stepped forward, his movements slow, as though he were fighting her as well. "You're a student at the school?" he asked.

"Maybe. Who are you?"

Maybe this wasn't her big secret as I'd hoped.

"You shouldn't be wandering about," he said. "There are dangerous creatures lurking outside these woods. The Raven Court, for one."

"Are you one of them?" She laughed.

The man stepped past me, so close I could smell his cologne. His features were in shadow as he stepped toward Periwinkle, but I was able to make out his red hair. He didn't glow like she did. I could see enough of him to note the kilt and traditional clothes.

"My name is Brogan McLean." He sat beside her on a mossy rock.

I could see his face now. He looked like the man who had met Khaba in town as we'd looked for Derrick. I had been afraid he intended to lure Khaba away from being my chaperone as a trap, but nothing bad had happened. Now this man was here, on the grounds to the school for some reason. His eyes raked over Gertrude Periwinkle's voluptuous curves.

She leaned back, her smile growing.

"I'm a friend of Khaba's," Brogan said. He still hadn't answered her question about whether he was a dangerous creature or from the Raven Court. I couldn't tell if he intentionally avoided answering the question or if his mind was muddled by magic.

"A friend? Or a lover?" she asked.

"A wee bit of both."

I wondered if he was the man I'd seen in Josie's magic-mirror spell at the pub with Khaba. I hadn't examined him carefully at the time. Now I wished I had.

She leaned forward, purring like a cat. "And what were *you* doing in the forest alone? On your way to the school to see our Mr. Khaba?"

"Aye." He swallowed. "Khaba sent a message that he needed to stop going to Lachlan Falls to meet me. Ever since the Raven Court has been showing up, he thought it wise not to leave the school. Since he couldn't leave, I thought I'd pay him a visit."

"Is our Mr. Khaba breaking the school rules? Sabotaging wards to sneak a stranger in during these dangerous times?" Everything Periwinkle said came out teasing and merry, but under her words I sensed a predator about to strike. Her eyes were full of cunning. She was wheedling information out of him, whether he realized it or not.

"There wasn't going to be any sneaking about it. I can walk in the front door freely because I'm a former student. So long as I check in at the office first," he said. "That's the rule for visitors. And you know how Fae are with all that red tape."

"Rules." She lifted her silvery-blonde hair and piled it on top of her head.

He watched her breasts lift as she raised her arms. Her smile turned smug. I really didn't like her.

She batted her eyelashes at him. "Is Mr. Khaba truly that concerned with his own rules if he breaks them?"

The man wet his lips. "It isn't breaking them if I only rub his lamp."

She leaned forward. "Is this the truth?" She stroked his cheek with a finger. "Or did Khaba send you out here to spy on me?"

"Khaba didn't send me. I saw you walking in the woods, and I thought you might be a student. At first I thought I would leave you be. Students are always sneaking off to Lachlan Falls, and it's none of my business. But these be dangerous times, and I reconsidered. Then I felt something, a presence following you."

"I didn't feel anyone." Her eyes flickered to the trees, to the place I stood, and kept scanning the shadows.

"I'm a telepath," Brogan said. "When I touch someone, I can read minds."

She withdrew her hand from his cheek. Served her right! He would know she was up to no good.

Brogan swallowed. "From a distance, I sense feelings. I could tell the person following you didn't have your best intentions in mind. He or she—I can't tell—hates you. I didn't want you to come to any harm. But then I saw you bathing, and, well—"

I did not hate her! Well, maybe a little. But I did have good intentions—they were to prove her guilt. They were to help me find Derrick. I could see how following her might look suspicious, but if he knew what I knew, I doubted he would disagree with my intentions.

"That's sweet of you, thinking I couldn't take care of myself." She stroked his hair. "Have you ever been with a siren?"

He laughed. "I've never been with a woman."

She leaned forward and kissed him. I was done here.

Miss Periwinkle's big secret of the day was that she snuck off to the stream. And she was disgusting, seducing anything with a penis she could get her hands on, but I already knew that. I had to find another way to prove her guilt.

Once I returned to the women's dorm, I tried to wash the mud off the Snuggie in the sink, but as I did so, the fabric started to turn opaque. Oh no! Maybe there were special washing instructions for invisibility fabric. I wrung it out the best I could and hung it on a hanger. There wasn't any place to hang it without getting anything else wet or muddy, so I hooked the hanger onto the empty birdcage suspended from the ceiling and set a towel underneath to catch the drips.

When I told Josie what I'd done, her face turned red. "You were supposed to bring me with you! What were you thinking? You could have gotten seriously hurt by that psycho." She slugged me in the arm, harder than her usual punch.

"Ow! Sorry. It couldn't wait. I didn't have time to get you."

She crossed her arms. "And now you've ruined your invisibility cloak and washed out the invisibility. Do you know how expensive those things are?"

"I know. It sucks."

"As soon as it's dry, I want you to bring it to me to see if I can fix it. Otherwise, the copy is going to look just as horrible as this one."

She punched me in the shoulder again. "And don't sneak off like that again. I'm getting tired of covering for you."

I was lucky Josie was willing to put up with me. I considered going to Khaba and telling him what I'd seen, but he was already under Gertrude Periwinkle's spell. I didn't know how he would react to the news that one of his special friends was seeing her in the forest too. I had to figure out what to do about Miss Periwinkle and prove she was up to no good. More than that, I needed to figure out how her nefarious doings were related to the Raven Court and Derrick's disappearance.

## CHAPTER TWENTY-SEVEN
## Adventures in Babysitting

The weekend came and went. Not knowing where Derrick was drove me crazy. I didn't know how to help him. Saturday and Sunday morning, Thatch missed our lesson. I shouldn't have been surprised.

On Monday morning during my second-period prep, a timid-looking boy came in. Like me, he was covered in a million freckles and petite. He lacked my natural red hair, his being dark brown instead.

"Um. . . ." His voice was high for a high school student, like he hadn't yet hit puberty.

"Hello, are you new?" I asked.

"Yeah. It's my first day."

"Where are you supposed to be?" Not my class. I didn't have a class this period.

"You're Miss Lawrence? This is my class."

"Maybe you have me next period. What's your name?"

"Trevor Annis." Poor kid. There would be no end to the teasing he got with that last name. I checked my roster. According to the class list, I had him this period as well as *every* other period.

"Well, that's odd. I don't usually have students during my prep period," I said. "I'm not sure what to do with you right now."

He stared at his feet. "That's what Mr. Puck told me too. I'm a sixth grader. I'm not in high school. Mr. Thatch said I could just stay here today."

"Mr. Thatch said that?" I wasn't a babysitter. Why did he do this to me?

"He was the one who found me. I didn't mean to make the volcano for the science fair spurt out real lava this morning." He scuffed his shoes against the floor.

Maybe this was why Thatch had missed our meeting. I hoped that was the reason.

"You're going to be in art all day. Do you think you can handle that?" I asked.

"I like to draw!"

Thank goodness.

During my second-period prep, Trevor followed me around like a silent shadow. I sat him down in a chair with a pencil and paper so I could finish planning my lessons. A few minutes later, I caught Trevor at the supply desk, licking a glue stick.

I left my desk and removed the stick and cap from his hands. "That's a glue stick. You can't eat that."

"Oh," he said, his cheeks flushing pink between his tan freckles.

"Are you hungry?" I asked.

"Yeah."

I didn't have time to sneak down to the kitchen. I gave him some granola from my desk, the kind that didn't have marijuana in it. I'd purchased that one for the school brownies.

"When's the last time you ate?" I asked.

"Dinner last night."

That made sense why he devoured the entire bag of granola.

Because it was a B day, I only had even numbered classes. Following second period was fourth period. I caught Trevor chewing on paper. It had been a while since I had taught middle school art. Sure, there had been times I'd caught middle school students licking the salt off the watercolor palettes when we had used salt on our papers to create a snowflake effect. And there had been that time a girl with hot-pink pastels on her hands had asked what would happen if she licked her hand. I'd told her not to, but she'd done it anyway. Those were the silly and immature kinds of behaviors one expected from middle school students.

When I found Trevor nibbling on a crayon fourth period without the provocation of other students, I had no idea what to think.

I took him outside the classroom onto the landing where I could keep an eye on my class and speak to him with some semblance of privacy.

"Trevor, I've told you three times not to eat my art supplies in the last two hours. I have a limited amount, and I'm not going to be able to teach classes if you eat the supplies." I tried to go for my patient teacher voice, but I didn't know how well I managed it. "What's going on?"

"I know. I'm sorry, Miss Lawrence. I'm just nervous, and when I'm nervous, I need to chew on something." His brown puppy-dog eyes broadcast his earnest regret. "When we packed my bag to come here, my mom didn't pack any gum for me."

"Licking my glue sticks is not the same as chewing."

"I thought it was a push pop. My mom didn't pack my glasses either."

"Didn't the glue stick taste kind of . . . yucky?" I would think he'd be able to tell the difference.

"It wasn't that bad. It was better than my dad's mashed potatoes."

At least this kid had a family. "Let's see if you can get through the rest of the period without sticking anything in your mouth. We only have thirty minutes until lunch. Then you can eat your fill. I want you to find something in the cafeteria you can put in your backpack for a snack this afternoon so you aren't tempted to chew on my supplies."

"I didn't bring a bag. My mom forgot to—"

"Agh! Just fill your pockets or stuff them up your sleeves. Or whatever," I said, about to tear my hair out. Why was this kid getting to me? I dealt with way worse—kids who intentionally destroyed my supplies. I took a few calming breaths.

"Will you show me where the lunchroom is?" he asked.

"Yes. I have to go down there for my cafeteria duty."

"Will you sit by me? I don't know anyone here yet."

"We'll see."

When the bell rang, students rushed out. I walked around the classroom, picking up pencils and paper they'd left out.

"I'm ready for lunch," Trevor said.

My closet door burst open with such force it slammed against the stone wall. I expected to see Thatch, but no one stood there. The air shifted and shimmered. I thought I saw a patch of flesh color flash near a chair.

Ragged breathing sounded from the far side of the classroom. Something scuffed against the floor. A chair toppled over. I stared in confusion, uncertain what kind of magic caused this.

"It's a ghost!" Trevor screamed and leapt behind me.

Another chair skidded back, and something large thudded onto the floor. Ghosts didn't stumble into a classroom.

An invisible man did.

I rushed around the U-shaped arrangement of desks.

"Derrick?" I asked.

A groan answered me.

I tripped over one of his legs and nearly crashed into the wall. Crouching on the floor, I felt around until I found him. I peeled back his cap to reveal his face. My hope and half a second of relief curdled in my stomach.

He had a black eye and a swollen lip. His face was bruised and battered. I thought about the Raven Queen and her plan to leave him for me to find.

"Are you all right?" Without waiting for an answer, I fumbled with his invisible coat and unzipped it. I lifted his T-shirt to examine his chest. His skin was intact. No entrails hung out. His ribs were bruised, and a blistered burn covered one side of his stomach.

He opened his eyes. His voice came out a raspy croak. "Water."

My water bottle was on my desk. I pointed to Trevor who stood next to the supply desk. "Get my water bottle."

He stared at Derrick. A crayon fell out of his mouth.

"Now," I said.

He shuffled over to my desk and threw the water bottle at me. It hit the wall and rolled. I dove for it and crouched at Derrick's side again. I lifted his head and tipped water into his mouth. He momentarily choked and then kept drinking. He didn't try to sit up or grab the bottle. He closed his eyes, and his head sank into my hand. This didn't bode well.

I snapped my fingers at Trevor. "Go downstairs and tell Mr. Khaba I need help. It's an emergency. Tell him it's Invismo."

He froze. His hand was in the tub of crayons. "I don't know who Mr. Khaba is."

"The first person you see, tell them Miss Lawrence needs Khaba. It is an emergency."

"What about lunch? You said you were going to show me where the lunchroom is."

"For the love of God, get help! You can eat lunch afterward." I didn't mean to shout at the poor kid, but my patience had evaporated.

Trevor ran off.

I removed my sweater and placed it under Derrick's head to make him more comfortable. He groaned. I locked the doors before returning to Derrick's side. I didn't want anyone walking in and seeing him.

"What happened?" I asked. "Where have you been? How did you get hurt?"

He opened his eyes. He managed a single word, fury and fear alight in his eyes. "Thatch."

# CHAPTER TWENTY-EIGHT
## Abra-Cadaver

Ten minutes later I sat with Derrick's head on my lap, dabbing at the crusts of blood and dirt on his face. Khaba materialized in my classroom in a puff of smoke. He exclaimed something in another language and rushed forward. "What happened?"

"I don't know." I filled him in on what Derrick had said and how he'd arrived. "What are we going to do?"

Khaba paced my room. "I can tell you what we *aren't* going to do. We aren't bringing him to the infirmary. I don't want anyone to know about this."

"Thank goodness. Nurse Hilda is a nightmare." She would probably make him drink her bat-dung elixir, and he'd get E. coli. As if he didn't have enough problems.

"And you aren't going to try to confront Thatch or do anything rash. I need to talk to Derrick when he wakes and find out what happened."

"Rash? Why do people always use that word? I'm not rash."

Khaba held up his hands in a placating gesture. "Impulsive, then. Promise me you won't do anything impulsive like gouge Thatch's eyes out."

Derrick moaned. I leaned closer, smoothing my fingers over his face. "It's okay. You're safe now. You're with Khaba and me. We'll take care of you."

Derrick's brow furrowed, but he didn't reply.

"Who's on duty downstairs in the lunchroom?" Khaba asked.

Craptacular. "Me?"

He grimaced.

"This is more important," I said. "You aren't going to make me monitor the lunchroom now, are you?"

"Ask Josie to cover for you. Meet me in Derrick's room when you're done. And bring some water and something for him to eat. Soup."

I rushed downstairs. Josie stood at a table, heaping food onto her plate, looking like she was about to sneak out of the cafeteria. I quickly filled her in. From her sigh, I could tell she wasn't happy about covering for me, but she said she'd do it.

I piled a plate with food and grabbed a pitcher of water before trekking across the school to Derrick's wing. Khaba sat in the chair next to Derrick's bed. He'd removed Derrick's hat and shoes. It was disconcerting not seeing the lower half of his body, encased in the invisibility socks and kilt he'd found.

I set down the tray on the low table next to the bed, scooting art supplies aside to make room. "Has he said anything?"

Khaba smoothed a hand over his bald head. "No."

I kneeled on the bed and shimmied Derrick's coat down his shoulders to free it from him. Khaba scooted closer and helped me. Derrick grunted in his sleep when I grabbed his bruised arm. We removed the invisibility clothes and the bloody T-shirt he wore. I blushed when I found he wasn't wearing anything under his kilt. I covered him with his blankets.

This was like the time he'd undressed me when I'd puked all over myself after my sister put something in my drink in high school. He had felt embarrassed and had feared I would feel violated and taken advantage of later. But I hadn't. He'd behaved honorably, his actions reasonable. I could only hope he would feel the same way about me undressing him.

I smoothed his blue hair out of his eyes and kissed his forehead. I would do anything for Derrick.

"Lunch break is almost over," Khaba said. "I'm going to need you to go to class."

I nodded, staring at Derrick's face. Even in the refuge of sleep, his jaw was clenched, and his forehead creased with worry lines.

"I need you to make it through the rest of the day." Khaba patted my shoulder. "Behave normally. Don't let on we've found him. Understand?"

I nodded again. My throat tightened, and I found I couldn't answer. I trudged to the door.

"Clarissa," Khaba said. "Be careful around Thatch."

I struggled to make it through the afternoon. Worry consumed me. Every minute away from Derrick tormented me. Halfway through fifth period, I found Trevor with a wad of paper in his mouth. I should have chided him, but my own stomach grumbled, and I remembered I hadn't eaten lunch.

I didn't have any more granola either. My brain was in a fog. The hours passed as slow as molasses, but whatever those minutes contained eluded me. Students were rowdy and threw supplies at each other. I lost track of the time and didn't give them enough time to clean up. They left a mess when the bell rang, and I didn't tidy up the room for eighth period.

I feared Thatch had tortured Derrick. Or the Raven Queen had. Chills prickled my skin when I thought about those glimpses of memory the Queen of Pain and Pleasure had given him.

At three p.m. the bell rang, and students rushed out. I robotically picked up papers and pencils from the floor. Trevor followed me from table to table like a lost puppy. I tried to recall what I had planned for my A-day classes.

"That was fun. Now what should I do?" Trevor asked.

"I guess you could go to the library." Let Miss Periwinkle figure out what to do with him when he ate her books. "Or one of the school clubs."

His voice was high. He sounded more nervous than ever. "Can't I just stay with you?"

"I have something to do after school. I can't bring you with me."

"Does it have to do with that ghost with blood all over himself earlier?"

I tried to phrase the words for what I wanted to say without piquing his curiosity. "It might be a good idea not to talk about that ghost. I don't want you to start any rumors and for people to be upset by it."

"Oh."

Hailey Achilles walked through the door. "I'm here. Let's get this party started."

"What? Why are you here now?" I asked. I needed to leave. I couldn't have students coming in.

"Duh. Art Club. Don't you remember?"

Craptacular.

Hailey looked Trevor up and down. "Who's this rug rat?"

"Hi, I'm Trevor. I'm going to try not to eat any more glue today."

Hailey's eyes narrowed, and she looked to me. "Is he for real?"

"Mr. Thatch found Trevor. He's in the sixth grade, but he needs somewhere to go because of his magic." I added in my firm teacher tone. "Be nice."

Hailey shrugged.

Imani, Greenie, and Maddy skipped in a moment later.

"It's a boy," Maddy whispered. "I thought only girls were going to be in Art Club."

"No," I said. "I'm not excluding anyone from Art Club. Boys and girls are allowed."

I was confident she could handle being around young men now that she was learning how to channel her affinity.

Trevor smiled shyly at her. "Are you a teacher?" he asked.

Even with the glamour spell on Maddy that Miss Periwinkle had used to tone down her siren beauty, she was still tall and blonde with high cheekbones. Her curves gave her the buxom appearance of an adult, but she was only a freshman.

The girls giggled.

"I need to run some errands," I said to the girls. "Watch Trevor while I'm out, and make sure he doesn't eat any art supplies. Take him to dinner with you and show him around. When it's time to get ready for bed—"

"Whoa, are you asking us to babysit this kid?" Hailey asked.

"I'm not a baby," Trevor said. "I'm eleven."

Greenie patted a chair next to her with a green hand. "Come on, little guy. We don't bite."

"Much," Hailey said.

Trevor timidly stepped forward, seating himself between Greenie and Maddy.

I continued, "When it's time for bed, find one of the male teachers to show Trevor where he's going to sleep."

"Where are you going?" Imani asked.

Two more students walked in the door.

"Is this where Art Club meets?" the boy asked. He looked human in aspect, but a scaly tail protruded from the seat of his pants.

I pointed to Imani and Greenie. "I leave you in charge of Art Club." I pointed to Hailey. "No fire. No magic. No burning down my classroom."

"Sheesh. You'll never let me live that down, will you?"

Khaba was gone from Derrick's room when I returned. I didn't like the idea of him leaving Derrick alone and not locking the door, but I didn't have a key, and I didn't know where he kept his room key. It worked in my best interest Khaba hadn't locked the door; I just didn't know if it was in Derrick's best interest.

The room smelled of herbs. When I sat on the bed, I found places on his face and arms covered in green salves. Derrick slept, occasionally stirring. I sat beside him in the bed, sketching in one of his books. I used quick lines to draw the angles of his face, trying to capture his essence in a caricature like he did. I omitted the black eye and bruises.

When I thought back to the drawings I had tried to do from memory a few days before, I had accidentally drawn him with a black eye. Could that have been a prophetic drawing? I wasn't sure.

He woke once asking for water. He cringed as he sat up and touched a hand to his ribs. The fact that he was sitting up was a slight improvement.

He gulped the water and drank the cold soup, leaving chunks of potatoes and carrots in the bowl.

"Do you want more?" I asked. "Something hot?"

He lay down and didn't answer. He was already asleep. Even his good eye was dark. I didn't want to leave him, but I knew he would eventually wake and want more food.

I didn't know what time it was. The skylight overhead was dark, so it was probably dinnertime, maybe later. If I left now, I could bring food, go back to my classroom and grab lesson plans, and prep while I sat at his bedside.

I left him a note in case he woke and wrote that I would be right back. I took his empty bowl with me and the tray. Students ran down the main corridor outside the great hall that housed our cafeteria. I shouted at the students to stop running inside. I supposed the lockdown was having its toll on them.

A boy from my sixth-period sculpture class whose name I hadn't yet learned, stopped in front of me, out of breath. "Is it true? I can't believe it."

"Is what true?"

A girl wailed as she came out of the cafeteria. She leaned heavily on one of her friends.

I rushed over to her. "Are you hurt? What's wrong?"

She sobbed, her words almost incoherent. "He was my favorite teacher. Why would anyone do that to him?"

I looked to Becca Harmon, one of the students I'd had last semester. "What happened? What is she talking about?"

"There's a rumor. . . ." Becca swallowed. "Is it true? Is Mr. Reade dead?"

# CHAPTER TWENTY-NINE
## Dead as a Doornail

Sebastian Reade was our foreign language teacher. This couldn't be true. I gaped in horror.

"Who told you that?" I asked. "Why would you think he's dead?"

"You mean it isn't true?" the first girl asked, wiping her eyes.

Becca fidgeted with the hem of her pleated skirt. "Jaimie McCarthy heard Jill Anderson tell her boyfriend that she heard Mrs. Keahi tell Mr. Puck he was going to have to figure out what to do with Mr. Reade's classes. And my best friend's cousin said Pro Ro covered for him this afternoon. And I heard Mr. Pinky tell Principal Bumblebub he found someone facedown in the stairwell, and they sectioned the area off and wouldn't let kids use those stairs. It must have been Mr. Reade."

News traveled fast in a small school. Gossip even faster.

"I don't know if it's true," I said. But I intended to find out. It couldn't be a coincidence that the day Derrick returned, injured, another staff member may have been found dead.

"And some new kid said he saw Mr. Reade's ghost!" Olivia Spencer said.

Another wail came from the cafeteria. I carried the tray, my knuckles bone white. Students stopped me along the way, peppering me with questions. I spotted Trevor sitting with Imani and the other students from Art Club.

Trevor chattered away with his mouth full, basking in the attention. "The ghost was covered in blood. Miss Lawrence tried to save him, but it was too late. It was the first time I'd seen a dead person. Well, the second time. I peeked in my grandma's casket at the funeral home."

Students ran and yelled, rowdier than usual.

Vega stood on the dais, her voice thundering across the expanse of students. "Settle down, the lot of you, or there will be no dinner at all."

The nearest students quieted, but the tables farthest away continued to shout. Students ran in the aisles.

I approached the dais, setting the tray on the table. "What's going on? Did Sebastian really die?"

Vega pointed a finger at me. "You were supposed to be here for dinner duty." She waved a hand at the chaos of the cafeteria. "This is what they're like unattended for twenty minutes."

Craptacular. Another duty I had forgotten. "I'm sorry. I really am. An emergency came up."

"Like what?"

There was no way I could tell her the truth. I opted for my old standby technique of avoidance. "Do you know what happened to Sebastian Reade?"

She crossed her arms and snorted. "Like I'm going to do you any favors and tell you." She nodded to the students. "You can deal with this for the rest of dinner. And I'm adding one more hour to our deal for this. I'm out of here." She strode off, leaving me to deal with the zoo of the cafeteria.

I ate dinner in the rowdy cafeteria, did my best to manage students, and brought Derrick food afterward. His chest rose and fell peacefully under the covers. Seeing he was all right, I ran to my classroom and retrieved my lesson-planning book. Along the way I stopped by Josie's room, but she wasn't in. I heard her voice on the way to my room as I passed the student dormitories.

She chided two boys in the hallway outside the girls' dorms.

"We weren't going in to spy on the girls—promise," Balthasar said. "We just wanted to talk to Hailey. We heard she saw Mr. Reade's ghost."

This was how rumors started.

"I don't care what your excuse is," Josie said. "No boys are allowed up here. Period. You both have detentions tomorrow."

They trudged away.

She ran to me and hugged me. "How's Derrick? Was he drained too?"

"Drained? Is that what happened to Sebastian Reade?"

"Yeah, Pinky found him. He told me all about it." She adjusted her lacy hat to keep it from falling off her head. "His face was all dried, and his veins had turned black. It was super creepy. Probably the work of some Fae."

"Are you saying there was a Fae on the school grounds?" I asked.

"I don't know. That's what the big uproar is about. Everyone is afraid the Raven Court got him."

I wouldn't put it past the Raven Court to find a way onto our school grounds to leave a message for me. I shivered. It was only a matter of time before they got me. I had thought the school was safe, but what if Thatch had let them in?

I hurried up to my room and packed a bag to stay overnight in Derrick's room. I didn't want anyone to see me carrying a bag through the hallway and ask questions, so I went outside around the back of the school. It was only seven but dark enough I couldn't see the path around the school and kept stumbling off it. Someone carried a glowing wand up near the woods. It was too far to tell who it was, but as the figure held the wand, I thought I detected a witch hat silhouetted against the light.

The figure slipped into the forest and disappeared. Was that Miss Periwinkle again? Curiosity prickled inside me. If I followed, I could see if that was Miss Periwinkle and where she was off to. The day a dead body turned up at the school, she just happened to venture into the woods? I doubted she intended to go skinny-dipping.

I could follow, or I could go to my boyfriend. I couldn't do both. The choice battled inside me.

I chose Derrick.

He was sleeping soundly as I tiptoed in. He didn't stir as I sat beside him and worked on my lessons. Several times he grew so still I wasn't sure he was breathing. I placed my hand on his chest. The beating was fast, not a heart at rest. He inhaled and exhaled, his breathing was shallow.

More green paste had been left in a terra-cotta bowl next to the bed. The salve smelled of mint and comfrey and the herbs of Grandma Bluehorse's greenhouses. When I closed my eyes and inhaled, I tasted her magic in the air. I applied more of the paste to his wounds.

Derrick's bulky frame took up most of the space in the little bed, but there was just enough room for me to curl up beside him on the edge of the bed. I set my alarm on my forbidden battery-operated alarm clock, and placed it on the floor so it wouldn't drain his powers.

At nine p.m. I fell asleep, an hour earlier than my usual. It had been a long day.

I don't know how long I slept before I felt him stir. I used the incantation for the flashlight spell. A sphere of light hovered above my open palm.

"Are you all right? Do you need anything? Water?" I asked. One-handed, I fumbled for the water bottle on the table and held it out to him.

He shielded his eyes from the light and blindly groped for the water. He drank, turning away from me. I dimmed the light in my palm so that it didn't hurt his eyes.

"Are you hungry?" I asked.

"Only hungry for you."

I laughed. That was Derrick, always the tease. I took the empty water bottle from his hand. "Do you want more?" I flashed my light over the pitcher containing more water. I scooted to the edge of the bed.

He caught my wrist as I started to stand. "Don't leave."

"I'm not going anywhere. I was just going to get you water from the table."

He shielded his eyes. "I don't need water. I just need you." His voice was rough, deeper than usual. "I need your touch."

I let the magic flashlight fade away. He pulled me closer, squeezing me so tightly against him I could barely breathe. I tried to set the water bottle down, but instead dropped it on the floor with a clatter.

"Derrick, you're crushing me."

He didn't apologize or make a joke like he usually would have. But I supposed these weren't normal circumstances. I didn't know what he'd been through. He released me only to capture my face in his hands and kiss me. He drank me in as though I were the last drop of water on earth. There was no tentativeness or hesitation in this kiss. He probed my mouth with his tongue and tugged at my lower lip with his teeth.

When he released me, I gasped for breath. I was light-headed after that kiss.

He scooped me up and sat me on his lap. "Take off your clothes. I want to feel your skin against mine."

The words sent a flush of warmth through me. His fingers explored under the edge of my pajama top, sending a shiver of longing into my core. I fumbled with the buttons as he nibbled on my neck. He pulled the shirt off over my head. His every touch was urgent and hungry. He reminded me of a wild animal about to devour its prey.

He kneaded my hips, massaging my muscles. It felt good, but it was on the verge of being painful.

His mouth tasted sweet and salty. Something bitter and minty touched my lips, and I wiped it away. Already I was feeling sticky from his medicine. Maybe the medicine had helped. And the sleep. He had more energy now at least.

He dipped his head down and tasted the skin of my neck, nibbling his way down to my belly. All thoughts of salve or sleep left my mind. Desire swelled inside me and along with it, my affinity awakened. It grew harder to control the magic inside me, harder to focus on anything other than the urges of my body, but I knew I would have to contain my affinity to channel it with intention rather than letting it run wild. I didn't want it to explode. I never knew if what resulted would be good or bad.

He bit my neck, the pleasant sensation blurring into a spike of pain. I didn't enjoy the sharp sting of his teeth, yet part of me did. I was wet with longing and moaned as his mouth grazed my flesh. My fingers instinctively clutched his back. His skin was sweaty and slick.

His breath was hot against my neck. "Take off all your clothes."

I kneeled next to him as I pulled down my pajama bottoms and panties, then shifted onto my bottom to finish the rest of the work. He tugged the pants away and dropped them on the floor.

He took hold of my hips and dragged me lower on the bed. This was so different from before, his passion burning through him like a fever.

His breath was ragged, and he sounded pained.

"Are you all right?" I asked. "Are you sure you should—?"

He claimed my lips with his, silencing my words. "Spread your legs for me."

He positioned between my knees and plunged into me. I cried out, startled by the suddenness of it. It hurt, but not like last time after I'd still felt raw inside.

He grunted and gasped and sank against me. He dropped his head onto the pillow, nuzzled his face against mine.

That was it? Well, that wasn't so bad. I didn't even have to visualize my affinity getting smaller. It was over.

Only I couldn't breathe.

I shook his shoulder. "Crushing me."

He rolled off me onto his back. Fluid trickled out of me. This was exactly what I had imagined sex would be like. Sweaty and messy. Rushed and unsatisfying.

Guilt followed up my initial assessment. Two out of three with Derrick had been great. And the last time he'd been so patient and considerate. I'd hurt too much to satisfy him, and he hadn't complained. He'd been completely indulgent. Why shouldn't I satiate him this time? I didn't know what he'd been through. Maybe he needed physical contact to ground him and slake his desire to feel whole again.

He lay beside me, panting.

I placed a hand on his arm, and he twitched. "Derrick? What happened to you?"

He closed his eyes and didn't answer.

"Derrick? Where were you? Who attacked you? You said Thatch had something to do with this."

He drew me to his side. "Just hold me. That's what I need right now."

Perhaps he would feel up for talking the next morning. I had questions. He had answers.

## CHAPTER THIRTY
## Secrets and Staff Meetings

It was a good thing I set my alarm to rise extra early to get the shower before Vega was awake because I found one more thing to do in the morning before class. We had an emergency staff meeting at seven thirty. Vega didn't chew me out about not being in bed by teacher curfew, so I hoped that meant she didn't care.

Everyone was in the staff meeting except Mrs. Keahi, the secretary, who I learned was serving Pinky's cafeteria duty. The room was more full than usual with some of the certified staff there in addition to the teachers. I was fortunate I arrived early with Josie.

Teachers crowded around the table and the perimeter of the room. Pro Ro shamelessly flirted with Miss Periwinkle, and if I wasn't mistaken, it looked like she flirted back. Silas Lupi and Jasper Jang couldn't take their eyes off her.

At seven thirty sharp Jeb started the meeting. Thatch was absent. I was kind of relieved, but also suspicious.

"I reckon y'all may have heard the rumors that somethin' happened to our dear teacher, Sebastian Reade, bless his heart. His time of death occurred sometime between lunch and eighth period. Mr. John—err—Pinky found him in the stairwell to the men's dormitories."

I shuddered thinking of how often I used that stairwell to go visit Josie in her room.

Jackie Frost raised her hand, but she didn't wait to be called upon. "Is it true he was drained?"

"By Fae?" Jasper Jang asked. "The Raven Court?"

"First, let me put your minds at ease." Khaba stepped forward. "My defensive wards haven't been tampered with, and my alarms haven't been triggered by intruders. As far as I can tell, there is no indication Fae are, or were, on campus."

"Except for you, Mr. Khaba," Pinky said, eyes narrowing.

Coach Kutchi and Jasper Jang whispered something to each other, glancing at Khaba with suspicion now.

I looked to Pinky in horror. Khaba may have been a full-blooded djinn, but he didn't count as Fae. He was loyal to our school. I understood Pinky's concern, him being new to the school and not knowing Khaba. When my biological mother had hired him—or indentured him—Khaba's presence had been controversial. But he'd been here for years now.

Jeb tugged at one of the curls of his mustache. "No, Mr. Johnson. Mr. Khaba isn't—wouldn't—ahem."

Khaba stood before us, his eyes rimmed with dark circles from lack of sleep. "Thank you, Mr. Pinky. Point acknowledged."

"Julian Thistledown," Vega said loud enough to be heard. "Your precious wards didn't detect his Fae presence."

Heads turned to look at her.

"What?" Vega sat taller, nose lifted into the air. "I'm correct, aren't I? Julian Thistledown was Fae. He killed people all the time and went undetected."

Gasps came from all around the table.

"Aw, hell," Jeb said.

The cat was out of the bag now. Jeb wasn't going to be able to keep denying Julian had preyed on students.

"Who did he kill?" Grandmother Bluehorse asked.

Vega glanced at me. "Besides the previous art teachers?"

"Ahem, getting back to business." Jeb cleared his throat. "Mr. Khaba, you wanna explain security for these folks?"

Khaba ran a hand over his bald head. "When we hire teachers, we do a background check and a few preliminary spells to make sure we aren't hiring anyone dangerous. As far we could tell, Julian Thistledown was Amni Plandai. What we couldn't see with how well he masked himself, was how powerful he was. His Fae magic went undetected.

"Our wards are constructed to allow all staff and students to go about without setting off alarms. Unless it's after curfew. Then I have alarms in place to detect a student leaving the premises. As you can see, the system isn't perfect."

Evita Lupi stood against the wall with her husband, their fingers intertwined. "So that means someone *here* killed Sebastian?"

"Here's what we know," Khaba said. "The Raven Court have made their presence known just outside our school's boundaries. The same day we found Sebastian Reade, one of our classified staff was attacked, possibly off campus."

"One of the brownies?" Grandmother Bluehorse asked, her brow crinkling up in concern.

Khaba inclined his head to her in apology. "He or she will remain unnamed until further questioning is possible."

I admired Khaba's ability to add Derrick to the list without calling out it had been his security guard who had been attacked. This meant staff might assume it was the secretary, custodian, librarian, the brownies, or any of the other nonteaching staff.

"Jeb and I have examined Sebastian Reade's body. We can see he was drained, yes, but the Raven Court seldom leaves a body when they drain a victim. And when they only partially drain a victim or are interrupted and unable to finish, there are no markings on the body. The corpse's capillaries had turned black, and his skin was almost transparent."

"His body was mummified." Pinky stood. "What kind of Fae do that? Tell us, Mr. Khaba."

From the way he glared at Khaba, I suspected he meant djinn.

Josie shook her head at Pinky, mouthing. "Dude, stop hating on Khaba."

Jeb adjusted his bolo tie. "Mr. Pinky, please sit. I realize you found Sebastian Reade, and that must have been more shockin' than all get-out, but let me assure you, Mr. Khaba had nothin' to do with it."

Pinky plopped down in the chair, the wood creaking ominously. "Maybe you should have some other teachers examine the body and see if they come to the same conclusions you do."

Vega raised her hand, sounding far too eager. "I can help examine the body."

Ick. She would say that. She would probably want to stuff him into the coffin under her bed and keep him around to play dress up.

"Ahem." Khaba's cheeks flushed with heat. I'd never seen his confidence falter until this moment. "As I was . . . as I was saying, I don't believe the draining originates from a Fae. I believe the perpetrator was Witchkin, either one of the students or another staff member. Whether this person was acting under the coercion or mesmerism of the Raven Court is currently unclear. It is also possible the incident is completely unrelated to the Raven Court's presence in Lachlan Falls."

His conclusion that this was a Witchkin mesmerized by the Raven Court made me immediately think of Derrick. They'd already had their eye on him. What if they'd snatched him in Lachlan Falls and made him do this? But Derrick had been in no condition to attack anyone. And he'd specifically said Thatch's name? Could Thatch be behind his attack and Sebastian Reade's?

Khaba went on. "The dehydration could have been caused by a

secondary spell to disguise a piece of incriminating evidence or it could indicate a draining done by an individual with an affinity related to heat such as an Elementia, a jorogumo that uses venom to liquify and suck out a victim's insides, a Bas Celik whose strength depends on water, a water Elementia such as a siren, or—"

Josie gasped. Heads turned in Gertrude Periwinkle's direction. The librarian lifted her nose in indignation.

Jackie Frost shook her head, her spiky hair turning blue. "A heat Elementia would burn a body."

Pinky looked to Josie. "A Japanese jorogumo would have punctures and be puffy from the venom, wouldn't it?"

Josie shrugged. "Why are you asking me? I'm not an expert on every Japanese demon just because I'm Japanese, Mr. Pinky."

Thatch strode forward. "A siren did not cause Sebastian's injuries."

I hadn't even seen him slip into the room.

"What about that girl with the rainbow affinity?" someone asked.

I shook my head. I didn't want Imani to get blamed for something she didn't do again.

"We have a student who is a siren and a staff member who is a siren. Have you questioned either of them?" Evita Lupi asked.

I bet she would like Miss Periwinkle to be the culprit—it might cure her husband of drooling over the librarian.

Miss Periwinkle's eyes narrowed at Evita Lupi. "How about werewolves?"

Our staff meeting descended into chaos. Students were being named: Hailey Achilles, Imani Washington, and Maddy Jennings among them. I knew none of those students would hurt someone.

At least I didn't think they would.

Jeb raised his hands in a placating gesture. He spoke, but his voice was lost in the commotion. I looked to Josie. Her face was pale and scared, mirroring my own emotions. I tried not to look at Thatch and give my loathing away.

"Do you think we should—" I started.

I didn't get any further. My voice stopped. All the voices in the room abruptly died away. My ears rang in the silence. Jeb stood, purple light emanating from his palms. White sparkles flickered above our heads before fading away.

His voice thundered across the room. "This meetin' ain't over. While this matter is bein' investigated, we got ourselves another pickle. Ahem. Mr. Puck."

Puck stood and stepped forward. His puff of blond hair was even more wild than usual. "Okay, guys, don't shoot the messenger, but here it is:

Sebastian Reade taught an elective, but the subject matter is essential for students for the spring exams. They need to know the basic grammar and pronunciation of foreign languages so they can pronounce spells correctly. The Latin helped students in Evita Lupi's zoology and animal-magic classes and Grandmother Bluehorse's herbalism and plant magic. The Gaelic, Fae dialects, Old English, and other languages were useful for Felix Thatch's alchemy and potions and for Vega Bloodmire's spells, charms, hexes, and wards classes." He drew in a deep breath. "When situations come up and teachers need a substitute that often falls on Jeb, Khaba, and myself. Currently our principal is seeing to other duties off campus trying to raise funds, Khaba needs to focus on security and investigating Sebastian Reade's death, and I'm still juggling schedule changes."

He allowed that to sink in.

"Oh no," Vega said with a moan.

"So you're asking us to fill in for the foreign language teacher?" Jackie Frost's tone was as chilled as her Elementia affinity.

Pinky raised his hand. "Would there be a pay increase with an added class?"

Jeb stroked his beard. "Hadn't thought of that yet. It ain't our usual procedure to pay for short-term subbing. When the need arises, we all just pitch in and help. I reckon it depends on whether we fill the position with a permanent sub or not."

Pinky's shoulders sagged.

"Oh please, as if bigfoot can speak Latin," Vega said.

Pinky lifted his chin, throwing out a phrase in fluent Latin. Or at least it sounded Latin. It was beyond my beginning skill level. Vega said something back in a snotty tone, which he answered in a snooty tone of his own.

He added in English, "Just because I'm a sasquatch and use a different magical system doesn't mean I'm not educated in Witchkin studies. I can speak nine modern languages and six dead ones. Also, I'm proficient in three different sasquatch tongues of the North Americas. They're closely tied to Native American dialects, so it would help students with those spells too."

Pinky knew a lot of languages. Maybe he could speak Middle High German. That could be helpful.

"Nice!" Puck said, completely oblivious to the tension in the air. "Mr. Pinky, I'll talk to you about Latin after the meeting. We need to fill Gaelic, Demon Tongues, Fae, and our Survey of Romance Languages Class. If someone has a different language skill they can share, even if it's only temporarily, that would be fine too. The more exposure kids have to as many languages as possible, the better it is for them." He looked to Josie. "You could even teach Chinese."

She said through clenched teeth, "I'm not Chinese, Mr. Puck. I'm Japanese. And I think the kids will have a pretty good handle on the language and culture from my Bushido elective."

The following ten minutes teachers argued about who would teach what. Everyone had some excuse they couldn't teach a foreign language. Eventually it was decided Evita Lupi, Silas Lupi, Pro Ro, and Jackie Frost would each teach one language temporarily. Pinky gave up his preps, intending to teach two.

The moment the meeting adjourned, Pinky made his way over to Josie. "Hey Jo, I wanted to talk to you about jorogumo for a sec."

Thatch snagged my elbow. "A quick word with you, Miss Lawrence."

I shook my head, trying to think of some excuse that sounded plausible. "I have class."

"You'll be late. Your students will wait."

Khaba stepped forward. "Pardon my intrusion, but I need to borrow Miss Lawrence for a moment."

Thatch glowered at him. "What I wish to speak with Miss Lawrence about cannot wait."

"As the school's dean of discipline, I disagree."

Thatch crossed his arms, eyeing me menacingly. "I will find you later."

"Ooooh, someone's in trouble," Vega said.

I had never felt so happy to be called into the disciplinarian's office.

Pinky lingered in a corner, speaking low to Josie. Her face was red, and it looked like she was holding her breath. She kept shaking her head. It wouldn't surprise me if he was asking her about something Chinese, not Japanese.

Khaba's office wasn't far. The moment Khaba closed the door, he asked, "Is Invismo any better? Has he said anything?"

"Um," I didn't know if midnight sex counted as better. He'd seemed pretty exhausted afterward. "He hasn't said much, except Thatch's name that once, but he was pretty vague."

"I'll check on him this morning during first-period homeroom."

"Can I be excused from my lunch duty to see how he is and bring him—"

Khaba crossed his arms. "Nice try, but no. You are not skipping duties. You are going to act as though everything is normal until I speak with Derrick myself and have a better understanding about what is happening. I need to know if the perpetrator who killed Sebastian Reade also attacked Derrick and if it was Thatch."

Khaba escorted me to my classroom. I was glad he did. Khaba wouldn't allow Thatch to make me break school rules and be late for my class.

So much had happened in the last twenty-four hours, my brain was still having difficulty processing it all. I didn't like how all the teachers had turned on each other during the first sign of trouble. It was a regular witch hunt in there. For the first time that I remembered, I hadn't been the one who had been blamed.

Only, I couldn't believe anyone would blame Khaba. He did so much for the school.

I worked to keep up with Khaba's quick strides toward my class.

I panted, out of breath. "Why was Pinky so . . . adamant you were at fault? You aren't like other Fae, right?"

"Not anymore, honey." Khaba sighed. "I can't blame him. Sasquatches are technically Fae themselves—just don't say that to their faces. They've been oppressed more than any other subspecies, perhaps more than Witchkin. I'm technically Fae as well, but I serve my master, and my master is the school."

"So when that raven lady offered to free you. . . ."

He snorted. "Even in my most opium-induced state, I wouldn't buy that line. A *free* djinn has unlimited power. I was once more powerful than the Raven Queen herself. Djinn were the worst of Fae—demons—until the major houses worked to punish and condemn us to live a life of servitude for all eternity. Our service limits our magic to wishes. No djinn is free anymore. Nor would any Fae house ever wish to free us because our power would pose too great a threat."

"So you were once evil?" I asked.

"I don't talk about those days. What's important is what I am now." He hugged me around the shoulder. "And how good I look in these pants."

I indulged him with a smile. I had never known all this about my friend. Pinky's accusations made more sense, even if they were unfounded.

During first period, I sent a student with a note to Josie's classroom, asking her if she would cover lunch so I could check on someone. I was careful not to say who. She would know. I wished I could tell her how peculiarly he'd acted the night before.

Her note came back with a student a few minutes later.

*Again? How many lunches do I need to cover for you? I don't want to be like Vega and tell you that you owe me for this, but you do. You're going to have to paint a mural for me or something to work this off, girl!*

I was so fortunate I had a friend like Josie who was willing to cover my duties and not make me pay her in blood. I probably should have offered to do something nice for her without her demanding it. After all this was over and Derrick was safe, I would ask what I could do to make up for taking advantage of her like this.

At lunch I snuck to the ruins, continually glancing over my shoulder to make sure no one followed. The door to Derrick's room was open. I rushed forward. The room was empty. His paintings were knocked over, and tubes of paint littered the floor. White feather down was scattered like snow over the entire scene. One of his paintings had been slashed.

I ran to tell Khaba. He wasn't in, so I left a note. I kept sending students with notes to his office, but he didn't reply. By the time dinner rolled around, I had heard the next round of student gossip.

Another body. No one knew who he was.

I feared the worst.

# CHAPTER THIRTY-ONE
## Dead Wrong

After school I returned to Derrick's room and then went to Khaba's office again. The moment I learned Khaba was in Jeb's office, I rushed past Mrs. Keahi who sat at her desk, something I'd never dared do before.

"You can't go in there!" she shouted after me. "The acting principal is in a meeting with representatives from the Witchkin Council."

Yeah, right. She always made excuses why Jeb was unavailable. It didn't surprise me she would try to stop me from seeing Khaba.

"Khaba! Is he all right? Was it him?" I burst into Jeb's office where Khaba sat at the principal's desk. Two elderly witches with pointed hats who I'd never met before were seated across from him. I halted in the doorway, realizing my mistake. Mrs. Keahi hadn't lied when she'd said he was in a meeting.

"Oh," I said. "I'm sorry."

Mrs. Keahi's hand clamped around my wrist like a vise. She yanked me out of the room, apologizing profusely.

"It's all right," Khaba said. "We're almost done here."

I took that to mean I could stay. Mrs. Keahi didn't. She pushed me into a chair in the waiting room and closed the doors.

She shook her head at me. "You need to show your superiors some respect at this school. Maybe you're not expected to use manners and have patience out there in the Morty Realm, but in the Unseen Realm we do things differently." She chided me for five whole minutes until the two witches exited, escorted by Khaba.

His face was drawn. "Please leave the paperwork with the secretary, and we'll see to it that the necessary arrangements are made." Even with his grim expression and the worry in his eyes, he still sparkled with so much magic, one of the witches couldn't tear her gaze away from him.

I stood. Mrs. Keahi wagged a finger at me. "Not yet. He hasn't said you can—"

"I'll see Miss Lawrence now." He waved me forward.

I dashed inside before Mrs. Keahi could stop me. Khaba closed the doors behind me. He drew me to him and hugged me.

His chest trembled. "I'm failing in my duties to protect this school. They're going to close us down if I can't keep people from dying. I don't know what to—"

I hated to interrupt, but I still feared the worst. "Is he . . . dead?"

"Invismo—Derrick? No." His voice came out rough, and he cleared his throat.

Relief washed over me. I hated for anyone to be dead, but at least it wasn't him. I could still hope everything would be all right.

"Who died, then? A student?"

"A friend of mine from Lachlan Falls. You don't know him. He was coming here to see me."

My lunch settled into a brick in my stomach. "Brogan McLean?"

He drew away. His eyes swam with tears. "How did you know?"

I regretted not explaining what I'd seen in the woods.

"I need to tell you about Miss Periwinkle."

# CHAPTER THIRTY-TWO
## Confessions of the Heart

I explained to Khaba all I'd seen in the forest while I'd used the invisibility clothes. He sat on the couch beside me, grimly listening.

"Why didn't you tell me this earlier?" he asked.

"When would I have had time to? You were on the go with murders and attacks. Jeb isn't here, and you're doing everything. This seemed far less important."

He stood up. "What part of 'this guy might be Khaba's boyfriend about to be seduced by a conniving witch' kept you from telling me?"

"I didn't know he was your *boyfriend.* I didn't know you had a boyfriend. I thought you and Jeb were together."

Khaba grimaced. "That old geezer? Why would you think that?"

I didn't want to recount the Brokeback Hogwarts scene I had witnessed that one time through the magic mirrors. There was no good way to talk about my eavesdropping habits. And of course, there was the other reason. "The last time I tried to tell you something about Miss Periwinkle, she seduced you."

He waved me off. "No, she didn't."

I gave him my teacherly I-know-your-dog-didn't-eat-your-homework look.

"She . . . rubbed my lamp."

"Like your boy toys rub your lamp?"

"Don't call Brogan that." Tears filled his eyes.

"I'm sorry." I regretted my impulsive word choice. "I just mean, she uses people sexually. She seduces men with her magic to get what she wants."

"My mind is a little hazy when I think about that interaction with her," he said. "I would never have thought a mere Witchkin could best me. A pureblooded Fae with magic—yes—but not a siren. There it is, I suppose.

The confines of my magical contract with the school keeps me from being as strong as I need to be to protect myself or others." He sank onto the couch next to Jeb's minibar.

I moved closer. "It's not your fault."

He stared into the unlit fireplace across the room. We sat in silence. I tapped my foot against the floor in impatience. Sitting here was agony. I wanted to do something.

"Have I ever told you why I hated your biological mother?" Khaba asked.

"You never told me that you did." I thought he'd been grateful she'd freed him from the bondage of his lamp and gave him employment.

"It wasn't because she turned evil and killed people. I suppose I should feel angrier about her destroying the school and murdering staff members, but there must still be a bit of demon left in me because I found that more curious and titillating than shocking or evil. The mystery of why she did it still intrigues me."

I knew some of the reasons she'd done it, but I didn't dare mention them.

"Alouette Loraline created the spell to keep me from living inside the lamp and being a slave with a master. Because of her, the lamp lives within me. I was thankful, and to some extent, I still am. But because of that spell, your mother knew me better than anyone else. She knew what I needed.

"I can't just make magic happen when I want. She came to me every morning and asked me what I needed—what *I* wished. No matter where my lamp was, she rubbed it so I could store up enough power to use later in the day for any task required of me by my job. I think she knew I would grow to resent her and hate being dependent on her. Every time I wanted something, I had to ask her. She never refused me, whether it was something dictated by the necessity of the job or something I desired for personal reasons—that is, if I could word my wish in a way that it satisfied the parameters of my contract and couldn't be used for sole personal gain." He laughed and shook his head. "That's a magical contract for you. It's always about the wording."

Yeah, I knew how those were after my experiences with Wiseman's Oath.

"It wasn't her being cruel that made me hate. It was that she was so kind and sympathetic. Funny how that is." He glanced at me, his smile turning sheepish. "It's petty, I know, but I did resent her. Then one day she brought a student to me. I can't even remember what it was he had done, something minor, not even worthy of a detention.

"His name was Brogan. I think he just needed someone to talk to, and she thought it should be me. It was late eighties, and those raised in the

Morty Realm were less comfortable talking about their sexuality than those raised in the Unseen Realm. It was obvious he was gay, but he felt ashamed about it due to his religious upbringing."

So that was how he had met his boyfriend. I took Khaba's hand, wanting to comfort him.

Khaba stared through me as he spoke, his gaze focused on the past. "The young man started hanging around my office more and more, opening up and talking to me. I knew Brogan probably had a crush on me—I mean, who doesn't?—but he was a student, and I wasn't going to do anything about it.

"One day he said to me, 'Mr. Khaba, who rubs your lamp to grant your wishes?' He must have seen the anguish in my eyes, but I wasn't about to tell him about my personal life. I just figured it was his awkward attempt at a cheesy pickup line and quickly forgot about it.

"I don't celebrate Yule or Christmas or any of your pagan holidays. In those days when Alouette was still alive, no one made me go to the holiday parties. I was fine not receiving gifts from anyone.

"Wasn't I surprised to find a gift outside my door on Christmas morning. It was a present from all the staff for a massage from the healer in Lachlan Falls. Written in handwriting I didn't recognize was a note that the healer had been paid and therefore was bound not to ask for anything if she rubbed my lamp. Your mother later told me the massage, and the clause that had been added so that the healer couldn't take my wish, was Brogan's idea. He had asked not to be named as the organizer of this, but . . . teachers talk." Tears swam in Khaba's eyes. "It was the nicest thing anyone had ever done for me—aside from your mother coming to me every morning and making sure I had enough magic to perform my duties.

"I can't explain why, but I didn't resent Brogan. Maybe it was because it wasn't done out of obligation, and I didn't feel beholden to anyone. I didn't even need to acknowledge Brogan as having thought of the idea. I felt so relieved. For once, I didn't owe anyone anything.

"That has been my entire existence as a Fae. I'm ruled by rules and obligatory boons.

"Grandmother Bluehorse helped Brogan find an appropriate apprenticeship outside of the school, and eventually Brogan graduated. I knew he was studying with a healer, but I didn't ask who. I didn't know it was the woman in Lachlan Falls who had given me the massage. At least, I didn't know until I showed up one day, after having paid for one for myself. The old woman asked if her apprentice could massage me since her arthritis was ailing her.

"Wasn't I surprised to find him in the healing room!

"He was so shy and awkward it was cute. 'Will this make you

uncomfortable, Mr. Khaba?' he asked. 'Since we knew each other when I was a student?'

"I tried not to laugh at his concern. I'd never been uncomfortable being nude in front of anyone. It's only school rules and my desire to show off my fabulous fashion sense that gives me the impetus to wear clothes." He winked when he said it, some of his old self glowing in his eyes as he recounted the story. "So Brogan gave me a massage. I came back the following week for another. And another. He was professional, and there wasn't anything sexual about it. Nor was there any hint he might ask me for anything in return. Neither he, nor the healer, rubbed my lamp to ask for wishes. I got to keep them all to myself. I think that alone made me fall in love with him." He smiled wistfully, and his breath hitched in his throat.

Tears filled my eyes. Every time I'd seen Khaba in Lachlan Falls sneaking off, I'd been so dense. It wasn't that he wanted just anyone for his kilty pleasures. He had a boyfriend in town. Of course they would want to spend time together.

Khaba cleared his throat. "I enjoyed the professional distance between us, the division that allowed me to keep my wishes and not have to share my magic with anyone. But as I grew to know Brogan—we often talked during the massage session—I felt uneasy about our patient-client relationship and the fact that he hadn't asked for any wishes. Ever. Months went by before I asked him if he would like to go over to the pub after work. It was easy talking to him, and I liked getting to know him outside of our professional domains. As we walked out into the night afterward, I did ask him then what it was he wanted, what wish I could make come true.

"Even in the moonlight I could see him blush as he said, 'I don't need magic to make my wishes come true. And if I did have to use magic for my wish, it would be stealing, and I wouldn't do that. Not to you. Not to anyone.'

"So I kissed him and asked if I had made one of his wishes come true. He said I had. I think we spent quite a bit of time that night making each other's wishes come true, sans magic."

I wiped my eyes. How could I have not known Khaba was in love?

"Brogan is—was—the one person who never asked me for anything in return for rubbing my lamp. I offered to grant his wishes many times. The one time he took me up on the offer was to help someone he couldn't heal. He had a good heart. He was my truest friend in all the world and my lover. And now he's gone forever." Khaba dropped his face into his hands and cried. "He had the same markings, the black veins like Sebastian Reade. It was the same murderer. I just can't understand why anyone would hurt him. He didn't deserve this."

I cried with him. Not for Brogan—I had hardly known him—but for

Khaba's loss. I shed tears for my own loss, at the fear of not knowing whether I had lost my own boyfriend and friend. Derrick and I understood each other like Khaba and Brogan.

Sorrow and guilt welled up in me, making my throat tight.

"I'm so sorry," I said. "I never knew. I didn't understand how your magic worked until recently, and when I did, I should have asked if you needed someone to rub your lamp." I'd been selfish and too focused on my own world to think about his.

More than ever, I had to prove Miss Periwinkle was behind the murders. It was too late for Sebastian Reade and Brogan McLean. I prayed there was still time to find and save Derrick. If I delayed, someone else might end up dead.

# CHAPTER THIRTY-THREE
## The Mysteries of How Vega Spends Her Spare Time

My first order of business was looking for Derrick. When that proved fruitless, I turned to the other problem at hand.

In order to prove Gertrude Periwinkle was the murderer, I needed someone who could resist her siren charms to help me. I required someone who wouldn't blink an eye at my ability to resurrect the dead so I could interview the deceased using my affinity in order to ask them who their murderer was. As much as I wanted to confide in Khaba, he went by the rules. I couldn't tell him I'd recently discovered I could talk with the dead. Nor did I have any faith he'd be able to resist Miss Periwinkle.

Josie had suggested Mrs. Keahi, but there was no way she would be willing to help me. She loathed me.

That left Vega to serve as a credible witness. I only had to figure out how to entice her.

Vega sprawled across her bed reading a magazine. I stared, perplexed when I saw it was a *Scholastic Art* magazine. I wouldn't have thought anything I liked would interest her, but I could see it was an issue featuring Edward Gorey's macabre artwork. It was one of *my* magazines.

"That is mine," I said, my ire rising.

She turned a page. "It was on the desk. You shouldn't leave your things around if you don't intend to share."

I waved my hand at the decorative glass bottles she'd placed yet again on *my* wardrobe. "Fine. I guess I'll start using your stinky perfume too." So much for trying to sweet-talk my roommate into doing a favor for me and bribing her with a promise to do more duties.

Vega laughed her wickedest witch cackle. "Go ahead and try. You wouldn't know the difference between the perfumes, acids, or poisons."

I carefully set the bottles back onto her wardrobe, in any free place available—and there wasn't much with the skull, crystal ball, candles, jar of eyeballs, mummified hand, bottles of herbs, voodoo doll, cauldron, potted plant, and scrolls of paper. I considered dumping one of the bottles into her wardrobe of clothes, but I didn't want to risk the entire room smelling like old-lady perfume.

Instead, I returned to my plan. "I could tell what was a poison when Thatch was puking up blood."

She sat up, dropping the magazine to the floor. "I had nothing to do with that." She pointed a finger at me. "Don't go accusing me of poisoning him."

"I didn't say you were. But Khaba still thinks it was you, doesn't he?" I didn't actually know that. It was a complete bluff. "He keeps giving you that look like he thinks you're guilty. He's waiting for you to mess up so he can catch you. I saw how he looked at you today at the meeting."

"Shut your mouth, or I'll shut it for you." She shook with rage. "I didn't hex anyone's fucking chocolate. And I didn't kill Sebastian Reade."

An idea crossed my mind, a long shot, but it might be better than trying to convince Vega to switch duties with me when I had missed part of two dinner duties already. I would be walking a fine line goading a powerful bitch-witch like Vega.

"The person who poisoned Thatch also attacked one of the school staff. He or she drained Sebastian Reade. Someone possibly in league with the Raven Court. A powerful Witchkin. If Khaba and Jeb suspect you of poisoning Thatch, they must be looking for links that connect you to the murders." I nodded toward her coffin. "I'm surprised they haven't questioned you about your coffin yet and who you plan to stuff in there."

She followed my gaze and nudged it farther underneath the bed with her foot. Or she tried to. It slid back an inch.

She twisted her hand, and her wand appeared in her fist. "Listen, bitch. If you're trying to scare me, you've got another think coming. I'm a powerful Celestor. I divined my future. I saw that I'm in no harm from being accused of these crimes again." She swallowed. Fear threaded through her posture, making her usually confident demeanor hesitant. Either she was lying about what she'd seen or there was something more she'd seen that she wasn't saying.

"Not if more bodies don't show up. But we both know that isn't likely with the way things are going. Wouldn't it be . . . convenient if you could prove you aren't guilty?"

Her eyes narrowed in suspicion. I could tell I had her ear, though.

She lowered her wand. "What do you mean? How would I prove my innocence? I've already tried foreseeing the truth."

"What if you interviewed the dead? You could ask Sebastian Reade who his killer was."

"Like a séance?" She rolled her eyes. "That is the kind of stupid suggestion someone from the Morty Realm would think up."

I hadn't been referring to a séance, but I didn't know why the idea was so stupid. "What's wrong with talking to the dead?"

"First of all, necromancy is forbidden. Second of all, the reason séances aren't allowed is that the dead are difficult to reach. You never know who you're talking to. If I attempted to call the spirit world, I might get someone else who will pretend to be Mr. Reade. No one would find information that comes about from a séance to be credible evidence."

"I'm not talking about a séance. What if you could temporarily resurrect Sebastian Reade's body and ask him who drained him?"

"I suppose it could work. In theory." She sat on the bed, staring up at the ceiling, lost in thought. "But as I said before, it's forbidden magic. It isn't like Witchkin schools have Necromancy 101 where one can learn the black arts. If we do have any books with those spells, I'm sure they'd be restricted. The books I've seen on the black market are usually incomplete and sometimes completely useless—not that I would know." She quickly added, "It's not like I've tried to resurrect the dead."

If Vega was the kind of person that enjoyed sex in a coffin, I didn't doubt she would try necromancy as well.

I licked my lips and then stopped, trying not to look nervous. "You don't need a book. I know of a way."

She skewered me with a look full of yearning. "You've got to be shitting me."

"I kid you not. I know of a way we can question Sebastian Reade." Here was the tricky part. "I'm willing to help you clear your name as a *favor* to you."

"A favor. What do you want in return?"

"Nothing much, since you're my roommate and we look out for each other."

"Just name your damned price."

"You have to be willing to report what Sebastian Reade says to Khaba and Jeb. You have to promise to tell them who the real killer is so you won't be accused."

"Is that all?" she asked.

"And I don't want you to tell them or anyone else I can do necromancy."

"*If* you're successful. No offense, Clarissa, but you can hardly get your wand to light up."

"I don't have a wand." Except the one I'd appropriated from a student.

"There's your problem."

"Will you perform Wiseman's Oath for this if I help you?" There was no way I trusted Vega not to tattle on me to Thatch or anyone else. A magical oath would ensure she didn't break her word.

She pursed her lips. "Fine. Hold out your hand."

Vega gripped my hand. She incanted a long spell in another language. Maybe it was Old English. The air between us crackled gold and then blue. The air smelled like old mushrooms and starlight. My mouth tasted off, metallic and tart.

"I, Vega Bloodmire, promise that if we successfully reach Sebastian Reade through necromancy and he says I am not the killer, I will not name Clarissa Lawrence as my source of forbidden magic when I tell Khaba and Jeb what I learned."

"And Thatch," I said. "You won't tell him either."

She rolled her eyes. "I promise not to tell Felix Thatch either."

Like any contract, Wiseman's Oath was only as good as the wording used. I wasn't a lawyer, but it sounded pretty safe. I tried to think if there was anything else that could go wrong. "And you promise you haven't already set up some secret message to anyone to get me in trouble like you did when you tricked Hailey Achilles that one time?"

"No." A smile curled to her lips. "But I wish I had thought of that." She cleared her throat. "I, Vega Bloodmire, have not and will not contrive to get Clarissa Lawrence in trouble for what she is about to do."

I didn't see how she would get out of that.

"Now, you repeat after me," she said. "I, Clarissa Lawrence promise to resurrect Sebastian Reade's body through necromancy."

I repeated.

Her smile widened. "And if I, Clarissa Lawrence, fail in this task, I give Vega Bloodmire my entire wardrobe to use as she pleases without complaint."

I shook my head. "I'm not agreeing to that."

"Yes, you will."

"I'm doing *you* a favor," I said.

"Not if you waste my time. If this turns out to be a bust, I want compensation for my disappointment."

"Never mind," I said.

"*You* never mind." She jabbed her wand into my stomach. "It was your idea in the first place. I bet you just want to talk to Sebastian Reade so he clears *your* name."

"No one accused me of poisoning my department head."

She crossed her arms. "Fine. How about this instead: If I, Clarissa Lawrence, fail in the task to resurrect the dead, I will allow Vega Bloodmire to use the top of my wardrobe without complaint."

I had a feeling that was the best compromise I would get out of her. I repeated the phrase, though I left out the part about "without complaint."

There was no way that would be feasible, and I wasn't going to risk a permanent explosion of boils on my face if I broke the oath accidentally.

It must have been good enough for Vega. She swirled sparkling magic around us with her wand and released my other hand.

She rubbed her hands together. "We need to prepare for this. When are we going to go?"

"As soon as possible. Tonight. I guess we should wait until everyone goes to bed."

"Good. You go run and get supplies: candles, a cape in case it's cold down in the crypt, maybe a blanket, and the items you need for your spell." She strode to her wardrobe and opened the cupboard. "I have to decide what to wear for this occasion."

I left to collect supplies. I pillaged a threadbare blanket from a closet outside the girls' dormitory and some nubs of candles from Ludomil Sokoloff's custodial closet. I didn't own a cape. I would wear my wool coat since that was the warmest item of clothing I owned.

Vega expected me to use a spell to perform necromancy. She didn't know about my affinity. I needed to keep it that way, which is why I tried to find items for a pretend spell. I picked a used tea bag out of the garbage outside the staff room and scooped the herbal contents out and wrapped it up in a piece of discarded paper. Probably I needed something more than that to look authentic, so I grabbed a piece of chalk from my classroom. My errands took me an hour.

I made it back to our room before curfew to find Vega in a beautiful beaded gown. It was longer than most of her flapper dresses, but it still felt authentically vintage. She had touched up her makeup and applied red lipstick and nail polish. She wore a beaded headband. While I had been busy scavenging, Vega had been beautifying herself. Why didn't that surprise me?

She retrieved a fringed shawl from where she had draped it over a chair and wrapped it over her shoulders. "There you are. I was wondering what was taking you so long."

"Why are you dressed up? Aren't we going to the crypt?"

"Of course we are, you fucktard. This is how I always dress when I visit the dead. They're all dressed in their finest clothes; I don't want to be the most underdressed person in the room." She looked me up and down. "Not that I have to worry if I'm in your presence."

As smart as Vega was, I had no idea how she could also be so ridiculous. I grabbed my coat, scarf, gloves, and hat.

"Ugh! I can't be seen with someone dressed like that," Vega said.

"The point is to not be seen by anyone."

Vega's brows drew together in concern. "Sebastian Reade is going to see us, isn't he?"

"I think he'll understand if I dress practically rather than in my party clothes."

"How would you know? It's not like you ever talked to him."

Vega threw open my wardrobe. She selected a lacy scarf with fringe and placed it over my coat, as if it could disguise what I wore. We waited half an hour after curfew before setting out.

"Do you know how to get to the crypt?" I whispered.

"Of course I do. I go there all the time."

Surprise, surprise.

Vega lit our way with her wand. I followed Vega to her classroom. She headed straight for the closet. It was like mine, with a flight of stairs that led to a storage area. There were fewer cobwebs in her stairwell. We descended the stairs, passed two more storage closets and made it to the lowest level.

She placed a finger to her lips, as if I needed reminding to be quiet. "This is the dungeon," she said.

We tiptoed down a hallway that led to Thatch's room. A woman giggled somewhere nearby. Miss Periwinkle? I prayed we weren't going to get caught. Vega must have had the same thought because she doused her light. She grabbed my arm, her nails digging into my wrist as she pulled me along. The passage was dark, and I bumped into her several times.

A moment later her wand glowed with light and not a moment too soon. We stood at the top of a stairwell. If nothing else, Vega came in handy for not allowing me to plummet to my death.

She counted under her breath as we walked. She halted at thirteen.

"Watch that step. It's booby-trapped," she said. She easily skipped the step as she glided down the stairs. I leaned against the wall as I eased my shorter legs past the thirteenth step.

"Why is it booby-trapped?" I asked.

"To keep students from desecrating the graves of honorable teachers of the school's past. The first booby trap was Thatch's quarters, of course. Don't worry, there are only two more traps left."

The stairway descended for what felt like three floors. At the bottom, Vega showed me another place to avoid. "Step on that stone and you'll land yourself right in Khaba's office, tied to a chair until he finds you in the morning. After I realized that was where it led, I removed all my clothes and stepped on the stone on purpose to see what his reaction would be."

"What was his reaction?"

"Nothing. That's how I found out he was gay. That was ten years ago, of course. I know better now."

I was surprised the hot-pink pants hadn't given it away, but maybe Khaba had dressed more conservatively ten years ago.

Vega sauntered over to a heavy wooden door with Celtic knotwork covering the frame. I found it curious the decorations were made of what looked like iron. Fae and many Witchkin were allergic to cold iron. Maybe the door needed to be made from a Fae-resistant material in case we were overcome by a zombie apocalypse and that was all that would protect us from the dead.

Vega jabbed her wand into the keyhole, and it clicked inside. She peeked inside. "It's clear."

"That lock was iron, but you still got magic to work on it." Derrick couldn't even pick up a cell phone with his bare hands.

Vega sighed dramatically. "Does Merlin-class Celestor mean nothing to you? Never mind. It's better you don't answer that and prove how stupid you are."

Vega was always boasting about how strong and superior she was. Apparently she wasn't all talk.

We marched across a stone ledge at the edge of a pit. The scuff or our feet on the stone floor echoed in the vaulted room. An undulating mass writhed below. I wouldn't have known they were disembodied hands if I hadn't previously fallen in. The hands didn't greet me today. Maybe they knew I was on a mission.

Or maybe Vega scared them.

On the other side of the chamber, we descended another flight of stairs.

"Is that considered a booby trap?" I asked. "It seems kind of dangerous compared to the one that lands a delinquent student in Khaba's office." Especially since the hands supposedly fed on fears. Any emotion a student projected was multiplied threefold.

It was fortunate I had been able to think sexy thoughts and tame the supposed demons with my feminine wiles. Or my affinity. It was hard to say which.

"That wasn't a booby trap. The hands are the reason the booby traps exist. Jeb doesn't want students falling in and getting hurt." She harrumphed. "My first year teaching at Lady of the Lake, we kept finding decapitated skulls that students snuck out of the crypt and left in the hallway. If we'd had something like this at my previous school, this would have put a stop to those students being disrespectful to the dead."

Vega jabbed her wand into another keyhole. The door creaked open. A cold breath of air washed over me, sending shivers up and down my spine even though I was completely clothed. I hugged the blanket and bag of supplies to my chest. The light of her wand suddenly felt too dim for where we were going.

"Honeys, I'm home." Vega laughed and strode forward confidently.

Already, I was creeped out by my choice of witness. I remembered what had happened the last time we were here. She'd tried to nail me into a coffin.

She closed the door behind us.

"Is that necessary?" I asked. "What if we can't get out?"

"Of course it's necessary. I don't want any moisture or rats getting down here and deteriorating the bodies. It's already risky enough with all the bacteria *you're* bringing in."

The air smelled of decaying leaves and the cloying fragrance of blood. The crypt didn't smell like apples and vanilla like the room with the dead body below the library. But it wasn't moldy either. The air was dry and cold.

I followed Vega along the perimeter of the room. She waved her wand over the shelves in the stone walls. Each was open with bones or bodies in various states of decomposition. Some even housed two. Many of the bodies were dried, the skin over the faces taut and shiny. The quality of the air must have mummified them.

Vega pulled on my scarf, nearly strangling me. "Check out this one. He's one of my favorites. Sleeping Beauty."

Obviously, Vega had been here often. All those times she wasn't in her classroom or our dorm room that I had suspected she was off campus, I now wondered if she had been here.

Vega held her wand close to the face of a corpse in one of the higher shelves. The man was beautiful, just as she'd said. His dark bronze skin was smooth and unblemished, the proportions perfectly placed and symmetrical. It was an honest face. He was cute in that boy-next-door way.

His dark skin tone contrasted sharply with his blond hair, just long enough to curl in a rakish sort of way. I could tell he was mixed race, but I didn't know what he was, nor could I guess his affinity or Fae heritage. He couldn't have been more than twenty-five or thirty when he'd died. He was so well preserved he looked as though he could simply be asleep. The old-fashioned suit reminded me of something Thatch would wear. There was something familiar about him.

"Who was he?" I asked. "When did he die?"

Vega waved her wand over the inscription on the plate in the wall, though it was too dark to see it. "Dox Woodruff. He was a teacher here. He died in 1932."

Now I knew where I'd seen him. He'd been the hot teacher Vega had drooled over in the old yearbooks from the twenties. He'd been a teacher at the school when Thatch had gone there.

"They did an excellent job of preserving him. I would do him if he still worked here." She placed a hand on his arm. He held a book to his chest. "I read about his life in his diary. He fell in love with one of his students, Millie. She was in love with him, but he was too gentlemanly to compromise her virtue, so he told her he would wait until she graduated before he married her."

She smiled, tears filling her eyes. "Millie's parents objected, saying she was too young and asked her to wait. Dox patiently waited, courting her and exchanging no more than a chaste kiss with her. Millie went to college to become a teacher and when her parents discovered she landed a job here—so she could be with him—they were enraged. The lovebirds decided to elope without her parents' blessing, but on the day of their planned wedding, they intervened."

"What was their objection?" I asked. "Was it racial?"

"Yes, in a manner of speaking. Millie's parents objected to his Fae lineage." She lowered her voice as if one of the cadavers might overhear. "He was a Fae prince! Can you believe it? His mother was human, so technically he was Witchkin, but his father was a prince of the Silver Court, and Dox lived amongst the Fae his entire life before coming here. He kept his lineage secret—but Millie's parents found out, and they demanded that no one in league with the Fae be permitted to teach impressionable young minds!"

If that was the attitude, I could see why people had objected to Khaba—and why the principal hadn't been particularly forthcoming with the news about Julian Thistledown's lineage. Though I didn't like the way Jeb had gone about it, trying to erase the mistake of not spotting a Fae predator from everyone's minds rather than admitting the oversight. Jeb was a jerk for trying to make Darla and other girls feel like nothing had happened.

Vega caressed the corpse's arm lovingly. "Dox was fired from his position as the magical defense teacher. It was a scandal, but ultimately Womby's decided to rehire him because his father donated money to the school. Of course, that was all going on while he was courting Millie, waiting for her to graduate from college. By the time she took the job here and the parents got wind of their plans, they hired a freelance fairy godmother to intervene on their behalf.

"The thing about that 'fairy godmother,' she wasn't Witchkin like they'd thought. She was a *real* fairy—my guess is someone affiliated with the Raven Court. She knew her way through a magical contract like nobody's business. The parents had said to stop their daughter. They hadn't specified how. It wasn't just one Fae that attacked Millie while she was in Lachlan Falls with a group of students, but several Fae. Millie didn't stand a chance."

This was the juiciest gossip I had ever heard about the school. And it was coming from my wicked roommate? I couldn't believe Vega even deigned to tell me this story.

Vega placed a hand over her heart, leaning closer to Dox's face. "Thatch told me that your mother told him Dox tried to revive Millie with a kiss. He pushed all his magic into her, trying to resurrect her from the dead. He didn't care if he died so long as she lived. But it didn't work. He was completely drained, and his heart stopped." She sighed longingly.

"Did my mother know them?"

"Probably. She worked with him." She shrugged. "You want to meet Millie, the young woman Dox died for?"

Millie wore a beautiful white gown with a high collar and a long train that draped down from her shelf and obscured part of the corpse below her. It was difficult to tell from the way her bridal headband and veil draped over her if her dark hair was cut in a short bob or curled and tucked up. She reminded me of Snow White with her cherry-red lips and pale complexion. I hoped there weren't any vampires in the crypt.

"She's beautiful," I said. She looked a lot like Vega, though her face was rounder, whereas Vega was slender.

Vega waved her wand over the inscription on the plate in the wall. "Millicent Pettigrove. 1932. I hope I'm as well preserved as she is when they give me a tomb here. She died saving the lives of her students and colleagues from Fae. They got her, but they didn't get her students." She turned to me, her eyes wide with awe. "Do you believe in past lives?"

Was she asking if I thought she might have been one of them? I didn't believe in past lives, but I didn't want to tell Vega that.

"I don't know. Anything is possible." Except that Vega could possibly have been reincarnated from a woman who cared about her students. More likely she just wanted Dox to be her past-life boyfriend. I couldn't blame her either. He was the hottest cadaver I'd ever seen.

Vega showed me the corpses of the teachers who had died in recent years. Lisa Singer, one of my predecessor art teachers lay on a low shelf close to the floor. Pieces of Jorge Smith were housed in a small cubby of his own. He was the one who had supposedly been attacked by students the year before I'd been hired. At least, that was what Thatch had told me to scare me. I now knew Julian Thistledown had killed him because Jorge Smith had put together the clues that Julian had killed Lisa Singer and Agnes Padilla.

Vega nodded to Lisa Singer who was almost as intact as Millicent Pettigrove. "Sometimes I come down here and listen to the silence. I talk to Lisa and tell her about my bad days and wonder if she can hear me."

"I didn't know you were friends with any of the previous art teachers," I said.

"Well, I wasn't when they were alive, but they aren't as annoying now that they don't complain about their stupid curriculum or lack of art supplies."

That sounded more like the Vega I knew.

I was surprised Lisa Singer was down here. People had said she'd mysteriously disappeared. Then again, Jeb might have been trying to cover up her death, not wanting the school to have more bad publicity.

"This is John Bingham. He tripped down a flight of stairs and broke his neck the year I was hired on. Probably pushed by the students." She introduced me to more corpses.

The way she talked about the dead, indignant on their behalf at the threadbare state of the clothes they were entombed in, or the manners in which they'd died, was touching. She spoke about them as though they were her friends. I'd never thought about how probable it was Vega might not have living friends. She was rude, snobby, and arrogant. In the past few months when I'd seen her speak with other teachers, she tolerated their presence, but she didn't talk to people as though she liked them. Even Thatch, Miss Periwinkle, and the other Celestors who were equal to her skill level weren't her friends. She didn't act as though she enjoyed hanging out with them.

And no one seemed particularly fond of Vega either. She sat on a high horse where there was only room for one queen bitch. It had to be lonely.

I never thought I would feel sorry for Vega, but I did.

When we came to Sebastian Reade, Vega leaned closer, peering inside the alcove. His complexion was waxy and pale. Black veins covered his face and hands. It was creepy. He wore the same brown suit and bow tie he always wore.

She tsked. "Those mother fuckers didn't even give him his own tomb." She shoved her wand into the shelf past him, showing me the bones of his roommate.

"Are all the teachers buried here?" I asked.

"No, some are buried in the graveyard in the woods, but they're the ones who die of natural causes. Sometimes families request cremation or want the bodies entombed elsewhere, so we don't have all the teachers' corpses. Plus, they only keep the corpses who die of mysterious circumstances here, probably so it's easier to exhume the body to examine later. Mr. Reade didn't have a family, though." She smoothed the older man's bangs to the side of his forehead, tenderly, as though she cared about him. "Did I tell you he was my foreign language teacher?"

"No," I said, wondering where this was going.

"I went to Lady of the Lake School for Girls. He had to put up with me for two foreign languages during the same day. It isn't like Womby's over there. Students have to take a minimum of eight classes, but they can take more if they want early-bird or independent studies. If you want to get ahead, that's the way to go. And Mr. Reade was there every step of the way." She smiled wistfully.

My roommate never shared personal details like this. I didn't dare speak and break the spell.

"Foreign language truly is the foundation for good spell work. I learned six languages from Mr. Reade. The rest I learned after I graduated. When I became a teacher, I thought I might . . . I don't know . . . hang out with him now that I was his equal. But a year after I was hired on, he moved to Womby's. I can't understand why he took the job. It was a huge pay cut. He said it was because he cared about students. He wanted to ensure the teenagers here graduated with a good education. As if he could do that alone."

"Is that why you took the job here?" I asked.

She abruptly turned away. "I don't know. It was ten years ago. One can hardly expect me to remember the reasoning of my stupidity from that long ago." She waved a hand at the blanket I carried under my arm. "Are you going to get this show on the road or what?"

I didn't see Brogan's body down here. That meant we would be questioning Sebastian Reade and no one else.

I spread the blanket on the floor and set out the candles. Vega lit them with her wand. I sat cross-legged, focusing on my affinity swelling in my core. I imagined the ball of energy growing and flowing into my veins. That was all I needed, maybe more than I needed, but I had to make a show of it. Already Vega suspected too much about my magic and affinity. I needed to misdirect her.

I gestured with my hands and tried to spell a few words in the sign language I could remember. I sprinkled the tea leaves on the ground. Through slit eyes I watched Vega watching me. Her arms were crossed, and she leaned casually against a wall, skepticism painted across her face.

I mumbled a few Harry Potter charms under my breath. I doubted she had read the books.

In a spark of inspiration, I said, "Abra-cadaver." I rose and approached Sebastian Reade's shelf. A moment of trepidation shivered through me. Necromancy was the kind of forbidden magic Alouette Loraline would have done. I didn't want to be like her. I told myself I was doing this for good, not evil.

Vega shook her head, her expression more disgusted with me than usual. "That isn't going to work. I'm glad I made you promise me your wardrobe."

It was only the top of my wardrobe, but it didn't matter. I knew I could talk to the dead. At least, I thought I could.

I reached into the cubbyhole. It was high enough to be awkward; I had to stand on tiptoe. I rolled back Sebastian Reade's socks and placed my hands on his cold ankles. His skin didn't feel like human flesh any longer. It was more like leather. I tried to think of happy, sensual thoughts; Derrick's lips on mine, his thumb brushing across my knuckles, the way he looked into my eyes and made my stomach flip-flop.

"Abra-cadaver," I repeated.

Vega's cackle was cut short when the foreign language teacher sat up. He bonked his head on the stone ceiling and fell back down. Startled, I let go and jumped back.

Vega jumped back too. "You killed him!"

"He was already dead," I said.

Even though I knew he would come back to life once I touched him, my insides trembled with nervousness as I took hold of his ankles again. Vega rushed forward, placing an arm over the deceased teacher's chest. He opened his eyes.

"Careful," she said. "We don't want you sitting up too fast." She helped ease him out of the nook so that he sat on the ledge. His feet dangled off the side. I crouched down so I could hold on to his ankles.

Sebastian Reade looked from me to Vega to the flickers of candlelight casting ominous shadows over nearby bodies. He flinched. "What are we doing down in the crypt? Did someone die?"

Vega cooed at him like he was a baby. "Aren't you precious? This is exactly what I imagined talking to someone down here would be like."

"I'm sorry to tell you this, Mr. Reade," I said. "But you're dead."

"No, that can't be right. I'm talking to you." He felt his forehead. "I just hit my head. That's all."

Vega took his hand in hers. "No, Mr. Reade. Someone murdered you."

"What? How can we be speaking? Miss Bloodmire, please don't tell me you're dabbling in necromancy. As one of my former pupils I should hope I instilled at least some moral values in you." His hand gestured and fluttered fluidly as he spoke. He must have been past the rigor mortis stage.

"Don't worry. I didn't resurrect you," Vega said with a pleased air. "Clarissa did."

He crossed his arms. "Well, I suppose there's no point in chiding her. I knew she'd turn out to be just as wicked as her mother."

In death, one might think the guy would give me a break, but no. Even corpses judged me.

"Was it a nice service?" he asked Vega. "Did you tell any stories about the days when you were my student back at Lady of the Lake?"

She wet her lips. "You only just died earlier today. We haven't had a service yet."

"What? But my body is down here. Are they going to have a funeral without my body?" He wagged a finger at her. "They are going to have a funeral, right?"

"I'm sure they will. People have just been a little high strung with the Fae attacks and your recent death. I'll make sure the principal organizes a nice service for you."

He nodded approvingly. "Good. And I don't want one of those wakes or memorials. People are too happy at those events. I'm dead. I expect people to cry and be sad."

Vega nodded. "I completely agree."

"I hate to interrupt your funeral plans," I said. "Can we talk about your death? Do you know who killed you?"

"No. Was it a Fae?" he asked.

"Do you remember that one time when you were my teacher and—" Vega began, a wistful smile on her face.

"Excuse me." I snapped my fingers at her. "Have you forgotten why we're here? We need to interview Mr. Reade so that your name will be cleared of being the murderer."

Vega gave me the evil eye as if I was some kind of party pooper.

"What's this about them blaming you for my murder?" he asked.

"Nothing. No one has accused me . . . yet. They only blamed me for Thatch's poisoning—which I didn't do."

"But they might think you killed someone if the bodies keep piling up," I said. I gazed up at Sebastian Reade. "What's the last thing you remember? Do you recall what you were doing in the stairwell?"

"Oh, bother." He looked away and coughed, though I was certain he wasn't breathing. "I may have experienced a . . . my discretion seemed to have . . . that is to say. . . ." He frowned at Vega apologetically. "I apologize. This may come as a bit of a surprise. Gertrude has fallen in love with me. She told me so herself. How is she taking my death? She must be heartbroken."

She hadn't sounded broken up about anything when we'd heard her laughing in Thatch's room.

Vega eyed him skeptically. "You are telling us you were with Miss Periwinkle?"

"Yes. We were . . . ahem. I only intended to give her one kiss, but one turned into more. I was kissing her when I started to grow light-headed and felt my magic being wicked away."

"Are you certain?" I asked.

"Oh yes. There's no way I would forget that kiss. I lost consciousness and woke up dead."

That was it! Miss Periwinkle drained Sebastian Reade. Vega was my witness.

# CHAPTER THIRTY-FOUR
## Putting the Romance Back into Necromancy

"So you're saying Miss P killed you?" Vega said.

"No. My darling would never do such a thing," Sebastian Reade said. "Someone must have snuck up behind me while we were kissing. Yes, the more I think about it, that's the only rational scenario."

Ugh, now he sounded like Thatch.

Vega patted his hand as though he were a particularly dense child she was fond of. "Mr. Reade, no. Gertrude is a backstabbing, soul-sucking siren. She was using you to gain strength from your magic."

He drew his hand away. "No, she wasn't. You don't know what you're talking about. Gertrude is a Celestor now."

"Hey, maybe this is a conversation we don't need to have right now," I said. This wasn't the kind of news one just dumped on some poor guy who was dead.

Vega ignored me. "A double affinity. It's rare, but not unheard of, though the siren magic seems to be overpowering her Celestor magic—and her common sense. Not only is she a powerful siren, but Clarissa told me she's dating Thatch."

I shook my head at her. I did not want to be the bad guy here.

He shifted, standing on both his feet so that I had to scoot back to give him room. "Gertrude and Mr. Thatch are simply friends. She told me she has a thing for older men. He's too young for her."

"That succubus has a thing for anyone with a dick." Vega said. "She doesn't deserve you."

He wagged a finger at her. "Miss Bloodmire, you watch your mouth! I will not have you using that language in my presence."

"Sorry, sir, but it's true. You deserve to be with someone who won't cheat on you."

"I'm dead! It doesn't matter what I deserve." His chest shook, and he covered his eyes with his hands.

Vega stood there shifting from foot to foot awkwardly. The problem with Vega was she hadn't even been trying to be a bitch for once. She seemed to admire Mr. Reade, and she probably liked him more in her morbid way now that he was dead. But she had to have the final word in everything, and that didn't coincide with compassion.

Vega scowled at me. "Are you happy now? You just used necromancy to make a dead man cry."

I shook my head at her. She so didn't get people—especially herself.

"Mr. Reade," I said in my nicest teacher tone. "Why don't we help you back onto your shelf so that you can go back to sleep?"

"I wasn't sleeping. I was dead. I don't want to be dead. I want to see Gertrude."

Vega glared at me as if this was all *my* fault. Sebastian Reade kicked past me, knocking me onto my butt. He staggered and lurched a few steps before falling flat on his face.

"Let's get him back into his tomb," I said.

Vega rolled him over. She grabbed him under the shoulders, and I lifted his legs, careful not to touch his skin. We heaved him into his shelf.

I set the candles aside and shook out the blanket. "Okay, now let's tell Jeb and Khaba what Sebastian Reade told us."

"No."

I froze. "Please tell me you didn't believe him about Miss Periwinkle being innocent after he explained she was the last person he was with. She probably sucked the magic right out of his face as she kissed him."

"I don't doubt it, but I'm not telling Khaba. Think about how bad this will look." She waved a hand at the candles nonchalantly. "They'll just say I'm trying to prove my own innocence—which they'll be even more doubtful of than ever. If I don't say *you* performed necromancy, they'll think *I* did. If they assume I've used necromancy, they'll insist I did other dark arts as well. Things I haven't done, like poison Thatch, and things I have done, which will remain unnamed."

A sneaky smile crossed her face at that. "Think about it. Am I a reliable witness?"

I gaped at her. "You made the oath. You can't change it."

"I'm not changing it." She picked up the lit candles and placed them closer to Mr. Sleeping Beauty. "I said *when* I told Jeb and Khaba, I wouldn't mention you. The fact of the matter is, I never intended to tell them."

Craptacular. Once again, my scheming roommate had outwitted me.

"What was the point in coming down here and waking the dead in the first place? Why did you agree to the oath? Why bother to agree to question

Sebastian Reade?"

She scooped up the remaining candles. "I was curious about who's been killing everyone so I could be nicer to him or her. I don't want to end up dead, after all. Now I know."

"What?" I backed away from her, unable to believe her level of evil.

"Here's what I'm thinking: if Gerty accidentally kills Thatch—or if she gets jealous enough about you stealing his attention from her she might do it on purpose—I wonder if I'll become department head. I wouldn't mind teaching potions and alchemy next year either." Any compassion she might have had for the dead was buried under the malicious gleam in her eyes.

I backed away into the shadows where I thought I remembered the door was located. Hopefully it was unlocked.

"You aren't leaving yet," she said sternly. "I'm not done with you. I had a more important reason to bring you down here than to resurrect Sebastian Reade."

A more important reason than to prove her innocence?

"To kill me?" That was typically what villains did after they told you their diabolical plans.

She cackled. "You're going to put the romance back into necromancy." She placed a hand on Dox Woodruff's arm.

No way.

I continued backing away.

"Clarissa, get back here. I want a stiff with a stiffy."

I may have puked in my mouth at that, and not just a little.

"Do the spell yourself," I said. "You're a Celestor. You saw me do it. You can figure it out."

She tapped her nails against her chin as if considering it, shrugged and turned to Dox Woodruff. I stumbled through the darkness, collided into a wall, and accidentally groped a set of dusty bones. Behind me, Vega muttered, "Abra-cadaver. Abra-cadaver."

A moment later I found the door. It was unlocked! I ran out, tripped into a set of stairs I'd forgotten were there, and crept through the underground labyrinth. I managed to avoid booby traps all the way up to Vega's closet stairwell before exiting her classroom.

I didn't know what Vega would do to me once she figured out she wasn't going to be able to make the spell work. She *probably* wouldn't kill me in my sleep. It was a school night after all. And of course, if she killed me, she wouldn't be able to coerce me into bringing her past boyfriend back to life some other night.

Lucky me.

I managed to avoid my room and an encounter with Vega for a little while because I packed a bag and slept in Derrick's room that night. I wanted to be there for him if he came back. He wasn't well. He might have just wandered away or passed out somewhere in his invisibility clothes.

He didn't return.

The next day after school, I walked into my dorm room, finding Vega bent over the desk studiously writing. Three open books floated in the air around her. I considered backing away slowly and quietly to sneak off before she caught me. After last night's expedition, I could only imagine how well she'd take it to have failed at her necromancy goal after I'd ditched her.

On the other hand, this was my room too. I would have to face Vega's wrath sooner or later. I stepped inside and went over to my wardrobe to select a warmer sweater.

Vega turned a page in a maroon book that looked as though it was made of vellum. It took me a moment to realize the floating tome was *my* book—the one I'd borrowed from the dead scribe in the secret library room. I was about to object, but then I saw the Old High German and Middle English dictionaries and another book that looked like it was some kind of German grammar book.

I understood what she was doing.

"You're translating the spell!" I said. "I didn't know you could speak Old High German."

"I decided to teach myself last night." She draped herself over the chair, managing to make slouching look sexy. Her eyes were bloodshot, and her eyelids drooped. "And for the record, it's Middle High German."

"Did you stay up all night working on this?"

"Not all night. Most of the night I spent with Dox."

"Oh. How did that go?"

"You think you're so clever." Her eyes narrowed. "You think I couldn't get your stupid abra-cadaver spell to work, don't you? I will have you know I am a Merlin-class Celestor. I can make any spell work."

"I don't doubt it. You're the one I go to for the big magic." And for assistance with morally questionable tasks.

She turned back to the dictionary, flipping the pages. "I did resurrect the dead last night, thank you very much."

"Oh? Nice," I said.

That spell had been made up. I didn't know if she really had done necromancy or this was the equivalent of *The Emperor's New Clothes*, and she was too embarrassed to admit she had failed. It was probably for the best to allow Vega to continue to act superior so she wouldn't turn into another Periwinkle who wanted to kill me in earnest.

"Good job," I said. "Did your former dead husband say anything interesting?"

"He's my late *future* husband. And no, we didn't do much talking." She scribbled a few notes down.

Her words sank in. Ick. I sincerely hoped necrophilia hadn't been on her to-do list last night.

"In any case, your spell was temporary and incomplete. Once I'm done with it and have collected all the ingredients, I'll be able to permanently resurrect Dox."

That's how she thought I had revived Sebastian Reade? It was better than her knowing about my Red affinity. She was the last person in the Unseen Realm I trusted with that knowledge.

"I couldn't acquire a dragon egg," I said. "Thatch said it was too dangerous to collect."

Vega pulled the grammar book closer. "For you, obviously."

Maybe it wasn't such a dreadful idea for her to be onboard with this spell. She wasn't going to help me without a motive. If she thought it cured death, it didn't hurt to let her think that. The more translating she did, the more it benefited me. It might be the solution to cure Derrick.

She held up what she had translated so far, obviously proud of herself. I had to admit, as wicked as Vega could be, she had an impressive mind.

Her translation was like reading Chaucer in Old English. I muddled through the description, trying to translate Old English into modern. "It sounds like you need someone from the Lost Red Court." No one talked about the Red affinity other than a few obscure references in old textbooks.

"Sometimes I don't realize how much of an idiot you are until you open your mouth. It clearly says the purpose of this spell is for when one *doesn't* have a Red affinity. This spell—it's a potion really—is so powerful it won't require forbidden magic to work. However, if one wanted to infuse more power into it, she could. That would take several Witchkin with a spectrum of affinities or one with a Red affinity to assist. Since the Lost Red Court died out a few hundred years ago, that's out of the question." She arched an eyebrow at me. "Unless you know something I don't. . . ."

"No," I said quickly. "Why would you think that? Anyway, what's the spell specifically for?"

"This spell is the answer to your mother's research. It could be used to cure Fae of their fertility problem or bring back the dead." Vega leaned back, looking smug. "It's the reason Thatch asked you to go on a wild goose chase, collecting unicorn horn for him."

"Could a spell like this cure a curse?" Thatch had claimed he needed the ingredients to cure Derrick, but for all I knew, he might have been using the spell from my mother's diary to solve the Fae Fertility Paradox.

"This spell can make a hex, curse, or enchantment. It can create a counter curse and so much more." She cackled ominously. "I can use it for anything I want."

That sounded ominous. I sincerely hoped she had no idea what I was. There would be no end to my problems if that was the case.

Now that I knew the spell had a use, I wasn't sure what to do with that knowledge. I supposed I could use it to help someone—if I had all the ingredients—which I didn't. I still hadn't seen Derrick or heard news about him from Khaba.

That meant I needed help from someone who might be able to find Derrick through divination.

I left Art Club early after school, awarding Imani and Greenie the task of overseeing activities.

I went to the kledstaff room and studied the schedules. If I had a prep period while Pro Ro taught yoga, I could offer to teach his class for him. Unfortunately, our schedules didn't line up. Pinky had a prep during Pro Ro's yoga class, though Puck had filled it with Latin. I was pretty sure Pro Ro spoke Latin. He could potentially teach that subject. And Pinky had boasted of his yoga skills enthusiastically several times. I wondered if I could get them to switch. If I convinced Pinky to agree to this, perhaps Pro Ro would then use his powers to search for Derrick.

I hiked across the school to Pro Ro's room.

He groaned, seeing me. "Not you again. I'm still recovering from my last encounter with you."

"Sorry about that. Hey, I was wondering if it would be helpful if I found someone else to take yoga off your hands. Maybe if you switched electives with someone." I didn't dare say who, lest he go speak to Pinky himself.

He glowered at me. "Fine. You find someone to switch classes with me and administration approves, I'll happily perform any spell you want."

That was all I needed! My nose guided me to the ripest part of the wing, Pinky's classroom. Setting foot in Julian's room momentarily creeped me out. I was sort of glad the door was locked. I knocked, but no answer came. I ventured to the male dormitories next. I tapped on the door. Pinky peeked out. He wore a pair of black-framed glasses, similar to Josie's.

"Hi, Clarissa." His voice was timid, wary. "It's a surprise seeing you here."

"In the male dorm wing?" I asked, breathing through my mouth. "I think it's okay if I stay in the hall. I'm just not supposed to be in your room."

"No, I mean, it's a surprise to see you here talking to me. To see *any*one here talking to me. Everyone treats me like I'm a pariah."

"Oh," I said. "Probably people are just busy."

He crossed his arms, looking unconvinced.

I plunged on, not wanting him to thwart me from my mission. "I wondered if you would help me with something. Pro Ro teaches yoga class, but he hates it. He said he'd agree to do a favor for me if I can find someone to switch classes with him. I noticed you're teaching Latin at the scheduled hour of yoga class. If Pro Ro speaks Latin, I thought it might be a nice trade since you enjoy yoga, and he doesn't."

"Huh," Pinky said. "I do like yoga more than Latin. It would be way less work for me."

"Will you do it?"

"What are you getting out of this? Maybe you think I'm just a dumb sasquatch, but I've noticed the social dynamics here. It isn't like you and Pro Ro are BFFs."

"He's performing a spell for me, a divination spell to locate someone I know. I'm afraid Invismo has been snatched by the Fae, and I need help finding him."

Pinky nodded. "I *could* talk to Pro Ro about it." He sounded hesitant.

"That would be great! We can go see him right now."

"Every time I try to talk to him, he always makes an excuse why it isn't a good time. He isn't rude, just. . . .What is it about him? Pro Ro and Vega Bloodmire, I get that they're both Celestors, and they're the most academic and powerful of Witchkin, but neither will talk to me. Miss Bloodmire is condescending and mean. Mr. Thatch is curt. I thought the Amni Plandai teachers at this school would be friendly at least, but they aren't. The Lupis are standoffish. Grandmother Bluehorse walks the other way when she sees me. I thought Josie and I might be friends—we used to work with each other and were friends—but she keeps avoiding me too. Why does everyone treat me like I have a contagious disease?"

"I don't know." My eyes watered from the proximity to him.

"But you must. You do it to me too. The only reason you're talking to me right now is because you want something from me."

Guilt churned in my stomach along with nausea at his odor. "I'm sorry. I don't want to be like that and use people."

"I don't care about that. I just want to know why people won't talk to me. I haven't done anything wrong, not like that one staff member. I heard one teacher here tore off Pro Ro's turban. I didn't do anything like that."

Did he seriously not know that was me? "If I tell you, will you promise not to be mad?"

He nodded, his fur flopping around. It sent up fresh waves of toxic musk into the air.

"And you'll still consider going to Pro Ro and trading classes? Even if you don't like what I have to say?"

"Yes! Just tell me!" His high nasally voice rose.

My chest tightened in panic. This was an introvert's worst nightmare. "So, um, the thing is. . . ." I grasped for the right words. I didn't want to hurt his feelings. "Some people feel. . . . Maybe you've heard people talk. . . . Vega put it bluntly to you several times. . . ."

His eyebrows rose in expectation.

I would rather have yanked out my fingernails one by one than be the bearer of the unwelcome news. "Do you know where I'm going with this?"

"No."

Eloquence eluded me. I blurted it out. "You smell."

"What? No, I don't."

"You do."

He laughed. "What's the real reason? I committed some kind of faux pas, didn't I? It was because I showed up the first day without clothes?"

Did I want to make this easy on myself or tell him the truth? "No. That's the real reason. You have an . . . odor."

"That's such a Witchkin thing to say. It's so anti-sasquatch. You're as bad as the Fae." He crossed his arms, looking indignant.

"I don't know anything about that. You asked me to tell you the truth, so I did."

"And just what do they say I smell like?" He huffed little breaths that reminded me of an animal.

There was no delicate way around this. This wasn't going to be easy to hear. "How often do you shower?"

"Shower? Like stand in a rainstorm? Occasionally."

"No, use a hot shower inside the male teachers' restroom?" I asked.

He looked absolutely perplexed.

"Or take a bath?"

"Oh, that. A couple times a year. In the spring and summer mostly. I prefer ponds."

No freaking way. No wonder he smelled as ripe as a dumpster in summer. He probably hadn't washed since September.

"Well, you might have to change that. Many Witchkin shower and bathe more frequently. Like every day."

"No." He shook his head adamantly. "No one would do that."

"Yeah, they do. Ask around." I casually backed a step away, giving myself more fresh air. "How about deodorant? Do you use antiperspirant?"

"That isn't healthy. Antiperspirants clog pores and get caked in fur." He clenched his fists at his sides.

"Maybe there's something more natural you can use." I offered him an encouraging smile. "After you figure it out, I think you're going to find it easier to make friends." I tried to soften the words as best I could, but his body language told me I wasn't succeeding.

He shifted from foot to foot in agitation and threw up his hands in disgust. "Sure, and while I'm at it, why don't I just shave off all my fur and wear a full set of clothes? The real problem is that I'm a sasquatch. You Witchkin can't accept a beautiful hairy man into your ecosystem of cool because you're too busy imitating our Fae oppressors who are keeping everyone down." He pointed an accusing finger at me. "Just because I don't conform to your Witchkin hygiene doesn't mean I smell." He stepped back and closed the door in my face.

I had a feeling he wasn't going to trade classes with Pro Ro.

# CHAPTER THIRTY-FIVE
## A Lunch Duty to Remember

On Thursday, I showed up to my cafeteria duty on time. As I neared the teacher table up on the dais, Thatch skulked out of the shadows and snuck up on me. "I thought I'd find you here. Khaba isn't here to rescue you this time."

I tried not to let my panic show. "I need to—"

"Yes, of course. Monitor our juvenile delinquents. By all means. I'll walk with you."

I wove through the crowd of students coming in from the nearest archway. It took everything in me to keep a cheerful smile on my face and not let my suspicion show. I passed students seating themselves at tables for lunch.

Thatch strode by my side. "It seems you've been keeping secrets from me, Miss Lawrence. Again."

"Oh?" Crap.

"One would think you'd learned the futility of this by now."

"Nope. Not me." I tried to sound unconcerned. I casually wiped my sweaty palms against my skirt.

It had to be about Derrick. I'd expected him to be angry. From the haughty amusement in his expression, I grew less certain.

"Let's talk about Derrick, shall we?" He smiled, a little too victoriously.

"Here? Now?" I glanced at another wave of students pouring in from the far end of the round room. "With all these students who might overhear us?"

"You were the one who was complaining about delays, about *interruptions.*"

I scooted back toward the dais where there were no students. The raised area would be ideal where I could watch the students while they would serve as witnesses to anything he did to me.

"There's no need to keep pretending," Thatch said as he shadowed me.

A student shrieked somewhere behind me. That was in no way unusual considering I was surrounded by hormonal teenagers. I turned away from Thatch, glancing over the students to see what was going on, but I was shorter than most of the students darting about. More students cried out. Thatch turned now too.

That was about the time I noticed the change in the students. A ripple of movement cascaded away from the center of the room. Human traffic leapt and ran away. As the crowd parted I caught a glimpse of a glowing sword, blue fire dancing over the blade.

I recognized that sword. Thatch had used it to temporarily put Bart to sleep.

Like a vision out of a mirage, flickers of tan skin bobbed closer before shifting out of sight. It was only when Derrick peeled off his invisible ski cap and I saw his blue hair that I knew it was him.

"Merlin's balls. What is he doing with my sword?" Thatch asked.

Derrick ran straight toward us.

"Derrick." Thatch put up a hand in a placating gesture. "Stop. Now."

His voice was lost in the screams of students. Derrick's eyes fixed on Thatch. He raised the sword.

Thatch stepped in front of me. He held out his wand. A burst of light shot out of his wand like lightning.

Derrick crumpled to the floor. The blue flames dancing over the blade extinguished. I ran to Derrick and dropped to my knees. His skin grew translucent. He faded away, along with my hope. By the time I reached out to where he lay, he was gone.

Tears filled my eyes. I turned to Thatch. "What did you do with him? Did you kill him?"

Thatch's face was a splotchy red. "How could you be so careless? I thought you understood the importance of keeping your magic under control. I trusted you to use common sense and behave reasonably, and this is what I get."

His words flowed past me like water. I floated above his chiding, clinging to the life raft of desperation. "What did you do to him?"

"What I should have done a long time ago. He's gone. Forever."

# CHAPTER THIRTY-SIX
## And I'll Get Your Little Dog Too

The cafeteria broke into chaos. Students screamed and ran in different directions. Khaba appeared in a puff of smoke in the doorway. Vega ran in from the hallway and collided into him.

Thatch grabbed my arm and hauled me to my feet. "You're coming with me."

"No, I don't want to go with you." I tried to wrench my arm away, but he held on to me too firmly.

"You don't have a say in the matter. We have things to discuss." He swept his other hand over my head in a gesture I recognized from the times he'd used his transportation spell.

I didn't know where he intended to take me, but I already knew I didn't want to go there. He would enslave me and make me the Raven Queen's servant like he was. He would curse me and take away my will.

He would do the same thing to me as he'd done to Derrick.

"No!" I said, but my voice came out reedy and thin.

The air was sucked from my lungs, and a cyclone of wind whipped around me. My hair came free of my ponytail and fell into my eyes. The world was a black-and-pink blur. When the movement stopped, my stomach continued to flip-flop. I wobbled and reached out to steady myself.

Thatch shoved me into a chair. I pushed my pink hair out of my face. I was in his office, not the dungeon. The Raven Queen was nowhere in sight. I sat in the metal torture chair.

He plopped himself into his comfortable ergonomic chair. "I specifically told you to stay away from Derrick. I told you he was cursed and you would only make things worse for yourself and him. And you did."

Hot tears spilled down my cheeks, blurring my vision. "You killed Derrick. You just killed my boyfriend."

He grimaced, not looking all that broken up about it. "You left me no other choice but to remove him from this equation."

I stood up, ready to launch myself across the desk and strangle him.

Of course, if I had been thinking logically, I might have remembered my tendency for physical violence was what had gotten me in so much trouble with Pro Ro.

Thatch flicked his hand at me. An unseen force pushed me back into the chair. My arms fell onto the armrests. Pressure squeezed my limbs. It felt like invisible ropes held me in place, similar to the spell Vega used to threaten me with, only this was firmer. I had a feeling I wasn't going to be able to kick myself free. The ropes shifted and tightened. I froze. These weren't ropes. They were snakes. Their scales raked over my bare arms. Another slithered across my belly and coiled around me, binding me to the chair.

The bonds were invisible when I glanced down, but I didn't doubt they were serpents—either brought out by my own fears from the fear chair—or brought out by Thatch's sadistic streak because he knew I was afraid of them.

Thatch steepled his long fingers in front of him. "Do I have your attention now? Or are you going to exhibit further displays of juvenile aggression?"

I sobbed and tried to wipe my face on my shoulder. "I hate you," I said.

"That may be the case, but it has little effect on the matter as it now stands. Your arrogance and selfish disregard for the rules I set in place for your safety have endangered you, as well as your students. You—"

"I broke his curse. My affinity and virgin's blood broke the Raven Queen's hold on him."

He snorted. "You wish."

"You still work for the Raven Queen."

His lips thinned, and his nostrils flared. "I do not." He fought to keep his anger in check, but I could already see I'd ruffled his feathers.

I pressed the proverbial blade deeper. "I know you tortured Derrick. He told me." I had seen it. "He said you attacked him. You were the one who cursed him with invisibility."

"You don't know what you're talking about."

That proved it right there. Thatch wouldn't even admit he'd lied to me. He was as much of a villain as Derrick had thought he was. "You're a liar. I'm not going to listen to you anymore."

"I omitted certain details about my knowledge of Derrick's whereabouts and concealed his identity for your protection. I found him a job at this school and looked after him so that no harm would come to him. If you weren't such an ungrateful, spoiled brat, perhaps you would be able to see that." He lifted his chin in his superior, snooty way. "I can see more than ever I was justified in my reasoning to conceal the truth, as you've shown how sneaking, conniving, and untrustworthy you are."

"You're the sneaking, conniving, untrustworthy one!"

He removed his wand from his vest pocket. "Truly, I don't know what to do with you. I've tried to be firm. I've been more than patient. But I can see it has finally come to this." He lifted his wand.

"No," I said, shaking my head. I didn't know what he intended: to erase my memories like he had with Derrick? To drain me? Abduct me?

Like clockwork, I heard Miss Periwinkle's voice behind me. "Felix? Is everything all right? I heard someone tried to attack—"

I craned my neck to see behind me. Miss Periwinkle glowered at me.

"Now is not a good time, Gertrude." Thatch closed his eyes, looking weary.

"What is *she* doing in here? You promised me you wouldn't allow her into your private rooms anymore."

"This is my office. It isn't a private room. Students can walk through that door to ask for tutoring—if they don't get scared off by the torture equipment in the dungeon." His lips curved upward into a smile at that. "We are having a meeting regarding the incident that just occurred. It would be unprofessional for me to chastise Miss Lawrence in front of another staff member. I request you take your leave until we are finished here. I will join you in the library afterward."

She remained in the doorway, biting her lip and looking torn.

Did I want Miss Periwinkle to leave? She obviously hated me and would love to see me dead. On the other hand, I didn't know what Thatch intended to do with me now. If he was going to erase my memories so I would forget Derrick—or do something worse—I had to stop him.

Though I was limited in my abilities to do so at the moment.

I made my best attempt at reverse psychology. "That's right. Get out of here, Miss Periwinkle."

Her pretty face pinched together in fury. "Don't tell me what to do, you little whore."

"Merlin's balls," Thatch muttered.

I tried to sound confident. "You're interrupting our latest attempt to have a conversation that doesn't concern you. Felix just asked you to leave. And I want you to leave." I desperately searched for the right words that would tick her off and make her stay so that his plans would be foiled. "Felix was about to tell me I've been a naughty girl. Do you know what he does with naughty girls?"

Her wand was already drawn. She stomped forward. I didn't know if this was going to be bad—or really bad.

Thatch stood. "Gertrude, don't. She's goading you. If you attack, Khaba will find out, and he'll fire you." He came around the desk to meet her. His voice remained calm and gentle. He held his hand out and she took it. "Put your wand away, love."

"That's right. Put your wand away like your boyfriend asks," I said. "Khaba might not have been able to catch you trying to poison me. He might not have seen you kill Sebastian Reade or Brogan McLean. He didn't observe you sending secret messages to the Raven Court, but he'll catch you this time."

"I didn't kill anyone!" she screamed. "I'm not a murderer."

I gave her my best impertinent expression. "That's not what Sebastian Reade said."

She dove toward me, her fingers curled like claws. I turned my face away, but she still managed to gouge her fingernails into my ear before Thatch yanked her back.

I continued. "Sebastian Reade said you were kissing him in the stairwell and you drained him."

"How do you know what Sebastian Reade said?" Thatch raised an eyebrow. "He's dead."

Damn it. I'd just outed myself as a necromancer. Then again, maybe not necessarily. I might regret this later, but I lied. "Vega told me. She took me to the crypt, and she brought him back to life—temporarily." She wasn't going to be able to blame me when they questioned her because of the oath, though she would kill me in the middle of the night for certain now.

Miss Periwinkle sagged against Thatch in defeat. He looked from me to her. "As usual, everything you said is obviously a lie. Gertrude would never cheat on me."

I struggled against the invisible restraints, but they wouldn't budge. "She's cheated on you with Pro Ro, Silas Lupi, and Sebastian Reade. I think she even seduced Khaba—and his boyfriend."

Thatch shook his head at me. "You are doing it again. You're being an immature, jealous imbecile who—"

Periwinkle cut him off. "I did not seduce Dean Khaba! I only rubbed his lamp."

"Yeah? And where was his lamp located at the time?"

Khaba's deep voice came from behind me. "Someplace I would prefer not to mention."

## CHAPTER THIRTY-SEVEN
## Djinntastic

"I hope you don't mind me crashing this party, but I thought I'd bring some djinn and tonic," Khaba chuckled at his own joke. He remained cool and collected as he leaned against the doorway. "One of you—or maybe more than just *one* of you—has a shitload of explaining to do."

I tried to rise from the chair, but the invisible snakes continued to hold me tight.

Miss Periwinkle opened her mouth. A high beautiful note erupted from her lips. Khaba held up a hand, and the note died away. Miss Periwinkle grabbed her throat. She coughed. She opened her mouth again, but no sound came out.

Khaba pointed a finger at her. "Not a word from you."

Yes! He was onto her! There was hope for me yet.

That small gesture must have cost him the last of his wishes—and possibly more. His eyelids drooped in what could have been a sultry come-hither look, but I suspected was actually the result of fatigue and extreme effort.

Khaba nodded to me. "Are you going to release Miss Lawrence? Or am I going to need to force you?"

The usual sparkle of magic that surrounded him had dimmed. He didn't look as casual in the doorway now, more like he leaned against it for support. If I noticed this, Thatch and Periwinkle must have as well.

Thatch spoke slowly, a glacial edge of warning in his voice. "The restraints are for her safety. I feared she might injure herself or someone else." He made no move to remove the invisible bonds, but they slowly melted away.

I jumped to my feet and scooted away from Thatch and Periwinkle, watching them warily until I came up beside Khaba. He had to be hurting for magic. I wrapped my arms around his waist and rubbed his back.

*I wish for Khaba's wishes to come true*, I thought.

One corner of Khaba's mouth lifted into a mischievous smile. He lowered my hand to cup his butt cheeks. "Say it out loud, hon."

My face flushed with warmth. I kneaded his muscles, trying not to think about how embarrassing this was in front of an audience.

I stood on tiptoe, whispering my wish into his ear. "I wish you had more power than Thatch and Periwinkle combined."

He stood taller. His skin radiated a healthy bronze shimmer. He was so beautiful it was hard to look away. Even Gertrude Periwinkle was transfixed by his Fae magic, her gaze unfocused. She swayed on her feet and leaned against Thatch's desk.

Khaba grinned and patted me on the head. "Aren't you a sweetie?" His gaze shifted to Thatch and Periwinkle. "Now, what did you do with my security guard?"

Thatch said nothing.

"I'm waiting. I trust Miss Periwinkle hasn't cast a tongue-twister jinx on you." Khaba's chuckle died into a tense silence. "Tell me what you did with Invismo. If you refuse to speak willingly, I will force you to explain through magical means."

Thatch's expression remained stony. "Invismo, your security guard, was not who you thought he was. His real name is Derrick Winslow." Thatch spoke slowly, enunciating each word with care. "He'd been brainwashed by the Raven Queen, which I managed to cover with a charm to erase his memories. When Miss Lawrence accidentally released him from the protective wards and charms I cast on him, he went on a killing spree. I believe he tried to poison Miss Lawrence's chocolate, though his plan was foiled when Miss Bloodmire switched staff members' chocolates as a practical joke. Sensing dark magic at work, I ate the chocolate to prevent anyone else from ingesting it."

"You're saying you consumed poisoned food out of the kindness of your heart? How noble." Khaba's skepticism was thick enough it could have been spread onto a slice of bread and served with a healthy helping of disbelief.

Periwinkle rubbed Thatch's shoulder affectionately like he was the most thoughtful, heroic knight in all the land. I wasn't sure what to think about Thatch at the moment.

Thatch's stiff frame stood as rigid as a tree. He gave away no indication of fear or guilt. "While under the spell of the Raven Queen, Derrick murdered Sebastian Reade and Brogan McLean to gain strength and power. In Lachlan Falls, he called emissaries of the Raven Court and served as the queen's spy. He would have severely injured Miss Lawrence only moments ago had I not intervened."

"No!" I said. "He was going to attack you, not me." I rubbed Khaba's backside, focusing all my will into my wish to make him stronger.

"Miss Lawrence cannot comprehend the gravity of this situation." Thatch's gaze remained glued on Khaba's face. "Had Derrick Winslow successfully struck me and incapacitated me, he would have kidnapped her and taken her to the Raven Court by force. Necessity dictated I take immediate action to remedy the situation, which I did efficiently and painlessly without risking injury to students or staff." He spoke smoothly as if discussing a matter as banal as the weather.

Khaba patted my arm, his gaze flickering from Thatch to me. "That's really nice, honey, but you can stop rubbing me."

I stopped massaging his butt, embarrassed I'd apparently gone overboard.

He took my hand in his and gave it a reassuring squeeze. "Where is Invismo now?"

"I'm not at liberty to say. I've concealed his body where Miss Lawrence will be unable to find it."

"Why?" Khaba's eyes narrowed. "If Invismo is dead, why not let me examine the corpse?"

Thatch hesitated. Miss Periwinkle stared at him curiously. Did Thatch know I could resurrect the dead? It was possible Vega had told him—or he suspected I could do as much from my innate abilities or from use of the spell in Alouette Loraline's journal.

Thatch wet his lips. "I believe it would be in everyone's best interests to let the dead rest."

"Dead men tell no tales," Khaba said with a wan smile. "Only, I don't believe Derrick is dead. I think you've sent him back to your queen—or if you haven't done so yet, you intend to do so soon."

My eyes went wide. There was hope, then? Derrick might still be alive?

"The reason I prefer not to share the location of Derrick Winslow's body is that it would upset Miss Lawrence."

Khaba tugged me back behind him. "And what about me? Invismo Winslow is my employee. Are you afraid of *upsetting* me?"

"I believe it is in your best interest, and the school's, for him to remain locked away."

Khaba lifted his chin. "I believe it's in my best interest to know where he is."

Thatch said nothing.

Khaba waved a dismissive hand at Thatch. "Fine, then. I'm firing you. And Miss Periwinkle."

Periwinkle tugged at Thatch's arm. She tried to speak, but she still had no voice.

"That would be a breach of contract," Thatch said. "Neither of us have broken any school rules."

"Oh really? First we have Miss Periwinkle, who I may have evidence to prove is the actual culprit behind several crimes." Khaba held up his hand, ticking off infractions on his fingers. "Among this list we have attempted poisoning, murder, conspiring with the Raven Court, jinxing another teacher's tongue, using siren magic to take away the free will of staff members, and an attempted assault on Miss Lawrence's person that I just witnessed with my own eyes."

Periwinkle shook her head and opened her mouth, but no voice came out. She tugged on Thatch's lapels, her face turning red as she tried to communicate something to him. He circled an arm around her and crushed her against his chest.

Only now did a hint of desperation leak through Thatch's voice. "Gertrude did not poison or murder—"

Khaba held up his hand. "Stop, before I remove your voice as well." He smiled. "We have your infractions to add to the list. Kidnapping, torturing, and assaulting one of my employees, lying to me in your letter of reference and not disclosing Invismo's past associations with the Raven Queen, and threatening and restraining Miss Lawrence against her will. We can also add you as an accomplice to murder and conspirator with the Raven Court."

Khaba looked quite pleased with himself. "Oh yes, and breaking the school rule of having a relationship with another staff member and fornicating with each other on school grounds. Ironic after *you* were the one to institute this rule for Miss Lawrence's supposed safety."

Periwinkle sobbed silently, her face buried against Thatch's chest. He stroked her golden tresses absentmindedly, as though she were a cat. Thatch's voice rose in anger. "Mrs. and Mr. Lupi also have a relationship. Do you intend to fire them as well? The rule was simply meant to keep sexual energies away from Miss Lawrence. The Lupis live off campus and perform recreational duties off campus. So it is with Miss Periwinkle and myself."

Khaba crossed his arms. "Sure you do."

"Have you any evidence we have ever behaved unprofessionally in the workplace or engaged in sexual conduct on campus?" Thatch didn't bat an eyelash.

Had I not caught an eyeful of Thatch and Gertrude Periwinkle together, I would have never known he was such a convincing liar.

"I don't need evidence," Khaba said. "You're a danger to this school and the students within. I want you gone."

I could see Thatch had lost even if he couldn't.

Thatch spoke just as slowly and calmly. "You don't have the authority to fire either of us. Only the principal can do that. Currently he isn't here."

"I'll send word to him. When he returns from fundraising, I'll inform him of your actions. He'll be forced to fire you and Miss Periwinkle for endangering Miss Lawrence, the staff, and the students due to your affiliations with the Raven Court, your murderous ways, and the smaller infractions you've both committed." Khaba held out his hand. "Until then, I'm confiscating your wands. And Miss Periwinkle's voice."

Thatch gritted his teeth. He reached into his breast pocket, his wand clenched in his hand.

Khaba scooted me farther behind him. For a second I thought Thatch might try to use it on Khaba. Instead, he released it, and the twisted stick of black wood floated into Khaba's palm.

Miss Periwinkle shook her head and kept pointing at me. Thatch removed her wand from her belt and tossed it to Khaba.

Having them hand over wands didn't make me feel a whole lot better. I could perform magic without a wand. So could they. All a wand did was focus powers.

Khaba twisted his wrist, and the wands disappeared. "Until Jeb arrives, you are both on unpaid leave. Neither of you are to interact with the students. I expect you to stay confined to your private quarters. Separately."

"Who is going to teach my classes?" Thatch demanded.

"It is no longer your concern." Khaba tugged me out of the room. "Come along, Miss Lawrence, you need to fortify your strength with food before teaching your afternoon classes."

I should have been happy. Thatch and Periwinkle had failed. I had won. Except, I hadn't really succeeded. I didn't have Derrick, and I didn't know how I would get him back.

Victory had never tasted so bittersweet.

# CHAPTER THIRTY-EIGHT
## Damned If You Do

Students were rowdy and unfocused during class, unable to concentrate after the events at lunch. *I* was unable to focus. Students peppered me with questions about the man with the sword who had been running toward Thatch and me in the cafeteria. It was obvious I knew Derrick considering I'd screamed out his name and fallen to my knees sobbing. Not to mention my public argument with Thatch.

I didn't want to believe Derrick could be dead. Thatch had implied it. He'd said he was gone. But gone wasn't the same as dead. Just like when Thatch said I couldn't "see" Derrick, he had been selective about his words.

If Derrick had been dead, Thatch would probably have disclosed where he'd hidden Derrick's body. I suspected Khaba was correct. Thatch had an ulterior motive.

I needed to help Derrick. Desperate times called for desperate measures. I was going to have to do something that would probably result in getting myself killed—or fired.

I didn't expect I would be able to get anyone to divine where Derrick was, nor was clairvoyance one of my natural talents. I wasn't telepathic. The closest I had managed was communicating with Thatch and Derrick in dreams.

Then again, that was something. If I meditated and used my lucid-dreaming techniques, I might be able to speak with Derrick if he was unconscious or asleep. If Derrick knew where he was imprisoned, he might be able to tell me. I could ask him what had happened and where he'd been. We could devise a plan to defeat Thatch together.

Before bed, I visualized what I needed to dream about. The moment Vega turned out the lamp, I sank deeper into a meditative state. I pictured myself in the garden where I had met Derrick in our dreams before. It was an exaggerated version of my childhood home, with my mother's plants growing as tall as bean stalks. A picturesque moon and stars that looked like cardboard cutouts floated in the sky. A sun brightened half the sky, incongruous with the symbols of night on the other side.

I tried to remember how I had called Thatch to me so I could invite Derrick into my dream. It had happened intuitively before, without effort. I pulled at the idea of Derrick from somewhere outside myself, but nothing happened. I imagined my boyfriend's beautiful cerulean hair and innocent eyes beside me. A ghost of his cheerful smile and goofy humor brushed against my soul. I tasted his magic of wind and faraway places. My affinity fluttered with yearning to feel his arms around me. I grabbed onto his essence and strained to bring him closer, but my dream fingers sifted through his presence. He melted away like mist.

I attempted again, catching a fleeting glimpse of Derrick but nothing more.

Maybe I had to go to him. I needed an exit. I pushed at the fabric of the dream and made room in a hedge of roses for a door. It filled an arched frame like one I might find in the great hall of the school, solid wood, and decorated with an iron ring pull.

The door floated in midair, surreal and out of place, but simultaneously natural in this strange dreamscape. Before my eyes, the door shifted from a natural wood to one painted red. The iron ring transitioned into a handle covered with swirling designs. I supposed that would work, but I wondered why my subconscious hadn't kept the door I'd imagined. Did the red represent my affinity? Or love?

Or danger?

I opened the door and glided through. Beyond my dream garden lay a desolate landscape dotted with lights.

I flew from my door and out across a horizon of rocks and dust. Sparkles caught my eye as I swept over the terrain. A green light glittered below, and it reminded me of Grandmother Bluehorse. A fiery orange one made me think of Hailey Achilles. Another tasted like Josie. I wasn't sure how I understood what I was seeing or where to go, but my intuition guided me. The landscape shimmered with a rainbow of constellations that tasted like the essence of each individual at the school.

A bright blue light glowed on the horizon, set apart from the other lights. Was that Derrick?

I ignored the stars speckled along the hills and valleys around me and journeyed toward the far dot of blue. The closer I drew to it, the farther away it felt. I pushed harder, reaching out my hand to touch that star. My arm stretched infinitely long, and my fingers turned into strings of taffy, time slowing and warping around me. The moment reminded me of science-fiction movies as travelers approached an event horizon.

That probably meant I would be trapped here.

Despair weighed down on me, tempting me to return to my own dream and my own body. Instead, I pushed harder.

Something popped, and vertigo washed over me. All at once, I held that light. I fell upon it, finding myself colliding into a new door.

It glowed with a cold cobalt reminding me of an arctic wind. There was no handle. I pushed, but to no avail. I dug my fingers into the surface. The smooth material remained impenetrable. There had been a doorknob the last time I'd entered Derrick's subconscious. His mind had opened to me, unlocked and unguarded.

I didn't know if my affinity could work for me while I was in this dreamland, or if I could possibly do anything from there that could give myself more power. I caressed the door, imagining Derrick's skin. I leaned my cheek against a patch of beryl wood, the surface warming under my touch. It no longer felt hard and unyielding, but softer. Muscle moved under the surface of skin as I massaged the door. I brushed my lips against the barrier to his mind and smelled him: Cheetos, Old Spice, and wind carrying the scent of faraway places.

My fingers tingled. Something shifted, but I couldn't place my finger on what until I drew back. A keyhole materialized about midway down.

I bent to look inside. The Raven Queen's dungeon waited on the other side, every bit as scary as it had been in his memories. Midnight feathers brushed the dungeon away. I saw a flash of naked bodies, an orgy of men and women intertwined. Like the shutter of a camera, darkness swept over the scene only to open to a new picture. Someone screamed as a cluster of ravens swooped down and pecked at a huddled form. It sounded like Derrick. The image darkened, but the wail continued as I glimpsed a different moment. His eyes were wide with horror, and he tried to claw his way out of a small enclosed space. It looked like a coffin.

In another flicker, I saw myself, but wearing patent-leather attire that would have been appropriate for a dominatrix. This other version of myself lashed out at Derrick with a whip while he was chained to the wall. A bird flew out of his mouth and up the stairwell to escape. Had the Raven Queen altered his memories to make him think I had been there torturing him? Or was that a dream of me as the Raven Queen?

The sight of this evil doppelganger sent dread shuddering through me. I didn't want Derrick to see me that way. It had thrilled me momentarily when teachers who had snubbed me thought I looked like my mother and reacted in fear, but I didn't want Derrick to be afraid of me.

The pain and fear in his voice melted into a moan of pleasure. A black rainbow, dripping like an oil slick, poured over my vision. The Raven Queen laughed. Pulses of dark disturbing images came and went.

"Like this, my child," the Raven Queen said. "This is how we drain those we find expendable."

She showed him how to torture and kill. The skin of her victim shriveled and blackened, energy and life wicked away as she demonstrated how to serve her needs.

I shivered and drew away from the keyhole. My affinity shrank to the pit of my belly, so small it felt as though it didn't exist. Pity rose up inside me, muddling my resolve. My magic didn't like what I was seeing. It was hard to bring pleasure to my body so that my magic could be strong when sorrow overwhelmed me.

This was Derrick's subconscious. I didn't want to enter Derrick's dreams. He was remembering, though I didn't know how some of those images were possible.

I hadn't been able to handle what I'd seen before in Khaba's office. My separation from what had happened to him became compromised as I sank in and felt what he'd felt. Now as I watched from a distance, I wanted to turn away. If I did, I couldn't help him.

If I walked through that door to his dreams, perhaps it could help me understand what he'd been through. Perhaps I could help him change the dream so he might become more empowered over his subconscious mind like I had done with Thatch's help. I couldn't leave him in his nightmares. He would have done anything for me.

I had to rescue him from himself.

Yet the door was locked. I had no key. Then again, maybe I didn't need one. I touched my finger to the keyhole and projected myself forward, squeezing through the hole and propelling myself through the door to the other side.

Thatch stood there, a lone figure under a spotlight. I stared at him, startled. He hadn't been there before.

He looked around, his brow furrowing in confusion. The flashes of memory were gone. I couldn't tell if Thatch was part of Derrick's subconscious, or this was a memory from being tortured in the Raven Queen's dungeon.

Thatch's gaze settled on me and his eyes narrowed. His voice was a cool monotone. "Clarissa Lawrence, I told you to leave Derrick be."

Apparently, this apparition was neither. It was the real Thatch.

"I'm not going to let you keep me from—"

"Get out." He held up his hand.

Energy pushed out of him and into me. I tried to stand my ground, but my feet skidded back. My body compressed and shrank. I squeezed out the keyhole to the other side. Thatch's magic blew me out across the expanse of the landscape, the lights below passing at a dizzying speed. I drew back into my own consciousness as though pulled by a rope. My belly flip-flopped, the same sensation I remembered from playing on a swing as a child at that moment I'd gone too high.

I snapped back into my body and opened my eyes. My winded breathing greeted my ears. Vega's shallow breathing came from the darkness nearby. I sat up in my bed.

I had succeeded, if only for a moment. I fumbled for my water bottle and took a swig before lying back down.

The moment I closed my eyes, Vega's voice startled me enough to make me jump. "Guess who Khaba appointed as the temporary Celestor department head?" Vega asked.

"Um . . . you?"

"Exactly!" She chuckled. "I've waited so long for this moment. I can hardly sleep! I have so many plans for tomorrow."

Wow. So all that time I'd been meditating to save the world—or at least save Derrick—she'd been imagining all the ways she intended to take over the world—or at least dominate the Celestor department.

"Did Khaba tell you why you're taking over for Thatch?" I asked.

"Don't know. Don't care." Her bed creaked. "Okay, so I do, just a little, and Khaba promised me he'll tell me after Jeb officially fires Thatch, but the reason doesn't matter. As long as he doesn't choose someone else in my department like Darshan or Josie over me for the permanent position I'm happy."

"And you'll get that room to yourself you always wanted."

"I'll get the entire dungeon."

I considered Vega's motives. I knew what she wanted. If I could use that to my advantage, I could convince her to help me.

"You're only going to get Thatch's room and the department head position if Khaba can prove Thatch has been conspiring with the Raven Queen. If you can help Khaba find Derrick—the invisible man—he'll be able to testify against Thatch and provide evidence that—" My voice cut out as though the volume had just been turned off.

"I'm not joining you in another one of your stupid quests," Vega said coolly. "If I involve myself in necromancy again and someone finds out, they'll sack me instead of giving me Thatch's position. Don't you dare do anything that would ruin this career move for me. Do you understand?"

So much for getting Vega to help me. I would need to find someone else.

When Jeb had thought students had stolen the answer keys to the spring exams, the three people who had been instrumental in the search had been

Pro Ro, Khaba, and Thatch. Obviously, I couldn't get help from Thatch. Khaba had already tried to locate Derrick and failed.

That left Pro Ro, a divination master. Unfortunately, he hated me.

Still, I had to try.

I had to make Pro Ro help me. I had asked nicely. I had offered to help him. I had tried to get Pinky to trade electives with him. There was only one thing left that I could do.

I was going to have to embrace my inner Vega and be evil. Blackmail was my only option left. I would do anything for Derrick, even become a wicked witch.

I knew from reading textbooks that diviners often needed an object that belonged to the person they wanted to locate. When Pro Ro had previously tried to cast wards on me, he had used a photograph. For that reason, I brought my sketchpad with me to show him the drawings Derrick had made.

Before school, Pro Ro wasn't in. During my prep, he was teaching. At lunch I had a duty. After school, he wasn't in his classroom, so I knocked on Pro Ro's dormitory door. He didn't answer. I knocked again.

All I had to do was tell Pro Ro I would tell Thatch about him and Periwinkle. Or I could tell Jeb, and then he'd lose his job.

As I stood there, I started to lose my nerve. Pro Ro was a powerful Celestor. He might not react as mildly as Periwinkle had with a tongue-twister jinx. He could probably wipe my memories away with the snap of his fingers, make my tongue fall out of my mouth, or some other horrible thing if I tried to tell.

It sucked being the least skilled witch in the workplace.

I had sunk to a new low if I considered blackmail the best way to convince my coworkers of helping me. Even so, it was all I had. I didn't care if my coworkers hated me if I saved Derrick.

I knocked again. There was no answer.

After dinner, I tried his dorm room again. Pro Ro didn't answer. I went to the library. Maddy said she hadn't seen him. He wasn't in his classroom or the astronomy tower either. Maybe he had divined that I would pester him, so he preemptively left his room to avoid me. He wasn't in the staffroom.

I trudged through the halls before curfew, asking students if they had seen him.

"He's with Mr. Pinky in his classroom," Chase Othello said.

Pinky? It was hard to believe Pro Ro would voluntarily go anywhere near the smelly sasquatch. I ran to Pinky's room, arriving out of breath.

Pinky and Pro Ro sat at the teacher's desk, going over some papers together.

Pinky looked up and waved. "Hello, Miss Lawrence. We were just talking about you!"

"Oh boy," I said. That didn't sound good.

"Don't worry." Pro Ro laughed, his belly shaking up and down as he did so. "I didn't say anything bad."

The two of them exchanged amused smiles and busted up. Right. Pro Ro had probably told him about the turban incident. On the other hand, Pro Ro was in the same room with me, and he was smiling. This was the friendliest Pro Ro had acted toward me in months.

It suddenly hit me what else was different. Pinky didn't smell. His fur was glossy and clean. The dark mud color that I thought had been the hue of his hair was actually a warm chestnut. None of his fur was matted.

Pinky had listened to me! Did that mean he had traded classes with Pro Ro? I didn't know how to broach the subject without being rude.

"So, um, are you two . . . have you been able to get Puck to agree to . . . um. . . ." I started. "Is Mr. Pinky teaching yoga?"

"Yessiree," Pinky said. "Pro Ro is getting my Latin class. Really, they should have just asked me to teach yoga to begin with, but no one thinks about asking a sasquatch if he can do yoga. It is so speciesist."

I sighed in relief. I looked to Pro Ro. "Does that mean you'll help me with. . . ?"

Pro Ro grimaced. "We're just about done here anyway. I'll help you divine your love life or whatever it is you need."

Score! I was on my way to finding Derrick.

Pinky gave me a thumbs-up. Pro Ro took me to his classroom. I told him an edited version of what I needed.

"Do you have a photo of your friend? Or anything that belonged to him?"

I held out my sketchpad and showed him my drawings of Derrick.

"Hmm," he said. "I don't know if a drawing will work."

I turned to the page where I'd nestled the sketch he'd done of me. "This belongs to my friend. He made this one. But I can go to his room and get something else if that helps."

"This will do."

He set a cauldron on a table and threw some herbs into it. He waved his wand over it and muttered something in another language. Shimmers of light spiraled out of the cauldron. His magic smelled like starlight and oddly enough, spaghetti with meatballs. The sparks blossomed in size, melding together and turning into blue and purple flames. Pro Ro stared into the flames, his eyes glossing over. This was a kind of scrying. I didn't know exactly how it worked, but from an outside perspective it didn't look like much was happening.

Pro Ro's eyes turned milky white. His lips parted. A long buzzing note that sounded like a thousand flies swarming around us came out of his mouth. The sound got under my skin and made me twitch. It took all my willpower to remain sitting there.

I'd never known how freaky his magic was until now.

When Pro Ro spoke again, his voice had returned to normal. "He's below the school. Not in the dungeon. Somewhere lower."

"The crypt?" I asked.

He blinked away the cataracts over his eyes. "There are corpses on the same level, but he's not in a crypt." His eyes returned to their dark shade of amber brown. "I think he's in the same chamber as the answer keys."

"Do you know where that is?"

"No. Only Jeb and Mr. Thatch have been down there." He studied me. "Why is your friend down there? Does this have something to do with the man that tried to attack you and Mr. Thatch yesterday? Did he hurt your friend too?"

I bit my lip, uncertain whether I should tell him more. Getting Pinky to trade a yoga class with Pro Ro didn't necessarily make him my BFF.

Pro Ro extinguished the fire in his cauldron and dumped the contents out a window. "Miss Bloodmire seems to think Mr. Thatch has committed some sort of crime—hence the reason she's filling in as department head." He made a face. "She gave me two of his classes to teach today and all her duties. I pray Mr. Thatch returns to teaching soon."

"Can you tell me where my friend is trapped?" I asked.

"I might be able to show you where he is on a map, but I don't advise you go looking for him. The room is guarded with booby traps and deadly creatures."

Of course it was.

# CHAPTER THIRTY-NINE
## Damned If You Don't

It was time to call in more favors. Aside from Vega—who had no reason to assist me—I only knew three other individuals who had successfully gotten down into the school's secret passages and survived: Hailey Achilles, Ben O'Sullivan, and Balthasar Llewelyn.

By the time Pro Ro had finished scrying more details, it was an hour past students' curfew, and they were in bed. I was supposed to be going to bed soon, but I didn't allow that to stop me from sneaking around the school, trying to rescue Derrick.

I tiptoed into the girls' dormitory under my dirty invisibility Snuggie. Most students were in bed, but several of the girls sat on each other's beds, whispering and talking. Hailey and Maddy shared a bed on the far side of the room in the corner. Hailey's face was lit by the blue light of what I suspected was a cell phone. The two of them held a magazine with some teen heartthrob's photo on the cover. Apparently they didn't get enough time to read about movie stars and musicians during the day.

"Hey," I whispered. "That better not be a cell phone."

Hailey's eyes went wide. Maddy looked around, her brow furrowing. Even though my cloak wasn't completely invisible anymore, and it was spotted with dirt, it still worked well enough in the dark. It was fun to see their confusion. Maybe I was turning a little bit evil.

"Miss Lawrence?" Maddy asked.

I pulled back my hood.

Hailey tossed the magazine aside. "I will have you know, I was using my wand, not a cell phone." She held it up, making a face at me.

"Good. I'm glad to hear it. I want you strong so Fae don't snatch you."

Maddy nudged Hailey. "See. Miss Lawrence cares about us. You should be thankful she sneaks in here to try to bust your butt for cell phones and stuff."

"Whatever," Hailey said. "What do you want now?"

I hesitated. Was I so obvious? I felt like all I did was use people these days.

"Is it Miss Periwinkle?" Maddy asked.

"No, I need to know about where the answer keys are stored." I looked to Hailey.

"I don't know anything about it," Hailey said quickly. "If Balthasar and Ben have been acting like morons and trying to break in—"

I held up a hand to stop her. "This doesn't have anything to do with them. I need to know about the room where the answer keys are hidden. You broke in last year, so I thought you could tell me." That was what she had once boasted anyway. I glanced over my shoulder. No one seemed to be paying attention to us, but I lifted the hood to cover my head anyway.

Hailey crossed her arms. "You told me I needed to turn over a new leaf. I have to try to be good so I can graduate, and you know, not die. I could get in a lot of trouble if I tell you where the answer keys are."

"It's a matter of life or death," I said. "I'm not going to get you in trouble. I'm the only one who will get in trouble. I need to know what the dangerous creatures are, about the booby traps, and how to get into the room."

Hailey looked unconvinced. "Why do you want the answer keys?"

"I don't. I want to find something else in the same room."

"The Ruby of Knowledge?" Her voice went up an octave in excitement.

"No. A person."

"Your boyfriend?" Maddy squealed.

I put a finger to my lips. "Don't tell anyone."

"Why would a person be down there?" Hailey shifted on her bed, leaning closer to me. "Did he try to steal the answer keys?"

"No. He got put down there by someone." Asking for help from students had been a mistake. It led to too many questions.

Maddy bit her lip. "Your boyfriend is the one who was with you that time you caught us in the secret passage? The security guard? He was the one Mr. Thatch . . . zapped in the cafeteria. He looked like he was going to attack you with his sword."

"He wasn't going to attack me. He wanted to attack Mr. Thatch."

"Did Mr. Thatch put him down there?" Maddy asked.

"Beeswax," I said, using the magic word to remind them of their manners that my fairy godmother had taught them.

It didn't work.

"Why did Mr. Thatch zap him?" Maddy asked.

"I don't think this is a good idea," Hailey said. "If Mr. Thatch put him down there, he probably did it for a reason."

"Mr. Thatch isn't himself," I said firmly. "Think about how he's been . . . behaving lately."

Maddy whispered something in Hailey's ear. Hailey's scowl turned to shock. "No fucking way. I thought he was . . . you know, inhuman and heartless."

"Language," I said.

Had she been completely blind lately? Either her surprise was triggered by the idea that Thatch was in love or that he had been weakened and seduced by siren magic.

"Will you help me?" I asked.

"I guess," Hailey said. "But only because I don't have anything better to do right now."

I knew from drawing class not to trust Hailey's skills in depicting accurate reproductions. Her map wouldn't be to scale, and a year had elapsed since she'd been under the school searching for answer keys, so she probably didn't remember where the booby traps were. Some of them might have changed since she'd been down there anyway.

The more I thought about this plan to venture into some unknown part of the school armed with an appropriated wand, an invisibility Snuggie, and a couple paltry magic spells—which included lighting a wand like a flashlight, cleaning tables, and taping posters to walls—the more I suspected this might be a bad idea.

Vega certainly was capable of helping me, but more likely she would turn me in to use me as a stepping stone in her quest for success. Even if I managed to entice her with the secret of necromancy or resurrect her future ex-boyfriend from her past life, she was too much of a wild card. I had no idea what she would do. Anything that served her best interests would always come first. I couldn't trust Vega to help me.

Khaba always followed the rules. Josie wasn't a strong witch. I dismissed the other powerful Witchkin, Thatch and Periwinkle, for obvious reasons. Unless . . . the price was right.

With Thatch I couldn't figure out his intentions, when he was sincere, or what he wanted.

Miss Periwinkle wasn't a great mystery. She loathed me. She would kill me rather than allow Thatch to be with me. It was possible she was in cahoots with the Raven Court. I wouldn't be surprised if she had joined up with the Raven Queen to try to get rid of me. If she hated me that much, there was the possibility she would do *anything* to ensure I didn't interfere with her relationship with Thatch.

Every solicitation for assistance was always met with a price. A bargain. If I could entice Periwinkle using her weakness, perhaps she would willingly help me.

I knocked on the library door. It was after hours. I didn't expect it to be unlocked. I pounded harder. No one answered. I needed a key.

Maddy probably had one since she closed the library on those occasions Periwinkle was out strengthening her siren magic and seducing men. I returned to the girls' dormitory. By that point, all lights were out, and I had to use my flashlight spell to guide me. Maddy cringed away from the light as I held it over her face.

She opened one eye. "Miss L, we have school tomorrow."

"No, you don't. It's Saturday," I whispered.

I had turned into the worst teacher ever. My guilt didn't stop me, though. "How can I get into the library after hours? Do you have a key?"

"No. There's a code."

Hailey covered her eyes with her arm.

"What do you mean by a code?" I asked.

"Insert your wand into the keyhole. The door will ask you a question that can only be answered by an adult who would be allowed in after hours. If you get the question right, the door will let you in."

"What's the question?"

She rolled over and mumbled into her pillow. "It changes all the time. Last week the question was, 'Who's the author of the *Count of Monte Cristo*?' This week it asked, 'Who is the cantankerous enemy and love interest of Elizabeth Bennet?'"

"But anyone could answer that," I said.

"Come on, Miss L, think about it? How many students do you think actually read those books?"

Hailey yawned. "What does cantankerous mean?"

I could see her point.

"But you only get one chance to answer," Maddy said. "If you guess wrong, the door stays locked."

I could do this! I knew my literature. I rushed down to the library. I jabbed my appropriated wand into the keyhole. The door spoke in a library-appropriate whisper. "What is the first book in *The Lord of the Rings*, written by J. R. R. Tolkien?"

This was an easy one. Then I hesitated. Was this a trick question? Did it mean the series or the trilogy? What if I got it wrong? I didn't want to get locked out.

"If you mean, the Lord of the Rings series, the answer is *The Hobbit*." I quickly went on, hoping it would allow me to continue. "But if you mean The Lord of the Rings trilogy, the first book is *The Fellowship of the Ring*."

The door creaked open.

The library was dark. I jabbed my wand into the keyhole of Miss Periwinkle's office door.

The door asked in an androgynous whisper, "What author wrote the fairy tale *The Little Mermaid*?"

Oh no! Was it the Brothers Grimm or Hans Christian Andersen? I could do this. I just had to use the trick I'd learned a long time ago about fairy tales. Grimm fairy tales were usually grim. The Danish fairy tales were moralistic and Christian. The mermaid sacrificed her happiness for the prince's happiness because she loved him so much. I'd always hated that story. I wanted the mermaid to have her happy ending with her prince like in the Disney movie. Though grim, it wasn't gory; I concluded the ending was a religious morality tale.

"Hans Christian Andersen," I said.

The office door creaked open. Yes!

There was no door in the wall that led from the office to the hallway to Periwinkle's room. I tried it anyway. I poked my wand at the wall. Nothing happened. I tried a different spot. I kept guessing where a keyhole might be. Finally, the wand sank in.

"What was Edgar Allen Poe's most famous poem?"

A chill settled over my spine. I didn't have to guess this one. Was it a coincidence the secret door to Periwinkle's chamber was guarded with a riddle so ominous? This had to be yet another indication of her alliances.

"The Raven," Miss Periwinkle whispered from behind me.

## CHAPTER FORTY
## Quoth the Raven

I whirled in surprise, my heart galloping in my chest at Gertrude Periwinkle's proximity. The light of my wand illuminated her grumpy expression.

"What are you doing here?" Miss Periwinkle asked.

I couldn't tell if Miss Periwinkle was whispering because Khaba still had possession of her voice or because this was a library and people were expected to be quiet here.

"Hi. I was just dropping in. I wanted to talk to you," I said.

She crossed her arms.

Yeah, it did sound lame. "So, um, I know you hate me and think I want to steal your boyfriend and ruin your life. But I promise I'm not trying to."

Her nostrils flared.

"I wanted to try to make things not as horrible for you by—"

"Dying?" she asked.

"No. I thought I would find my boyfriend and leave you alone for the rest of my life so you and Thatch can live happily ever after. And my boyfriend and I can live happily ever after. I just need to rescue him."

The loathing in her eyes turned to uncertainty.

"His name is Derrick, but you might know him as Invismo. He's a security guard who works for Mr. Khaba. Thatch hid him in the school—under the school. I have a map. But I can't get him because of the booby traps and secret passages, and I'm not very good at magic. I thought you might help me if I left the school after I retrieved Derrick." That was what Derrick had originally suggested anyway.

Her voice came out a raspy hiss. "What good will that do me if I'm already fired?"

Good point. "Maybe I could sign a paper or something attesting to your innocence?" Even though she *wasn't* innocent and should be punished for her crimes, I wasn't above lying about it if it helped me get what we both wanted.

I wanted Derrick alive and safe so badly I was willing to cover for a murderer working for the Raven Court.

Her smile turned smug. "I'll do it if you attest to my innocence. And Felix's."

"Okay." I would be covering for two murderers. This just got better and better.

She opened a drawer to her desk and retrieved a pad of paper. She sat in her chair and brought the quill closer.

"I'm not going to sign it now," I said. "What if you push me into one of the booby traps and I die?"

She lifted her chin. "What if you push me and *I* die? I'm not going to take that risk for nothing. Either you agree to this or you can leave and find your boyfriend on your own."

I needed her, but I didn't trust her. Witchkin bargains were all about negotiating. "I'll sign something to say I don't think you tried to kill me and I was wrong about you killing people. I'll attest to Thatch's innocence after I find Derrick."

"No." She stabbed the pointed end of the quill into the air in front of me. "We both know Felix is innocent. Clear his name now. You can clear mine afterward."

I hesitated. This had to be a trick. It couldn't be that she wanted his name cleared because she cared about him, could it?

She shoved the quill at me. "You cost him his job and sullied his name. You need to make it right."

I leaned over the desk, trying to think of words that would sound plausible for mistaking him as a murderer. Slowly I wrote, hating myself for making up these excuses for him. When I was finished, and Miss Periwinkle was satisfied, she finally looked at the map I had brought down.

Hailey had correctly identified the first booby traps. They were the same ones Vega had told me about on our way to the crypt. I wasn't sure about the rest, and I needed Periwinkle's help with those. The two of us walked toward my classroom. I was surprised Khaba hadn't confined her to the library with magic, but he did have his magical limits.

We used the back stairwell in my classroom and the secret passage that went past the closet to get to the dungeon. Periwinkle hesitated at the hallway past Thatch's rooms, her eyes filled with longing.

For all her cheating, she did look like someone in love.

She led me down the steps. "Be careful. There's a booby trap on the twelfth step down," she whispered.

"No, it's on the thirteenth step," I said.

"No, it's the twelfth."

"You're trying to trick me. You just want me to die."

"You're trying to trick me!" She jabbed me in the side. "And I've lost count now."

By that point I had lost count as well. I trudged back up the stairs. She followed me.

"One. Two," she said.

Oh, I saw what she was doing. She didn't count the top of the landing as a step like Vega had. Her twelfth was my thirteenth. Maybe she hadn't been trying to kill me. She pointed out the stone tile at the bottom that would transport me to Khaba's office. She jabbed her wand into the keyhole of the iron door at the bottom. Something scrabbled in the darkness beyond, sounding like a rat.

She leaned closer to the closed door, listening. "Can you make your wand brighter?" she asked.

I held my wand in both my hands and focused. She held hers out. As the door creaked open, she thrust her wand forward.

"Hold yours out," she said.

We held our light out in front of us. Scratching and scrabbling came from the pit below. I couldn't tell what was in the room, only that the sea below undulated with movement. I hoped it was only the hands I had encountered before.

"This is one of the most dangerous traps," Periwinkle said.

"We're okay. There's a ledge." I scooted to the side of the door where the narrow passage waited for us.

"The Pit of Lost Souls will sense your fear and multiply any emotion from you threefold," she whispered.

"Yeah, I know. Vega told me about it. I survived last time." I had tamed the hands using my affinity.

"Was that before or after Jeb and Mr. Khaba reinforced the lost souls with more magic?" she asked.

I hesitated. The scrabbling grew louder.

Maybe this wasn't such a good idea. Periwinkle cackled, the sound hoarse and hissing without her voice. I tried to dart to the side and push past her.

I wasn't fast enough.

She shoved me into the pit. I dropped my wand. The door closed with a slam.

I landed into the mosh pit, hands swarming over me. One of them pulled my hair.

Craptacular. I didn't have time to die right now.

# CHAPTER FORTY-ONE
## The Brad Pitt of Horrors

Just as the first time I'd fallen into the Pit of Hand Jobs, I had to focus on calming myself despite the distractions of my surroundings. Miss Periwinkle's attempt to kill me and ruin my plans for coming to Derrick's rescue were thwarted by my friendship with the lost souls. It took about ten minutes of clearing my mind, coming up with handy puns, and manifesting friendliness threefold to convince them to help me climb out.

Once on the landing, one of the supposed demons handed me my wand and patted me on the back, as if in a gesture for good luck.

The real problem was the door on the other side of the chamber. I jabbed my wand into the keyhole, visualizing my affinity swelling with power as I pushed my will into the door. I didn't know any magic spells for opening doors so I cheated and said, "Alohomora."

I didn't expect a spell for Harry Potter to work. It never had before.

Unexpectedly, the door creaked open.

Unlike the time I'd gone this way with Vega, the passage before me was filled with mist. Or maybe it was smoke.

A tall figure strode out of the shadows toward me.

I backed away, afraid it was Thatch. The light of my wand illuminated something bright pink.

A cheery voice greeted me. "There you are, Clarissa. I've been looking all over for you!" Khaba continued toward me, a smile on his face. His pink shirt and pants were now visible through the gloom.

My momentary elation turned to frustration. "I'm not going back. I'm here to rescue Derrick." I tried to close the door between us before he could magic me back to my room.

He put up a hand and grabbed the door. "Well, fancy that! So am I. What a coincidence." He grinned. "As it happens, I need *you* to help *me* rescue Derrick."

He wasn't going to make me go back? And *he* was going to break into the vault? "But the rules . . . I thought you were bound by school rules."

"I'm obliged to go where necessity dictates. Right now I'm on the clock, and this is official school business. Derrick is classified staff, *my* employee. I need to rescue the best invisible man I've ever hired." He swallowed, his usual confidence faltering. "You know I'm not free to use my powers for my own personal gain."

There was something he wasn't saying, but I didn't quite understand what. "This is official school business, right? So you can use your magic for saving Derrick?"

He stared into my eyes, his own mirrors of sorrow. "Yes, but I can't do it alone. I can't do any magic by myself. Ever."

"So you need *me*?" I asked.

"I require an assistant to rub my lamp and wish for the appropriate magics. I've already used up my last wish from . . . Brogan." His smile almost masked the shame in his eyes, but not quite.

I could only imagine how much it cost his pride to ask me, the daughter of the woman who had enslaved him to the school.

"You'd better not disappoint." He pointed to his back with a flamboyant wave of his hand. "Start rubbing."

I ran to him and hugged him. "Let me help you make your wishes come true."

We passed through the crypt Vega had previously taken me into and through a long chamber that held an older crypt. With my assistance, Khaba lit the passage so we could see better and disarmed two booby traps. With each wish I made, his lamp shifted position, and I had to rub a new place on his body. Each time, it migrated lower.

"Pretty soon this is going to cross our professional boundaries and become naughty," I said.

"Probably. It's a good thing we're alone in a dark passage without any witnesses." He winked.

Khaba's presence was a balm to my worries. I should have asked him to help me find Derrick sooner. I should have trusted him as a friend and colleague.

He pointed to his lower back. "Massage my back before we get to the next room so I can open the door and brighten the chamber at the same time."

He leaned against the wall as I kneaded his dense muscles. My hands were tired, but I didn't complain. Everything I did was for Derrick. I was pretty sure I was going to have to massage Khaba's butt again soon. I was going to handle the situation maturely and impassively—and not brag about it later to Josie.

Khaba straightened. "That's enough. Now say it."

"I wish the door was unlocked and the next room was lit."

Khaba snapped his fingers. "Your wish is my command."

The heavy door swung open. On the other side stood Thatch.

# CHAPTER FORTY-TWO
## Behind Door Number One

Felix Thatch strode toward us. He shook his head at me. I backed up.

"How does that saying go?" Khaba stood his ground. "The criminal always returns to the scene of the crime."

"No crime has been committed. I'm here to ensure it stays that way." Thatch pointed to me. "Miss Lawrence, go upstairs and return to your room."

"No," I said. "You go upstairs. You were supposed to stay confined to your quarters."

Thatch blocked the doorway. I couldn't see much past him, but I thought I saw a large slab of rock in the middle of the room. I didn't see Derrick.

Maybe he'd already gotten rid of him. But if he had, why would he still be blocking the door?

"You need to stop," Thatch said. "You're doing exactly what the Raven Queen wants you to do. Go upstairs, and we can discuss this."

"So you can erase my memories like you were going to before," I said.

"I wasn't going to erase your memories." The corners to his mouth turned down. "I was simply going to make your mood . . . more agreeable."

Khaba remained where he was. He waved me closer, his smile sly. I knew what he needed. He required my assistance to defeat Thatch.

"Don't move," Thatch said. "I don't want to hurt anyone, but I will do what I deem necessary." He lifted his hand. A large ball of red fire flared to life in his palm.

Khaba's eyes narrowed. "Don't you dare threaten me. I should have insisted Jeb fire you twenty-five years ago. Clarissa, come here."

Thatch's face remained emotionless. I didn't believe Thatch would try to hurt me. After everything, I supposed I didn't want to believe he was actually evil.

I stepped toward Khaba. Thatch threw the ball of fire. It crackled in the air between Khaba and me. I dove back. Khaba leapt to the other side. Thatch darted through the door into the room with us. He waved his wand in the air, incanting as he did so. Khaba lunged toward him and punched him in the stomach. Thatch doubled over, the air knocked out of him.

Khaba wrapped an arm around Thatch's neck in a headlock. "Clarissa, rub my lamp!"

I had my hand on him, rubbing frantically before the words were even completely out of his mouth.

I had to be fast, but I didn't know what to wish for. I said the first thing that came to me. "I wish you were free to make your own wishes."

Khaba released Thatch. He turned to me in shock. "Oh no, honey. Why did you wish that?" His voice didn't sound right. It echoed like multiple people were speaking at once, each slightly out of sync with each other.

Thatch's brow furrowed in disbelief. He shook his head at me.

"What?" I asked.

Khaba stared down at himself. Smoke billowed around him. He swelled in size. His clothes caught on fire. He twisted and writhed. Whatever was happening looked painful. It looked like he was fighting with himself. I didn't understand. I thought freeing him would be a good thing.

"Run," Thatch said. He shoved me through the door, separating me from him and Khaba.

The last thing I saw before the door slammed closed was Khaba exploding into a giant ball of fire.

# CHAPTER FORTY-THREE
## Cadavers Don't Complain

Khaba's supernova blinded me as the door slammed closed, and I stumbled around the nearly empty vault. The room shook. Dust and small rocks dropped from the ceiling. I fell to my knees as the vibration rattled through me. Another door lay on the other side of the room.

I could run like Thatch said. He'd seemed sincere in his concern about the danger. But he hadn't rushed into the room with me. He'd stayed behind with Khaba. I hoped they were both okay.

Khaba's transformation hadn't been reassuring. Maybe he'd turned back into a demon.

I knew I should run, but this is where Derrick rested. I was sure of it. I didn't see him, but this had to be the place Pro Ro had told me about. On a pedestal were sealed envelopes labeled "answer keys."

A long gray slab of stone dominated the center of the room. I swung my wand back and forth to illuminate the space better with my flashlight spell. I approached the slab, thinking it might be a sarcophagus, but it more closely resembled a bench about chest high. Something about the bench wasn't right. The top was uneven in places, and from where I stood, it looked like I could see inside a box. At other angles I couldn't see an interior. It reminded me of a hologram, fluctuating into and out of view. It shimmered and caught the light unevenly. Magic was at work. Tentatively, I reached out my hand and felt the stone. It shifted under my hand like fabric.

I felt around, my fingers encountering a mass I couldn't see under that sheet. I grabbed and pulled. Invisibility fabric shifted aside.

Derrick lay with his eyes closed. He looked peaceful and content, the corners of his mouth curled up as though he were about to snicker at some joke. A purple bloom of bruises marred one side of his eyes, and scratches were etched into his cheek and temple. Despite his injuries, his skin was clean.

Tentatively, I smoothed his cerulean hair out of his eyes. He was as cold as a corpse. My breath caught. He couldn't be dead. I'd seen his dreams.

I shook his arm and shouted his name. He remained still. Thatch had been in this room. He had known I would come for Derrick. He might have killed him.

I felt Derrick's neck for a heartbeat, my fingers trembling so much I couldn't be certain whether the thudding I felt was his or my own erratic heartbeat. I removed my hand and watched for the rise and fall of his chest. I thought I detected the slightest movement. When I placed my hand close to his nose, a tickle of breath brushed my fingers.

I wasn't sure if he was in a coma or in some kind of magical stasis. All I knew was I had to help. My Red affinity had been strong enough to break through his invisibility. I hoped it would break through this.

I boosted myself up on the slab. Awkwardly I twisted to place my hands on his chest. All I needed to do to wake the dead was touch him like I had with Sebastian Reade. Of course, the Red affinity's ability for necromancy had its limitations. I would have to keep touching him or he would die.

Nothing happened. Maybe it was because he wasn't actually dead. I thought about the time I had saved an old man from cardiac arrest with my powers. Maybe I could Frankenstein Derrick awake with my affinity.

Dox Woodruff had attempted to resurrect someone with his affinity, but he hadn't been Red. Nor did I intend to drain myself in doing so.

Derrick remained still. I shifted so that I straddled his torso, keeping my palms pressed to his naked chest. His heart lurched under my fingers and then returned to a soft, almost undetectable beat.

If this was a fairy tale, I would kiss him. He was my sleeping beauty. I had broken his curse once before through touch.

I pressed my lips to his. His heart thundered under my palm, and he gasped. I tried to pull back to look at him, but his hand grasped the back of my head, holding me there and drinking me in.

He tasted like wind and spices, not decay and death. His tongue brushed against mine, and he moaned.

"I need you. I need your touch." He mumbled against my lips.

He'd said that before, the night he'd returned. Our lovemaking had been unexpected—and unexpectedly brief. I didn't know how much Derrick understood about what I was and what my magic could do. Perhaps he had meant he needed comfort after his encounter with the Raven Queen. Or perhaps he needed my affinity to heal him with magic.

I kissed his neck and his jaw, the prickles of his stubble scraping my lips. His fingers found their way under my skirt, kneading my thighs. The frigid stone under us bit into my knees, hard and unyielding. It was going to be an effort to ignore the discomfort. I squirmed back, trying to shift the fabric of the invisibility cloth under my knees as a cushion.

At any moment, Thatch might throw back the door and find us. If he wasn't dead. I pushed all thoughts of him aside.

Derrick tilted his pelvis to grind against mine. A flash of pleasure shot through me. I didn't think I would have trouble getting my affinity to work to try to heal him. The red energy in my core swelled and danced. I let the magic radiate through me. He lifted his head and kissed me. My insides turned to molten lava, making my skin feel feverish under all the layers of clothes I wore. His hands were cold on the bare flesh of my hips as he slid my leggings and panties lower. I fought to wiggle them down my legs. He fumbled with the buttons of my coat. We were awkward and bumbling, like the first time we'd been together. We managed to remove my coat. I freed one foot from a shoe and slipped one leg from my leggings.

Like that first time we'd been together, there was a yearning in him so deep it was like a bottomless pit he couldn't fill. Yet he didn't rush. Each kiss brought with it the promise of more. He stroked me, electric chills washing over my skin, making my affinity spark in my veins.

His erection pressed against me, teasingly sliding against me. It was difficult to concentrate on my affinity with the wanting building in me. He nibbled my neck, tasting my skin as if he wanted to consume me. He kissed me urgently, like his life depended on it.

As if he would never see me again.

Even in that moment of passion, a part of me feared that his life did depend on this. For all I knew, he might fall back into oblivion the moment I broke away like Sebastian Reade had.

"I love you. We'll always be together," I said.

"No, Clarissa," he said between pants. "We won't."

"I'll save you. I'll fix you."

"You can't. There's no saving me."

He plunged inside me, and I cried out from the satisfaction of it. He thrust deeper, making me gasp. My pelvic muscles clenched around him. The affinity inside me fought to break loose. I couldn't tell if it would be rainbows or lightning. I wanted Derrick to be alive and his latest curse broken—I didn't want to leave him a charred lump like I had with Julian. I needed to focus.

The pleasure built inside me. I imagined it traveling up my arms and out of my hands and into him. Red magic flowed out of me, and I willed it to give him life. I didn't need Vega's do-anything spell.

I was the Red affinity. I was powerful.

Light radiated from my bare arms and through my shirt, illuminating his face. My hands on his chest glowed pink. It was about then I noticed the color of his eyes, no longer the vivid blue they once had been. They were solid black like those of the Raven Court. He crushed me against him for another kiss, stealing my breath away. He thrust harder, faster, pleasure and pain mingling as one.

"Slow down," I said. "If I'm going to . . . save you . . . I need my . . . to build slowly."

It didn't so much feel as though I was sending magic now as much as it was being sucked from my veins. My skin prickled like needles stabbed into my muscles. My hands didn't resemble my own. These hands were etched with red lines, squiggles radiating in fractals. They reminded me of varicose veins, like the pattern that had been on Sebastian Reade's face and hands. It was what Khaba had described had marked Brogan McLean's body.

The pain in my hands and arms intensified, only now it wasn't just my limbs that hurt. The sensation radiated up into my chest. It felt as though my stomach had turned inside out, all my organs yanked out of me.

"Something isn't right," I said, trying to pull away.

He squeezed me so tightly around my ribs it hurt. "I need your magic."

"I think you're draining me," I said.

Khaba had said those markings on the bodies were unusual. The draining had been done by the same person—by Miss Periwinkle, I'd assumed. Surely Derrick's magic couldn't create the same signature she had.

Which meant I had been wrong. Gertrude Periwinkle had never killed Sebastian Reade or Brogan McLean or anyone else. The realization crushed into me, making it difficult to breathe.

I watched the spidery veins darken. Derrick was doing the same thing to me. He was draining me.

I lifted my hips away from Derrick's and for the briefest moment, the intensity of that pulling inside me diminished. He grunted. His pelvis arched, his erection searching for me.

"Derrick, stop. You're going to kill me."

Venom laced his voice, making him sound gruff and unlike himself. "That's the point." He took hold of my hips and sat me on him again.

"What?" I thought I had misheard him.

I tried to pull away, but he wouldn't let me. When the pulling ache started up in my arms again, I knew I hadn't. He was draining me. He was a murderer.

I tried to twist away, but couldn't.

"Think about what you're doing," I gasped between spasms of pain in my chest. "You don't want to kill me. You love me."

"That's why I have to do this. She'll never get you this way. She'll never be able to torture you or kidnap you."

This wasn't Derrick talking. It couldn't be. It had to be his brainwashing. I tried to pull away, but he wouldn't let me. He thrust into me, the simultaneous pleasure of sex and the pain of the draining confusing my senses.

"Stop!" I slapped him hard across the face.

He didn't let go of me. Tears filled his eyes. "I will always love you, Clarissa."

The previous fever of my desire wicked away and was replaced with the frigid chill of the crypt. The cold of death sank below my flesh and into my bones. I shivered uncontrollably. The blooms of burst blood vessels under my skin darkened.

His fingers closed around my throat. I didn't want to hurt Derrick. I wanted to help him. He squeezed my esophagus, his eyes so sad as he looked at me.

I thought of Miss Periwinkle's door, unlocking with a question about *The Little Mermaid.* The mermaid in the story had sacrificed her happiness for the prince's. I had always hated that story with its lack of happy ending. Was that my life? Couldn't I save us both?

I loved Derrick. I couldn't imagine the world without him. For years I had dreamed we would be together. But this wasn't Derrick anymore. He was a brainwashed shadow of his former self. I wouldn't let him kill me.

I wouldn't allow the Raven Queen to triumph. I would break her spell on him.

I tried to stir up my affinity, to let it blaze inside me to send it rushing into him. The pain sucking away my soul was too great. I tried to block the discomfort as Thatch had taught me, but it was harder to get started when I already was in pain. I tried to concentrate on the bursts of pleasure building inside me. That was what would strengthen me. I sank into those pulses of enjoyment. My head floated, distant and detached.

I wasn't breathing.

I was distantly aware of the longing and adoration in Derrick's eyes. Bliss buzzed inside me in waves, cresting higher. The moment was coming. If I could just hold on a little longer, I could shoot lightning out of my palms and break our connection. I could save him and myself.

The world grew hazy and dark. The pulse of orgasm sparked inside me, igniting my affinity anew. I drove it out into him, a massive propulsion of energy. I forced it out of my palms, not the molten lightning it had been when I'd done this before, but just as intense. White light flared so bright it drowned out the darkness.

I jolted my magic into him, and Derrick screamed. I didn't want to hurt him. The idea of it made me want to throw myself across him and beg for forgiveness, but I couldn't make my limbs work. The pulsing spasm of light projecting out of me was too intense.

My magic flooded into him, arching his body in pain and pleasure. Yet even as he screamed, he yearned for more. He kept on taking that magic, unrelenting as he stole more of it away from me. I kept giving until I had nothing left.

"I'm sorry," he said.

Derrick's lips brushed against mine, the tenderness of his touch reminding me of how I loved him.

I had failed. My heart lurched and went still. All went dark.

## CHAPTER FORTY-FOUR
## Ding Dong, the Witch is Dead

Death was a peaceful, painless respite after all I had been through. The blackness was a dreamless sanctuary. Nothing mattered any longer.

Almost nothing mattered.

A string tethered me to the shell of a body where I had once dwelled. A man's voice shouted my name, his voice urgent and full of panic, but muffled through the barrier of worlds. I couldn't see him. I almost couldn't hear him.

Then all at once my soul yo-yoed back into my body, jolting me awake. My heart lurched, and I choked. I was blind in the darkness of the chamber.

A hand pressed against my chest, hot with electric magic. I tried to draw in a breath, but I found I couldn't. I clawed at my throat, trying to remove the crushing weight that had been there moments ago, but there was none. Stabs of pain throbbed in my neck. The hand shifted from my heart to my throat. The tingle of magic washed over me in hot and cold waves.

He leaned closer, his breath becoming my own. Wind pushed down my throat and into my lungs.

It was Derrick's wind affinity.

The numbing shock of death dissipated from my limbs, leaving me aching and cold. Arms enveloped me, comforting me with warmth. He held me in his lap, cradling me against his chest as he rocked back and forth. I sank into his embrace, comforted by his touch. I clung to his coat as though it were my anchor to this world. I choked in another breath, coughing and gasping.

I had almost died. Derrick had almost killed me. But it was all right now. I had stopped him with my magic. He had saved me just in time. Love had conquered the evil Raven Queen.

I trembled uncontrollably. Hot tears spilled from my eyes. I nuzzled against his shirt. That should have been the moment I had known.

Derrick hadn't been wearing a shirt or a tweed jacket.

"Hush. You're all right. You're safe." Felix Thatch's British accent raked against my ears.

"No!" My voice came out unrecognizable as my own.

This couldn't be right. I tried to examine his face as my eyes adjusted to the dark. His midnight hair flowed over his shoulders into the shadows. Surely my eyes were deceiving me. The person who had saved my life couldn't be Thatch.

A sob shook my chest. I didn't want him. I wanted Derrick.

Or at least, I wanted the person Derrick used to be, the best friend who would never have hurt me. But Derrick had betrayed me.

Thatch drew my coat around my shoulders and stroked my back. His hand shifted over my arm, rhythmically, his movements calming. He spoke in a flat unaffected tone, the monotone more soothing than I remembered. "You're alive. Keep breathing. Living people do that."

I sagged against him, my strength leaving me. I was so tired. My chest ached, empty and raw as though my heart had just been torn out.

My grief bubbled out of me in uncontrolled blubbery wails. "I thought he loved me. He tried to kill me. How could he do that to me?"

It was a wonder Thatch could understand anything I said.

He hugged me like a friend would do. "I know," he said. "Life isn't fair. Fae play dirty."

I couldn't tell if he was patronizing me or being nice. He found my hand under my coat and squeezed it.

"You saved my life?" I already knew the answer.

"Indeed." He rested his chin on my head.

"Even though I blamed you for everything bad that happened? Even though I accused you of torturing Derrick and working for the Raven Queen? I accused you of lying and—"

"Clarissa, I do work for the Raven Queen. I have no choice." He exhaled, deflating, his façade of stoic indifference gone. "I simply don't permit her to control me. I do everything I can to thwart her attempts to hurt the students and staff at this school. I tried to save Derrick in the only way I knew how, but I had to make my act convincing to her. I didn't *want* to hurt him. Derrick was . . . a nice kid. He was a good person. After I took him into my care, I did everything I could to suppress her spells." He cupped my face in his hand, lifting my chin so that I met his eyes. "I watched over him and did everything in my power to keep him safe from himself and safe from you."

I had been so angry at Thatch. I had loathed him. I had cost him his job, almost cost him his girlfriend—conniving bitch that she was, she did make him happy—and he had saved my life anyway.

"Why couldn't you have just told me?" I asked.

"Would you have stayed away from Derrick if I had? Would you have listened to me and believed me?"

I didn't answer. We both knew the answer was no. I would have done anything to be with Derrick.

I *had* done everything I could think of, no matter what the cost. I had shirked my teacher duties, taken advantage of people, and manipulated Vega and Gertrude Periwinkle. If I had needed to, I would have blackmailed Pro Ro. I didn't like that person I'd become.

The wicked witch.

"I'm sorry," I said.

Shame coiled around my chest and tethered me to my many misdeeds. Intending to do good, I had failed and hurt the people I cared about. I had become my mother.

His brow crinkled. Only now as I gazed at him did I notice the red blisters across one side of his face. One of his eyes was red and swollen, dripping blood down his cheek.

"What happened to you?" I asked.

"Khaba. I'm lucky this was all he managed to do to me before I banished him. I'm afraid to see what he did in his reign of destruction upon leaving the school."

"Banished? You banished Khaba? Why? For how long?"

"It's easier to send a demon away than to contain one. If we're fortunate, he won't come back."

Khaba was gone. I had lost yet another friend. In my attempt to help, I had made him evil, and now he was banished. No good deed went unpunished. Misery barbed into my heart and lodged itself there.

"Can I do anything to . . . help?" I asked.

One side of his mouth lifted into a smirk. "Miss Lawrence, haven't you done enough helping for the day?"

I laughed, sounding like a strangled mouse.

We sat in silence, the sound occasionally broken by one of my sniffles. He handed me a handkerchief. I leaned my head against his chest. Every part of my body ached. My hands were no longer spiderwebbed with broken blood vessels, but my skin hurt. I couldn't feel my affinity. All I could feel was my sorrow.

"Do I have any magic left?" I asked.

The storm clouds of his eyes were so full of sorrow, he didn't even attempt to mask it. "Think of your affinity like a battery. You depleted yourself trying to give your magic to Derrick. It's best that you refrain from using magic so you'll have time to recharge. If you don't give yourself a rest, you'll drain yourself permanently and will never be able to recharge."

So I had succumbed to the same fate as Dox Woodruff when he had pushed his magic into someone he'd loved, hoping to resurrect her but dying in the process. Only he hadn't had Thatch to revive him.

I hadn't thought my heart could hurt any worse, but I was wrong. It felt like death had claimed me and I'd woken up in hell.

"I'm sorry," he said.

I had lost everything I'd ever wanted. If only I had listened to Felix Thatch. He patted my shoulder awkwardly, like he didn't know what else to do.

I shifted and groaned as I realized how much I hurt. My gaze fell on my leggings and underpants, half off and dangling from one knee. No wonder Thatch had covered me with my coat. How embarrassing.

"I'd like to put my underwear back on now," I said. "Before Miss Periwinkle walks in and accuses us of being naughty."

He snorted. "That would be my luck."

He lent me his hand to stand and turned away while I pulled up my underwear and leggings.

"I think. . . ." I didn't know how to say it. The wound was still too fresh. "I think Derrick killed Brogan McLean and Sebastian Reade."

"You are correct. You owe Gertrude an apology."

Like that was going to happen after she'd pushed me into the pit. "She was kissing Sebastian Reade when he died."

"Yes, Gertrude came to me and told me about it immediately after it happened. Derrick would have drained her too if he hadn't been intent on finishing Sebastian off." Thatch strode around the slab, waving his wand light into the shadows as if searching for something. "He was out of his mind—driven mad by what the Raven Queen did to him. He wasn't the same boy you knew."

I couldn't think about what he was saying. I didn't want to. It was easier to focus on his relationship than mine.

I hopped around, searching for my shoe. "You know about her cheating on you?"

He crossed his arms, staring off into the darkness. "My relationship with Gertrude Periwinkle is none of your concern."

"It is if she uses her siren magic to put a spell on you and every other man in this school."

He sighed in exasperation. "How could I not know about her infidelity? She was born a siren. She may have successfully worked to become a Celestor affinity, but my affinity draws out her suppressed powers. Every time I touch her, my magic causes hers to swell, and it becomes difficult for her to control."

Just like I had done to Maddy.

I found something that I thought was a shoe. I lifted it, realizing too late it was a broken bone. I dropped it and continued prodding the ground with my foot.

"It doesn't bother you that she does that?" I asked.

"Of course it bothers me," he snapped. "But what am I supposed to do about it? Am I going to be jealous and blame her for *my* magic? Any relationship I have will result in the same problem. I'm just lucky she isn't a fire Elementia."

Thatch waited on the other side of the stone slab. I found my shoe on the ground on the other side and slipped it on. Thatch's brow was furrowed. He scanned the shadows.

It occurred to me that Derrick wasn't there. I patted the stone slab where he'd rested. He was gone.

"Where is Derrick?" I asked.

Thatch held up his hand, starlight swirling from his fingertips. The prickles danced around the room. His expression remained grim. We were alone. Did that mean Derrick was alive?

"The room was empty when I found you. I expect he left after he saw what he did," Thatch said.

I wasn't sure if I should be relieved or afraid. I wanted him to be alive. Even if he was under the Raven Queen's influence and had tried to kill me, it still meant there was a chance he might be able to be fixed someday. I wouldn't try to save him by myself again. If I asked Thatch, he would help me. Derrick was still a good person deep down.

"How can we save him?" I asked. "That spell? The ingredients we were collecting?"

"No. Derrick is permanently damaged. You cost him any chance he had for recovery." Thatch pointed a finger at me, all gentleness gone from him. "You aren't going to be helping him or anyone else. You have no magic and you'll need months to recharge. Don't get it in your head you can try to fix the world. Do you understand me?"

A scream echoed from far off.

I had a bad feeling about this.

"Oh, bother," Thatch said. "Let's go see who died now."

# CHAPTER FORTY-FIVE
## A Smoking-Hot Boyfriend

Thatch flung the door open and hobbled out. I ran after him. I was only able to keep up with his long legs because he was limping. He kept a hand against the wall to hold himself up. I slipped an arm around him to help him.

The secret vault led to the old crypt and beyond that was the newer crypt. All the bodies we passed were black and charred, their clothes now cinders. Some had turned to dust. Smoke still rose from the bodies, and embers smoldered from the remains of a few. When Khaba had exploded into a demon, he had left a trail of fiery destruction in his wake.

Yet, not all were burned. A woman in a white wedding dress sat in the cinders. It took me a moment to realize she was alive. She sobbed into the ashes, her hands covering her face. It looked like Millie, the preserved corpse Vega had been drawn to. She kneeled before one of the alcoves of charred bodies. I stared in shock, unable to fathom how she'd been resurrected.

Realization crept over me. Vega had used the spell from the book.

"My future husband!" the woman wailed. "Not again."

Hearing her voice, it became clear this wasn't Millie. It was Vega.

"What are you talking about?" Thatch asked sharply.

Vega hurriedly wiped her eyes with a lacy white sleeve, smearing it with black eye makeup.

"You did this, didn't you?" She rose, her gaze fixed on me. Murder laced her voice. "You released a demon from under the school just like your mother did! You destroyed and desecrated the graves of my friends."

I shook my head, wanting to be as far from here as possible. "Khaba did it."

"You're lying," Vega said.

"Vega, get ahold of yourself," Thatch said sternly. "Go upstairs and check on the status of the school. We need to see if anyone is injured or if Khaba damaged school property."

"Go check on your precious school yourself, you fucktards."

I tugged him toward the door. He didn't know how Vega could be. If Vega needed time alone to mourn, it was best to leave her. Thatch and I kept walking.

"What are we going to do about Khaba?" I asked. "Is he really evil? He can't be evil." I remembered what Khaba had told me about his days of unrivaled power.

"A free djinn makes the Raven Court look . . . friendly. There's nothing to be done about him. If my banishing worked, he's gone." Thatch's mouth remained a flat line.

I didn't want Khaba to be gone. I didn't want Derrick to be gone.

When we came to the stairwell cluttered with charred stone, Thatch limped faster. He cursed under his breath.

The upstairs floors were chaos. Smoke filled the air, stinging my eyes and making me cough. Students ran in every direction. Soot covered their pajamas.

A giant hole had exploded from the floor of the great hall, stone scattered across tables and benches. The avocado-green paint on the walls had blistered and turned black, and one of the stone archways from the hall was now in rubble. Pro Ro and Pinky directed a group of students in a bucket brigade. Jackie Frost and Jasper Jang worked to clean the smoke with wind magic. Water affinities doused flames. A group of Celestors wove magic with earth affinities to rebuild a stone wall that had toppled over.

I leapt back as a student shouted at me. "Excuse me!" The young man rode a white domesticated unicorn down the hall, carrying buckets of water on a broom like a yoke across his shoulders.

"What happened?" I asked.

"Khaba, apparently, didn't leave quietly," Thatch said. "We'd best hope he never returns."

He was talking about Khaba, but he might as well have been speaking about Derrick.

Miss Periwinkle stood at the edge of a small crowd. She shouted and pointed to a burning wall. Apparently she had regained her voice. She directed Maddy and two water Elementia from my classes, Jessica and a boy named Anatole, to douse the flames. They used their affinities to draw water out of the nearest bathroom and directed it at the fire. I had never imagined Miss Periwinkle to be a take-charge type, much less someone who would care about the school, but there she was.

One of the students pointed to Thatch and me. Miss Periwinkle turned, looking stricken.

"Felix! Are you all right? What happened?" She ran to him, shoving me out of her way. She hugged him around the waist. "We need to get you to see Grandmother Bluehorse and Sam. They're treating the injured."

"I'm well enough to help."

"We have everything under control. You need to rest." She waved her arm, flagging down one of the students. "Someone, get a healer."

"That can wait," he said. "The fires can't."

Her eyes narrowed as she noticed me. "You," she said.

Thatch groaned. "Gertrude, don't start."

She pointed at me. "She did this, didn't she?"

"Now isn't the time."

"It's never the time. Because of her, I've lost my job, half the library was destroyed, the dungeon is in ruins, and people I know are dead. Students have been injured all because of *her*."

The last words were like a sucker punch to my gut. Who had died now?

"The students?" I asked. "Are they all right? Who's hurt?" What if it was Imani or Greenie or Hailey? My throat tightened with fear, cutting off further questions.

Periwinkle's voice was a growl. "She released a demon under the school just like her mother, didn't she? She's the one who should get fired, not us."

I had. I was just like my mother. My actions had led to the destruction of the school. I was the reason my friends were now gone. Tears filled my eyes.

"No one is going to be fired," Thatch said calmly. "The school can be rebuilt. Books can be replaced." He didn't add dead people *could* be resurrected. That was probably for the best.

"I hope you're happy." Periwinkle jabbed a finger at me. "The least you could do is leave like you promised me. You found your dead boyfriend, didn't you? Well, get out of here."

"No one is leaving." Thatch leaned against a wall, looking weary.

"No, not until she promises to sign a new statement attesting to my innocence for those crimes she accused me of." She glared at me. "And I want you to sign a new one for Felix. You probably thought that clever, destroying my office in the fire. You aren't going to get away with this."

Another student rushed by on a unicorn, and we had to smash ourselves against a sooty wall to avoid getting run over.

"What are you talking about?" Thatch asked.

Periwinkle took in a breath and choked on the smoke. It was the first time she'd stopped ranting long enough for me to get a word in edgewise.

"Miss Periwinkle and I made a bargain. I agreed to sign a statement attesting to your innocence if she helped me find Derrick. I promised I would leave with him if I found him. But Periwinkle tried to kill me instead."

As usual, he missed the point I was trying to make. Thatch glowered at his girlfriend. "You assisted Clarissa?"

"I might have." She eyed me with disdain, her gaze roving over me. "Did your supposed boyfriend give you those?"

I looked down at myself in confusion, uncertain about what she referred to.

"The bruises." Her gaze drifted to my neck. "*My* boyfriend wouldn't do that to me."

"Merlin's balls! Is that necessary?" Thatch asked. "Listen to yourselves. You're like children. Worse than children." He pointed a finger at her. "Stop attacking Clarissa. If you can't keep your jealousy and possessiveness to yourself, I will end our relationship right now." He pointed to me. "Stop accusing Gertrude of trying to kill you. She didn't ever try to harm—"

"She tried to poison me," I said. "She tried to kill me by pushing me into—"

"As difficult as it may be for you to face the truth, you need to know Derrick was the one who poisoned your chocolate. Gertrude has never made an attempt on your life."

She coughed.

He eyed her. "What? Is there something you've kept from me?"

"I did push her into the Pit of Lost Souls tonight. But that's the only time I've tried to harm her." She lifted her nose as she said it, as though she didn't deign to lower herself to such a level often.

He looked from his lover to me. "This is exactly what I'm talking about. I will not tolerate this animosity between the two of you. If you don't stop, I will be forced to take drastic measures. . . . It happens I know a spell to make two individuals best friends. I will cast that spell if you force me to do it."

Periwinkle stepped back, horror crossing her face.

"Isn't that illegal?" I asked. It sounded like it should be.

"As if you should be one to talk after everything you've done tonight." Thatch gestured to the chaos of the students putting out fires and rebuilding walls. "Now, we have work to do."

That was an understatement. The school was in ruins and would have to be rebuilt. One of my good friends had become a demon by my doing. Khaba wasn't anywhere in sight. I supposed I should have been relieved about this. Instead, I kept thinking how much I was to blame. How would the school survive without our dean of discipline? How would I survive without him as a friend?

I didn't even know if Josie would talk to me anymore. When I thought of Derrick, I felt numb inside, like the wound was still too fresh to process the pain. I'd succeeded in resurrecting him, only for him to try to kill me. He had been the one working for the Raven Queen. My insides churned with turmoil. I'd lost my best friend, possibly for good this time.

I had accused Thatch and Periwinkle of deeds they hadn't been guilty of. In trying to save Derrick, I had isolated myself from everyone I had once befriended. I had become an island surrounded by burnt bridges.

I wished I could undo all I had done.

"I'm sorry," I said to Thatch. I turned to Periwinkle. "I really am. Please tell me what I can do to make this better."

She looked like she was about to make a biting reply.

"You are forgiven," Thatch said. "We're still . . . friends." He hesitated when he said the word, as if it tasted strange on his lips. He offered me one of his rare smiles, and I knew things weren't completely broken between us.

Looking at the school, I could see I had a lot of fixing to do. It wasn't going to be easy; I would need to make amends with those I'd wronged and undo what I'd done. Not with magic, but with hard work and determination. With friendship.

Thatch drew my attention to the present. "There's much mending that needs to be done to this school right now. We need to stand as a unified front to help those around us. People in the school are hurt." Thatch rubbed at one of the blisters on his face and flinched. His hand came away bloody.

"Like you," I said at the same time as Miss Periwinkle.

"Ah, isn't that cute. You agree on something." His smile transformed his face, a touch of something wicked in his eyes. "It's time for you to get over your rivalry. Now kiss and makeup." Thatch pushed Miss Periwinkle and me together like one would with fighting preschoolers.

I collided with Miss Periwinkle. She pushed me away, a look of disgust on her face. Thatch embraced us both in a bear hug and squished us together again.

I'd never seen him be this nice to anyone, let alone me. If Miss Periwinkle had bewitched him, it had to be backfiring on her now. Either that, or he was hugging us of his own volition. That was hard to believe, but not improbable if he thought it would make us both more uncomfortable than it made him.

Thatch released us. He stepped toward the chaos. I placed a hand on his arm, not ready to face the real world yet. "I never asked you about my prophecy chocolate. How did it taste?" I asked. "And don't just say it tasted like poison." I expected him to brush me aside.

His brow furrowed. He actually seemed to take my question seriously. "It tasted . . . bittersweet."

"Bittersweet? Or bitter and then sweet?" Had I lived through the bitter part of my chocolate? Would I have something sweet coming up in my life? Maybe that meant there was hope for me.

Thatch smiled wanly. "Come along. I'm certain I tasted repairs to the school in your future." He handed me a bucket.

I found Maddy busting out a waterbender move. She parted from the other water affinities and grabbed me. "We need you, Miss Lawrence." She tugged me toward them.

I understood why she wanted me, but it wasn't going to work.

"I can't help you," I said. "I don't have any magic." Thatch had said I needed to rest and recharge.

She held my hand, raised the other, and aimed it at the stream of water. It turned into a geyser, multiplying so strongly it plowed students over on its way to the flames in the other room. The unexpected flood momentarily reminded me of Missy accidentally flooding our basement with her magic when we'd been kids.

Maddy released my hand, and the water died down to a smaller stream. She took my hand again, smiling as the water gushed forth.

I still had magic to give to others? I thought I'd pushed it all into Derrick when I'd resurrected him. That was what Thatch had said, anyway. He'd insisted I not use my magic.

Then again, when wasn't he trying to get me to not use my magic?

I had lost a boyfriend, and somewhere along the way, despite all I had done to hinder myself, I had gained a friend out of Felix Thatch. Perhaps I wouldn't be alone as I set out to fix the world next time.

Thatch had said it was impossible to save Derrick, but he didn't say it was impossible to save Khaba.

With or without magic, I would get Khaba back.

## THE END

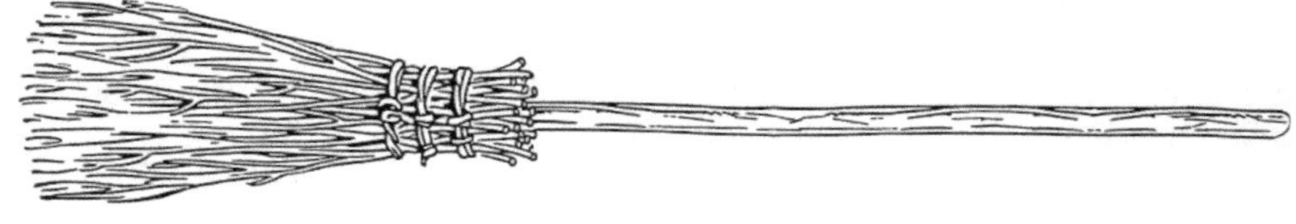

A Sneak Peak of

# Budget Cuts for the Dark Arts and Crafts

Sequel to

Reading, Writing and Necromancy

## CHAPTER ONE
## Another Year, Another Hex

My first year at Womby's School for Wayward Witches had been filled with students cursing me and teachers cursing *at* me. For my second year, I hoped for less dark arts and crafts, and more fine arts and crafts.

I sat in the sanctuary of my classroom amongst a dozen of my most artistic students. Monday, Wednesday, and Fridays I hosted after-school Art Club meetings. These were my favorite days, the excuse I needed to create my own art with my most talented and enthusiastic students.

I had transformed the gloomy stone tower of the art room into an inspiring classroom full of motivational quotes and cheerful paintings. Vincent van Gogh's *Sunflowers* and Georgia O'Keeffe's *Red Canna* hung above my beginning class's close-up drawings of flowers, leaves, and pine cones. The *Mona Lisa*, one of Chuck Close's grid-style self-portraits, and a Frida Kahlo self-portrait hung above my advanced class's self-portraits. Students sat in desks and chairs placed into a horseshoe shape, chatting amiably and working on their independent projects.

It was a much better start than the previous year. Students had realized I couldn't do magic and glued me to the ceiling on my first day. This year on my first day, incoming freshmen had already heard the rumors that my biological mother was the baddest badass witch of all time, and I was someone not to be meddled with. They had learned Alouette Loraline had released a demon and destroyed part of the school . . . and so had I.

Teachers stayed away from me, thinking I might explode with magic at any moment. Students respected me because they thought I was powerful. Little did they know how wrong they were.

Six months before, I had pushed my affinity into Derrick to resurrect him. Until my magic recharged, I couldn't actively use it, though something in me still brought out the magic in others. If I couldn't use magic, that meant I was defenseless against soul-sucking Fae, homicidal students, and teachers who probably wanted to kill me.

I couldn't protect myself against the boyfriend who had attempted to kill me once and would try to do so again.

At the start of last year most of the teachers had disliked me, now they hated me. Including my friend Josie. Mostly that was for releasing Khaba into his demon form. That was only the start of my problems.

Despite my attempts to combat my worries, uneasiness wormed its way under my skin and threatened to sink its teeth in. I distracted myself with other concerns about job security and the school's budget. At this point, I still couldn't figure out why they'd hired me back.

I flipped through my sketchbook, considering which of the renderings of the school might show it off in the best light. No matter what angle I chose to draw Womby's School for Wayward Witches, it resembled an architectural monstrosity. Arms stretched out from the great hall like a spider, constructed from mismatched brick, stone and wood. The boxy buildings were stacked onto each other, gables contrasting with turrets on round towers, reminding me of Howl's Moving castle—but on crack. I'd included the charred stones and wood from the school's most recent fire in my rendering, though I hadn't yet decided if I intended to include that in my final painting.

It seemed unlikely I was going to be able to capture a viewpoint of the school that would entice anyone to buy the painting in a charity auction to raise funds for the school. I'd said as much to the principal, but the scars of the fire were at least in part my doing, so I felt obliged to help the school in any way I could.

I would do anything to redeem myself in the eyes of the teachers and staff. After the explosion and the repairs needed after I had accidentally released a demon from the school—or as I thought of it, a djinn from his lamp—it was likely they would need to cut a teacher at the end of the year—if not sooner.

I selected the least hideous perspective of the school and sketched the building on a canvas.

"Miss Lawrence, look at my collage," Chase Othello said, waving me over. "Do you think it's good enough for the auction?"

Chase was a junior this year. She was tall, with purple hair and a lip ring. She didn't have time for art class so I was pleased she had joined Art Club after school.

I set down my sketchbook on my table and went over to see my student's work. I complimented what she had done well and gave suggestions for how she could improve her collage with contrast.

To my right, Imani Washington, a dark-skinned girl, sketched her friend Grogda, who insisted on being called Greenie, while the other girl more or less stayed still while she drew anime characters. Considering Greenie had mossy skin and leaves grew in her verdant hair, she'd never been able to leave the Unseen Realm, or else it would have drawn attention. She had never experienced Morty culture firsthand, so I didn't know how she'd been exposed to Dragon Ball Z.

Maddy and Hailey chatted while they sculpted using clay.

"Son of a succubus," Hailey Achilles swore. "This stupid clay keeps cracking."

"Language," I reminded her.

"Sorry." Hailey tucked her brown hair behind a pointed ear and cast her amber eyes downward.

I walked closer and said with my patient-teacher smile. "Think about the outcome you want and the path you need to take to get there."

"I want the clay to stop being so dry so I can work with it." Hailey looked to Maddy, the blonde water siren sitting beside her. Hailey clomped the gob of clay on her friend's desk and looked at her expectantly.

"What?" Maddy asked.

Hailey waved a hand at it. I hadn't been the most articulate high school student either. I stepped closer and spoke quietly so I wouldn't embarrass Hailey. "Use words to ask for what you want. She isn't a mind-reader."

Hailey lifted her chin. "Do your water magic and fix it."

Maddy rolled her eyes and sighed. "You could just get a cup of water."

Even so, Maddy picked up the crumbling brown mess in one hand. With the other she pinched something invisible in the air and drew it toward the clay. Blue light danced around her fingers, and she wove water back into the clay. Maddy's siren magic was subtle, the task easy for her skills. Her creamy skin turned pearlescent, and she grew so beautiful it hurt my eyes to look at her. She already was tall and blonde and could passed for a model, but when her magic shimmered through the wards used to tone down her siren affinity, boys tended to drool.

Like Balthasar.

Hailey smacked him on the back of his head. "Close your mouth before a fly lands in there."

The clay became moist and pliable in Maddy's hands. Too moist as a gush of water surged forward and mud splattered the front of Hailey's white blouse.

"Son of a fucking succubus!" Hailey yelled.

"Language," I said.

"Sorry," Maddy said. "I didn't mean for that much water to come out."

Balthasar laughed, his mop of black hair falling into his freckled face. "You always have accidents when you're in Miss Lawrence's classroom."

Maddy bit her lip, looking from me to Hailey. Imani ducked her head down. Balthasar was right. The more time she spent with Imani and me, the more her magic went overboard.

Hailey pretended to be more interested in drying the mud from the white shirt of her school uniform than our conversation, but her pointed ears twitched as though she was listening.

I tried to think of a valid excuse. "It must be that everyone feels so at home in the art room, we let our guards down." I strolled away from Maddy in case I was the cause.

After what I'd done last year, my affinity wasn't drained, just depleted, like a battery with some juice still left in it. I still had a knack for drawing out the powers of others. Over summer vacation while I had resided with my fairy godmother in Oregon, I'd inadvertently brought out plant magic in her. Either that or it had been Imani, who had stayed with us during the summer months, and also had that effect on people with her secret Red affinity.

We had been fortunate Gertrude Periwinkle had looked after Maddy, otherwise I would have needed to bring her home with me. Her proximity to so much of our magic would have drawn the attention of Morties and Fae alike.

Imani met my gaze. Worry tugged the corners of her mouth downward. One of these days I would give myself away, and when I did, it wouldn't just be myself I took down but Imani and Thatch.

The uncomfortable quiet of the room stretched on. Hailey coughed.

The awkward silence was broken by Trevor. "Look what I made!" he said, holding up a chunky clay animal.

Unlike most of the other students at the school, Trevor should have been in middle school. But his powers had manifested early, and he'd needed a place to go. I'd never been clear on what his affinity was, only that he had a talent for eating my glue and crayons.

"Is it good enough for the art show?" he asked eagerly.

From the way he'd overworked the clay, it had dried out. He'd mashed the cracked clay coils together so that it resembled a dinosaur made out of turds. A *Turdosaurus rex*.

I didn't want to break his heart, so I opted for a half truth. "Remember, these projects are just experiments. We don't even know if the clay from the stream banks can be fired or if it will fall apart. We need to let this dry out and build a kiln out of—" I stopped midsentence, eyeing Trevor warily. "Why is your mouth brown?"

Trevor's cheeks flushed scarlet. Quietly, he said, "I wanted to see if it tasted like chocolate."

"The clay?" I asked.

The wind outside rattled the shutters.

Hailey snorted. "Was it everything you hoped for and more?"

I shook my head at her. "Don't encourage him." I turned back to Trevor. The wind whistled so loud, I had to raise my voice to be heard. "Honey, we've talked about this before. "You cannot eat art supplies. If you want to be in Art Club, you have to—"

"*C'est pas vrai!*" someone said from the door. Pierre halted in the hall, a bundle of canvas under one arm. He scowled.

I waved to him and welcomed him in. He wasn't one of my usual Art Club enthusiasts—I could barely get him to do his assignments in my class—but Maddy had asked him to join and he'd attended three meetings so far. He was an Elementia with a rock affinity, which gave him the bulging muscles of the Hulk. Those body-builder muscles coupled with his baby face made him a favorite amongst the girls.

He glared at Balthasar Llewellyn. The smaller boy's goblin-like features couldn't compete with brawny and handsome Pierre.

Pierre grumbled, his voice rumbling like rocks rolling down a hill. "It was my turn to sit next to Maddy." Or that's what I suspected he said. Between the unusually low voice and his French accent, it was often difficult to understand what he said.

"Oh." Maddy looked from Pierre to Balthasar seated next to her. Her cheeks flushed pink. "I'm sorry. You didn't say you were coming and wanted me to save you a seat today."

"You snooze, you lose, loser." Balthasar chuckled. "That's what you get for being late."

Ugh. There would be no end to the teenage crushes and the hormonal conflicts that spilled over from classes into Art Club.

Pierre's words came out in a landslide of anger. "Shut up, penis breath!"

Even with his accent, I had no trouble mistaking that.

Balthasar whipped out his wand faster than you can say "abra-cadaver," the tip fizzling with magic. Pierre rushed forward, raising a meaty fist that either was going to break one of my tables or Balthasar's head.

Maddy squealed, diving for Trevor and yanking him back. Imani and Greenie grabbed their drawings and backed away, eyes darting between the two boys. Hailey leapt to her feet, a fireball in her hand and her eyes glowing as brightly as orange lava. Panic shot through my veins like a jolt of caffeine, switching me from calm art mode to teacher ninja in two seconds.

"Hey!" I shouted, wedging myself between the two boys, which, in hindsight, might not have been the safest move. "Stop, right there. This is Art Club. No fighting allowed, or I'll kick both of you out."

"If that happens, then neither of you will get to sit next to Maddy," Hailey said in her ever-so-helpful way.

The wind whistled through the cracks in the shutters, whipping my pink hair into my face. It should have smelled like fall, but it smelled like spring.

"Pierre, take a step back," I said. "Balthasar, hand over the wand. We are going to put it on my desk until Art Club is over." Grudgingly, they both followed directions. "Now, I want us to use words, not wands. Do you remember those I-statements and the active-listening exercises we've been practicing?"

"Oh no! Not this again!" Balthasar wailed.

The shutters burst open in a flurry of decaying leaves and biting droplets of ice. It was far too warm a day for ice, but we were at a magic school—nothing was impossible. Papers fluttered from my desk to the wall, where they pirouetted against the rough stone. One of the students squealed. I rushed to the window and fought against the wind to latch the shutters. The moment I succeeded, the shutters of another window popped open.

"Get those!" I pointed to the students and the window on the other side of me.

More shutters burst open.

I shouted to be heard over the banshee howl of wind. Students ran in every direction. The air whistling through the cracks of the shutters I held closed whispered against my skin like a lover's breath. The wind felt unseasonably cold for September, followed by a rush of warmth, carrying with it the perfume of spring flowers and exotic spices. I tasted faraway places and magic, reminding me of Derrick.

Derrick, my former best friend and the love of my life.

Derrick, whom I had loved and trusted above all others. Every time I recalled how I'd made his curse worse and turned him evil, a chasm of pain cracked open inside me and threatened to swallow me whole. Even after he'd tried to kill me, I couldn't bring myself to hate him.

My chest ached where the void of hope and love for him had once been. The memory of what had transpired six months before was still too raw to think about. I blinked the tears from my eyes.

When the wind had stopped, all of us picked up the scattered papers and art supplies that had fallen to the floor. Rhett Jacob's pallet of cool-colored paint had fallen onto his chair. I showed him where the rags were to clean up. Eventually we all returned to our seats to continue with our art. I found my sketchbook still open, but it was no longer turned to the angle of the school I intended to paint.

Instead, I found myself staring at the portrait I'd drawn of Derrick the year before. The sketch was whimsical and light, rendered in pencil. I had reworked his eyes, and when the pencil hadn't erased, the paper had become smudged with graphite. The haunted expression resembled Derrick as I'd last seen him more than the smiling, jovial man I'd grown to love.

It couldn't be a coincidence the wind had opened the shutters, smelling like Derrick's affinity, and my sketchbook had turned to the page showing Derrick. Icicles skated through me. I wrapped my arms around myself.

Derrick was haunting me from afar, reminding me of what he'd done, that he'd try to kill me again. For all I knew the Raven Queen might be torturing him at this very moment and forcing him to do evil.

"Miss Lawrence?" Imani asked, looking up from her art. "Are you all right?"

She stared at me, her brown eyes warm and full of concern.

"Fine. Thanks." I closed the book. I picked up my pencil, but my hand was shaking. She kept staring.

I crossed my arms to hide the tremble, noticing my sleeve was covered in a streak of blue paint. In the commotion of the wind, phthalo blue and cerulean paint had somehow collided with my pink-and-white polka-dot sweater. The advantage of acrylics was that it dried quickly and was water soluble. The disadvantage was that it was permanent and water resistant once it dried. I examined my sleeve, growing more disgusted as I realized some of the paint had smeared onto the side of the sweater too. Some of it was still wet.

My friend Josie had taught me a handy cleaning spell. I didn't know if it would work on paint as well as it did on dust. Felix Thatch, the equivalent of a Sith Lord of a magical mentor, had advised me not to use magic, claiming I needed to rest and recharge after resurrecting Derrick from the dead. Even so, I knew I still had magic. I had seen it at work in subtle ways.

Thatch had said to wait. It had been six months. I could sneak in a small spell that used hardly any magic. Besides, it was important to keep up my reputation so students wouldn't think I was powerless.

I reached for my new wand where I had shoved it up my sleeve like all the cool teachers did, but it wasn't there anymore. It wasn't on the floor under my seat or by the window. I felt along the waistband of my skirt, but it hadn't fallen there either. Those wands were more trouble than they were worth.

"Can I borrow someone's wand?" I asked.

Imani, Greenie, and Maddy all raised theirs at once.

"I can loan you mine," Greenie said with an eager smile.

Imani held hers in front of her best friend's. "No! Use mine."

"I already have mine out," Maddy said.

They were all so eager to please, more like middle school students than most high school students I'd taught. I was happy I'd made such a good impression on this many teens. I accepted Imani's wand because she was closest.

I waved it over my sleeve and shirt, imagining power from my affinity swelling inside me. It shifted up my arm and into the wand. I didn't have a lot of experience using wands, but this seemed like the best option because they were supposed to focus magic.

As I waved the wand over myself, the paint unpeeled itself from my arm and midsection, hovering in the air in front of me. The air didn't smell like lemons and flowers like when Josie used the spell. Instead it smelled like burned toast and rotten eggs.

Globs of cerulean and phthalo drifted together, the colors marbleizing in a mesmerizing undulation. When Josie cast the spell, all the dirt usually fell to the floor. I pointed to the wooden boards at my feet, but the paint didn't obey like a well-trained dog.

The paint bubbled and smoked. I stepped back.

"I don't think the spell is supposed to do that," Imani said.

"No shit, dumbass," Hailey said.

I was too distracted by the potential danger to correct her language. Everyone backed away except for Trevor who held a tub of paste and was licking his fingers. I grabbed him by the collar and yanked him back toward the door.

"Maddy," I said, waving a hand at the bucket of water in the broken sink. I didn't dare take my eyes off the smoldering paint.

"Got it," she said. After hanging out with a fire sprite like Hailey, she was getting to be quite the expert at putting out fires. She lifted her hands and motioned to the water in the bucket. A puddle of liquid rose and floated toward the blue gob.

The blue paint condensed into a smoldering ball. The moment the floating puddle collided into it, the paint and water exploded outward. I turned away and shielded Trevor the best I could, though I was no Goliath in size. The students dropped to the floor and shrieked.

The water was warm at least. When I straightened, I found all of us were covered in murky blue splatters.

"Everyone all right?" I asked.

Everyone's gray-and-black school uniforms were stained blue. Hailey looked at her white shirt, now muddy from clay and blue from the paint. She glowered at me.

I stepped toward the mop, wobbling as a wave of dizziness washed over me. A pang of lightning ripped through my core. Light danced before my eyes, and I fell to my knees. I gasped for breath.

"Oh my God! What's happening?" Greenie shrieked.

"Miss Lawrence, are you all right?" Imani grabbed my elbow.

Hailey pointed an accusing finger at Imani. "It's all because she used your stupid wand."

"No! There isn't anything wrong with my wand."

"Should we do that Heimlich maneuver thing?" someone asked. "That Morty magic Miss Lawrence did last year?"

I tried to speak and say no, but I could barely catch my breath.

Cool hands grabbed my arms. My affinity fizzled inside me, the red ball of energy sparked out of control. Another lance of pain tore through me. Someone shrieked. Hands released my arms, and I pitched forward. The descent to the floor felt as though I were drifting through molasses, the fall slowed by a distortion in gravity. Time slowed. Not enough that I didn't feel my cheek slam into the unforgiving solidity of the floor.

I didn't understand what was happening. My brain floated above my body, not completely anchored. First the wind, then the sketch of Derrick, now the haywire magic. Was this all Derrick? Had he cursed me now too?

"What should we do? Get Nurse Hilda?" Balthasar asked.

"Get Thatch," I said before another crippling spasm of pain gripped me.

# CHAPTER TWO
## Professor Grumpsalot

I don't know how long I lay on the floor, experiencing white-hot lightning dancing in my core. Pain shot through my limbs in surges. The pain faded between each interval, and I hoped it would be the last. I tried focusing on calming my affinity and diminishing it, but every attempt I made to reach out to the magic inside me only made it worse.

Felix Thatch's crisp British accent sliced through the ringing in my ears. "Everyone out," he said.

Feet thudded away, vibrating through my skull resting on the paint-splattered floor.

He crouched down before me. His midnight hair was tousled back rakishly. He kneeled in a blue puddle, staining his gray tweed pants. Already, blue had gotten on the sleeve of his old-fashioned suit. My gaze fell on his silver-and-black ascot, patterned with the school colors. Dizziness washed over me, though I hadn't tried to get up.

"Merlin's balls," he said. He would have been handsome if he hadn't been scowling. "What is wrong with you? I told you not to use magic."

I was in too much pain to answer. The school's most talented Merlin-class Celestor, who happened to be the most gifted healer—or at least better than Nurse Hilda—happened to have the bedside manner of a porcupine.

"Darling," said a woman. "You don't know she used magic."

"Indeed, I do."

From the melodious music in the woman's voice, she had to be Gertrude Periwinkle, though I couldn't see her. I tried to lift my head to determine whether she was casting a spell on me and about to kill me, but this brought on a new wave of pain. The spasm passed, leaving me panting.

"Derrick," I tried to say between gasps. It came out as "Daarreew."

Thatch rolled me over. "She definitely tried to use magic." He sat me up.

Gertrude Periwinkle held me around the shoulder while Thatch placed one hand on my belly and the other on the small on my back. Just as the white light flared behind my eyes, it ebbed away. Thatch inhaled sharply. The pain wicked out of me and into him. In its place, a numbing coolness washed over me. His cheeks flushed a healthy shade of pink, so different from his usual pale complexion.

My muscles relaxed. It grew easier to breath. I leaned against Gertrude Periwinkle, momentarily stiffening when she smoothed a hand against my shoulder. She wasn't going to do anything to me in front of her boyfriend, I reasoned. She would be on her best behavior after his previous plea for us to get along and be friends.

"Are you feeling better, dear?" Gertrude Periwinkle's cerulean eyes were infused with a façade of concern that almost made me believe she cared. Then again, with her singsong voice, she was able to make anyone believe anything.

I nodded. It hurt my head to do so. I touched a hand to my cheek, flinching at the tenderness of the puffy skin.

"That, I intend to leave." Thatch lifted his chin. "Let the bruise serve as a reminder of the consequences of using magic after I advised you against it." He imperiously stared down his long nose at me.

My temper flared. "You said I should probably wait a few months before I tried to use magic. It's not like you forbade me."

"I did not say 'probably.' Nor has it even been six months. What were you thinking? This is far too soon to even try magic." His monotone was clipped, an edge of anger threatening to break free from his crabby calm.

"Nurse Hilda said—" I tried to interject the advice the school nurse had given me.

"Nurse Hilda is a senile old bat. If you want one of her tonics with werewolf excrement in it, then be my guest. No? Then I advise you to listen to my instructions."

"I just thought it was a suggestion when you said not to use magic. You didn't tell me anything could blow up or lightning might shoot out of me."

"That's curious," Gertrude Periwinkle said. "She shouldn't have been able to do either." She tilted her head, studying me. Her witch hat, already heavy with roses and small animal skulls on one side, tilted as though it might fall off her corn-silk hair.

She was too preoccupied with me to see Thatch shake his head at me. I noticed though. I'd already assumed she knew all my secrets, but maybe I shouldn't have spoken so openly.

"There wasn't enough magic to shoot anything resembling lightning out of you." Thatch's eyes narrowed in warning. "It stayed contained *inside* you. And if anything did escape, it most certainly wasn't lightning. More likely you interpreted the pain as feeling that way. Had you bothered to follow my advice—"

"Look, I'm sorry. I didn't think it was a big deal. I get it now. I won't do it again." I drew in a shaky breath, my nerves bundling together into knots again at the thought of what else I needed to tell him. "Before the spell went all haywire and exploded, there was something else. . . . Derrick's magic."

Thatch's dark brows lifted. He opened his mouth to speak, but no words came out. Apparently, I'd taken him by surprise.

I told them about the wind smelling like Derrick and the drawing in my notebook. Thatch's scowl returned.

"He used magic on me, right? A hex?" I asked.

"You would try to pin this on Derrick rather than take responsibility for your own mistakes." He shook his head at me in disgust. "There was no hex. Simply your dormant affinity reacting to his. No wonder your magic combusted.

"As far as we know, Derrick believes you're dead and has no reason to think otherwise. If you sense him again, you are to come directly to me, do you understand? I will not have him on campus, nor anywhere near the students. He is not to come anywhere near you."

"Why do you say it like that?" I tried to scoot back, but Gertrude Periwinkle held on to me too tightly. "Do you think I want him near me after what he did?"

"Considering your history of poor decisions, yes."

A smile curved Periwinkle's lips upward. "Do you two always fight like this?" She gave my shoulder an affectionate squeeze. Maybe she wouldn't try to kill me later if she wasn't jealous of Thatch yelling at me.

Sure, Thatch was handsome in that emo Professor Snape sort of way, but she should have realized by now how he irritated me like no one else in this realm.

"Promise me you won't use magic until you're healed and recharged. You won't even try," Thatch said.

"How long will that be?"

"Until I say so. It's dangerous for others, and it's dangerous for you. You're lucky you didn't kill yourself just now."

"I don't understand. How could I have killed myself?" I didn't even understand why I couldn't use my magic. Like with all things, Thatch simply ordered me to do his bidding, expecting complete obedience without explaining how this world worked.

Gertrude frowned, eyeing him incredulously.

"Your affinity is depleted like that of a battery," Thatch said. "I told you to wait, and you will wait to recharge it."

"Just spit it out and get it over with." Gertrude Periwinkle clucked her tongue at him. "Tell her."

"There's nothing more to tell." Thatch shook his head at her, trying to give her the same warning look he often gave me.

"Tell me what?" I asked.

Periwinkle said with mock kindness. "Your former boyfriend *drained* you."

The words hit me like a stampeding unicorn. Was she truly saying what I thought she was? Maybe she meant he *used* my magic, not *drained* me of magic.

"You aren't being helpful, *kitten*," Thatch said between clenched teeth.

Kitten? Gross. They were the sappiest, most barf-worthy couple I'd ever met. Periwinkle batted her eyelashes.

I shook my head but stopped when it made my cheek throb. "You said my spell used up *most* of my magic, but I would recover."

"Indeed. Your spell used most of your magic. Derrick draining you used up *all* remaining magic. When you stopped breathing and your heart ceased beating, your affinity was gone. It took my magic and affinity to bring you back to life." He looked to Periwinkle. "I didn't use necromancy. Just healing."

"I didn't say you did." Her tone was cloying.

"But I still have *some* magic, right?" I asked. Hadn't I been the one to draw out my mom's magic and Maddy's? Or was it all Imani's presence that did it? "In a few months, I'll be back to normal, and I can go back to learning how to ride a broom and use cleaning spells and magic to defend myself. . . ." My voice petered out into a squeak. Panic squeezed my throat like a vice, making it difficult to breathe.

He didn't meet my eye. He swiped his wand over the blue stains on his clothes. "Perhaps." Murky blue water splattered to the floor.

"So I might not *ever* recover?" How could I live without magic? Now that I'd had a taste for it, I couldn't go back to the Morty Realm and be ordinary. I was Witchkin. Thatch knew how much I had always wanted this. And he'd kept me in the dark yet again. "Why didn't you tell me the truth?"

He stood. "I didn't want you to get it in your head to do something you would regret."

"Like what? What can I possibly do without magic?" Did he think I'd go to the Raven Queen and trade my soul for magic?

Thatch stuck his nose up in the air. "I can't say. Your impulsive nature often eludes reason. You've already proven yourself incapable of following instructions."

I didn't know if he meant my inability to stay away from Derrick, despite his previous warnings, or in general. He'd be right by both accounts. My anger deflated. "How long will it take to know if I can do magic?"

He retrieved the broom in the corner and swept up the blue puddles. He must have been using a spell because it worked surprisingly well. "It takes years to recover from being drained."

"One rarely recovers from being drained, period." Periwinkle's façade of enthusiasm faded as she studied him. "Except for you, darling. It took you record time to recover after Alouette Loraline drained you. Months."

"I will remind you, I was not drained to the point of death. That does make a difference." He pushed the blue water into a corner. Slowly it shrank, leaving remnants of blue paint crusted on the floor. "Furthermore, it was nearly a year before *hints* of my powers came back. I was weak for years."

Periwinkle raised an imperious eyebrow. He looked away. He was lying, and from her reaction, I could see she wanted to call him on his bluff. Maybe she wouldn't here in front of me, but she would later. Did that mean he had taken some other measure to recover that he didn't want me to know about? I wondered what else he'd lied to me about.

"Come along, Gertrude. Shall we be on our way?" Thatch extended a hand to her in a gentlemanly gesture.

She eyed my crotch, brow furrowed. Since she was a siren, I knew she could be sex-obsessed, but that was a little much. Her gaze flickered back to him, and she took his hand.

She smoothed out her black skirt and straightened the tiny animal skull set into her cameo at the nape of her lace collar. Somehow she'd managed to repel blue puddles from her ivory shirt. She eyed my lap again, so I finally looked down. Something poked out away from my crotch.

"Is that. . . ?" She cleared her throat. "Is that a wand in your skirt, Miss Lawrence?"

"No, I'm just happy to see you!" I said. I never got tired of that one.

No one laughed except for me. If only Khaba had been there to appreciate my corny humor. Sorrow tugged at my heart when I thought of my friend, now gone. It was bad enough Derrick had turned evil, but Khaba too? In the same day, no less.

I dug under the waistband of my skirt. My wand had somehow slid between my underwear and my striped leggings. I flourished my wand, pleased I had found it.

Thatch snatched it out of my hand. "You have done quite enough with that for the day. You won't be needing a wand for a while." He tucked it into the breast pocket of his vest.

He wouldn't even let me keep my wand? Fingers of gloom crept over me. There were no bright rays of hope on my horizon. How was I going to protect myself from the Raven Queen in the long run if I didn't recharge my magical batteries ASAP?

Thatch didn't offer me a hand. I clambered to my feet. Every part of my body ached, my head worst of all.

Desperately, I grasped for the slimmest sliver of optimism.

"How did you recover so quickly?" I asked. "Did you steal magic from someone?" From my mother?

He looked to me sharply. "No, of course not. Why would you even think such a thing? Do you truly think so little of me?"

"Well, it isn't like *you* volunteer to tell me anything. I have to keep guessing."

He walked over to my sketchbook and examined the drawing of Derrick. He tore it from the pad.

I rushed forward. "Hey, leave that alone. That's mine!"

"It isn't going to help you get over him." He folded it and placed it in his breast pocket. He made a face at the next drawing of the school I had sketched in pencil and looked to my canvas on the floor. "Please say you aren't going to paint that for the auction. No one wants to look at that rendition."

Did he have to shred every possibility of happiness in my life? I snatched up my book and closed it before he found more drawings of Derrick or anything else he could make snarky comments about.

"Thank you for your assistance healing me today," I said through clenched teeth, trying not to be ungrateful. "Is there anything else we need to discuss?"

He drummed his long fingers against his chin, thinking. "I advise you not to mention your lack of magic to the students or staff. Enough people already wish to kill you. There's no reason to tempt them further."

I stared at him in shock. "Who wants to kill me? Besides the Raven Queen? Or do you mean Derrick?" Or did he mean all the teachers who now hated me?

"We're done." Thatch offered Periwinkle his arm.

He headed toward the back stairwell that held my closet on the floor below and eventually led down to the dungeon where he lived and taught.

Periwinkle patted his arm affectionately. "I don't think I've ever seen you angry before. Do you always get like this around her?"

I could only hope her presence during one of our more vexing conversations might mean she wouldn't later accuse me of trying to seduce him like she was wont to do.

"I don't know what you're talking about." He touched his wand to the locked door, and it swung open.

She adjusted her witch hat as she stepped into the closet. "Does she always get you so . . . fired up? Passionate? I'd like to see you get that angry about me sometime."

I rolled my eyes. I bet she would. The rumble of his voice was too low to understand.

"All that shouting makes me rather. . . ." She giggled.

His voice slipped into his carefully controlled monotone. "I was afraid you might say that, kitten."

"Maybe if I'm a naughty girl later, you'll yell at me and . . . spank me."

I barfed in my mouth listening to the two evil lovebirds. I walked to the closet to close it, but not before I caught the tail end of their disgusting conversation.

"It was the wand and Miss Lawrence's lewd innuendo, wasn't it?" he asked. "That's what's got you hot and bothered?"

She laughed from the shadows. I slammed the door closed and leaned against the wall, eyeing the gloom of my classroom.

No magic. No spells. No flying on brooms. Was I even a witch anymore? How was I going to survive the rest of the year against Fae—or students—without magic?

Go to Sarina Dorie's website to learn more about the next book in the series, including where it is available: https://sarinadorie.com/writing/novels

If you enjoyed this witch mystery *in the Womby's School for Wayward Witches Series* please leave a review on the online retailer where you purchased this collection. You might also enjoy free short stories published by the author on her website: http://sarinadorie.com/writing/short-stories.

Readers can hear updates about current writing projects and news about upcoming novels and free short stories as they become available by signing up for Sarina Dorie's newsletter at: https://www.subscribepage.com/q6h1q2

Other novels written by the author can be found at: http://sarinadorie.com/writing/novels

You can find Sarina Dorie on Facebook at: https://www.facebook.com/sarina.dorie1/

You can find Sarina Dorie on Twitter at: @Sarina Dorie

Seventeen-year-old Sarah's life changes forever when a man falls from the sky—and she falls in love. As if teenage romance isn't hard enough in the times of the Puritans, imagine falling in love with an alien!

Magic. Jehovah's witchnesses. Karmic collisions. . . .Two unlikely friends—a witch and a Jehovah's Witness—discover the magic of friendship, as well as real magic.

Gothic Romance. Mystery. Ghosts. Imagine a whimsical fairytale world with the feel of Jane Eyre . . . only working in a house of were-wolves.

For more fantasy, science fiction and romance, go to: www.sarinadorie.com

# ABOUT THE AUTHOR

Sarina Dorie has sold over 150 short stories to markets like Analog, Daily Science Fiction, Magazine of Fantasy and Science Fiction, Orson Scott Card's IGMS, Cosmos, and Abyss and Apex. Her stories and published novels have won humor and Romance Writer of America awards. Her steampunk romance series, *The Memory Thief* and her collections, *Fairies, Robots and Unicorns—Oh My!* and *Ghosts, Werewolves and Zombies—Oh My!* are available on Amazon, along with a dozen other novels she has written.

A few of her favorite things include: gluten-free brownies (not necessarily glutton-free), Star Trek, steampunk aesthetics, fairies, Severus Snape, Captain Jack Sparrow, and Mr. Darcy.

By day, Sarina is a public school art teacher, artist, belly dance performer and instructor, copy editor, fashion designer, event organizer, and probably a few other things. By night, she writes. As you might imagine, this leaves little time for sleep.

CPSIA information can be obtained
at www.ICGtesting.com
Printed in the USA
BVHW041726110619
550727BV00012B/118/P

9 781722 645540